CONEY
ISLAND
AVENUE

ALSO BY J. L. ABRAMO

Jake Diamond Mysteries
Catching Water in a Net
Clutching at Straws
Counting to Infinity
Circling the Runway

Jimmy Pigeon Mystery
Chasing Charlie Chan

Stand Alone Novels
Gravesend
Brooklyn Justice

J. L. ABRAMO

CONEY ISLAND AVENUE

Down and Out Books, LLC
3959 Van Dyke Rd, Ste. 265
Lutz, FL 33558
www.DownAndOutBooks.com

The characters and events in this book are fictitious. Any similarity to real persons, living or dead, is coincidental and not intended by the author.

Cover design by JT Lindroos

ISBN: 1-943402-56-6
ISBN-13: 978-1-943402-56-4

*For all of our children, who must face
the dangers we have created.*

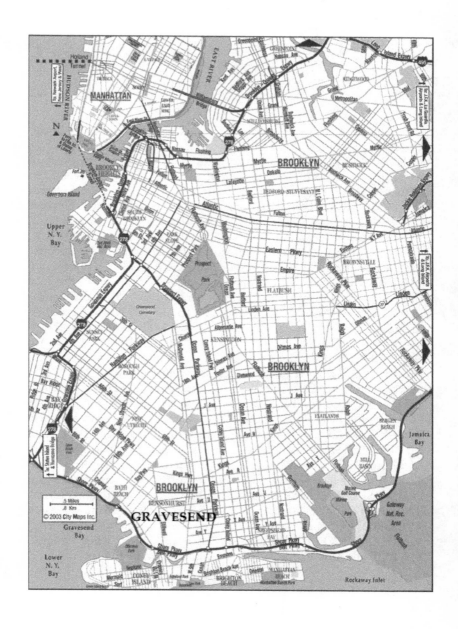

CAST OF CHARACTERS

BILL HELLER...an investigator
VINCENT SALERNO..a bus boy
ALISON DAVIS...Vinnie's girlfriend
ANGELA SALERNO..Vinnie's sister
EDWARD CICERO..Angela's boyfriend
THOMAS MURPHY.....................Detective, NYPD, 61st Precinct
AUGIE SENA.............................proprietor of Joe's Bar and Grill
PAUL GALLO...hired muscle
STAN LANDIS..................a uniformed officer, NYPD, 61st Precinct
REY MENDEZ.................a uniformed officer, NYPD, 61st Precinct
SANDRA ROSEN...........................Detective, NYPD, 61st Precinct
KELLY..Desk Sergeant, NYPD, 61st Precinct
JAMES SAMSON..............................Captain, NYPD, 61st Precinct
MARINA IVANOV..........................Detective, NYPD, 61st Precinct
MARTY RICHARDS........................Detective, NYPD, 61st Precinct
DEREK FIELDER...Crime Scene Unit, NYPD
DR. BRUCE WAYNE.............Medical Examiner, City of New York
BERNIE SENDEROWITZ.................Detective, NYPD, 61st Precinct
JOHN CICERO...............................Detective, NYPD, 68th Precinct
LORRAINE DiMARCO...an attorney
BOBBY HOYLE....a restaurant manager, neighbor of the DiMarcos
RIPLEY...a former FBI Agent
CONNIE SHOREY...Ripley's sister
CARMINE BRIGATI.........................a friend of Vincent Salerno
LEE WASKO.....................................a.k.a. Mr. Smith, an enforcer
RACHEL IVANOV.....................Detective Ivanov's younger sister
ALEX HOLDEN...Rachel's boyfriend
MARK CALDWELL.........Assistant District Attorney, Kings County
KEVIN DONAHUE...a building contractor

ROGER JENNINGS.....................Kings County District Attorney
STANLEY TRENTON...........................Chief-of-Detectives, NYPD
LINDA RICHARDS...Marty Richards' wife
ALICIA SAMSON..Samson's wife
JACK FALCONE..............................Detective, NYPD, 60th Precinct
JOSH ALTMAN..............................Detective, NYPD, 63rd Precinct
JIMMY SAMSON...Samson's son
JENNY GRECO...a high school co-ed
PATTY BOLIN..a high school co-ed
PETER DONNER........................a high school football star
SALINA MENDEZ...Rey's wife
JOAN MICHAELS.......................................Crime Scene Unit, NYPD
KENNY RAMIREZ...a fugitive
DAVID ROSE.....................................a school psychologist
PAVEL VASIN.....................................a private investigator
WILLIAM PABST...a high school principal
SARAH SANDERS..a journalist
VLADIMIR MARKOV.......................owner of the Lobnya Lounge
LEV GAGARIN.............................Chef, Lobnya Lounge
MIKHAIL GAGARIN...Lev's father
ROMAN CHURKIN..........................Chef, Lobnya Lounge
IRINA CHURKIN....................................Roman's mother
DANNY MAGGIO...........Detective, NYPD, on loan to 61st Precinct
KATRINA POPOVICH...................................a sales representative
VICTOR BRONSKI................................a murder suspect
STUMP.......................................a confidential informant
NICKY DeSANTIS.................................a murder suspect
MARCO ACEVEDO..................................a congressman
THEODORE WILSON.......................a Mayoral candidate

THE NIGHT BEFORE

Bill Heller could not shake the feeling he was being followed.

Heller was driving up 18th Avenue toward Ocean Parkway to pick up the Prospect Expressway.

When he stopped at a red traffic light on 77th Street, he noticed the OPEN sign in the window of Il Colosseo.

He decided to go in and have something to eat and try at the same time to determine if he was being tailed.

The restaurant was nearly empty at nine-forty on a Tuesday night.

They had stopped seating at eight-thirty. The sign on the front door had been flipped over to the side that read CLOSED.

A young couple rose from their chairs at the back of the dining room. The young man placed a tip on the table and escorted his girl to the front door.

Three *twenty-something* females were putting money together to cover their bill.

A man in his late-thirties sat alone at a table near the front window.

The bus boy had already started clearing vacant tables.

A waitress was refilling salt and pepper shakers.

The restaurant manager stood at the cash register.

The diner at the window spotted a big man in a jogging suit out on the street, straining to look inside.

He had paid cash. His waitress brought his change and his receipt—a carbon duplicate of the three-by-five inch guest check.

He asked her for a pen and a rubber band.

. . .

1

The large man in the jogging suit made his way back to a car parked on the opposite side of 18th Avenue. A second man was seated behind the wheel.

"Well?"

"He's still there. He's sitting alone in front."

They watched the young couple leave the restaurant.

"How many others inside?"

"Looks like three more customers. There are at least three others working the floor, and maybe one or two in the kitchen. They're shutting the place down."

"Let's wait," the man in the vehicle said.

A few minutes later the two men across the avenue watched as the three young women came out of the restaurant.

"Those are the last customers other than him," the big man said.

"Do you think he spotted you?"

"No, and what if he did. I'm just a guy on the street glancing into the place as I passed."

Just a big ape in a goombah outfit, the second man was thinking.

"Take the car, go around to the back and watch the rear exit. If he isn't out in five minutes, I'm going in," the man in the car said.

He climbed out of the vehicle and handed over the keys.

The man at the table near the front window scribbled a note on the back of the guest check.

He called the bus boy over.

"Where is the rest room?" he asked the kid.

"Down at the end of the hall in back."

"Can you hold this for me?"

He placed something into the bus boy's hand and without waiting for an answer he walked toward the rear.

It was a small solid item.

2

It was wrapped in a paper guest check receipt held by a rubber band.

"Go back there and see what's taking him so long," the manager said. "We need to lock up and get finished here."

The bus boy walked back to the men's room.

He had slipped the small package into his apron pocket.

He returned a moment later.

"He's gone. He went out the rear door," he said, just as a well-dressed man opened the front door.

"We're closed," the manager said.

"I'm looking for a friend who said he would be here."

"All of the customers are gone. The last seems to have used the rear exit for some reason. Maybe he was parked back there."

"Can I go out that way?"

"Go ahead. I need to lock the doors before someone else wanders in."

The well-dressed man exited through the back door and saw the ape in the jogging suit getting into the car.

"Did you see him come out?"

"I was about to drive around front to pick you up. I sandbagged him when he came out the door. He's in the back seat, gagged and tied."

"Did he have it?"

"I thought it might be a better idea to get away from here and find a more private place to pat him down."

Thirty minutes later, only the bus boy and the restaurant manager were left in the restaurant.

The young man had forgotten the small package until he removed his apron.

He placed it into his jacket pocket.

"Are you all done?" the manager asked.

"Yes."

"Then go, I'll see you tomorrow."

The bus boy stepped out onto 18th Avenue to wait for Alison, who was on her way to pick him up. Her roommate was out-of-town and he was looking forward to being alone with her in her apartment.

Alison was a very playful girl. Maybe she would let him spend the night again.

While he waited, he pulled the small package from his pocket. He removed the rubber band and the paper guest check, revealing a small tape recorder and a fifty-dollar bill.

He noticed there was writing on the back side of the check.

Keep this safe. I'll make contact. There's another hundred in it for you.

He stuffed it all back into his pocket as Alison's Chevy Impala pulled up to the curb.

PART ONE

THE SIX-ONE

How do you know love is gone?
If you said you would be there at seven
and you get there at nine,
and he or she has not called the police yet,
it's gone.

—Marlene Dietrich

ONE

The face in the mirror returned a dazzling smile.

The lips, complete with a fresh coat of Covergirl Fairytale 405 lipstick, mouthed three words. *I feel pretty.*

It was her twenty-fourth birthday, Eddie had made dinner reservations at New Corners Restaurant and Angela Salerno knew that Eddie Cicero was going to pop the question.

Eddie would be arriving soon to pick her up, with a fistful of flowers and a ring hidden in a jacket pocket. Angela turned from the mirror and redirected her attention to the new dress neatly laid out on the bed. It was a little black number, short black satin with spaghetti strings. When Angela had tried the dress on at Cue Boutique in Fort Hamilton her best friend Barb had assured her: *You look so hot you are going to burn New Corners down.*

It was Barbara who had confirmed Eddie had a ring. It was Barbara's boyfriend Albert, Eddie's best friend, who let Barbara in on the *secret*. Barb had not been able to keep it to herself.

Angela didn't mind, she could act surprised. She was thrilled knowing Eddie had finally decided to take the big step.

Angela was about to pull the new dress over a short black silk slip when there was a knock on the apartment door. Eddie was early. Better than late.

She danced over to the door and she looked through the peephole.

It was her brother Vincent.

She reluctantly opened the door. Vincent rushed in, moved her back into the living room and quickly pushed the door shut.

Vinnie was carrying a large green gym bag and he was visibly upset.

"I need money, Angie," he said.

"Hi, sis, it's been awhile, you look great, happy birthday," Angela said.

"Hi, sis, happy birthday, you look great," Vinnie said. "I need money."

"I have an address for his parents' place and one for his sister. I want both watched until he shows up."

"Give me the addresses, I'll call Gallo," Mr. Smith said.

Thomas Murphy took possession of a stool at the bar.

Augie Sena, from the opposite side of the bar, set a bottle of Samuel Adams Boston Lager within Murphy's reach a moment later.

"I haven't seen you move that fast since the last visit from the Health Department," Murphy said. "How did you know I wanted a beer?"

"Wild guess. It's on me."

"My birthday is not for another five months."

"I might not live that long," Augie said. "The beer, my friend, is meant in way of congratulations."

"You heard I won two bucks on a ten dollar lottery ticket?"

"I heard you're up for lieutenant."

"Bad news travels fast," said Murphy. "Thanks for the beer anyway."

"I'll bet you the two bucks you would love the fried calamari over linguini for dinner."

"Wild guess?"

"Just call me Sena the Psychic, but the calamari is *not* on the house."

"That, my clairvoyant friend, even I could have guessed. I'll take it with the hot sauce."

Angie Salerno gave her brother Vincent all of the cash she had on hand.

Seventy-seven dollars.

Vinnie thanked her with a bear hug.

"Okay, Vincent. You'll ruin my makeup. And what's with the gym bag? Did Mom's washing machine break down or are you planning a trip to Monte Carlo?"

"Cute. I have to run. By the way, you *do* look great."

"Thanks. Go, before Eddie gets here and I beg him to slap some sense into you," Angie said. "Be careful."

Vinnie ran down the two flights of stairs and was about to exit through the front door when he suddenly decided against it.

He continued down to the basement instead, opened the metal door at the rear of the house, skipped up the concrete steps and slipped out to the back alley.

He headed down the alley toward Avenue U, turned east on the avenue, and hurried over to the elevated train station on McDonald Avenue.

He rushed up the stairs and anxiously waited for an F Train.

A man in a gray suit slipped into the front passenger seat of a black Lincoln sedan on the opposite side of the street from the house entrance.

"Are you sure he's in there?" he asked the man behind the wheel.

"I watched him go in and I called you, I haven't seen him come out. I checked the mailboxes. His sister lives on the top floor."

"I would rather deal with him out here."

"We can wait."

"Fuck."

"What?"

"Who is that?"

They watched a young man walk into the building.

"How the fuck should I know?"

"On second thought, let's not wait."

. . .

"There's a kid in a hurry," Augie Sena said, seeing a young man with a green gym bag race past the front window of Joe's Bar and Grill. "Maybe you should go after the kid. He may have knocked off the Jerusalem Pizzeria."

"He'd deserve a medal. The pizza there tastes like soaked cardboard."

"How is the linguini?"

"Not bad," Murphy said. "How did you get it delivered here so fast?"

"Anyone ever tell you you're a laugh a minute, Tommy?"

"I hear it every sixty seconds," Murphy said, slipping a fork-ful of calamari past his smile.

"My sister's boy is popping the question."

"What question is that? Why is the eggplant always greasy?"

"He bought a ring for his girlfriend."

"Jesus, Augie, what kind of uncle are you? Couldn't you talk him out of it?"

"You're a hopeless cynic, Tommy. I haven't met her, but my sister says she seems likes a very nice girl."

"They all seem like nice girls, and then they grow into their mothers. Which sister?"

"Rosie."

"The sister who married Cicero? I'm not too sure about her judgment."

Murphy shook his head and let out a deep sigh.

"What?" asked Augie Sena.

"The cynic and the psychic," Murphy said. "We're quite a pair."

It was all Eddie Cicero could manage to say when Angie opened the apartment door wearing the short black spaghetti string dress.

"Wow."

"Not bad, right?"

"How am I supposed to give the osso buco at New Corners

the attention it deserves with you sitting across the table in that thing?"

"Chew slowly," Angie said, beaming.

Eddie handed her a dozen red roses.

Then there was a rapping at the door.

"Expecting your other boyfriend?" Eddie said.

"Everyone is a comedian. It's probably my worthless brother. He was just here for another handout."

Angie opened the door half way.

The two men in the doorway did not look friendly.

"We're looking for Vincent Salerno," said the shorter man.

He was well groomed and he wore a gray business suit. An expensive suit. He could have passed for a banker.

His companion wore a blue jogging suit and looked like something she might have seen in a zoo.

"Vincent is not here," Angie said, Eddie close at her side.

"We saw him come in."

"He was here, he left. I don't know where he ran off to."

"Mind if we take a look?"

"Yes. I do mind."

The ape violently shoved the door open, knocking Angie and the flowers to the floor. Eddie reacted and went after the big man. The gorilla laid Eddie out cold with a roundhouse punch. The two men walked into the apartment. The well-dressed man shut the door while the big man kept an eye on Angie.

"We can do this the easy way or the hard way," the banker said.

"Very original. God, you really hurt him," Angie said, looking over at Eddie.

The big man kicked her in the side.

"Where is Vincent?"

"I told you I have no idea where my brother went," Angela screamed from the floor. "Keep that animal away from us."

The big man kicked her again. Then he pulled a gun out of his jacket and pointed it down at Eddie. Eddie was still unconscious.

"Please, don't," Angie said, terrified. "Take whatever you

want. I swear, I won't say anything to anyone."

"Where is your brother?" the man in the business suit said.

"I don't know."

"I am not going to ask you again."

"Please, I don't know."

"Fine. I believe you."

Suddenly the big man made it official and then Mr. Smith made it absolutely final.

Vincent Salerno hopped off the F Train at 42nd Street and he walked the two blocks to the Port Authority Bus Terminal. Vinnie used most of the money he had scored from his sister, his girlfriend and the man in the restaurant for a one-way bus ticket to Chicago. The bus was scheduled to leave in less than an hour. He walked into Casa Java, located an empty chair at a small table near the rear exit, placed the gym bag under his seat and held it between his feet.

Vinnie nearly jumped out of his skin when he finally noticed the waitress standing beside him.

"Can I help you?" she asked.

"I doubt it."

"Excuse me?"

"Coffee," Vincent said. "Light. Lots of sugar."

Mary Valenti had been attending evening Mass at Sts. Simon and Jude every Wednesday since losing her husband to a massive heart attack fourteen months earlier. As Mary crossed Avenue T on her way home from the church she could hear her dog barking.

"Hold your horses," she mumbled as she picked up her pace. When Mary reached the house she found the front door wide open. Unusual.

She rushed to her apartment door to let the pooch out before he put a new design on her living room rug. The dog raced right past Mary when she opened the door and headed straight up the stairs.

Mary followed.

"What in God's name has gotten into you, Prince?" she said as she reached the third floor landing. The door to the top floor apartment was opened. Prince had disappeared inside and continued to bark wildly.

Mary called out her tenant's name. When she received no answer she entered the apartment. She found the dog and saw what he was yapping about.

Mary held back a scream, quickly made the sign of the cross, scooped up the animal and ran down the stairs to call 9-1-1.

"I have to say, Augie, the garlic bread was particularly good this evening," Murphy said after polishing off the last morsel.

"Tell your friends at the precinct."

"Unless I swallow an entire bottle of Listerine before I head back, I won't need to tell anyone anything."

The siren turned both their heads toward the front window.

The patrol car raced up Avenue U and turned sharply onto Lake Street.

"One of yours?" Augie asked.

"Yes."

"Are you going to check it out?"

"Not unless I have to."

The siren went silent.

"It's close," Murphy said.

"Are you going to check it out?"

"Not unless I have to."

Vincent Salerno stepped up onto the bus.

He showed his ticket to the bus driver, made his way to the back of the coach and put the bag under his seat.

He would be arriving in Chicago the following day, late in the afternoon. Carmine Brigati would be meeting him at the end of the trip and then he and Carmine could argue about how Vinnie was going to get out from under the mountain of trouble he found himself in.

Vinnie thought about his big sister. As often as he had disappointed Angie, she had always come through for him. He wondered when he would see her again.

Vinnie was determined to stay awake. To protect the bag. To guard the tape recording that was causing all the turmoil.

When the bus pulled out of the Port Authority Terminal ten minutes later and entered the Lincoln Tunnel, Vinnie was asleep.

Officers Landis and Mendez were first on the scene. They were greeted by a woman who was nearly hysterical. Trembling, sobbing, babbling. She clutched a small, wiry-haired dog tightly to her chest like it was a life raft.

Landis gently eased her into a chair at the kitchen table. Mendez scared up a glass and filled it with water from the kitchen sink. When he placed the glass on the table the woman reacted to it as if it had eight legs.

Landis finally managed to calm her down somewhat by assuring her she would not have to accompany them to the third floor. Landis asked her to wait and the two officers headed up.

When they reached the second floor landing they both pulled out their weapons.

At the third floor landing, they found the door to the apartment opened wide. Landis entered first, slowly, holding his weapon out in front of him with both hands. Mendez followed suit.

"Jesus," Mendez said.

"Check if either victim is alive, nothing more," Landis said, fairly certain about the answer. "I'll make sure there is no one else in the rooms."

A few moments later Landis was back.

"Clear," he said.

"Both dead," Mendez said. "Should we check for identification?"

"We call it in and leave it to the guys making the big bucks. But I can tell you who the boy is. That's John Cicero's kid."

"Detective Cicero from the Sixty-eighth?"

"Yes."

"Fuck," said Mendez.

"Pretty dress," Landis said.

TWO

Sandra Rosen sat at her desk, alone in the large squad room.

Detective's Squad. Second floor. 61st Precinct. Coney Island Avenue. Brooklyn. New York.

Rosen looked around the room. Six desks. Ivanov and Richards out trying to track down two teens who had robbed a coin-operated laundromat wielding metal softball bats. Senderowitz completing a seminar at John Jay College of Criminal Justice called *New Directions in Evidence Collection for the 21st Century*. Murphy taking a dinner break.

The last desk, once occupied by Lou Vota, remained unassigned.

Samson was in his small private office in back, door closed, window shades drawn, not to be disturbed. Buried under a mountain of thankless paperwork.

It was unusually quiet in the precinct and abnormally calm out in the street. Particularly for this time of year, during the dog days of August, when breaking the law in the Borough of Churches was a popular pastime rivaled only by baseball.

The call was transferred up to the detectives' squad by Sergeant Kelly down at the front desk. Rosen answered on the third ring and she kept the conversation short.

She grabbed her jacket, her shield, and her holstered .38.

Moments later she was tapping on Samson's door.

"Come in, Rosen."

Rosen opened the door and entered the captain's office.

"How did you know it was me?"

"I can identify all of you by the way you knock. Although you are becoming less and less tentative as you settle in here. I almost mistook you for Senderowitz."

"Think you will ever mistake me for Murphy?" Rosen asked.

"Not unless you start using a battering ram. What's up?"

"I just took a call from Landis. I'm on my way out."

"What?"

"Two dead. That's all I got. I asked Landis to hold the gory details, work at locating the medical examiner and a crime scene investigation team instead. Want to ride along?"

"Do you need me to?"

"No."

"Where is Tommy?"

"Out to dinner. I know where to find him. I'll call him on my way."

"I'm glad you came over to us, Sandra."

"So you've said."

"And you?"

"Glad I came over? The jury is still out."

"Because of you and Murphy?"

"It's tricky."

"Call me from the scene. Let me know what you think happened there and yell if you need more uniforms."

"I will," Rosen said, turning to leave.

"And, Sandra," Samson said, briefly stopping her in her tracks.

"Yes?"

"It's only tricky when you're not sure what you want."

Ivanov and Richards used their legs, leaving their vehicle parked out in front of the laundromat and moving east along Avenue S.

The first confirmed sighting was reported by a Pakistani grocery store manager.

"Two boys walked in and tried to buy cigarettes and beer. I told them it was not possible. They insisted they were old enough. I asked for ID and told one of them if he didn't stop waving his bat, I was going to wrap it around his neck. They left."

The two detectives walked into a pizzeria further down the avenue.

"Two boys, ordered three large pizzas. One was on his cell phone the whole time they waited for the pies, inviting friends to a party at the school yard. David A. Boody Middle School, two blocks down on the right."

"Did they have softball bats?" Ivanov asked.

"One blue, one gray. One of them paid for the pies, pulled forty-six dollars from a fistful of small bills."

"Thanks for your help," Ivanov said.

"In my day, they called them Junior High Schools," the man said.

"Junior High Schools?" Richards said.

"Things change," Ivanov said.

She dragged Richards back out to the street.

"What was the rush? That kind of thing interests me."

"Let's go back for the car and find these delinquents while there is still daylight. You can come back here for a history lesson later."

"You're no fun," Richards said.

"You may change your tune when we get to the school yard."

Like Sandra Rosen, Marina Ivanov and Marty Richards were new recruits to the Six-one. Ivanov had come over from the 60th Precinct, Coney Island, four months earlier after working as a member of a joint task force that included Samson, Vota and Murphy from the 61st and Rosen, at that time with the 63rd Precinct, Flatlands. Marty Richards had come over less than two months earlier after finally realizing he was not cut out for the Internal Affairs Bureau.

They found eight teens, five boys and three girls, sitting on the ground under a basketball net. Gathered around three open pizza boxes. Someone had scored beer.

Two of the boys were holding court, side by side with two softball bats resting between them, likely bragging about their daring adventures.

A boom box was pounding out a rap tune Ivanov did not recognize and Richards could not stomach.

"How would you like to approach this?" Ivanov asked.

"By the book."

"What? *Police, you're under arrest?* Have you taken a good look at that sorry bunch? *By the book* is seldom effective when dealing with *comic book* characters. And with that suit you're wearing, they'll make you from a mile away and scatter before you say a word."

"Do you have a better idea?"

"The Russian-American junkie prostitute approach. Wait here. Pay attention."

Ivanov handed him her jacket, let down and mussed her hair, opened the top three buttons of her blouse, and strutted toward the pizza party.

Murphy was draining his second bottle of beer when the bar phone rang.

"Joe's Bar and Grill."

"Augie, this is Sandra Rosen."

"Hello, Detective Rosen. Nice to hear your voice."

The salutation captured Murphy's attention.

"Likewise. Is Tommy there?"

"Right beside me, trying to get the marinara off his necktie. Hold on."

Augie handed the telephone to Murphy.

"Rosen?"

"We have what appears to be a double homicide, just up the street from where you are. Lake Street, between Avenues U and T, east side of the street, the only three-story house, brick façade. I'll be on the top floor."

"I'm on my way," Murphy said.

"How is that going," Augie asked, as Murphy threw on his jacket and placed a twenty-dollar bill on the bar.

"How is *what* going?"

"You and Rosen stationed at the same precinct."

"I'd love to stay and chat, Augie, but I have a crime scene to get to."

"It's a simple question."

"There is nothing simple about it. Thanks for the beer."

"Can't you tell me if you think it is going to work out?"

"You want to know what I *think*."

"Yes."

"Read my mind," Murphy said, and he was out the door.

Rosen stepped out of her car and crossed Lake Street.

As she approached the building entrance, she spotted Mendez coming toward her from the north.

"I moved the patrol car up to Avenue U," he said. "Attract less attention here, at least until the CSU rig and the ambulance come screaming in."

"Good call. When are they expected?"

"Any time now," Rey said, "and the M.E. is on his way over from Brooklyn Hospital."

"Let's get inside."

Mendez led her into the ground floor apartment and back to the kitchen.

Officer Stan Landis and Mary Valenti sat at the table silently, which was very unusual for Landis and a good indication he had finally managed to calm the woman down.

"We're going to need at least four more uniforms, to canvass neighbors and for crowd control," Rosen said.

"I'll call it in," said Mendez.

"I would like to go up alone. Watch for the forensic team and Dr. Wayne. No one else gets in. Except Murphy, he should be here any minute."

Rosen climbed the stairs to the third floor. She walked through the open door into the apartment. She looked down at the bodies, had to quickly look away for a moment, and then she got down to business.

Ivanov strolled right through the circle and stopped in front of the two alleged laundromat burglars.

"I need a cigarette," she said.

"And I need a blow job," said the older of the two.

"In front of all of these boys and girls?"

"That's up to them."

"I prefer a little more privacy."

"How much?"

"Fifty."

"I don't have fifty. The pizza cost a fortune."

"Twenty?"

"That might be doable. Why don't you show me a little more of what you have under the shirt."

Ivanov reached into her blouse and pulled out her detective shield.

"Police," she said. "You're under arrest."

"You've got to be kidding me," the kid said.

Everyone else in the group was suddenly very quiet.

"Do you want to see my gun also?" Ivanov asked and then added, after a palpable silence, "I'll take that as a *no*. I want the two of you face down on the ground, hands behind your backs. The rest of you beat it."

Richards saw the group breaking up and he hurried over. Ivanov already had the older boy handcuffed, the second boy wasn't moving a muscle, and the other six kids were running out of the school yard at breakneck speed.

"Thank God they took the boom box," Richards said as he pulled out his own cuffs. "Do we have to clean up the food and drink?"

"I'm sure there's a night janitor around here who will appreciate the beer, let's get these tough characters out of here," Ivanov said, pulling the older boy up to his feet.

"Want a slice?" Richards asked, standing the second boy up.

"I'll pass."

The detectives ushered the boys across the school yard and to the unmarked car. They roughly deposited the boys in the back seat of the vehicle.

Richards climbed into the driver's seat.

Ivanov climbed in beside him.

"Ivanov."

"Yes, Richards?"

"Your blouse is open."

The promotion was not all it was cracked up to be.

There was much about being in the lower ranks that Samson missed.

After recovering from a gunshot wound that nearly demolished his elbow, he had been itching to get back to the trenches. Fortunately it was his left arm so he could still throw a baseball with his son, still corral his two young girls in his right arm, and still draw his service revolver.

Then, on the eve of his return to the Six-one, Chief of Detectives Stanley Trenton had visited Samson at home.

The news was Lieutenant Samson would be rejoining the troops at the 61st Precinct as Captain Samson.

The news was not a huge surprise.

The position had been vacant since before Christmas, when Captain Pulaski had lost his battle with lung cancer. Samson had been running the squad by default since. And Stan Trenton had threatened Samson with the permanent assignment a number of times.

The captain sat at his desk in the small office behind the deserted squad room staring distastefully at a pile of paperwork. Samson often felt isolated in the small space even when the larger room was bustling with activity. He took consolation in the thought that, so far, he had been doing a good job.

Samson had succeeded in pulling together a strong detectives' squad.

He had recruited Sandra Rosen and Marina Ivanov, spiriting them away from neighboring precincts, after witnessing their diligence and good instincts while they worked the Joint Task Force in the Gabriel Caine case.

Samson first ran across Marty Richards when Richards was the junior member of a two-man team sent by the Internal Affairs Bureau to interrogate Murphy. Samson saw something in the young man that inspired him to try rescuing Richards from a dreadful fate, a despised life with IAB. It took some convincing, but Richards was eventually persuaded to come over to the 61st.

And then there was Bernard Senderowitz.

Bernie and Samson had once worked as a team, longer ago than either cared to remember. Senderowitz was on the verge of an early out, being fed up and dismayed about how things were being run at his precinct in Staten Island. Not to mention it was *in* Staten Island. When Senderowitz told his old friend about his decision, Sam offered Bernie the option of sticking it out at the Six-one and getting in his time for full retirement. Bernie took the offer.

Senderowitz was a clever, seasoned detective, a priceless source of wisdom for the younger members of the squad.

Samson's greatest challenge was finding someone to fill Lou Vota's spot at the Six-one.

Lou had been shot and killed in February.

For Samson, Vota could not be truly *replaced*. Samson had sincerely admired and cared for the slain detective.

But Samson had finally made a choice, deciding on someone who he believed would complete the landscape at the Gravesend precinct.

Samson still missed being out in the streets regularly, like the theatre director who on opening night wants nothing more than to be down on the stage. But at the moment, gazing at the load of paper on his desk, Samson wanted nothing more than to get the hell out of the precinct house. Get home to Douglaston to be with his wife and children.

He cherished his family time. Sitting down to dinner with Alicia and the three kids. Putting Lucy and Kayla to sleep with a bedtime story. Picking up from his teenage son all the knowledge that had not been offered, or was not paid very much attention to, when Samson was at school in Bedford-Stuyvesant.

As badly as he wanted to get out, Samson felt obliged to wait until he heard from Detective Rosen.

After quick deliberation he decided, rather than waiting for a call, he would visit the crime scene at Lake Street on his way home.

When Murphy reached the landing he found Rosen sitting on the floor, her back against the wall beside the opened door.

"That bad?" he asked.

"That bad."

Murphy took a quick glance into the front room.

"What a fucking mess," he said, sitting down next to Rosen.

She was holding a small black velvet covered box in her hands.

There was a pair of driver's licenses on the carpet at her side.

"Horrible," she said.

"What do you have there?"

"Looks like an engagement ring to me. I found it in the boy's pocket. I also found close to two hundred dollars cash in his wallet."

"I guess we can rule out robbery. Are those their ID's?"

"Yes."

Murphy picked up one of the licenses.

"Please tell me that wasn't John Cicero's kid."

"I can't."

"Jesus fucking Christ."

"Worried about how Cicero is going to react?"

"I know exactly how he will react," Murphy said. "He's going to go to war. What I don't know is how I am going to break this to Augie Sena."

"Augie?"

"The kid was also Augie's nephew. His sister Rosie's son."

"Oh, Tommy, I'm so sorry."

"Sometimes I really hate this fucking job."

"It gets more tragic," Rosen said, handing Murphy the other driver's license.

"Angela Salerno? I didn't know her."

"Take another look."

"Am I missing something?"

"It was the girl's birthday," Rosen said, placing the small black velvet box down on the carpet between them.

THREE

When Samson arrived on the scene all the wheels were in motion.

Both ends of Lake Street, at Avenue U and Avenue T, were blocked off by patrol cars manned with uniformed officers. Samson parked his car on Avenue T and walked up to the house.

The CSU van and an ambulance sat in the middle of the street out front. The area between the north and south walls of the house and out to the curb was taped off. A uniformed officer was posted there to control entry.

Samson spotted Mendez and another officer canvassing door-to-door on the east side of the street. Two other uniforms were working the opposite side.

"Officer Landis is in the ground floor apartment with the landlady," the patrolman out front told Samson as he let the captain through the barrier.

He found Landis standing near the kitchen table. The woman was at the stove lighting up a gas burner underneath an old-fashioned coffee percolator.

Landis made the introductions.

"Mrs. Valenti, we are very sorry you had to experience this tragedy," Samson began. "We greatly appreciate your help and patience. We will do all we can to complete our business here as soon as possible. We realize you will have much to deal with in the following days and we have people who can assist you. For the moment, if you would please excuse us, I need a word with Officer Landis."

"There will be fresh coffee in ten minutes," was all she said.

"I may take you up on the offer."

Samson moved out of the kitchen toward the apartment exit with Landis on his heels.

"She discovered the bodies when she returned home from church. The second floor tenant has been out-of-town since Sunday. We found a door in the basement, leading up to the back alley, wide opened. It is always locked from the outside, but can be opened from inside. One of the CSU techs took prints from the door. Detectives Rosen and Murphy, the M.E. and CSU are up on the top floor."

"Do you think she'll be alright alone in there?" asked Samson. "I could use you out on the street."

"I'll go back in and feel it out."

"Thanks, Stan," Samson said, and he started up the stairs.

At the second floor landing he ran into Detectives Murphy and Rosen coming down.

"Did Batman kick you out?" Samson asked.

"We didn't give him the opportunity."

"So, where are you headed?"

"I need to make the long walk back over to Avenue U to tell Augie Sena his nephew was shot to death before having the opportunity to propose marriage to his girl."

"Rosie's son?"

"Yes."

"I'm sorry you have to break the news, Tommy. Will you go with Augie to see his sister?"

"If he wants me to," Murphy said.

"How about you?" Samson said, turning to Rosen.

"Off to see the girl's family. Want to ride along?"

"Do you need me to?"

"No."

"Then I guess I'll stay awhile and get in the way up there," Samson said. "Let me know if you need anything."

"What I need is a fucking desk job," Murphy said, starting down.

Samson and Rosen made brief eye contact and broke off in opposite directions.

. . .

Samson looked into the apartment on the top floor.

The CSU team, Derek Fielder and Joan Michaels, were moving through the front room armed with latex gloves and metal tweezers.

The medical examiner, Dr. Bruce Wayne, a.k.a. Batman, was down on his knees at the girl's body.

Before going in, Samson made a quick phone call.

Veteran detective Bernie Senderowitz exited the classroom following the final panel discussion of the three-day seminar at John Jay. A young woman in uniform came up to his side.

"What did you think?" she asked.

"About what?"

"The presentations. All of the remarkable new tools for investigating a crime scene."

"Very interesting."

"But?"

"But I think I will continue to rely on my most effective tool," Bernie said.

"Which is?"

Senderowitz simply touched his nose. Then his cell phone rang. After a very short conversation he told the young officer he had to run.

"A double homicide in Brooklyn," he explained. "My captain wants me to get over there and sniff around."

"Good evening, doctor," Samson said when he finally walked into the front room.

"Nothing much good about it," the medical examiner said looking up from the girl's body. "Good to see you out in the field, though. It's been a while. Do you still remember how to stay out from under my feet?"

"I do. What can you tell me?"

"The girl was kicked in the side. Twice. Brutally. She was shot two times in the chest. Large caliber by the look of the entrance wounds. The ballistics report will tell more. The shooter would have been standing very close to where you are standing now. Which, by the way, is *too* close."

Samson moved back a few steps.

Wayne stood up off his knees before continuing.

"I believe the girl was already down on the floor when she was killed," he said. "The boy was shot once in the forehead. Close range. I'm fairly certain it was a smaller caliber gun. His jaw is broken. I'd say he took a nasty punch. He may have been unconscious when he was shot."

"Two shooters?"

"Or one with two guns," Wayne said. "But don't quote me on *any* of this. Nothing is official until I get them down to the lab, which I am ready to do. As soon as you tell me they can go."

"Give me a little time, Bruce," Samson said. "I promise I will watch my step."

"I could use a cup of coffee," the M.E. said.

"There is a fresh pot waiting for you down at the ground floor apartment. I'm sure Mrs. Valenti would appreciate the company."

"How long?"

"Just until Bernie Senderowitz gets here and has time to take a quick look."

"Do you think Senderowitz is going to see something CSU won't find?"

"Maybe. He has a good nose."

"He has a large nose. I hope the coffee is strong."

"I have no doubts," Samson said. "If you run into the ambulance guys, ask them to sit tight."

"Sure."

"And, Bruce."

"Yes?"

"Thanks for being patient. I know it's not easy for you."

"Nothing about this job is easy for me, Sam."

. . .

Murphy stood on the opposite side of Avenue U staring at the door of Joe's Bar and Grill for nearly five minutes before working up the courage to cross over.

"Back for seconds?" Augie said, gazing up from the bar when Murphy walked in. "Jesus, Murphy, you look like hell."

"It's not good, Augie. It's your nephew, Edward, he was shot."

"What are you talking about?"

"At his girlfriend's place, less than a block away on Lake Street. I'm very sorry. I really don't know what else to say or how else to say it. They were both killed."

"My God, Tommy. Why?"

"We don't know what it was about, but I promise we're going to find out."

Murphy neglected to tell his good friend the young couple had been executed.

"Rosie?"

"She hasn't been told. I thought it best if she heard it from her big brother. But I can do it, or at least go with you to see her."

"No. I need to do this alone," Augie said. Sena looked so much smaller than he had before Murphy walked in. Like a de-flated balloon. "You *can* do something for me."

"Anything."

"Can you track down the boy's father? He's on duty tonight, out of the Sixty-eighth. I don't want him to hear about it from somewhere else."

"I'm on it, Augie," Murphy said, thinking it was absolutely the last thing he wanted to do. "What about this place? It's almost a full house."

"I'll get my day manager down here, he's five minutes away. I'll tell him to stop serving and to shut down when these people are done. We won't open again until sometime after the funeral."

"Are you sure you don't want me to come with you?" Murphy asked.

"Find John Cicero, Tommy," Augie said.

. . .

After dropping the two delinquents off at the Crossroads Juvenile Center on Bristol Street, Richards and Ivanov took East New York Avenue out to Kings Highway and headed toward Gravesend. Richards behind the wheel.

The detectives agreed they were both hungry.

"How about L and B?" Richards suggested.

"Pizza? If I wanted pizza I would have dined at the school yard," Marina said.

"They serve more than pizza."

"For instance?"

"Outstanding hero sandwiches. Veal parmesan, meatball, sausage and peppers, peppers and eggs."

"Multi-grain bread?"

"What?"

"Think they know how to throw together a vegetable salad?"

"I'm sure they can," Richards said. "Pretty sure."

"Fine. Columbus took a chance."

"Were your parents from Russia?"

"Interesting non-sequitur."

"You mentioned Columbus, it brought transcontinental travel to mind."

"My paternal grandparents. They both came to America when they were small children, in the late-twenties, after Lenin died and Stalin came to power. They met at a clothing factory on the Lower East Side in Manhattan. She was a seamstress and he was a presser," Ivanov said. "My dad was the first of seven children."

"And your mother?"

"All-American girl. Brooklyn born and raised. And *her* parents before her. My great-grandfather helped build the Manhattan Bridge. How about your people, did they come over on the Mayflower?"

Before Richards could answer, Ivanov's cell phone buzzed.

"This is Kelly. Did you crack the laundromat case?"

"Wide open."

"Where are you?"

"Kings Highway. Crossing Ocean Parkway," Detective Ivanov reported. "Did someone break the law or is this a social call?"

"There's a guy holed up in his house on West Twelfth. Between S and T. He's threatening to kill himself. His wife called it in."

"Called it in from where?"

"From inside the house. They had just finished dinner with their two kids. He rises from the table, takes a gun from a high cabinet in the kitchen, gives them all a warm farewell and locks himself in the bathroom."

"The wife and children are still inside?"

"She said she wouldn't leave him there alone."

"Very romantic. Do you think they are in danger?"

"I don't know. There are two uniforms outside. They're both as green as spinach. Everyone else is out. I've been trying to hunt down a negotiator."

"Give me the address," Ivanov said.

"Sounds like we're not going to make it to L and B," Richards said when the call was through.

"No. But we will be landing very close."

When Senderowitz walked in, the first thing he noticed was the victims.

Then he turned to Samson, who stood nearby.

"Not a pleasant picture."

"You don't know the half of it," Samson said.

"What can I do, Sam?"

"Do what you do. Use your senses. First impressions. Gut feelings. I want to know what you think happened here, without intellectualizing. But make it quick, Wayne is in a yank to get out of here."

"Batman left," Bernie said. "He told Landis he'd be down at the morgue waiting for the bodies, but wouldn't wait all night. I don't see clear indications of self-defense. That door will automatically lock when it is shut. There are no signs of forced entry. Whoever killed these kids came into the room. Someone opened the door for them from the inside."

"Someone they knew?"

"Not necessarily, it could have been carelessness."

"Go on."

"I am going to assume there were two shooters," Senderowitz said. "Don't ask me why. I'm not sure what it is, but I am going to proceed using that assumption."

The medical examiner had already suggested that possibility, based on the appearance of the gunshot wounds.

Senderowitz had looked down at the bodies for only a moment when he first walked in.

"Go on," Samson repeated.

Now, Senderowitz took a closer look at the two victims. He circled the bodies, closed his eyes, opened them, looked over to the front door and back and finally walked around the bodies once more.

After a minute or so he was back beside Samson.

"I don't believe this was a crime of passion. It was an execution, cold and business-like. By the look of the nasty bruise on the boy's face, he may have done something that made someone angry enough to pound him. Or, the boy may have been withholding information. The more I look at it, the more it feels as if they came for information, not for bounty or to settle a score. Look at the young man's body, both arms at his side, like someone who was asleep when he was shot, maybe unconscious. Not like someone who was staring up at a weapon pointed at his head."

"According to Wayne, the girl had been kicked in the side, twice. She may have also been down on the floor when killed," Samson said.

"I think the boy was killed first."

"Why is that?"

"The position of the girl's body. It looks as if she was moving toward the boy, trying to reach him, just before *she* was shot."

"Do you think they got the information they were after?"

"Possibly. If the boy was out cold, they were interrogating the girl. If she had the information, she may have given it up to try to save the boy's life."

"So, why *kill* these kids?"

"To avoid being identified maybe. It was done without conscience. They killed the couple, probably walked out of the house cool and calm. Now they could be off trying to find out whatever it was they may not have discovered here," Senderowitz said. "These children were innocents. After all these years, it still breaks my fucking heart. Have you notified the parents?"

"Murphy and Rosen are on it," Samson said. "By the way, as if it isn't bad enough, the boy's father is John Cicero."

"Terrific."

"Yes."

"Can we get out of here?"

"Sure," said Samson. "I'll let the EMS team know they can take the bodies. I'll leave Landis with the landlady and Rey Mendez to handle the canvassing."

"I could use a drink," Senderowitz said.

"I'll call my wife and tell her I'll be late. The drink is on me."

FOUR

The 68th Precinct sits on 65th Street, between 3rd and 4th Avenues, in the shadow of the Gowanus Expressway where it meets the Belt Parkway.

Murphy knew he should not waste any time getting word to John Cicero about his son's death, as unpleasant as the task would be.

But Murphy had another duty that would not wait, at his three-room flat on Marine Avenue.

And it was not out of the way.

Murphy double-parked in front of the building. Before leaving the car he slapped an eight-by-ten inch laminated card reading OFFICIAL POLICE BUSINESS on the dashboard and he turned on the emergency flasher. He rushed through the lobby and up the short flight of stairs to Apartment B9.

"It's me," Murphy announced from the hall outside the door, the customary method of identifying himself, and he let himself in.

Ralph sat just inside the threshold motionless as a statue, looking as if he had been staring at the door for hours. Murphy was certain Ralph was relieved to see him, but the message in Ralph's large brown eyes was anything but understanding or forgiving.

"Sorry, pal," Murphy said. "Let's go."

Ralph jumped to his feet, ran past Murphy, and hurried down the stairs. Murphy locked the door and quickly followed. Two short blocks to John Paul Jones Park, two quick circles around the perimeter and a side-by-side sprint back to the car.

Murphy decided to take Ralph along for the trip. He would treat Ralph to a few hotdogs after their mission was accomplished.

"Want to go for a ride?"

Ralph wagged his tail wildly. Murphy opened the back door of the car and the dog jumped in. Murphy slipped behind the wheel, started the car, drove to the end of Marine Avenue, and turned onto Shore Road in the direction of the Six-eight.

Rosen rang the doorbell. The woman who answered opened the door only as far as the safety chain would allow.

"Mrs. Salerno?"

"May I help you?"

"Detective Rosen. Sixty-first Precinct."

The woman unlatched the chain and opened the door. She was wearing a muumuu—a loose fitting flowered housedress.

"My God. I knew it. I have never seen him so upset. I begged him not to go out. What has Vincent done? Is he alright?"

"Vincent?"

"Aren't you here about my son?"

"Mrs. Salerno," Rosen said, "may I come inside."

The police car was in front of the house on West 12ᵗʰ Street when Ivanov and Richards pulled up. Marina saw two children in the back seat of the car, a boy and girl, both pre-teen. The detectives climbed out of their own vehicle and Marina approached one of the uniformed officers.

"I talked the woman into allowing the kids leave the house," he said. "She's still inside, trying to talk her husband out of the bathroom."

Suddenly there was an older man standing beside them.

"I'm sorry, sir," the uniform said. "You need to move away from here."

"Detective Ivanov?" the man said.

"Do I know you?"

"Frank Sullivan. Sully. The last time we met I was on the ground with a bullet in my side."

"Of course, Mr. Sullivan," Ivanov said as Richards joined

them. "It's good to see you up and about."

"I live just a few doors down," Sully said. "What happened here?"

"Do you know the people who live in this house?"

"I know them well, Robert and Maggie Marconi, they have two young children."

Ivanov pointed over to the patrol car. Sully spotted the children, clearly frightened, and he walked over to the vehicle. He said a few words to the boy and girl and they seemed to relax a bit. Then he came back to the detectives.

"Mr. Sullivan, can you think of a reason why Mr. Marconi would want to harm himself?" Marina asked.

"He ran an auto parts business on Avenue U. The business went under and he has been out of work for half a year. Did you say harm himself?"

"He is threatening to take his own life."

Sullivan shook his head and sighed deeply.

"I can understand his desperation, if not what he is considering as a solution," Frank said. "I've been there. And please, call me Sully."

"Sully, his wife is still inside," Ivanov said. "She refuses to leave him in there alone. Do you think she is in danger?"

"I don't believe he would harm Maggie," Sullivan said. "But then, I never imagined he would be thinking about suicide. If you would permit me, maybe Maggie will listen to someone she knows."

"I don't think that's a good idea, Mr. Sullivan," Richards said.

"It might be, Marty," Ivanov suggested. "Mr. Sullivan has a much better chance of gaining her trust. Go ahead, Sully. Please be careful."

Frank Sullivan moved toward the front door.

When Murphy and Ralph walked into the lobby of the 68th Precinct the desk sergeant looked down from his elevated post.

"No pets allowed," the sergeant said.

"I'm Detective Murphy, from the Six-one."

"I know who you are, Murphy. I was talking to the canine. How can we be of service?"

Murphy gave Ralph a moment to answer before speaking himself.

"I'm looking for Detective Cicero."

"Up the stairs to the right."

"Can I leave Ralph down here with you?"

"Does he bite?"

"Only if you tried taking a roast beef sandwich away from him."

"If there was a roast beef sandwich in this damn place, I might take my chances. Leave the dog with me, maybe he and I will order in. Up the stairs, to the right."

Murphy entered the squad room and spotted Cicero immediately. He took a deep breath, let it out, and walked over.

"Hello, John."

"Hello, Tommy. What brings you to our neck of the woods?"

"Is there somewhere we can talk?" Murphy asked, looking around the room. There were two other detectives working at their desks.

"What do you mean?"

"Somewhere private."

"This place isn't exactly Grand Central Station."

"Somewhere else," Murphy said.

Cicero stood up from his desk. He was a big man, at least a head taller than Murphy. He looked as if he was about to say something argumentative, but had changed his mind at the last second.

"The captain is out. We can use his office," Cicero said, leading the way.

Richards and Ivanov watched as Maggie Marconi opened the door to Sullivan.

The two exchanged a few words and then Sully stepped inside.

And the door was closed again.

"That's not good," Richards said. "I thought the idea was to get the woman out."

"I'll admit this was not exactly what I had in mind," Ivanov said.

"What do we do now?"

"Think positive."

A few minutes later the woman came out.

She shut the door behind her and walked away from the house.

"Unbelievable," Richards said.

Richards and Ivanov moved to meet her.

"Are you all right?" Ivanov asked.

"Not really. But I'm not hurt if that's what you're asking," Maggie said. "Where are the children?"

"Sitting in the back seat of the patrol car," Richards said.

"May I sit with them?"

"Of course you can."

As she moved to her children, Richards looked over to the front door of the house and then back at the woman.

"Mrs. Marconi?"

"Yes?" she said, turning to the two detectives.

"What about Mr. Sullivan?" Richards asked.

"Frank is a wonderful man."

"We're sure he is."

"Sully said he would stay with Robert, so I could come out and see the children."

She climbed into the back of the patrol car and took the children into her arms.

Richards and Ivanov turned back to the front door.

Richards broke the silence.

"How are we doing so far?"

Marie Salerno had been trembling, on and off, for nearly thirty minutes—since learning Detective Rosen had not come about her son, but about her daughter. She spoke occasionally, incoherently.

Vincent was in some kind of trouble.

It was Angela's birthday.

Rosen sat quietly by Marie's side until the woman's husband arrived. He had been working late at his office when he got the call from his wife. He took Marie into his arms and the woman finally broke down, breathless sobs, cries of lament. Rosen watched uncomfortably as Fred Salerno slowly managed to calm his wife. The detective knew it was time to leave.

She told the Salernos they would be called in to identify Angela's body. No matter how many times she had been required to say those words they always felt cold and cruel. She told them how sorry she was. She told them to call the 61st if they needed help with anything.

Rosen said goodbye and walked out to the street.

Back in her car, she called Kelly at the precinct.

"I needed an APB out on Vincent Salerno. White male. Twenty-two years old. Five-ten. Approximately one hundred sixty pounds. Brown hair. Brown eyes. Wanted for questioning."

"Done," Kelly said.

"Thanks," Rosen said, and then she headed back to the crime scene on Lake Street to check for any progress.

"So, what is this about?" Cicero asked, once they were inside the office.

There was no easy way to say it so Murphy simply said it.

"It's about your son, John, he was shot."

"What the fuck are you saying?" Cicero said, loud enough to turn heads in the squad room.

"In Gravesend. At his girlfriend's apartment. They were both killed."

The look in Cicero's eyes could have shattered glass. He picked up a letter opener and imbedded it in the captain's desk. He grabbed a desk phone and was about to hurl it against the wall, but he stopped himself. He sat at the desk and placed his hands over his face. He sat that way without making a sound for nearly five minutes. Then he uncovered his face, placed his hands palms down on the desk and looked up at Murphy.

Murphy had been standing by quietly hating every minute.

"Tell me everything you know about what happened," Cicero said.

Murphy didn't have much to tell.

There had been little in the way of solid evidence when he left the scene and he hadn't heard anything new. All he could relate was what he saw when he walked into the apartment and it was no less ugly and tragic in the telling.

"Rosie?" Cicero asked when Murphy was done.

"Augie is with her," Murphy said. "We'll find out who did this, John."

"We?"

"Everyone at the Six-one will be on this around the clock."

"You do what you have to do, Murphy, and I'll do what I have to do."

"Look, John, I understand what you are feeling. When Lou Vota was killed we were ready to tear up the entire borough. But the case belonged to the Seventy-sixth Precinct and Trenton warned us all to stand down."

"Stan Trenton's warnings don't scare me. I have been ignoring them for years. And the scum who shot Lou Vota, if I remember correctly you ran him down with your car."

"I was lucky to be in the right place at the right time."

"I hope to be as lucky."

"Just don't forget it's our case, John."

"Just don't fucking forget it was *my* son, Murphy. Thanks for coming to see me, I know it wasn't easy. Now, if there's nothing else, I need to get home to my wife."

"Sure. Do you need a ride?"

"Thanks, I can take care of it myself. All of it."

Murphy watched Cicero leave and waited a few minutes before going back down for Ralph. Murphy could only hope he and his team would wrap this case up in record time. There was no chance in hell Detective John Cicero was going to stay out of their way for long.

"How about, while we're waiting, I run over to L and B and grab a sandwich and a salad?"

Ivanov gave her partner an unfriendly glance.

"I'm kidding," Richards said. "We have to do something. We have no idea about what's going on in there."

Before Ivanov could respond Sullivan led Robert Marconi out of the house, his hand on Marconi's shoulder.

"The weapon is on the kitchen table," Sully said when they reached the detectives.

One of the uniformed officers was moving to take Marconi into custody.

"Hold on," Ivanov said.

Marconi's wife jumped out of the patrol car and ran over to embrace her husband.

Ivanov gave them a minute before speaking.

"You will have to go to the hospital," she said, "for evaluation."

"I made a huge mistake," Marconi said. "It won't happen again."

"I'm glad to hear that, but I'm afraid it is standard procedure."

"I understand. I'll do whatever is necessary to get this behind us."

"Can I ride with my husband?" Mrs. Marconi asked.

"Of course," Ivanov said. "What about the children?"

"I can watch the children," Sully said. "I'll take them over to visit with Sal and Fran DiMarco. I am sure Fran has some homemade cookies or cake handy."

"Thank you, Frank," Maggie said. "For everything."

"Just take good care of Robert," Sully said, "there are many people who care about your family. You will get through this."

"Do we need to cuff him?" one of the uniforms asked.

"No," said Richards. "Just drive them to Coney Island

Hospital. They may have to keep you overnight, Mr. Marconi, in which case the officers will bring your wife home."

The children had stepped out of the patrol car and they stood quietly at the curb.

Their parents hurried over to them and Robert Marconi took the children into his arms.

"Thank you, Sully," Ivanov said. "Mind if I ask what you said to him in there?"

"I told him his children were very frightened and his wife needed his help. Robert is a good man, a hard-working man. Bob *will* find work. In fact, I have been checking on several leads. Is he under arrest?"

"Yes and no," Ivanov said. "Attempted suicide is not against the law, but he is being brought in for suspicion of endangering the safety of others. It's a formality, for mental evaluation purposes. If he has a permit for the gun he'll be released once it is determined he is not a threat to himself or his family."

"And if he doesn't have a permit for the weapon?"

"Then it could get a lot stickier," Richards said. "Recent changes in the law could mean a jail sentence. If that's the case, I'd recommend finding a lawyer right away."

"Let's pray it doesn't come to that," Frank Sullivan said.

They watched the patrol car drive off, the children stood patiently.

Sully waved them over.

"Are you guys okay?" Sully asked the boy, the older of the two.

"Yes," the boy said bravely.

"Would you like to visit with the DiMarco's while we wait for your mother to come home? I'm sure there will be cookies."

"Yes," the boy said.

"Me, too," said the girl.

Sully took them both by the hand.

"Good seeing you, Detective Ivanov," he said, "and meeting you, Detective Richards."

Marina and Marty watched them move up the street.

"I could use a cookie," Richards said.

. . .

Vincent Salerno opened his eyes when the Greyhound bus came to an abrupt halt.

Vinnie looked out of the window at a large sign in front of the building.

WELCOME TO THE BLUE MOUNTAIN SERVICE PLAZA

He waited while the other passengers left the coach, grabbed the gym bag from under his seat and walked to the front.

"Where are we?" he asked the driver.

"On the Pennsylvania Turnpike in the beautiful Poconos. You can leave the bag onboard."

"I'd rather carry it with me. How long?"

"You have exactly sixteen minutes. If you're late, you miss the bus."

"Story of my life," Vinnie said.

"Give me a break, kid. What are you all of twenty-five-years old?"

"Twenty-two."

"Better yet. You have your whole life ahead of you."

"I hope you're right," Vinnie said before stepping down to the pavement.

When Detective Rosen arrived at the house on Lake Street everyone had left, except Landis who was eagerly waiting to be cut loose.

Landis gave her a quick update.

"Samson said to call it a night. The bodies are gone. The landlady was picked up by her son. She will be spending a few days with his family," Landis reported. "It was getting a little too late to bother neighbors, so we shut down the canvassing until morning. Nothing major so far. Well, next to nothing. One neighbor saw two adult males standing at a car that had been parked in front of his house across the street. One got into the car and drove off. The other walked up the street. He said he didn't see where they had come from."

"Descriptions?"

"One well-dressed, in a gray business suit. The one who got into the car was in a blue jogging suit and was built like an NFL defensive lineman."

"The vehicle?"

"Big and black."

"Great."

"I was hoping to get out of here, unless you need something else."

"No, you can go," Rosen said. "I'm sorry we kept you waiting. We'll hit it hard in the morning. Has Murphy been back?"

"I haven't seen him."

"Okay then. Good night, Landis."

"Good night, Detective."

Rosen went back to her car and called Murphy.

"Where are you?" she asked.

"I just left the Six-eight. No fun. Ralph is with me. I'm going to grab a few hotdogs for him on Eighty-Sixth Street and drop him at home before heading back to Lake Street."

"I'm at Lake Street. There's nothing happening here, Samson closed up shop for the night."

"So what are you doing now?" Murphy asked.

"I was hoping I could meet you at your place. I would rather not be alone tonight."

"Absolutely, come on. Do you want a hotdog?"

"No thanks, but I could use a hug."

"I'll have one waiting," Murphy said, "with all the fixings."

FIVE

Samson called in all 61st Precinct detectives and uniformed officers for a mandatory meeting at eight o'clock on Thursday morning.

The call was not well received by those who had been looking forward to a scheduled day off, but Samson wanted the entire precinct to be made aware of any solid progress in what was being called the Lake Street Homicides. If in fact there was any progress to report. The captain also called in Derek Fielder from CSU, Matt Beck from Ballistics and Robin Harding, Dr. Wayne's assistant in the Medical Examiner's Office.

When the troop was fully assembled Samson asked Officers Landis and Mendez, first on the scene, to kick off the proceedings.

"The victims were discovered in the top floor apartment of a detached three-family brick house at one-twelve Lake Street by the house owner, Mrs. Mary Valenti, at approximately ten past seven last evening. Valenti, a widow, lives alone in the ground floor rooms. She had just arrived home when she found the victims. The only other occupant of the building, who rents the second floor apartment, was reportedly out-of-town," Landis began.

"Did you get anything on the second floor tenant?" asked Senderowitz.

"Richard Sherman. Male. Single. Thirty-two years old. Out-of-town since Sunday, due back late this afternoon."

"Out-of-town where?" Bernie asked.

"A business conference in Boise, according to the landlady."

"We'll need to question him," said Samson.

"Should we try to confirm Sherman was actually where he told the landlady he would be?" Landis asked.

"I'm sure he was in Boise," Murphy said. "Who would make up a story about having to go to *Idaho*? How long has he lived in the apartment?"

"Three years."

"I think we can safely rule him out."

"We still need to talk with him," Samson said. "Sherman may have heard or seen something around the house lately that could help us. And we need to do more canvassing. Landis and Mendez, when we're done here take two more uniforms with you and cover both sides of the street, starting where you left off last night. Keep your eyes open for Sherman's arrival and question him when he turns up. Anything else come out of the door-to-door yesterday?"

"Just a neighbor across the street who spotted two men at a car in front of his house around six-thirty," Mendez said.

"We heard. The big black car," Murphy said, "the odd couple."

"He may simply have trouble with verbal description," Senderowitz said. "Did he think he could identify the men if he saw them again, Rey?"

"He said *possibly*. Should we bring him in to look at mug shots?"

"No. It would be a waste of time, it could be nothing. Let's put him with a sketch artist instead. And try to get more from him about the car. Old. New. Foreign. American. Two door. Four door. Cadillac. Ford. Try getting him to picture it in his mind. Jog his memory somehow."

Rosen listened attentively whenever Senderowitz spoke. She understood she could learn a lot from the veteran detective.

Murphy's attention tended to drift.

"What do you have, Fielder?" Samson asked.

"Michaels and I went through most of the apartment and we went over the stairs, although there was a lot of traffic up and down after the crime and before our arrival. We'll go back and finish up this morning. The victims were definitely killed where they were found. It didn't look as if the intruders, there seems to have been two, went further than the front room. We lifted a number of prints last evening. We are in the process of running those that don't belong to the victims through our database. I lifted some prints from the rear door in the basement that matched prints found in the apartment and did not match those of either victim or the landlady."

"So whoever went out the back door to the alley may have been in the apartment last evening," Richards suggested.

"Definitely at some time, possibly last evening," Fielder offered.

Samson thanked Fielder and called on Beck, wanting to move ahead quickly.

"The victims were killed with different caliber weapons," Beck confirmed. "We are most likely looking at two shooters, but there is no way of knowing for certain. There were no bullet casings discovered. Of course, we cannot match the bullets to specific weapons without the weapons. We can try to determine if they match any we have in evidence from other shootings."

"What is the argument for two shooters, other than the use of separate weapons?" Rosen asked.

"Bullet trajectory" Beck said. "One shooter would've had to move at least ten feet before shooting the second victim, regardless of which victim was killed first. I don't buy it. On top of that, one perp using two guns is not logical."

"Nothing about killing two young people is logical," Ivanov said.

"There is work to do at the lab, Captain," Robin Harding interrupted. "Dr. Wayne needs me back there as soon as possible."

"Go ahead then," Samson said. "What do you have so far?"

"Not much more than we may have guessed," Dr. Harding began. "Both victims were struck with great force. However, the cause of death in both cases was the consequence of the gunshot wounds, loss of blood and the destruction of vital organs. The approximate time of death for both victims is the same, but Dr. Wayne seems to think the boy was killed first. Something about the position of the bodies at the scene."

Samson and Senderowitz exchanged glances.

"For what it's worth, I personally agree the idea of one shooter wielding two guns doesn't fly," Harding added.

"Thank you all," Samson said. "Harding, Beck and Fielder can get back to work. Landis and Mendez, choose canvassing partners and get over to Lake Street. All other officers check with Desk Sergeant Kelly for assignments."

Everyone broke away except the detective squad.

"Rosen, tell us about the APB on Vincent Salerno," Samson said.

"I went from the crime scene to the home of the girl's parents to make notification. The girl's mother, Marie Salerno, was alone at the house. Mrs. Salerno became very upset when I identified myself as a detective, thinking I had come about her son. She allowed me into the house and I had to explain I was there about her daughter, make her understand her daughter had been killed, and then it became very difficult getting coherent responses from her. I managed to learn a few things but had to tread softly.

"She could think of absolutely no reason why anyone would decide to harm Angela or her boyfriend. I don't think she knew about the engagement ring. Her son, Vincent, lives with his parents. He never came home Tuesday night. He showed up on Wednesday afternoon extremely agitated. He asked his mother for cash, she had none available. She said she would phone his dad and ask her husband to bring money for Vincent but he told her not to call his father. She begged him to wait, but he took off," Rosen said, "with a gym bag full of clothing. I learned that Vincent works as a bus boy at Il Colosseo Restaurant on Eighteenth Avenue and Seventy-seventh. I called the restaurant and was told he had worked on Tuesday night and had failed to show up for his scheduled shift yesterday."

"Did you say a gym bag?" Murphy asked.

"Yes."

"I think we saw the kid run past Augie's bar before Rosen called me."

"There are a lot of kids in Brooklyn running around with gym bags," Richards said.

"Sure. But this kid was in a big hurry, less than a block away from the crime scene."

"I hate the idea, but we need to speak with the parents again as soon as possible," Samson said. "If he hasn't shown up yet, we need help to locate the boy. Names of friends. Particularly girlfriends. Murphy, go along with Rosen. Maybe you can talk with the father while Sandra talks to the mother. And if the boy lived at home, try to get something with his prints."

"Fingerprints?" Rosen asked.

"Maybe he went to see his sister for help after he left his mother," said Senderowitz, on the same page as the captain.

"We should at least check to see if the boy is in the system," Samson added. "How did it go with John Cicero, Tommy?"

"Cicero is going to be trouble, Sam."

"No surprise. I'll talk to Trenton about it."

"Cicero doesn't care about Trenton," Murphy said.

"No surprise either," said Samson. "Bernie, find out when they open the doors of the restaurant where the Salerno kid works. See if there's anything to discover down there. I want all of you back here at four sharp this afternoon. Drop whatever you are doing for a short time."

"What's the occasion?" Murphy asked.

"It's a surprise. Get to work."

"Do you have anything for Ivanov and me?" Richards asked. "Or do we hang here and send out for donuts."

"Doesn't anyone in this place know how to pick up a damn phone?" the desk sergeant said, barging into the squad room.

"What is it, Kelly?"

"A call came in on a dead body in a car under the elevated train tracks on McDonald at Avenue T. Gun shot. A big man in a blue jogging suit. The vehicle is big and black."

"Does that answer your donut question, Richards?" Murphy asked.

"Guess we'll have to pick up a dozen on the way."

"Get going, I'll call CSU and the M.E.," Samson said.

"Take a photograph of the victim," Senderowitz said. "It should save having to use a sketch artist."

"Do you really think it's one of the two men spotted on Lake Street last night?" Ivanov asked.

"I'll bet my pension on it."

Frank Sullivan rented the basement apartment in the DiMarco house on 12th Street, a few doors down from the Marconi residence.

Sully received a distressing phone call from Maggie Marconi on Thursday morning.

After the call, he went upstairs to see Salvatore and Frances.

Sal greeted him at the door.

"Frank. Good morning. Frances walked down to Campo's store for milk. She should be back any minute. Fran expected she would find you there."

"Joe gave me the day off," Sully said. "He and I took care of all the major deliveries yesterday."

"Well, come in, would you like coffee?"

"I wanted to thank you for helping with the Marconi children last night."

"Of course, it was our pleasure. They're great kids."

Sully was silent for a moment before responding.

"They are very good people, Sal," he finally said.

"I know. I also know they have been going through a rough time, and we have all been concerned. But they have friends here, good neighbors who care. They will get through this."

"I could use that coffee."

"What is it, Frank?" Sal asked, sensing there was something else.

"The family may be in more serious trouble, Salvatore. I'm hoping your daughter Lorraine can help."

The car parked under the McDonald Avenue El was a four-door black Lincoln sedan. Marty Richards circled the car while Ivanov peered into the front passenger door window.

The victim was in the driver's seat, his head resting against the steering wheel.

"No license plates," Richards said, arriving beside Ivanov and looking in. "Wow, talk about getting your brains blown out. Whoever capped this guy had to be right on top of him. Is that a gun in his lap?"

"Smith and Wesson nickel plated thirty-eight."

"Nice piece."

"The doors are locked," Ivanov said.

"That shouldn't be a problem, we're cops."

Detective Richards turned to the uniformed officers who were first on the scene and had called it in and asked if they had something in their patrol car to do the trick.

A minute later they had the door opened.

"This is a real mess," Richards said. "I'd rather not touch anything."

"We need to get the weapon," Ivanov said.

She pulled out a latex glove, carefully lifted the gun out and placed it into a plastic bag Richards held ready. She asked the uniforms to wait for the CSU techs and the medical examiner.

"Ask CSU to take a Polaroid of the victim and get it over to Landis and Mendez on Lake Street. Make sure they get the jogging suit in the photo."

"Do you think Senderowitz is right about this being one of the men seen last night on Lake Street?" Richards asked.

"Yes, I think Bernie's pension is safe, and I think the doer is going to need a new gray business suit. Let's get this gun over to ballistics."

Senderowitz arrived at Il Colosseo Restaurant at ten, hoping to find someone at work before the doors opened to the public. The detective spotted a man setting up the cash register in front and tapped on the door.

"We open at eleven," the man called out.

Bernie pressed his detective badge against the window.

The man closed the register and walked over.

"We are very busy now, getting ready for the lunch crowd," he said from behind the closed door.

"I just need a few minutes."

The man opened the door, let Senderowitz in, and locked up again.

"Are you the owner?" Bernie asked.

"I'm the manager. What can I do for you?"

"Detective Senderowitz, Sixty-first Precinct. I'm looking for an employee of the restaurant, Vincent Salerno."

"Join the club. I haven't seen him in two days. He missed his work shift yesterday and didn't call. If you find him, tell him if he doesn't call today he's out of a job."

"Do you have any idea why he failed to show up?"

"I have no idea why any of these kids *do* show up. He's a bus boy. They come and go like the days of the week."

"What is your name, sir?" Senderowitz asked. "Just so I know what to call you."

Besides asshole.

"Atanasio. Mike Atanasio."

Senderowitz took a business card from his jacket pocket and handed it to Atanasio.

"Do me a big favor, Mike. If Vincent turns up, please give me a shout."

"Sure. Is there anything else?"

"I'll let you know if I think of anything. Thanks for your time," Bernie said. "You can let me out now."

A moment after the detective left, a young man who had been setting napkins and silverware approached Atanasio.

"I need a smoke break," he said.

"Are the tables done?"

"Everything but the water glasses."

"Salt and pepper shakers?"

"Topped off and set."

"Okay, but make it quick. We open in less than an hour."

"It'll be done, Mike," Bobby Hoyle said. "Don't I always get it done? You need to chill out."

"When I need your advice, Bobby, I'll ask for it. Make it quick."

"Got it, I heard you twice the first time."

When Bobby got out to the street he spotted the detective leaning against a car on the opposite side of 18th Avenue.

Senderowitz was looking at the restaurant entrance as if he was expecting someone to come out.

Bobby walked across to meet him.

"You were asking about Vincent," Bobby Hoyle said.

"Yes, I was."

"I may be able to help you."

"I'm all ears," Bernie said. "Let's take a walk."

Lorraine DiMarco was working at her desk in the law office when the telephone rang. It was her assistant, Victoria Anderson.

"You have a call from Frank Sullivan."

Lorraine had been expecting the call. Her father had phoned and given her a heads-up earlier.

"Put him through, Vickie."

"Lorraine?"

"Sully, it's good to hear from you. How have you been?"

"Fine, thanks. And you?"

"Very well, also."

"Lorraine, I need some legal advice and I would rather speak with you about it in person. If you could find the time."

"As a matter of fact, I have a meeting in Bensonhurst at one-thirty and I need to get something to eat before I perish. What about lunch at the Del Rio Diner on Kings Highway at twelve?"

"That would be terrific, as long as you let me buy."

"We can arm wrestle for it."

"Fair enough. I appreciate your time."

"It's no problem, Sully. I'll see you at noon."

Mickey, Denise and Claire were running around the back yard, yelling like the wild Indians they were pretending to be.

54

Kyle was keeping an eye on his brother and cousins.

A *special assignment* delegated to the eight-year-old by his dad.

"Try being *quiet* Indians sneaking through the woods," Kyle said. "The cowboys can hear you from a mile away."

Surprisingly the ploy worked and the three younger children turned it down a few decibels. Ripley and Connie watched from the kitchen window.

"He's good," Connie said.

"He's turning into a little man right in front of my eyes. But I can't wait until school starts up again," Ripley said. "Summer vacation was not designed with parents in mind."

"How are you feeling about this afternoon?"

"Feeling?"

"Nervous?"

"I'm just hoping I will fit in."

"They'll be glad to have you, and lucky."

"Thanks."

"It's a big step," Connie said.

"One I had to make. The boys have been uprooted and moved around enough already. New York is their home, and mine. I want us all to stay close to friends and family. I want the boys to grow up with your girls and I can't imagine how I would manage without you and Phil nearby."

"We are all happy you decided to stay," Connie said.

Ripley suddenly noticed his older son standing at his side.

"Dad?"

"Yes, Kyle."

"Can you teach me how to throw a curve ball?"

"When the three little Indians go up for a nap, son," Ripley promised. "Right now I need you to tell them it's time for lunch."

"Should I send a smoke signal?"

"I think two little words will work faster," Connie said, laughing.

"What two little words?" Kyle asked his aunt.

"Grilled cheese."

. . .

"He was brought before a judge this morning and he was charged with possession of an unlicensed and unregistered lethal weapon," Sully said. "He could face a jail sentence."

"Was it Judge Epstein?" Lorraine asked.

They were sitting at a window booth in the Del Rio Diner.

"Yes," Sully said, wondering how she had guessed.

"Norman Epstein is a good and fair judge, but in this case it is not great news for Mr. Marconi."

"Why?"

"With the increased incidence of gun violence in the past decade, often resulting in multiple deaths, a line has been drawn in the sand. Legislative, Executive and Judicial elected and appointed officials have been compelled to make it very clear as to where they stand. On the side of stronger gun control or second amendment rights," she explained. "Judge Epstein is a zealous advocate for greater gun control and is prone to articulate his point of view by making examples of those who break existing gun laws."

"It was his father's gun," Sully said. "Robert never considered licenses or registration. If he goes to prison the family will really fall to pieces."

"I understand that, and I know Mr. Marconi. I know he is a good man and I care about Maggie and the children, but Epstein can be stubborn and unsympathetic."

"What do we do?"

"You try to assure them it will be alright and collect names of any friends and neighbors who will speak for him. I will try reaching out to some friends of my own, in the prosecutor's office," Lorraine said, as the waitress brought their plates. "For the moment, we can eat."

Lorraine dug in.

Sully sat quietly, pushing the food around in his dish.

"Lorraine?"

"Yes, Frank?"

"How do we convince someone things will work out when we are not confident ourselves?"

"We do it all the time, Sully. Now please stop worrying. And please, stop playing with your food. I don't like eating alone."

"Sorry."

"Listen to me, I sound like someone's mother."

"I think you would be a great mother."

"That's a very nice thing to say," Lorraine replied, and sadly thought of Lou Vota.

Vincent Salerno stepped off the bus in the Greyhound boarding area on West Harrison Street in Chicago. It was just before three in the afternoon on Thursday. He had been traveling for nearly nineteen hours.

Carmine Brigati was waiting for him inside the terminal.

Vincent and Carmine had grown up together since infancy. The Salerno home was next door to the Brigati home on 82nd Street between 3rd and Ridge Avenues in Bay Ridge. The boys had gone to school together, from PS 102 to JHS 259 to Fort Hamilton High School.

They were as close as brothers.

After their sophomore year at Fort Hamilton Carmine's father, who had been a New York City firefighter for fifteen years, took a job with the Chicago Fire Department and moved the family to his wife's home town.

A year later, Carmine's dad was killed in the line of duty when a stairwell collapsed in a burning warehouse.

Vincent barely made it through high school in Brooklyn. Carmine fared much better in the Windy City, despite the loss of his father. And because he was the son of a firefighter, Carmine Brigati qualified for a Chicago Police and Fire Scholarship, which granted full tuition for four years at the University of Chicago. He studied Computer Sciences.

Today, Carmine had an entry-level position with a software development company and was taking graduate courses at night and Vincent had less than twenty dollars in cash after leaving a job as an underpaid bus boy in an Italian restaurant. Of course, Vincent did have his green gym bag, which he clutched tightly to his chest when he greeted Carmine.

"I hope you have a couple of slices from L and B in that thing," Carmine said.

"Don't you have pizza in Chicago?"

"They call it pizza. You must be starving after that bus ride. I'll take you out to eat."

"After that bus ride I would rather not be around other people. Can we pick up something to go?"

"Anything you want, Vinnie. I took this afternoon and tomorrow morning off from work. We can pick up food and beer, go to my place and settle in. And later, maybe you will tell me why you finally decided to visit after more than six years and why you were suddenly in such a hurry get here."

SIX

The detectives began drifting into the squad room shortly before four in the afternoon. The door to Samson's office was shut, the shades drawn. They all had news to report, but decided to hold off until the captain appeared and revealed his *surprise.*

"Any ideas?" Richards asked.

"Not a clue," said Rosen.

"Knowing Sam, it must be big," Senderowitz said. "He's not in the habit of being mysterious."

"Maybe we are all getting pay raises," Ivanov said. "What do you think, Murphy?"

"Pay raises? The captain said he was going to surprise us, not shock us."

The door to the captain's office opened and Samson ushered another man into the squad room.

"Well, this *is* a surprise," Murphy said, as the two men approached. "I would never have guessed a visit from the FBI."

"I brought you all in to welcome a new member to the Six-one Detectives' Squad," Samson said when they reached the group. "George Ripley. Some of you have already met him."

"Good to see you," Murphy said, moving to offer a handshake.

"Likewise."

"That's the first time I've ever heard your given name."

"Please forget you ever heard it," Ripley said.

Samson introduced Ripley to Richards and Senderowitz, the only two who had not met the former FBI agent back in February.

"What made you decide to leave the Bureau and join the proletariat?" Ivanov asked.

"They were going to transfer me to the West Coast. I didn't

want to drag my boys across the country. They have been moved around enough already," Ripley said. "On top of that, I was feeling guilty about making so much more money than you guys."

"Ripley will be teaming with Bernie," Samson said. "I filled him in on everything we knew this morning. Now that we are all here, what's new?"

"The murder victim in the black Lincoln on McDonald was identified as Paul Gallo," Marty Richards began. "We found a thirty-eight in the vehicle. Ballistics confirmed it was the gun that killed Edward Cicero. We had the witness on Lake Street identify Gallo from a photo. His face wasn't in great condition after the gunshot to the head, but the witness felt certain. So I think we can take for granted Gallo was on Lake Street last night, and he appears to have been in possession of one of the guns used in the double homicide."

"And we know Gallo will not be doing much explaining," Murphy said. "What do we know about Gallo?"

"Not much yet," Ivanov said.

"I can tell you about Paulie Bonebreaker," Senderowitz said.

"Nice nickname," Murphy said. "I'll bet it made his mother proud."

"Go ahead, Bernie," Samson said.

"Gallo was mob muscle, part-time driver. Last I knew he was working for the Colletti's, before Tony Territo sent Dominic Colletti and his two sons to Boot Hill."

"I never properly thanked Tony for that," Murphy said.

"You may get a chance someday," Samson said. "Anything else, Marina?"

"Batman pulled the bullet out of Gallo's head," Ivanov said. "We received a call from ballistics before we got back here. It matches the bullets that killed Angela Salerno. I agree with Murphy's implication, I believe the second shooter decided very early on Gallo could be a liability."

"If they were doing a job for someone else, I would like to find the second shooter before someone decides *he* is a potential problem also," Samson said. "Murphy, Rosen, what did you get from the girl's parents?"

"The father was out, making funeral arrangements," Rosen began. "We talked with her mother at home. She gave us a list of names, Vincent's close male friends and one girl he had been seeing. We took a few items from his room and sent them over for prints. We split up the list. No one we tracked down had seen or heard from Vincent since Tuesday, except the girlfriend."

Murphy's cell phone rang. He took a quick look at the caller ID.

"It's Joan Michaels from CSU, I should take this."

"Go ahead," Samson said, and they all waited while Murphy took the call.

Ripley had been quietly listening to the others, taking notes occasionally.

Senderowitz had been watching Ripley, sizing up his new partner.

"They matched prints from Vincent Salerno's hair brush to prints on the rear basement door at his sister's place," Murphy said.

"Okay, he may have been there last night, before those kids were killed, or he may have left prints on the door at some other time," Samson said. "Tell us about the girlfriend."

"Alison Davis. Twenty-three years old. Works as a sales girl in a bridal shop a few doors down from the restaurant where Vincent works," Rosen said. "Vincent spent Tuesday night with her, at the apartment she shares with another girl in Dyker Heights. Alison had the day off yesterday."

"Did she have anything relevant to say?" Richards asked.

"Patience is a virtue, Marty," Murphy said. "Detective Rosen is getting to it."

"She said Vincent got a phone call, late Wednesday morning, which seemed to upset him. He wouldn't tell her what it was about, but he did ask if she had any cash handy. She had less than fifteen dollars, she gave it to him and he left quickly. *Rushed off* is how she put it," Rosen reported. "And that was all she wrote."

"I'm pretty sure I can tell you about the phone call," Senderowitz said.

"I wouldn't doubt it," Sandra said. Rosen often suspected Bernie knew everything.

Ripley remained silent, taking it all in.

"I spoke with Bobby Hoyle, an assistant manager at the restaurant."

"I know that name," Ivanov said.

"We all know someone called Bobby Hoyle," Murphy said.

"Hoyle told me a very big man in a jogging suit came into the place when they opened yesterday morning, around eleven. He asked if anyone had found a small tape recorder, the kind that uses the mini-cassettes, which may have been accidentally left behind the night before. Hoyle told the guy that, to his knowledge, it wasn't found. He suggested the man leave a phone number where he could be reached in case it turned up. Hoyle said if it was left at a table it might have been found by the bus boy, who hadn't mentioned it. He said he would ask Vincent when he came in to work."

"He named Vincent?" Ivanov asked.

"Hoyle said he didn't think anything of it until the guy asks for Vincent's address or telephone number. Hoyle tells him he can't give out that kind of information and the guy gives him a look he described as real scary," Bernie said. "Then a group of lunch customers walk in and maybe save Hoyle some grief. The guy turns to go, Hoyle asks if he wants to leave a phone number and the guy walks out the door to the street without another peep."

"And Bobby called Vincent."

They were the first words Ripley had voiced since the reporting began.

"Bingo."

"He's gone," Ripley said.

"Gone?"

"Gallo and the business suit were looking for Vincent."

"Go on," Samson said.

"They must have just missed him and when his sister and her

boyfriend were no help to them, they became expendable. Vincent found something they want back very badly. Not a twenty-dollar tape recorder, but something on the tape itself. And Vincent knows what he has, and he knows he is being hunted. He asked his girlfriend, his mother and his sister for money. He packed a gym bag full of clothing. Vincent is running, and I don't think we are going to find him anywhere in the neighborhood," Ripley said. "In fact, I seriously doubt he's still in Brooklyn. Or in New York for that matter."

"Anyone on the list of friends who lives out-of-town?" Captain Samson asked.

"No, but we weren't thinking out-of-town," Rosen said.

"We are now. We'll need to talk to his mother again."

"How about if Ripley and I go," Bernie said. "The poor woman may not care to see Tommy's mug again so soon. No offense."

"None taken," Murphy said, "and who could blame her. Besides, it will give you and the new guy the opportunity to do a little bonding."

"Is that your desk, Murphy?" Ripley asked.

"Yup, right next to yours."

The desk Lou Vota once occupied.

"I love the photographs."

"It's my renowned wall of fame. Harry Callahan. Frank Pembleton. Andy Sipowitz. John McClane. Martin Riggs. A montage of the toughest fictional cops of all time."

"I have a 'Popeye' Doyle signed by Gene Hackman at home that would look really good up there."

"Ripley, my friend," Murphy said, "welcome to the Six-one. You are going to fit right in."

Lorraine had news for Frank Sullivan she wanted to relate to him in person, so she called her mother.

"I was thinking I could come over for dinner, and then we can have Sully up for coffee and dessert."

"That would be perfect, Lorraine," Frances said. "Your

father and I will be so happy to see you."

Six months earlier, just after Lorraine's surgery and Lou Vota's death, Salvatore and Frances had insisted she stay with them for a while. And she did, for short time. She knew she had not been seeing them enough since and she was looking forward to one of her mom's home cooked meals.

"Can I bring anything?" Lorraine asked.

"Don't be silly."

And Lorraine loved it when her mother called her silly.

"How about a really good bottle of Chianti for Dad?"

"I'm sure your father would like that, Lorraine," her mother said.

After sharing four Hackneyburgers and half a twelve-pack of Heileman's Old Style beer, Vinnie finally let the cat out of the gym bag.

"What is it?"

"A tape recorder."

"I know it's a tape recorder, Vinnie, but what is it? You're holding the thing like it has teeth."

And then Vinnie told Carmine what it was.

"The night before last I was working at the restaurant and after most of the dinner guests were gone I began clearing tables. Plates, glasses, napkins, silverware."

"I get the picture."

"This dude asks where the toilet is, he hands me a package, goes back to the john and disappears out the back door. It's a small tape recorder wrapped in a note and a fifty-dollar bill. The note says he'll be in touch and hook me up with another hundred to get the thing back. Are you with me so far?"

"Yes, Vinnie. And if you don't get to the point soon I might pull ahead."

"The next morning, yesterday, I get a call from the assistant manager at work and he tells me some big ape came in looking for the recorder, and wasn't too happy when he didn't find it there. Bobby tells me the guy is sporting a jogging outfit, a thick gold chain around his neck, like some Tony Soprano wannabe, and I'm wondering what the deal is."

"And?"

"And, I've got the fucking thing and I'm looking it over while Alison is in the shower."

"Alison?"

"A girl I've been seeing. Very hot but maybe talks too much."

"Got it, go on."

"So I listen to the tape and I realize who one of the two men on the tape is, like maybe the biggest building contractor in all of Brooklyn. Restaurants. Office buildings. Condominiums. Nearly all the Erie Basin waterfront in Red Hook. His fucking name is on everything."

"And?"

"And this," Vinnie said, and he pressed the play button.

"I'm going to run down to the New Times for coffee and a sandwich to go, can I bring you anything?"

"Mind if I tag along?"

"Of course not," Murphy said.

"How do you feel about Ripley coming on board?" Rosen asked as they walked to the restaurant.

"I don't know if I feel anything about it, but I think it will be good. I liked him when I met him," Murphy said. "You know my opinion of the FBI, gang of blowhards. Ripley wasn't like the federal cops I'd met, who think all other cops are amateurs. The last time I saw him we were together on that roof with Gabriel Caine, making Butch and Sundance jokes just before the poor guy got blown away."

"That *poor guy* killed three young people. The first was only eight years old."

"I never condoned what he did. I remember talking with Lorraine about Caine when she was in the hospital, before we caught up to him. I asked her if she thought he was responsible for his actions or driven insane by his grief. I had just lost my brother Michael and I guess I was thinking about all of the people out there who need help and don't find help."

"Or won't accept help," Rosen said.

"That too. In any case, I felt sorry for the poor bastard."

"Speaking of Lorraine, have you seen her lately?"

"It's been a few months. I keep telling myself to call her and then I don't. It seems whenever we get together, we get each other thinking about Lou," Murphy said. "And it's still hard for both of us."

"How do you feel about Ripley taking Vota's desk?" Rosen asked. "And please don't give me the *I don't feel I think* routine."

"No problem. It will be better than talking to the pictures on my wall."

"Have you talked to Augie?"

"No. I thought I should give him time with his family," Murphy said. "It's funny you mention Augie."

"What's funny about it?"

"When you called me over to the scene on Lake Street and I was trying to get away, before Augie knew about his nephew, he decides to ask me how we were doing."

"How who were doing?"

"Us. He asked if it was working out, being together on *and* off the job."

"And what did you tell him?"

"I dodged the question, told him I had to run and I would get back to him on that."

"That *is* funny," Rosen said, remembering her little chat with Samson on the same subject.

"What do *you* think?" Murphy asked.

"We're here," she said, as they arrived at the door of the restaurant. "Let me get back to you on that."

"Wow."

"That's one way of putting it," Vinnie said.

"And the guy who gave you the tape recorder?"

"Didn't do me any favors. He must have guessed someone

was after him so he dumped it on me."

"And that someone knows you have it?"

"That someone, probably the other guy on the tape, believes I have it and once he realizes I flew the coop he'll know for sure."

"You could have stayed and said you knew nothing about it."

"People like that never believe you, even if you're telling the truth. And if he found me, or I should say *when* he found me, I would've spilled my guts and told him everything he wanted to know."

"You could have given it back," Carmine suggested. "You could still give it back."

"Carmine, you've been away from Brooklyn too long. He will assume I heard the tape, no matter what I say, whether I did or not. And he'll put me with the gorilla in the jogging suit and I could swear on my mother's life and on a stack of bibles I would never say a word and it would do as much good as telling the ape I dig his gold chain."

"What are you going to do?" Carmine asked.

"I have no fucking idea. That's why I came to you. You're the only friend I have whose IQ reaches double digits."

"I'm flattered. Do you know who the other guy is?"

"The other guy?"

"On the tape."

"No. Someone who cleaned up his mess, right? I mean, you heard it."

"Unfortunately."

"Fuck," Vinnie said, suddenly realizing he had put his friend in the same leaking boat he was in.

"That's one way of putting it."

"I'm sorry I got you into this, Carmine. I should leave right now, before anyone knows I was here."

"Where would you go, what do you have for money?"

"Seventeen dollars and fifty-eight cents."

"You counted it?

"Twice."

"Forget it, Vinnie. We'll work something out."

"How?"

"I'm not sure. I need to sleep on it. In the morning we'll try to figure a way out of this mess. Right now, I would rather you help me knock-off this twelve-pack and I would like to hear some juicy details about your talkative friend Alison."

Samson came out of his office and found Ivanov at her desk working on the Paulie "Bonebreaker" Gallo report.

"Where is everyone?" Samson asked.

"Sandra and Murphy ran out for coffee, Richards had to go over to the Crossroads Juvenile Center to testify on the laundromat softball bat stick-up."

"Senderowitz and Ripley?"

"At your service," Bernie said as the two detectives walked into the squad room.

"Get anything?"

"Do we have a travel budget?" Ripley asked.

"This isn't the FBI, the NYPD doesn't pay for gas mileage," Samson said.

"How about air mileage?"

"What do you mean?"

"Plane fare," Ripley said. "We think Vincent Salerno may be in Chicago."

"May be?" Samson said. "What do you have?"

"An address and phone number. A kid he grew up with. According to Vincent's mother they were like two peas in a pod," Bernie said.

"Wouldn't it be cheaper to call and find out if he's there?"

"If Vincent doesn't want to talk to us he might skip again," Ripley said.

"So, you want to go to Chicago."

"Actually," Senderowitz said, "we would both like to go to Chicago."

"That won't be an easy sell," Samson said. "I'll do whatever I can to get it authorized, but I sincerely doubt it is going to happen before morning. And if it doesn't fly, we will have to call the kid and cross our fingers."

"Fair enough," Ripley said.

"Meanwhile get the information you need on plane flights."

"Planning the company retreat?" Murphy asked, as he and Rosen strolled in.

"Bernie and Ripley are going to Chicago," Ivanov said.

"In mid-August?" Murphy said. "You may as well stay in Brooklyn and get baked alive right here."

"Yes?" Fred Salerno said when he answered the door.

"Sorry to bother you, sir. I'm Detective Andrews."

"We already told the other detectives all we knew about Carmine," Salerno said.

"Carmine?"

"Carmine Brigati, Vincent's friend in Chicago. Don't you people communicate with each other?

"I'm sorry. I thought I might catch the other detectives here."

"Listen, we know you are doing your jobs, but my wife is still extremely upset and we need time to ourselves. If we hear from our son, or think of anything else, we'll call."

"I understand completely, and I apologize again for the intrusion. We truly appreciate your help."

"I may have some good news, Sully," Lorraine said.

Frank Sullivan had joined her and her parents at the dining room table for dessert and coffee.

"Tell me."

"Does Mr. Marconi have any skills as a car mechanic?"

"Absolutely. He ran an auto parts store. Robert could *build* a car if he had all the pieces."

"I spoke to a friend in the DA's office," Lorraine said, "who would rather remain anonymous. Prosecutors don't like being known as compassionate. I think we can plead for a suspended sentence and community service, if Judge Epstein is having a good day. And here is where it gets more hopeful. One of the community service options is at a public trade school in

Brooklyn teaching automobile mechanics, and something very good could come out of this mess."

"What do you mean?"

"It could work into a full time teaching position, a decent salary and all of the city employee benefits. We go before Epstein in the morning to propose the plea bargain."

"Do you think the chances are good, Lorraine?" her father asked.

"I do."

"Lorraine, I can't thank you enough. I want to pay you for your services."

"Not necessary, Sully. I have to meet my self-imposed pro bono quota."

"I don't know what to say."

"You don't have to say anything, Sully, just pass the plate of cannoli please."

He made the call from a public telephone on the corner of Chambers and Broadway in lower Manhattan.

"This is Mr. Smith," the man on the receiving end answered.

"I could use some good news for a change."

"I got him."

"You have him?"

"Not exactly, but I'm pretty sure I know where I might find him."

"*Pretty sure* and *I might* are not my favorite expressions."

"I went to his parent's place, claiming to be a police detective."

"And?"

"His old man dropped a name."

"I hope you didn't have to kill the father too."

"I told you it was Gallo, the guy was a maniac. He put one in the boy's head without a warning," Mr. Smith said. "What was I supposed to do about the girl?"

"You were saying the father dropped a name?"

"Yes, and unfortunately the NYPD caught it too. But I found

an address, and with all their red tape I'm certain I can get to him before they do. I'll jump on it as soon as possible."

"Are you too busy right this minute?"

"I have to make travel arrangements, the address is in Chicago."

"Then the boy does have it. He's running."

"I'd say so."

"By the way."

"Yes?"

"The young man Gallo killed. His father is a cop. As, of course, was Investigator Heller."

"Terrific."

"Well put. There is going to be a lot of heat."

"I guess Gallo is lucky he won't be feeling it."

"Please don't disappoint me again. Find the tape."

SEVEN

Vincent Salerno woke to the aroma of coffee and the smell of bacon.

He found Carmine at the kitchen stove, cracking eggs into a skillet.

"Good morning, van Winkle," Carmine said. "Do you like your eggs up or over easy?"

"Over burned."

"Make yourself useful. Pop some of that bread into the toaster, and pull the butter and the cream out of the fridge. The coffee mugs are in the cabinet above the sink. And set this bacon on the dining table."

Vinnie also found and set plates and silverware.

"Nice work," Carmine said.

"It's what I do."

"Watch the bread, the toaster is erratic," Carmine said, sliding a couple of fried eggs onto each plate.

"Did any thoughts about my problem visit you during the night?" Vincent asked, carrying the toast over.

"I have an idea. But let's dig in first, before the food gets cold."

"I'm sorry, sir, that flight out of Newark is fully booked. The next flight is at ten."

"What about another airport?"

"JFK or LaGuardia?"

"It doesn't matter, the soonest available."

"Let's see, give me a moment."

He felt like throwing the cell phone through the windshield.

"Okay," said the reservationist after a few long minutes. "I can get you on a non-stop out of JFK at eight-fifteen, arriving at O'Hare at nine-fifty-eight. That's only eighty-four minutes after the Newark flight arrives."

"Fine, book it," he said, thinking about his impatient employer.

Eighty-four minutes would seem like a lifetime.

Samson had called the Chief of Detectives, asking for Trenton's clout to get timely authorization for the travel request. Senderowitz and Ripley climbed aboard a United Airlines flight from Newark to O'Hare at seven Friday morning.

"How did Samson pull it off?" Ripley asked.

"Late calls to friends in high places. Sam can be very persuasive, he was afraid if we didn't jump on it someone else might get to the kid first."

"Do you think Vincent knew about what happened to his sister and it scared him all the way to Chicago?"

"No. I don't believe we are dealing with a bad kid, just a young man who did something to seriously piss-off the wrong people," Bernie said. "I think if he knew his sister was killed he would not have bolted. I think he'd want to be with his family, and try to help nail whoever did it."

"So, when we break the news, he should be willing to come back to New York with us and talk," Ripley suggested.

"That's the thing," Senderowitz said. "You just never know."

John Cicero came into the precinct and stormed up to Kelly's desk.

"Is Murphy in?"

"Should be here by ten," the desk sergeant said.

"How about Captain Samson?"

"Sitting in traffic on the Belt Parkway. Maybe I can help you, Detective."

"Why is there an APB out on Vincent Salerno?"

"We just want to talk with him. He may have been one of the last people to see his sister alive."

"And to see my son alive. I need to speak with Vincent's parents. I don't remember where they live. Can you give me the address?"

"It's our case and we have it covered. His parents convinced us they don't know where the boy is. Don't forget the Salernos lost a child also and they have been questioned a number of times since it happened. Listen, we understand you want to help, Detective," Kelly said, "but we should give them some time to themselves."

"No, you listen. Fuck you. I'll find them myself."

"What's up, Sam," Murphy said, answering his cell phone.

"Tommy, where are you?"

"Shore Road Park under the Verrazano Bridge, trying to keep Ralph from following a squirrel up a tree."

"I need you to get to the Salerno home right away," Samson said.

"Did the kid show up?"

"No. But John Cicero showed up at the Six-one asking about the kid and according to Kelly he was not very cordial."

"Did Kelly mention Chicago?"

"No, but Cicero is going over to grill the boy's parents. I need you to head him off."

"That's just swell," Murphy said. "I'm on my way."

"Great breakfast," Vinnie said. "Thanks."

"You're welcome."

"Can you stop chewing for a minute and tell me about your idea?"

"You have to go back to Brooklyn and let them find you," Carmine said.

"Are you nuts?"

"No. Listen. You are safe as long as they don't have the tape.

Like you said, they will eventually find you. You admit you found it, say you left it in the restaurant and tucked it away somewhere in case someone came back looking for it, and you forgot to mention it."

"How do I explain the little trip to Chicago?"

"You never came to Chicago."

"So where have I been for two days?"

"Say you got a wild hair and went to Atlantic City."

"Atlantic City? What if they decide to check it out?"

"Do you remember my cousin Geno?"

"Tall gawky kid, used to play baseball with us?"

"He works in Atlantic City. He'll say you were down there if I ask him to, he owes me big time."

"What if they don't believe me, or don't care? What if they think I heard the tape? Once they have it, I'm a threat."

"You'll need to make a judgment call, go on intuition. Once they get the tape, if you see anything or hear anything that convinces you it's not over you let them know about your insurance."

"Insurance?"

"It's sitting right in front of you."

"The salt shaker?"

"The CD."

"Come on, Carmine, you're killing me."

"It's a copy of the tape."

"How did you make a copy of the tape?"

"I have an analog to digital converter. I use it to input my father's old record albums to my computer, so I can burn CDs to listen to them in the car."

"You made a copy of the tape so you could listen to it in the car?"

"I made a copy so you would have something to bargain with."

"Bargain for what?"

"Bargain for your safety. As long as there is a copy out there, you're protected."

"And if they don't believe me?"

"You show them the CD."

"You're not making sense."

"Then you tell them you have a second copy, I have the entire recording on my computer. You tell them you made arrangements to have it delivered to the police if anything should happen to you."

"It's too complicated," Vincent complained, "and it's fucking dangerous. Why don't I just take the damn thing to the police in the first place?"

"Because then you can't name your price for keeping quiet."

"What are you talking about?"

"It's called blackmail," Carmine said.

Murphy caught Cicero before the other detective reached the front door.

"John, hold up."

"Back off, Tommy."

"They don't know anything I can't tell you, let them be. Let's grab a cup of coffee and talk."

"They lost a daughter, I lost a son, I only came to commiserate."

"Come on, John, let it wait," Murphy said, stepping between Cicero and the door.

"Get out of my way, Murphy," Cicero warned.

And then Fred Salerno opened the front door.

"What's going on here, haven't you people intruded enough."

"Fred, it's John, Eddie's father," Cicero said.

"John, I'm sorry, I didn't recognize you. Do you have any news?"

"No, Fred. I just came to give my condolences. My wife and I cared a lot for Angela."

"Thank you. Marie and I have thought of your family also, but she is still very upset and can't see visitors right now. And I need to get back to her."

"I understand," Cicero said. "Have you heard from Vincent?"

"I told you yesterday I would let you know if we did," Fred Salerno said, addressing Murphy, who was standing by hoping Cicero would maintain control. "And then after you left, still another detective came and I had to go through the whole thing again."

"Did you get his name?" Murphy asked.

"I can't remember. I would say he was in his early-thirties, on the short side, five-seven or eight, well-dressed for a police detective."

"You told him about Vincent's friend Carmine?" Murphy asked.

"Yes," Salerno said. "Is there a problem?"

"Not at all," Murphy said.

"Thank you for coming, John. Please give our sympathies to your wife. I need to get back inside."

Cicero just nodded his head.

"Thank you, sir," Murphy said. "We are very sorry to have bothered you again."

"His friend Carmine?" Cicero asked when Salerno had gone back inside.

"We believe Vincent may have run off to Chicago."

"Chicago?"

"Detectives Senderowitz and Ripley flew out this morning to try to find the kid," Murphy said. "John, whoever came here after we left yesterday was not one of ours, not a detective at all. It was someone looking for Vincent and for something he may have. And I think it may have been one of the men who killed Edward and Angela. Let's get away from here and find a place where we can talk. I'll tell you everything."

"It's about time. Let's go."

"Fuck."

"What?"

"I need to call Senderowitz," Murphy said, "warn him they could be expecting company."

. . .

"Well?" Carmine asked.

"I don't know."

"I have money. I can get you on a flight back to New York this afternoon. You go straight to your parents' house, try to sell the Atlantic City story. How many days did you miss at work?"

"Just Wednesday. I wasn't scheduled again until tomorrow."

"Good. You call work, apologize for missing your shift, promise it will never happen again, plead for another chance, and then hopefully you go in tomorrow and remember finding the tape recorder."

"I'm having trouble deciding what to do, it sounds crazy," Vinnie said. "Is there a park nearby, somewhere I can sit alone awhile and think?"

"Hoyne Park."

"Where?"

"Go left when you leave the building, and left again at Thirty-fourth Street. It's a few blocks down. I think this could work, Vinnie, but you can't waste time. You need to make up your mind."

"I won't be long," Vincent said.

Carmine Brigati's residence was in a two-family on South Bell Avenue in the McKinley Park neighborhood, west of the South Loop.

Senderowitz and Ripley parked the rental across the street from the house, left the car, and walked to the front door.

"It's on the second floor," Bernie said, checking names on the mailboxes. "Go around back. See if there is another way in or out."

Ripley returned in a few minutes.

"A fire escape with a landing accessing two windows. Could be the kitchen and bedroom."

"Do you mind keeping an eye on the escape?"

"Not at all," Ripley said. "Yell if you need me."

Bernie climbed the stairs and knocked.

"That was quick," Carmine said as he opened the door.

"Mr. Brigati?"

"Who are you?"

"Detective Senderowitz, NYPD."

"Do you have identification?"

Senderowitz showed his detective shield.

"NYPD. You must have taken a terribly wrong turn somewhere."

"I'm looking for Vincent Salerno," Bernie said, resisting the urge to smack the kid.

"I haven't heard that name in a while. The last time I spoke with Vinnie he was still living in Brooklyn."

"We have reason to believe he may come to visit you here."

"I'm sorry you had to travel all this way, Detective, but I haven't heard from him in years. Is he in some kind of trouble?"

"I'm not at liberty to say. Are you expecting someone?"

"What do you mean?"

"You said *that was quick* when you opened the door."

"No. Well, yes," Brigati said. "I'm working at home today and I'm waiting for a messenger to run something over from my office. I'm sorry I couldn't help you."

Senderowitz pulled out one of his cards.

"If you hear from Vincent, would you please ask him to call? You would be doing him a favor."

"I will. And I will call you as well."

"Thank you for your help," Bernie said, and headed back down.

"He claims he hasn't heard from Vincent," Senderowitz said, after joining Ripley in the back of the building.

"Did you believe him?"

"I don't know. He was cool as a cucumber, to the point of being an obnoxious little shit. I'm not sure."

"What do you want to do?" Ripley asked.

"We came all this way. We may as well sit and watch for a while. What do you think?" Senderowitz said just as his cell phone rang.

The call lasted less than a minute.

"What was that?"

"That was Murphy. He said someone else from New York might be on the way here."

"Well, I guess that settles it," Ripley said, "let's sit and watch for a while."

Mr. Smith took a taxi from the airport to South Bell Street to save time. He paid the driver and let the cab go before walking to the building entrance.

As soon as he was inside, Detectives Senderowitz and Ripley jumped out of their car.

"Take the back," Senderowitz said.

"Got it."

Bernie entered the building and stood quietly at the foot of the stairs listening.

Carmine opened the door expecting Vincent.

"Detective Andrews, Chicago PD," Smith said. "I'm looking for Vincent Salerno."

"What the hell," Carmine said. "I just went through this with a dick from the NYPD. Show me some ID."

"Will this do?" Smith said, pulling out a gun.

He ushered Carmine back from the door and entered the room.

"Don't waste my fucking time, kid. I fucking hate plane rides. Either you are Salerno or you know where he is, what is it?"

Senderowitz stood right outside the door, service weapon in his hand.

"Carmine?" he called from the hall.

"Answer him."

"Yes?"

"It's Bernie. You left your car headlights on."

"Who is it?" Smith whispered, pointing his weapon at Carmine.

"The guy who lives downstairs," Carmine said, thinking fast. "Get rid of him."

"Thanks, Bernie, I'll take care of it."

Bernie pushed the door open and stepped in, his gun held out in front of him.

"Drop it," Senderowitz said, feeling a little foolish saying it.

Smith grabbed Carmine with an arm around the neck and pulled the boy close.

He pressed his weapon against the boy's head.

"No, you drop it, or I put one in his ear."

"Who gives a fuck? I hardly know the kid, and he's a wiseass. Besides, if you kill him we won't have to bother proving you killed the two kids back in Brooklyn."

Mr. Smith turned the gun on Senderowitz, who didn't have a clear shot. Bernie dropped to the floor and Smith pulled the trigger missing Senderowitz by inches.

Smith wheeled around to a sound behind him and he squeezed off two more shots before taking two in the chest.

"Nice shooting," Senderowitz said, getting to his feet. "Maybe too good."

Carmine stood like a statue, if a statue could shake uncontrollably.

"He was shooting at us," Ripley said.

"I'm not really complaining, it would have been nice to chat with him is all," Bernie said. "Carmine, calm down. Do you need a glass of water?"

"Yes."

"I got it," Ripley said.

Senderowitz sat Carmine down on the sofa.

"Listen, son. This is not the end of it. If you know where Vincent is, tell me now. We can protect him."

"Vincent walked over to the park, a few blocks from here. Less than an hour ago," Carmine answered without hesitation as Ripley handed him a glass. "You go left when you hit the street and left on Thirty-fourth."

"Ripley, call this in and wait for the CPD to take over. I'll walk down and try talking to the boy."

"Go," Ripley said.

"Carmine, come with me. I'll need help telling your friend his sister was killed."

It didn't take long for Murphy to tell Cicero all he had to tell.

"So you're saying the two men who showed up on Lake Street were actually there looking for Vincent Salerno," Cicero said, "or something he may have had that belonged to them. And one of them killed the other under the El on McDonald Avenue and may now be hunting for Vincent in Chicago."

"That's what we have, from ballistics, an eye witness on the street, and Vincent's co-worker," Murphy confirmed.

"And you are saying because of a cheap fucking tape recorder Vincent may have picked up in a restaurant, my son and Fred Salerno's daughter are dead."

"That's what it looks like."

"And no one has any idea what was on the thing that necessitated the execution of two innocent young people?"

"No one we've been able to talk to."

"So we need to find the second shooter, because he definitely fucking knows. And find Vincent, who *may* know. And both might be in Chicago."

"Yes. And so are Senderowitz and Ripley."

"Have you heard from them?" Cicero asked.

"Not yet."

"Does that worry you?"

"Not yet," Murphy said.

When Senderowitz arrived back at the house, with Carmine and Vincent in tow, the corpse had been removed and the crime scene techs were wrapping up. Ripley introduced Bernie to the lead CPD detective, Tyrone Jackson.

"Driver's license identified him as Lee Wasko. I have Detective Ripley's statement," Jackson said. "It works for me. It reads like a righteous kill."

"My partner saved my life."

"I need for you and Mr. Brigati to sign off on it."

"No problem," Bernie said. "I wonder if you could help us out."

"Go on."

"Wasko fired three shots. I was hoping we could take one of the three slugs back to ballistics in New York. For comparison."

"I think we can spare one," Jackson said. "Perry, let me have one of those slugs you took out of the wall. Put it in a separate bag."

"And maybe a snapshot of the deceased," Senderowitz added.

"Sure. I'll fax it over to Brooklyn."

After the exchange, everyone left except Bernie, Ripley, Carmine and Vincent.

"Ripley, see if you can get Vincent a seat on our return flight."

"It's already done, I was being optimistic."

"I need to give Samson a quick call, tell him it looks as if both suspects in the Lake Street case have been spoken for," Bernie said.

After calling the captain, Senderowitz got down to business.

"Alright, we have a few hours. We need to decide how it is going to go down when we get back," Senderowitz said. "So let's sit and get comfortable."

There was a knock on the door.

"Jesus, now what?" Carmine said.

"It's probably the pizza," Ripley said.

"You ordered pizza?"

"I never tried Chicago deep dish here in Chicago, I figured it was as good a time as any."

"How did you find a place that delivers here?" Bernie asked.

"Actually, my phone found it."

"Amazing," Senderowitz said.

"That's all I know. Now I have to get to the precinct, and I need to stop at home first to shave and shower. When I got the call this morning I was literally running around a park trying to rescue squirrels."

"Promise you'll keep me in the loop, Murphy."

"I will. As soon as I hear about Chicago I'll give you a yell."

"I don't want to cause you trouble, but I can't just sit on the sidelines in the dark."

"I understand. I'll let you know."

"And Murphy."

"Yes?"

"Tell your desk sergeant I'm sorry if I was rude this morning."

"Kelly thrives on rude, but I'll tell him."

"Okay, I'll talk to you later."

"Okay," Murphy said. "Later."

Murphy walked away wondering if he had done a terrific job of talking Cicero down or if the man was a terrific actor.

Lorraine walked out of the courtroom and called Sully at Campo's grocery.

"It looks good," she said. "Epstein went for the deal. Mr. Marconi will begin his community service teaching on Monday. They're taking care of the paperwork now. He should be home in time for a late lunch."

"That's great news, Lorraine. If there is anything I can do for you."

"You can keep your eye on Robert. Make sure everything is going alright. If he tries anything foolish again there won't be much we can do."

"I will," Sully said.

Ripley, Bernie and Vincent returned the rental at O'Hare and shuttled to the terminal.

After checking in they went to the departure gate, waiting to board.

Vinnie was sitting, tapping his foot on the floor like Fred Astaire on amphetamines.

"Can I speak with you for a moment, Ripley?" Senderowitz asked.

"Sure."

"Let's take a little walk."

"What's up?" Ripley asked, when they were out of Vincent's range.

"I feel like I was a bit bossy today," Bernie said. "Telling you what to do. Go around the back of the building, use the fire escape, stay and wait for the Chicago police, make arrangements for Vincent's plane ticket."

"No problem, I admire those who can delegate. I'm used to doing things the FBI way. I need to learn how it's done in the NYPD, and I understand Captain Samson put me with you for a reason."

"I just don't want you to think we are not a team, or that you can't tell me if you feel I'm making a bad call."

"I'm not shy, Bernie, you'll be the first to know."

"Good. Now I need to talk to Samson and get everything in place for our arrival and I need you to sit and talk with that kid, he's a wreck."

"What do I talk to him about?"

"Vincent," Senderowitz asked when they returned. "Are you a Mets fan or a Yankee fan?"

"Mets, totally."

"There you go," Bernie said to Ripley.

Detective Murphy was tapping on Samson's office door ten minutes after Senderowitz called.

"Come in."

"Good afternoon."

"Tommy, you fooled me. I couldn't tell it was you."

"Rosen told me you think I abuse your office door."

"What I failed to mention to Rosen was it is part of your appeal."

"You should point out my appeal to her at every opportunity."

"How did it go with Cicero?" Samson asked.

"When I got over to him he was ticking like a time bomb. I managed to sit him over a cup of coffee and I think I diffused it somewhat. Then again, he may have been playing me. In any case, I had to tell John everything. He knows about the tape recorder and also knows about Vincent and the second shooter, he is as anxious as we are to find them both and get some answers."

"The second shooter is dead," Samson said. "Ripley took him down in self-defense."

"And Vincent?"

"Bernie and Ripley are bringing him home. That's all I'll say for now, because I hate repeating myself. We'll all go over it together here at six."

"Hating to repeat yourself is a big part of *your* appeal."

"Tell that to my kids."

"One other thing. I sort of promised John Cicero we would keep him informed," Murphy said.

"Do you think we should call him in?"

"I'm worried about how he may react if we don't."

"Well, let me put it this way, do you think he'll behave if we invite him to join us this evening?"

"I'm really not sure, Sam, it's a crap shoot."

"Give him a call," Samson said.

EIGHT

Detective Marina Ivanov received the call from her mother just after two on Friday afternoon and rushed over to her parents' house in Mill Basin.

Her mother, Natalie, greeted Marina at the door and led her back to the kitchen where Rachel sat at the table.

Marina could tell Rachel had been crying and she looked as if she had been hit by a truck. The left side of her sister's face was deep purple.

"My God, Rachel, did Alex do that to you?"

"No, of course not, Alex would never hurt me," Rachel said. "But when he sees me he will want to hurt *someone*. A lot."

"Who did this?"

"A creep at the social club, the owner's son. He shows up there almost every night bothering all the girls and they're too afraid to say anything to his father. He's been hitting on me for weeks. I kept telling him I have a boyfriend but he's relentless. I would have quit long ago if the money was not so good."

"What happened?" Marina asked.

"Last night after closing he cornered me on the way to my car. I pushed him off and then he punched me. Alex will go crazy and I can't let him go over there, you know how violent the Russians can be."

"Rachel, please," her mother said. "Your father's people are Russian."

"No, Mother," Marina said in Rachel's defense. "Unfortunately some of these people are nothing like our grandparents—criminals who belong to a club that makes today's Italian wise guys look like troublesome kids. So when you mess with one, you are messing with them all. When I was back at my old precinct even the police walked on eggshells down at

Brighton Beach. I warned you about this, Rachel."

"You did and I'm sorry I didn't listen and I'm not going back. But that does not change the fact Alex won't be hesitant to *mess with one* of them when he finds out. And he *will* find out. I refuse to lie to Alex, for any reason."

"I wouldn't ask you to," Marina said. "I'll talk to Alex. Can you get him over here?"

"I'll call and ask him to come when he's done at the bakery."

"Good, try to relax, we'll work it out," Marina said. "Right now, I have to call the precinct and tell the captain I need to miss the meeting scheduled for later today."

"You don't have to do that for me, Marina."

"Yes, little sister, I do."

Senderowitz had the cab driver stop a block from the house, to avoid the risk of one of Vincent's parents seeing him arrive with the two detectives. Bernie climbed out of the car with Vincent while Ripley remained to hold the taxi.

"Tell your folks you just heard about Angela, you had been at your girlfriend's place for a few days, are you sure Alison will cover for you?"

"Positive," Vincent said.

"Call work. Be very apologetic to your manager. He is not too happy with you but it would be a lot better for us if you can at least get in the door. I will speak to Bobby Hoyle and ask him to back up your claim the tape recorder never left the restaurant, if it comes to that. Do not leave your parents' house until you hear from us, we will have someone watching the house around the clock. We will be in touch as soon as the captain and the other detectives in the squad decide how to proceed. Any questions?"

"No."

"And are you going to do exactly as I said?"

"Yes."

"Okay, go."

Senderowitz stood for a minute and watched Vincent walk off before returning to the taxi.

"Sorry I made you wait, Ripley. I delegated once again, didn't I?"

"Yes, partner, but who's counting."

"Where to now?" the driver asked.

"Sixty-first Precinct," Senderowitz said. "Do you know where it is?"

"Unfortunately," the driver answered, "I know it very well."

"It's been almost three fucking days and you're telling me to calm down."

"You know how Heller works. If Donahue was having second thoughts, Bill would have reminded him of his options and would have given him time to decide to do the smart thing."

"So why hasn't Bill let us know?"

"That is also how Heller works. Bill prefers reporting in with good news. Not to mention you asked him to stay away from this office until the deal was done."

"Did I say that?"

"You said that."

"So I shouldn't worry?"

"I didn't say you shouldn't worry, I just suggested you calm down."

Senderowitz and Ripley arrived back at the Six-one shortly after five on Friday evening. Senderowitz pulled a plastic bag out of his jacket pocket and walked over to Kelly at the desk sergeant's post.

"Do you have someone who can run this down to the ballistics lab right away?"

"I think I can dig someone up, what do you have?"

"A spent bullet from Chicago, I'm almost sure it will match the ones that killed Angela Salerno," Senderowitz said. "I simply need confirmation, and I need it right away. Please have whoever takes it over say Chief Trenton gave it top priority."

"Did he?" Kelly asked.

"What difference does that make?"

"Is Angela Salerno the girl killed two nights ago on her birthday?"

"Yes," Senderowitz said.

"I'll take it over myself."

"Thanks."

Senderowitz and Ripley climbed to the second floor and walked into the squad room. They found Richards, Murphy and Samson gathered around Murphy's desk.

"Are you alright, Ripley?" Samson asked as soon as they came over.

"I'm good."

"I only ask because I know what having to use deadly force is like."

"I didn't have much choice," Ripley said. "And the good and bad of it is it wasn't the first time."

"Second day on the job and you've already chalked one up for the good guys," Murphy said. "Are you bucking for a spot on my wall of fame?"

"Would you put me next to Bruce Willis?"

"You'll probably need to talk with Internal Affairs," Richards said.

"Don't sweat IAB, Ripley," Murphy said. "They think a bad cop is one who doesn't live with his mother. No offense, Richards."

"If you guys are done, I would like to see Bernie and Ripley in my office," Samson said, just as Murphy's cell phone rang.

He checked the caller ID.

Mendez.

"Bed Bath and Beyond, beyond department," Murphy said and then after a moment, "he's standing right here, hold on. Mendez for you, Sam, he claims you're not answering your phone."

"I can't hear it from here."

"He said he called your cell."

"I can't hear that from here either."

"Doesn't that defeat the purpose?"

"Let me have your phone, Tommy," Samson said impatiently. He exchanged a few words with Officer Mendez.

"Goddamnit."

"What's up?" Senderowitz asked.

"Landis and Mendez are at the Marlboro Houses. A maintenance worker stumbled on a dead body in one of the boiler rooms. Shot. I need two of you to run down there. Rosen will be here at six. I can't send her or Murphy, they're the primaries on the Lake Street case. And Ivanov asked to be excused from the meeting this evening. She had personal family business so I cut her loose. Bernie, I'll need you or Ripley to hurry over with Richards. Batman is already on his way."

"I'll go," Ripley volunteered. "Bernie should stay. He knows the Salerno kid's story much better than I do."

"Good. It's House Five, can you find it, Marty?"

"I think I know it, the closest to Stillwell Avenue," Richards said. "I'll look for the patrol car."

Richards and Ripley grabbed what they needed and they headed out to the scene.

"Did you call Cicero, Tommy?"

"He'll be here by six."

"Let us know as soon as Rosen and Cicero arrive," Samson said. "Bernie, let's talk in my office."

"Sam, this place is not Buckingham Palace, I am sure we'll know when they get here. And as you pointed out I'm one of the primaries," Murphy said. "Is there any reason why you can't talk in front of me?"

"Just one, Tommy," Samson answered. "Deniability."

Rosen was thinking about Wednesday, spending the night at Murphy's place. It was good. She had needed someone to make her feel like the world wasn't one big catastrophe and being with Tommy had done the trick. But when he brought up the idea of living together, and not for the first time, she had felt a knot in her stomach.

It was not that she didn't care for him. She cared for him very much. Loved him in fact. But she had made a mistake before, with a detective from her old precinct, and it had turned into a total disaster. Rosen had promised herself it would never happen again. Then along came this funny, goofy, tough, gentle, confident, troubled, adult-sized kid named Thomas Murphy.

Working with him in the field was not as problematic as she had feared when she accepted Samson's invitation to join the Six-one. They were a good team, their skills and methods complimented each other. And their off-duty time together had been uncomplicated without being shallow. A walk in the park.

But a decision to cohabitate was a horse of an entirely different color, and having to make that decision was a dilemma.

Then Sandra thought of the birthday girl and the boy with a ring in his pocket who no longer had any choices to make and she felt guiltily thankful that, at least for the moment, what to do about Thomas Edward Murphy was her biggest problem.

Rosen walked into the squad room with six coffees in paper cups on a cardboard tray and a white paper bag of creamers, sugar packets and wood stirrers.

Murphy was alone in the room.

"You look good," he said.

"Thank you. Where is everyone?" she asked, setting her bounty on Murphy's desk. "Don't we have a meeting in less than fifteen minutes?"

"Ripley and Richards pulled what looks to be a homicide at the Marlboro Projects. Ivanov is excused. Family business. Sam and Senderowitz are having a little powwow in the captain's office."

"Concerning?"

"Something Sam thinks I'd be better off not knowing about."

"Do I have to drink all of this coffee myself?"

"Maybe not," Murphy said, taking a cup from the tray. "John Cicero will be joining us."

As if on cue, Detective Cicero walked into the squad room.

Murphy made the introductions.

"What's new?" Cicero asked.

"I don't really know. The captain was waiting until everyone got here before bringing us up to speed," Murphy said.

"Is the coffee up for grabs?" Cicero asked.

"Help yourself," Rosen said. "Take as many as you like."

"That was Beck from ballistics," Senderowitz said after taking the call.

"And?" Samson asked.

"He said it may not hold up in a courtroom without the gun handy, but he is convinced the bullet we brought back from Chicago matches those removed from the Salerno girl *and* Paul Gallo. Same caliber, same type gun, and he would be willing to bet the farm all from the same weapon."

"That's good enough, in terms of what we are looking to decide today."

"I agree. And CPD has the weapon if we need it down the line. Wasko must have been very fond of his forty-four, holding on to it for so long."

"We proceed with the assumption Gallo and Wasko were the two shooters on Lake Street, they were hired by someone and given carte blanche to find the tape. Now all we need to do is get whoever was behind it all to show his face."

Samson peeked out from behind the window shade and confirmed Detectives Rosen and Cicero had arrived.

"We're all here," he said, taking the disc from his desk. "Grab the CD player. Let's see if the others think we are brilliant or out of our minds."

"Jesus, this poor bastard looks like he had a bad day at Guantanamo," Richards said.

"I don't know about Cuba," the M.E. said, examining the victim, "but his bad day definitely wasn't here, and it wasn't today. He was dumped after he was killed. Watch where you walk, I'll be with you in a minute."

Richards and Ripley stepped back carefully and stood waiting.

Samson and the four detectives sat close to Murphy's desk in chairs pulled from around the squad room.

Senderowitz had placed the CD player on the desk.

"Let me begin by welcoming John Cicero and thanking him for being here," Samson said. "John, I am sure I speak for all of us when I say we are profoundly saddened by the brutal death of your son and Angela Salerno. We are all sympathetic to your personal loss and totally committed to finding all those responsible."

"I'm glad you included me," Cicero said. "Unfortunately, I'm a pressed for time. I need to be back at Graziano Funeral Home by seven."

"Then we will get right to it, I'll hand the ball over to Bernie."

"The man who assaulted us in Chicago was Lee Wasko. He was a known enforcer-for-hire. We are stipulating the following with great confidence. Lee Wasko and Paul Gallo went to the house on Lake Street searching for Vincent Salerno with the belief Salerno had a tape recording they needed to retrieve. Wasko and Gallo shot Angela Salerno and Edward Cicero after they could offer no help in locating Vincent. Wasko shot and killed Gallo sometime after. Wasko went to Chicago following the same lead we had as to Vincent's possible whereabouts and he was killed by Ripley in a gunfire exchange."

"So both of the alleged Lake Street shooters are dead, and as useful for questioning as Lee Harvey Oswald," Murphy said. "Where does that leave us?"

"With the recording," Bernie said, and he put the disc into the CD player.

Donahue: *Kevin Donahue.*
Unknown: *Good afternoon, Mr. Donahue.*

Donahue: *Are you crazy? I told you never to call me here. And why are you calling at all, our business is done.*

Unknown: *I need two hundred thousand dollars.*

Donahue: *You already got two hundred grand.*

Unknown: *My needs have changed. I saved you at least twenty times that amount and a good deal of bad publicity. I don't feel as if a ten percent commission is asking too much.*

Donahue: *We had a deal. I don't know what world you bureaucrats live in, but where I come from a deal is a deal.*

Unknown: *Spare me the lecture on business ethics, Mr. Donahue.*

Donahue: *Why should I give you another dime?*

Unknown: *Because just as easily as I made incriminating evidence disappear, I can make it miraculously appear again. We are talking about a scandal that could severely damage reputations and hurt the city. Working together to keep New York City great should be our most pressing concern. Consider my request for additional funds a contribution to that effort.*

Donahue: *Save the stump speeches. My biggest concern is how long you will continue to milk me.*

Unknown: *Satisfy this request and you will never hear from me again.*

Donahue: *What if I decide I would rather face the consequences than trust you again? I can just as easily throw you to the dogs. It wouldn't take any more than a suggestion of impropriety to derail you.*

(End of tape recording.)

"What's his name, Rachel?"

"Alex, please calm down, I'm alright."

They were sitting in the living room. The girls' mother was preparing dinner in the kitchen.

"What is his name?"

"Alex, I said I would take care of it. I know you're angry, but so am I. She's my sister, I am not going to let some punk punch my sister in the face and get away with it," Marina said. "I will go down there tomorrow, in daylight, with backup, and we will find him and take him in for assault."

"I want to hurt the son-of-a-bitch."

"I understand, but if you go down there all fired up *you* could wind up with an assault charge, or you could get hurt yourself. These people can be very nasty, let me do it my way."

"Please, Alex," Rachel said.

"Okay."

"Promise you won't do anything foolish," Marina said.

"I said okay, Detective, but that bastard better pay."

"Girls, would you please set the table," their mother said, looking in from the kitchen. "Dinner is nearly ready and your father will be home any minute."

"Okay, Mom," Marina said.

"You are welcome to stay for dinner, Alex," Natalie said.

"Thank you, Mrs. Ivanov, but I have more work to do back at the bakery. Cakes to be completed for an early pick-up tomorrow morning."

Alex left, having to assure the sisters once again he would stay clear of the Lobnya Lounge.

Marina and Rachel began setting plates and dinnerware.

"Damn it," Marina said. "Dad."

"What about Dad?"

"When he sees you he won't be too thrilled either."

The medical examiner had completed the preliminary examination and had told Detectives Ripley and Richards all he could relate with confidence before doing the lab work.

"Was there any identification?" Richards asked.

"No," Batman said.

"I can tell you who he was."

The detectives and M.E. turned to the man who had silently come up beside them.

"And who are you?" Richards asked.

"Kings County Assistant District Attorney Mark Caldwell."

"And the victim?"

"Investigator Bill Heller," Caldwell said. "Heller worked for us."

"So you are suggesting we wait to see who comes looking for the tape recorder," Rosen said.

"Yes," Senderowitz answered.

"We have Kevin Donahue cold for paying bribes to cover up illegal activity," Murphy said. "Why not just pick him up?"

"Because now we are looking to indict someone for murder and we have nothing to connect Donahue to Wasko or Gallo. We can't even be sure Donahue was behind the killings."

"The other voice on the recording?" Rosen said.

"Exactly, and we don't know who that is. Hopefully Vincent can go back to the restaurant tomorrow and get the tape recorder back in. Someone wants it very badly. Sooner or later someone may come looking. We will make it seem as if the recording never left the place. Vincent found it, dropped it into his apron, forgot about it and no one had listened to it. We put the tape recorder on a hook, and then we sit patiently and keep watching to see if anyone bites."

"What about the guy in the restaurant who handed Vincent the tape in the first place?" Rosen asked. "Could he be the second man?"

"We have no idea who he was or why he ditched the recording," Samson said, "or how he came to have it."

"I'll be damned, we never thought of that," Senderowitz said.

"Thought of what?" Murphy asked.

"What if the man in the restaurant taped the conversation himself, with a phone bug perhaps, and he was planning to use the recording to blackmail the second man, or Donahue, or both."

"Great," Murphy said.

"What?" Samson asked.

"Senderowitz may have just come up with a third suspect."

"Wow," Rosen said.

No one had anything more profound to add.

"So, we're arranging to let the tape out of our hands?" Murphy asked.

"It might be worth the gamble," Samson said, "if it leads us to a killer."

John Cicero had not said a word.

"What do you think, John, are you on board?"

"You're not worried you may be tying Vincent to a stake?" Cicero asked.

"We will be protecting Vincent every moment," Samson said.

"And he's not a threat if we sell the idea he never heard what was on the tape," Senderowitz added.

"And what if no one comes looking for the tape?"

"Then we bring Donahue in on the lesser charge. We sweat him or deal with him for the identity of the other man on the recording. Meanwhile we try connecting him to the killers. And now, I suppose we need to try finding the man who had the damned thing to begin with."

"I'm willing to give it a little time," Cicero said. "But if someone hired Gallo and Wasko to kill my boy, I won't rest until I know who. Right now, I need to get to the funeral parlor. My wife will be waiting."

After Cicero left, Senderowitz called Vincent Salerno to map out a plan and he reported to the others.

"Vincent will be going to the restaurant tomorrow to ask his manager if he can start back at his job after his sister's funeral. One way or the other he can get the tape back into the place, and tell the manager he found it Tuesday night and forgot about it. Vincent's girlfriend will drive him there. Mendez and Landis, in plainclothes and an unmarked vehicle, will follow them and remain at the restaurant to watch. We will continue to stake out both the restaurant and Vincent's home around the clock. The manager, Mike Atanasio, will be arriving at the restaurant by nine tomorrow morning to start setting up for lunch and Vincent needs to be at church by eleven for his sister's memorial service and burial."

"I'll let Landis and Mendez know they need to replace the overnight team by eight tomorrow morning," Samson said.

"Do you think this plan will pan out?" Rosen asked.

"I think it's worth a shot," Samson said. "I don't see why dealing with Donahue can't wait, but we all need to agree."

Before they could tally the votes they received the call from Ripley.

NINE

Samson, Murphy and Rosen waited for Richards, Ripley and Assistant District Attorney Caldwell to arrive at the Six-one.

Samson quickly brought Caldwell up to date on everything they had on the Lake Street case. Vincent Salerno, his sister Angela, Edward Cicero, Paul Gallo, Lee Wasko, Chicago, the tape recording, and their thoughts about using the recording as bait.

"And when did Kevin Donahue enter the picture?" Caldwell asked.

"We knew nothing about Donahue's possible involvement until earlier today," Samson said.

"Okay. Let me try to fill in some of the blanks."

The Kings County DA's Office had been looking at Donahue Contracting for nearly six months, conducting an investigation into alleged illegal business practices. An inquiry that now appeared to have resulted in the deaths of two innocent victims, two alleged killers and a DA Special Investigator.

The investigation was instigated by an anonymous tip that Donahue had been underbidding for city contracts by illegally cutting labor costs.

The Brooklyn-based company was suspected of using workers without valid work permits, or without authentic union affiliation, for labor on several building projects funded by the City of New York. At sub-standard wages.

The DA's Office had reached out to the City Comptroller's Office, looking to find anything on Donahue Construction that would support the accusation.

When nothing incriminating turned up, two possibilities were suggested.

Either the suspicions were unfounded or someone inside city

or state government made evidence disappear—perhaps for personal gain.

Kings County District Attorney Roger Jennings was not ready to let it go.

DA Jennings managed, with the help of a judge who owed him one, to sanction a tap on Kevin Donahue's office phone. Then he handed the ball to his Assistant DA, Caldwell, and his special investigator, Detective Bill Heller.

"The conversation you are all now familiar with was a result of that phone tap," Caldwell said. "Heller contacted Donahue and gave him a hint of what we had. Heller asked for a meeting, suggesting there might be a way to make Donahue's situation less damnable. Kevin Donahue played dumb, but he agreed to meet Heller as a gesture of respect to the DA's office. Heller took the recording to Donahue's office on Tuesday night. We were as interested in identifying the second man on the recording as we were in nailing Donahue, if not more. Heller was to propose a deal for that ID and Donahue's future court testimony. Then Heller fell off the radar until his body turned up a few hours ago. We can only speculate as to what transpired."

"What is your guess?" Samson asked.

"We are presuming that after hearing the recording Donahue asked for a little time to consider the deal and Heller granted him a short reprieve. We are also assuming that after leaving Donahue, Heller felt he was being followed and he stopped somewhere to be certain the coast was clear. Heller knew we would not want Donahue's visitor tailed to the DA's office."

"So it was Heller who slipped the recording to Vincent at the restaurant," Murphy said.

"It had to be."

"And obviously he *had* been followed," Rosen said.

"We think he was abducted leaving the restaurant and interrogated. Heller was subjected to serious physical abuse before he was finally killed. We believe they were after the recording and when they didn't find it they tortured him in an attempt to discover where it was."

"You said *they*, are you guessing Wasko and Gallo?" Rosen asked.

"From what you've told me," Caldwell said. "Yes."

"If all of your suppositions are correct, then Heller was followed by Wasko and Gallo from Kevin Donahue's office and they not only knew of the recording, but knew Heller left the office with it. Doesn't that drop the whole business right in Donahue's lap?" Murphy asked.

"Not positively," Senderowitz said.

"Explain," Murphy said.

"I'll let our new man explain."

All attention turned to Ripley.

"Wasko and Gallo could possibly have been employed by someone else to keep an eye on Donahue. One or both of them could have spied on his meeting with Heller and would have known what Heller had and also known he took it away with him when he left," Ripley said. "When Heller could not produce the recording, they might have guessed he ditched it at the restaurant, which would explain why Gallo popped up there on Wednesday. When Gallo was led to suspect that the bus boy might have found the recording and kept it, they began the hunt for Vincent Salerno."

"I don't get it," Murphy said.

"Don't get what?" Samson asked, hoping Ripley wouldn't have to run through the whole thing again.

"I don't get the importance of the tape," Murphy said. "I'm sure you guys at the DA's office have a copy. Even we have a damn copy."

"A *copy* does not hold as much weight in court, particularly now that we are looking at multiple homicides including the death of a police investigator. And Ripley is correct, we cannot be certain Donahue sent Gallo and Wasko after Heller."

"So we are back to the other voice on the recording," Murphy said.

"And back to deciding if we let Vincent return the original to Il Colosseo," Senderowitz added.

"Who had the most to lose?" Samson asked.

"Before anyone was killed," Caldwell said, "Donahue had *less* to lose. There would be fines and wage compensation, the company would fall off the city's eligible contractors list, but there wouldn't be jail time involved. We're talking about a lot of money, but it wouldn't break the bank. The majority of their contracts are with private corporations and Donahue would not lose too many of those due to a hand-slapping by the city. The bottom line is everyone who is building anything is looking only for the lowest price, the city included. However, anyone inside the city or state bureaucracy involved in suppressing evidence of misconduct would definitely be looking at prison time."

"So, the second man on the tape was most in jeopardy," Samson said.

"Before the killing started, yes, but now it's a new ball game."

"How so?" Richards asked.

"If we can connect him *or* Donahue to Gallo or Wasko, the DA's office will not rest until one or both are indicted for murder. And killing Heller was a capital crime. But trying to find someone in city or state government who may have tampered with damning evidence against Donahue would be like trying to find Jimmy Hoffa. There could be hundreds of suspects, from who knows how many different bureaus. Department of Labor, Division of Labor, Division of Labor Standards, City Comptroller, Attorney General's Labor Bureau, and the list goes on."

"Why can't we simply confront Donahue again?" Richards asked. "We break him down and get a confession or compel him to finger the other man. Wasn't that your plan in the first place?"

"It won't be easy to get a confession when we are talking about the murder of a police detective, carrying a possible death penalty. But it would certainly be worth considering if we can find him?" Caldwell said.

"Find him?" Samson asked.

"No one has seen or heard from Kevin Donahue since his visit from Bill Heller on Tuesday evening."

It was nearly eight when the gathering at the Six-one broke up.

Caldwell would go directly from the precinct to his office and speak with his boss, Roger Jennings.

How to handle Vincent Salerno and the original tape recording would be the District Attorney's call. Caldwell would inform them of Jennings' decision first thing in the morning.

Richards, Samson and Ripley were all anxious to get to their homes and their respective families.

Murphy and Rosen decided on dinner together.

Bernie Senderowitz decided he needed a few drinks.

Before settling on a place to dine, Murphy and Rosen had to make a stop at Tommy's apartment to see to Ralph's culinary and biological needs. Finding a parking spot in Bay Ridge on a Friday night was going to be near impossible, so they left Rosen's vehicle at the precinct.

Whether it was a miracle, or simply the luck of the Irish, a car was vacating a parking space on Marine Avenue just as they arrived.

After taking care of the dog they walked to a Middle Eastern restaurant a few short blocks from Murphy's apartment building.

"What do you make of this entire mess?" Sandra asked after they had been seated and served cocktails and salad.

"I don't know. It gets more complicated by the minute, and it has all the markings of a hazardous road leading to a dead end. On top of that, it seems as if our part of the case is done. Our job was to discover who shot those two young people on Lake Street, and it looks as if that particular mystery has been solved."

Murphy took a swallow of his bourbon.

"What do you think is worse..."

"The watered down drinks or the bitter salad dressing?" Murphy said before Rosen could finish her question.

"You are a remarkable comic, Tommy. Ever think you may

have chosen the wrong profession?"

"All the time."

"What do you think is worse," Rosen said, trying once again, "dying for a reason or a cause, or dying as a result of being in the wrong place at the wrong time?"

"For the survivors, the Salernos and the Ciceros for example, it is much more difficult to accept when an innocent is killed." Murphy said. "As for the victims, I can't see that it makes much difference."

Whenever Marty Richards arrived home he did two things immediately.

First, he kissed his wife Linda. Second, he found his eight-month-old daughter Sophia, lifted her from the crib or the playpen, cradled her in his arms, and marveled at her fragility and her beauty.

When he had accepted the invitation from Samson to join the 61st he was aware Linda was not all for it.

The job of a detective on the streets was a lot more dangerous than that of an IAB investigator, barring the chance of being assaulted by an irate police officer under scrutiny. But he needed to make the move, for his own sense of self-worth.

He needed to do the kind of work that would make his daughter proud.

"Are things going well for you at the precinct?" Linda asked her husband, as he held the baby snug against his chest.

"Very well. I mean Murphy still ribs me at times about having been Internal Affairs, but that's just Tommy. He gives everyone a hard time. I try not to react because it only encourages him. But I am much happier there than I was at IAB. The detectives at the Sixty-first are an exceptional group, a group who I know I can trust to watch my back."

"So, you had a good day."

Richards spared Linda any details that might worry her unnecessarily. As much as the sight of Heller's battered body had affected Marty, he knew it was better left unmentioned.

"Yes, I did. But now I'm very happy to be home with my girls."

Samson was pleased he was able to get away from the precinct by eight.

Taking the eastbound Belt Parkway out to Douglaston would not be too bad.

Most of the traffic at that hour would be headed in the opposite direction toward Manhattan.

He would be home in time to visit with his two young daughters before they were off to bed, and he knew Alicia would have something warm for him in the oven.

He would try to put police business out of his mind until morning, try to clear his head, relax and enjoy being where he most preferred to be.

The girls were delighted to see him when he walked into the house.

Kayla, his eight-year-old, sprinted to the door to reach him first.

"Hi, Dad. Did you eat?"

Samson tried to recall when she had graduated from calling him *daddy*.

"I'll eat later," he said as five-year-old Lucy ran up to join them, "but first I want to hear all about *your* day."

"Are you going to ask me about *my* day," Alicia said, coming in from the kitchen.

"I think I will hold that inquiry until *after* I eat," Samson said, smiling, and he walked over to give his wife a hug and a kiss.

Once the girls were safely tucked away, Samson sat at the kitchen table working on a surprisingly tasty bowl of vegetarian chili complimented by a few homemade jalapeno corn muffins.

Alicia straightened-up around the kitchen while he ate.

When he was done they moved to the living room.

"So, how *was* your day?" Samson asked.

"I'm a little concerned about Jimmy."

Jimmy was their seventeen-year-old son.

"Aren't you the one who is always saying *I* worry too much about the boy?"

"Yes, and you do worry too much, but now I'm worried."

"What's the rumpus?"

"The rumpus?"

"An expression from a movie I saw," Samson said. "Something like *what's going on.*"

"Was the character who said it an African-American?" Alicia asked.

"No."

"I'm not surprised. The rumpus is Jimmy's grades last semester. The poorest since he began high school. Not bad by average standards, but very disappointing considering what we know he is capable of. He is starting his senior year in less than two weeks and he will have to do particularly well to compensate. Acceptance to a good college and hope for a tuition scholarship are on the line."

"Why did his grades take a dive?"

"I don't know. He hasn't offered any explanations or excuses, and I have given him ample opportunity."

"And why am I hearing about this now, and not sooner?"

"Because I hoped I could spare you the extra worry, but I'm running out of steam. It's time you had a talk with him."

"Where is Jimmy, by-the-way?"

"Out with friends."

"Maybe that's the problem."

"It's Friday night, they went to a movie, that's not the problem. There is something going on with him he's not inclined to talk with me about."

"I'll talk to him," Samson promised. "Do we have any ice cream?"

Ripley had to contend with the heavy Manhattan-bound traffic Samson had been lucky to avoid.

When he arrived at his sister's house to pick up the boys, they were already in bed and asleep.

He and Connie looked in on Kyle and Mickey.

"Don't wake them. They can spend the night and so can you."

"I need to get home. The house was like a disaster area when I left for Chicago and I haven't been back since."

"Stay for a bite to eat at least. Phil ran out for some milk and juice for the morning. He should be back any minute and he would be sorry to have missed you."

Connie fixed her brother a hot meatloaf sandwich.

"Do you remember my best friend from Junior High School, Justine Turner?" Connie asked, after bringing Ripley a plate and joining him at the kitchen table.

"Twigs Turner?"

"Granted, she was a skinny teen. You weren't exactly Mr. Universe yourself. But she was always a beautiful girl and she filled-in very nicely."

"How would you know? Didn't the family move out to California before you started high school?"

"Phil and I were at the children's school last night. St. Margaret's invites all the parents down every August, before classes start up again, to meet the new teachers. I ran into Justine, she's back in Queens and begins teaching at St. Margaret's this year."

"Twigs Turner is a nun?"

"No, she is not a nun, she's simply a teacher. Justine lost her husband in Afghanistan two years ago and she decided to come back east. You know what I think?"

"If I say yes, do you still have to tell me?"

"I think it might be nice if I invited Justine over for dinner sometime and you joined us."

"You know I love you, Connie. But you do so much for me and the boys already, you don't need to add matchmaker to your résumé."

"It's just dinner."

"Let me think about it," Ripley said, just as his sister Connie's husband walked in.

"My favorite brother-in-law," Phil said in greeting.

"Last time I checked I was your only brother-in-law."

"That too. Can I interest you in some Irish whiskey?"

"Why not."

The Palermo Social Club on Smith Street across from the park in Carroll Gardens was one of the few remaining establishments of its kind in Brooklyn.

A plain stucco façade painted a dark gray. Small high windows that let in some light but offered no view of the interior from the street. No identifying signage on the exterior.

A recessed door made of solid oak, displaying only a numbered street address and a white metal placard with two words written in bold black letters. MEMBERS ONLY. The fact it was *men only* as well was clearly understood by any who tried to venture past the sign.

The club had first been rented in the late-sixties and then purchased in the seventies as a place for members of Societa Villabate, named for a Sicilian town outside of Palermo, to gather for drinks, swap tales and play card games. The Society had been meeting in borrowed rooms since 1919 until finding the permanent home on Smith Street.

Bernie Senderowitz had grown up in Carroll Gardens, an area that had for decades been populated exclusively by Italian-Americans. His family was one of a small number of Jewish families in the neighborhood and Bernie was the only non-Sicilian allowed through the oak door. Bernie had run errands for members since his pre-teens and even now, in his early-sixties, Senderowitz was referred to by many of the old-timers as *il piccolo ebreo con il naso grosso.*

The little Jew with the big nose.

The Palermo Social Club was Bernie's drinking establishment of choice. It was only a block away from his house on President Street, and being within walking distance of home was a huge advantage to someone who took as much pleasure in the use of scotch whiskey as Senderowitz did. And it was private.

When Bernie walked through *that* door he was not a police detective, he was just another *paesano* from the neighborhood.

Senderowitz sat at a small table in the back of the club, working on his second double Johnnie Walker Black.

Silvio Batale brought a platter of *taralli*. Crisp Italian style pretzels, which are boiled and then baked. He set the snack down on the table.

"Thank you," Senderowitz said.

"Mind if I sit a minute?"

"Only if I don't have to hear your theory of why the Scots never ruled the world. Again."

"Actually, I was looking to *get* some advice for a change."

"I don't know if that's a great idea. The last time I gave advice to a friend it cost him three thousand dollars at the race track."

"I'll take the risk."

"Don't say I didn't warn you. Go ahead."

"My youngest boy, Andrew, graduated from Brooklyn College this past June. He excelled in criminal justice and pre-law courses. We expected he would go on to law school. In fact, Andrew was accepted to both Brooklyn Law School and the CUNY School of Law. But now, suddenly, he tells us he wants to join the NYPD. With all due respect to you, his mother and I aren't crazy about the idea and we don't know how to talk to him about it."

"And you think I can give you something to use to talk him out of it? Listen, Silvio, when I was young there was nothing I wanted more than to be a cop and no one was going to talk me out of it. It turned out to be the best and the worst decision I ever made, but it was *my* decision. I wouldn't recommend it for your son, but I could not condemn the choice either. Your boy is a man now, and he will do what he feels he needs to do. I'm sorry I can't help you more."

"I appreciate your thoughts."

"Enough to bring me another double?"

"Sure, and it's on the house," Batale said. "By the way, have you noticed the new Korean market going in at the corner of Court and Union?"

"It would be hard to miss."

"This building was an Italian produce store until the time it was acquired by the Society. It was one of dozens of Italian markets in the neighborhood. Now, you can't get a piece of fruit unless you buy it from an Asian."

"What's the difference," Senderowitz said. "An apple is an apple."

On Friday night, after failing to reach the man who he only knew as Mr. Smith, he was feeling very uneasy.

There were questions he needed answers to.

Evidently Donahue was considering throwing in the towel and making a deal with the District Attorney. He had apparently recorded damning evidence and handed it over to the DA Investigator on Tuesday night.

When Smith and Gallo did not discover the tape on Heller, he had asked them to locate Donahue and find out if what he had given to the investigator could name him. Donahue insisted it was the District Attorney's tape, not his, recorded from a phone tap, and swore there was nothing on it that could reveal the identity of anyone but Donahue himself.

Smith and Gallo had threatened Donahue physically and the contractor was terrified. He promised to hand over a considerable amount of cash and keep his mouth shut.

But in either case, if Donahue himself had taped one of their phone conversations, as some kind of liability insurance, or if it was obtained through a phone tap, there was no way of knowing *which* conversation it might be.

Heller never made it back to the DA. So if Donahue was lying, and no one other than he and Heller had heard the tape, he could perhaps dodge the bullet, no matter how incriminating the content might be. That is if no one else ever *did* hear it, or no one else was willing or able to say they did.

He couldn't trust Donahue was telling the truth, he needed to locate and listen to the recording to be certain he was safe.

In the subsequent attempts to track it down, two young people had lost their lives to no avail.

But there was still the chance Smith could find the tape in Chicago and secure it before it fell into the wrong hands.

Then Mr. Smith would deal with whatever it was the bus boy did or did not know.

His only consolation, if it could be called that, was that Smith could not name him either. They had never met face-to-face.

He thought about how well he had played Donahue.

Discovering proof of Donahue's labor law infractions quite accidentally, immediately recognizing the find as a windfall, contacting the contractor with an offer to make his problem disappear, phoning in the anonymous tip to the DA's office to turn up the heat and inspire Donahue to dig into his pockets for more hush money, and devising a fool proof plan to hide the evidence.

Simple. Effective. Relatively harmless. Done.

He should never have demanded more from Donahue. It had opened a deadly can of worms, but he had needed additional funds for his campaign.

The election was less than three months away.

He was not a religious man, but as he poured another drink he found himself praying he would not go from a front-running political candidate to a convicted murderer because of damned tape recording.

Detective Jack Falcone had been Ivanov's partner when she was back at the Sixtieth Precinct.

Falcone shook Marina Ivanov from sleep with a telephone call shortly before midnight.

"What time is it," Ivanov said, after managing to get the phone to her ear.

"Almost Saturday. Sorry if you were asleep, I didn't think it should wait."

"What's happened?"

"There's a young man down here who asked for you," Falcone said. "Do you know Alexander Holden?"

"Yes. Is he alright?"

"There's been an incident outside the Lobnya Lounge on Brighten Beach Avenue. The owner's son was killed. Holden has been arrested for homicide."

TEN

Senderowitz woke up Saturday morning with a harsh reminder of a very long battle of wills with Johnnie Walker. Walker won.

Before he had left the Palermo Club, well after midnight, Silvio Batale, apparently still uneasy about his son's decision to join the NYPD, posed one last question to the detective.

"Do you think it was the pressures of working on the police force that made you so fond of the scotch whiskey?" he had asked.

"It wasn't the job, Silvio, it was the taste."

Senderowitz dropped two tablets into a tall glass of water, watched them fizz, emptied the glass with one long drink, and found his way to the shower.

Murphy and Rosen woke up together in Murphy's bed, having enjoyed a very pleasurable night by avoiding subjects such as cohabitation and how the on the job/off the job arrangement was *working out*.

"I would not be horrible to stay exactly where we are for a while longer," Murphy said.

"I could think of more terrible places to be," Rosen agreed.

Ralph sat at the foot of the bed patiently waiting for acknowledgment.

Richards woke up to the sound of Sophia crying.

"Go see what all the fuss is about," Linda said. "I'll start breakfast."

He lifted his daughter from the crib and swayed her in his

arms with a gentle rocking motion.

"How about bacon and eggs?" he asked the infant.

Sophia stopped crying and Marty had to laugh when he caught himself wondering if it was the motion or the menu that had done the trick.

Ripley woke in an empty house that looked as if a Category 3 hurricane had roared through it.

He realized if he didn't do something about it before he picked up his boys it might never get done.

He rolled up his sleeves and got to work cleaning.

When it came to moving his service weapon to clear and wipe down the kitchen table he was reminded he had shot and killed a man less than a day earlier.

Ripley wondered how long he would be spared a visit from another ghost.

Samson woke up and immediately decided he would put off talking to his son about school grades until he heard what District Attorney Jennings had in mind for Vincent Salerno and the deadly tape recording.

Then he would be able to determine how to deploy his troops.

It was a defensible excuse for putting off the talk with Jimmy, if he was required to defend it, but it was an excuse nonetheless.

Samson understood he often avoided confrontations with his son.

Alicia was correct. Sam was overprotective when it came to his son. He lacked objectivity. Maybe because he was the male child, Jimmy reminded Samson of his own youth.

At Jimmy's age, Samson had been exposed to many influences that could have easily landed him on the opposite side of the law.

He wanted to be a strong father, as *his* father had been, a father who could be trusting and patient but could put his foot down hard when necessary.

He was well aware that having once been a teenager did not qualify him as an authority on adolescence.

He knew that simply being a father didn't afford him full understanding of the challenges his dad had faced being one.

He recognized that growing up in the Bedford-Stuyvesant in the seventies was not quite like growing up in Douglaston today.

But Samson felt that in many ways the world was a far more dangerous place today, and protecting the children was his job.

He wasn't looking forward to telling Alicia of his decision to postpone the father and son talk. His wife had recommended speaking to the boy as soon as possible and he had already missed an opportunity when Jimmy returned from the movies the night before.

On Saturday morning, Samson found Alicia and the girls in the kitchen.

Kayla and Lucy were totally involved in what appeared to be a breakfast cereal speed-eating contest.

"Slow down, girls," he said, joining them at the table. "Remember the first one who chokes loses."

Alicia brought her husband a cup of coffee.

"Daddy?"

"Yes, Lucy?"

"How come Jimmy went to the ocean and we can't?"

"Jimmy went to the ocean?"

"Yes, Sam," his wife said.

"Were we aware of his plans?"

"Jimmy told us last night, as he raced past us on his way up to his room, that he and some friends were leaving early this morning to beat the traffic out to Jones Beach," Alicia reminded him, "and you didn't protest. So, I guess you boys will have to reschedule your man-to-man."

"I guess we will," Samson said.

"Daddy."

"Yes, Lucy."

"I can't finish my cereal."

"That's alright, sweetheart, Daddy can finish it for you."

. . .

Detective Marina Ivanov woke up on Saturday morning with six words echoing in her head. *Holden has been arrested for homicide.*

She would visit her sister's boyfriend as soon as she was allowed, but not before the prosecutor had decided on a charge and filed it to the court.

Then there would be an arraignment, a formal reading of the charge and an opportunity for Alex to enter a plea, but not until Monday morning.

Alex would be held without bail until then.

It would be advisable to retain a criminal defense attorney immediately, an advocate to be present with Alex at the arraignment.

But first Marina had to face her most unpleasant task.

She had to inform her sister Rachel.

The murders on Lake Street, as horrible and tragic as they were, did not make front page news and less than three days later they were nearly forgotten by all but several persistent reporters, two stunned and grieving families, and a select group of law enforcers.

The assassination of Paul Gallo earned considerably less attention.

And the death of Lee Wasko may or may not have created any interest in Chicago.

However, when these events were connected the media would be all over it. It would then become the job the Public Information arm of the Deputy Commissioner's Office to deal with that certain eventuality.

And Public Information was receiving daily inquiries from those several diligent reporters who had latched on to the story and would not let go.

There was enough evidence to name Wasko and Gallo as the perpetrators on Lake Street, and throwing that bone to the media might give the DA and the NYPD some breathing room if they could make it appear an open and shut case and if business misconduct and political corruption, at least for the time being, could be kept out of the equation.

When Chief of Detectives Stanley Trenton collected the Saturday morning *New York Post* from his front lawn, and saw that the mysterious disappearance of "Brooklyn Business Tycoon" Kevin Donahue *had* made the front page, he was afraid the breathing room might not hold air very much longer.

Chief Trenton immediately scheduled a meeting with Henry Munro from Public Information and District Attorney Roger Jennings at the DA's office.

Roger Jennings woke up having to make a decision which, in his mind, defined the term *crapshoot.*

Withholding information about the recording, and using the recording to *possibly* lure a murder conspirator, was a tremendous gamble. It could give the Kings County prosecutors something to crow about, or it could blow up in their faces. For an instant, Jennings considered tossing a coin.

For the Salernos and the Ciceros, who in time might have become one family through marriage, Saturday was the day when both families would be burying their children separately.

Ivanov showed up at Rachel's door before eight.

Marina did not want to give her sister the terrible news over the telephone.

It had taken some time to calm Rachel down.

Marina refrained from using the standard *there's nothing to worry about* since she didn't believe it herself.

She assured her sister she would be talking with Alex as soon as possible and would work on retaining a lawyer for the Monday arraignment.

Rachel wanted to go along to see Alex, but Ivanov finally convinced her it would be best if Marina saw him alone.

Detective Jack Falcone called while she was still working at pacifying her sister. Falcone had arranged for Marina to visit Alex at nine.

"The District Attorney has entered a charge," Falcone said. "Second-degree murder."

"What is it?" Rachel asked after Falcone's call.

"I can go see Alex now."

"Tell him I wanted to come."

"I will."

"Thank you, Marina."

"Try not to worry, Rachel, everything is going to turn out alright," Ivanov said, not buying a single word of it.

Officers Stan Landis and Rey Mendez watched the Salerno house in an unmarked car and street clothes. They had arrived at eight and they were waiting for word from Samson about whether or not they would be following Vincent and the recording to the restaurant on 18th Avenue.

"I think my wife is going out on me," Mendez said.

"Is that a joke? You have three kids under six years old. You are hardly ever home with this fucking job, where would she find time to do anything but laundry? And why would you even think something like that?"

"I don't know it's just a feeling. It's hard to explain."

"You don't have to explain it to me, Rey," Landis said. "Just because I'm gay doesn't mean I haven't been cheated on. But that is not a conclusion I would jump to with no more to go on than *I don't know it's just a feeling.*"

"Something is a lot different, Stan. Salina doesn't seem as happy to see me anymore."

"Try doing the laundry occasionally, if that doesn't put a smile on her face we can talk about it again."

They both instinctively slouched down in their seats when a Chevy rolled past them and turned into the Salerno's driveway.

Alison Davis climbed out of the vehicle, walked to the front door and rang the buzzer. Landis and Mendez watched as Vincent let her into the house.

"Very attractive," Mendez said.

"Not my type, Rey."

Chief of Detectives Stan Trenton, District Attorney Roger Jennings, and Henry Munro from Public Information met at the DA's office at half past eight on Saturday morning.

Jennings handed each of his guests a transcript of the recording.

They quickly read through the short document, they were both seeing it for the first time.

"That's it?" Munro asked.

"That's it," Jennings said. "The other man hung up very abruptly after Donahue's statement about impropriety and derailment."

"Donahue threatened him, so he employed Lee Wasko's skills and had Donahue watched," Trenton said. "Wasko recruited Gallo, who probably never knew who he was actually working for. Not that it matters now with both of them out of the picture."

"Do we know where the call to Donahue originated?" Munro asked.

"A public phone in lower Manhattan," Jennings said, "and we received a printout of Wasko's cell phone history from the Chicago police. There were four calls to Lee Wasko from the same public phone between the time this conversation was recorded in Donahue's office and the time Wasko was killed, as well as a number of phone calls between Wasko and Gallo."

"So where do we go from here with the recording and the media," Trenton asked, "beside way out on a limb?"

"I think we should go ahead with the plan to put the recording back out there and see if anyone crawls out of the woodwork. Donahue knew what we had on him and he was considering a deal. He knew he would be facing a financial beating, but I doubt he would have considered it one worth killing for. I don't see him as the force behind Wasko and Gallo. The other suspect, on the other hand, has not heard the recording and can't be sure about how incriminating it may be. I believe, in his own mind, he has a lot more to lose than money. He has caused a great amount of trouble and destruction to get the tape into his hands before someone can identify him," the DA said. "If it's really that important to him it may draw him out."

"More to lose than money?" Munro asked.

"Power perhaps," Jennings said. "Maybe we'll get lucky and Kevin Donahue will resurface and give us the goods. Meanwhile, we send Vincent Salerno and the recording back to the restaurant. In the absence of a better plan, I think it's worth trying."

"I'll let Samson know we are going ahead," Trenton said. "So, how do we deal with the Press?"

"We give them Wasko and Gallo as the solution to the Lake Street case," Munro said. "They killed the young couple. Call it a robbery gone bad. Wasko killed Gallo. Wasko was tracked to Chicago and killed in a shoot-out with the police. If we can make a case against whoever was behind this down the line, we can introduce it as a *new development.*"

"So, we're all agreed," Jennings said.

"I suppose so," Trenton said. "And we might also agree we could be riding straight into the center of a shit storm."

Samson and Senderowitz had been at the precinct since half past eight Saturday morning waiting for the go ahead from Assistant DA Caldwell.

It came by way of Chief Trenton instead, just before nine.

Bernie called Vincent. Samson called Landis.

Then Samson assigned duties.

He, Senderowitz and Ripley would man the office phones. Ripley said he would be in by noon.

Murphy, Rosen and Richards would be off for the day but on call.

Ivanov phoned in after nine.

"Do you need me at the precinct?" she asked Samson.

"Not just now. Can you be available?"

"Sure. Captain, do you know a good criminal defense attorney?"

"I know a very good one, Lorraine DiMarco, a friend to the Six-one," Samson said. "I can't promise she will have the time or the inclination to help you out but she will certainly hear you out. DiMarco and McWayne on Remson Street in the Heights."

Landis and Mendez followed Alison's car out to the restaurant. Vincent was in and out in less than fifteen minutes. He and his girlfriend returned to the Salerno house where another pair of officers would be on watch.

Mendez and Landis would remain to stake out Il Colosseo.

Vincent reported to Senderowitz. He had successfully managed to place the tape recorder into Atanasio's hands, claiming he had found it and forgot it in his apron. He went to where his apron hung and brought the recorder back up to his manager. Atanasio, perhaps sensitive to the death of the boy's sister, told Vincent he could come back to work when he was ready.

Now all they could do was wait and watch.

He had not been able to reach Smith all evening Friday and by Saturday morning he knew he had to do something or he would lose his composure.

All he had to go on was Smith was following the bus boy to Chicago.

He needed to know where in Chicago and who the boy saw there.

He found the information with two short phone calls from a public phone on Columbus and West 77th, across from the Museum of Natural History.

The first call was to the home of Vincent Salerno's parents and if he was counting on luck he got it in spades.

Vincent's mother took the call. He identified himself as

Detective Heller and expressed both his condolences and his apologies for bothering the family again. He claimed he needed the name of Vincent's friend in Chicago.

Vinnie's mom, in a rush to get to the funeral home, gave him the name with no questions. Had Marie Salerno been in a different frame of mind she might have asked why he was calling them when the police already had that information and why it mattered since according to her son he never went to Chicago.

The second call was to Chicago directory assistance, to find Carmine Brigati's phone number.

Now he would have to count on human nature, the natural instinct to protect friends and family and the blind willingness to accept easy money.

He called Chicago.

"Hello?"

"Mr. Brigati?" he said, rolling the dice again.

"Who is this?"

"Someone who can offer you a lot for very little. I need some information I think you may be able to help me with. In return for your help, I will pay you ten thousand dollars. And I can assure you your friend Vincent will no longer be in any danger."

"Let's assume I know what you are talking about," Carmine suggested.

"If Vincent had a tape recording when he visited you, and if you heard that recording, I need to know without doubt if any of the voices on the tape could be identified. Think carefully before you respond, I demand complete honesty and total discretion."

Carmine Brigati decided to take the plunge.

"There were two men on the recording. One was a big time contractor from New York named Donahue. There was nothing on the tape that would identify the second man unless they could do a voice print or something, he was never named. That's all I can tell you."

"And that is the truth."

"Yes."

"And you never received this call."

"What call?"

"I will send you the money, in cash. I will mail it today. Vincent will have no problems from me from here on."

"Do you need my address?" Carmine asked.

"I have your address. I know where you live, Carmine. Please do not forget that."

After making the deal he learned from official sources available to him that Smith, identified as Lee Wasko, would not be returning from Chicago.

He resolved he would hold up his end of the bargain and send the payment to Carmine.

He decided to trust Brigati had been honest about what was on the tape recording.

He determined the recording could not hurt him and he would simply ignore it.

He had been extremely careful in his dealings with Mr. Smith. There was no way he could be connected to Smith or Gallo.

And as far as feeling responsible for the deaths resulting from the search for the recording, he had learned how to quiet a guilty conscience long ago.

He picked up two coffees, bagels, and a fresh-squeezed orange juice at a market on Amsterdam and walked back to his apartment to have breakfast with his wife.

He believed the nightmare was finally over.

Ripley and Senderowitz caught the call early Saturday afternoon.

A building superintendent at Marlboro House 2 in Gravesend had gone into one of the two basement apartments.

The apartment on the north end of a long hallway had been vacant since the previous weekend. Separating the unit from the one at the south end were a large laundry facility, a trash collection room with dumpsters which were fed by chutes on each of the floors above, an electrical room, and the heating and cooling works.

The empty unit was as isolated as any corner of a large busy apartment building could possibly be.

It had been the Superintendent's first opportunity to check out the unit since it was vacated.

The super needed to make note of all that had to be done to get the place in shape for showings to prospective renters.

He saw the victim the moment he stepped into the front room. He moved back into the hallway, closed the door after him, and immediately called 9-1-1.

When Ripley and Senderowitz arrived at the scene the medical examiner was already present. The body of the victim was lying face up on the floor and Dr. Wayne was ready to talk.

"The victim was tied into that chair," Batman said, pointing it out. "His mouth was taped shut, duct tape. There was a cloth bag pulled over his head, tied tightly at the neck. I would say he died of asphyxiation or dehydration or a combination of both if asked to speculate before I do the lab work. It would have taken days to die. It looks as if someone left him sitting here, tied and gagged, and forgot to come back to see how he was doing."

Senderowitz looked down at the body.

The victim had clearly been struck in the face repeatedly.

"Do we have an ID?" Ripley asked.

"It's Kevin Donahue," Senderowitz said.

ELEVEN

Chief of Detectives Stanley Trenton picked up the *New York Post* and the Sunday *New York Times* from outside his front door.

The front page of the *Times* featured no less than six-headlined stories of national and international concern ranging from politics to warfare to the regulation of the food industry to mental health in Argentina to robot labor.

The *Post* had one headline dominating the front page.

CONTRACTOR KEVIN DONAHUE
ABDUCTED AND LEFT TO DIE

The copy that followed reported that the Brooklyn building magnate had died from lack of air and water in a vacant apartment in Gravesend's Marlboro Houses where he had apparently been held hostage for several days.

The NYPD was withholding further comment until investigators from the 61st Precinct Detectives' Squad, CSU and the Medical Examiner's Office had more solid information.

A short biography of Donahue and an unflattering photograph completed the fact-deficient story.

A statement of some kind, probably in the form of a press conference, would be demanded by the media and the public no later than Monday.

The Office of the Deputy Commissioner had gone ahead and fed the print and broadcast media the little white lie that Lee Wasko and Paul Gallo were solely responsible for the Lake Street homicides.

The news of Donahue's death had effectively buried the Lake Street story deeper into the newspapers and the disguised resolution of that case was little mentioned in broadcast news except on local cable news programs.

That would all change drastically once the two events were connected.

And how to handle giving the media information about an unidentified co-conspirator lurking within the city or state government had never been effectively settled by Trenton, Munro and Jennings.

If they were not careful they could look a lot like *The Three Stooges*.

The message from the Commissioner of Police late Saturday night was unambiguous. The Mayor was expecting a prepared statement no later than nine on Monday morning, *and it had better be convincing*. The sharks would be circling and "His Honor" was not about to jump into the water alone.

The call to Trenton from Captain Samson later Sunday morning only served to muddy the waters.

Evidence collected by CSU and the medical examiner indicated District Attorney Investigator William Heller had definitely been held and probably murdered in the same basement apartment where Kevin Donahue's body had been found.

Trenton could feel a killer headache coming on.

Sixty-third Precinct detectives Aidan Reilly and Josh Altman sat in an unmarked vehicle on the corner of Avenue I and East 39th Street staking-out Amersfort Park.

There had been rumors of drug activity in the area.

The three-and-a-half acre park was fairly empty late Sunday morning.

Several parents looked on as their children leaned over the short wall of the fountain, reaching up for a cool spray of water on an August day that was already turning brutally hot and humid.

An old man, sleeping in the grass under a tree, was considered not worth a bother to the detectives.

"My wife is killing me," Reilly said.

"You've been singing that tune for so long I can't imagine how you are still alive. What is it this time?"

"She wants to have another kid. I need another kid like I need another gallstone."

"You have gallstones?"

"It's an analogy, sounds better than hemorrhoids."

"Have you tried either analogy on her?"

"No. With Megan I use a less effective method. I try reasoning with her."

"Unfortunately I'm not in a position to give marital advice," Altman said.

"Because you're not married?"

"Exactly."

"There is nothing unfortunate about that. Speaking of which," Reilly asked, "is there any truth in the talk you're seeing Sandra Rosen again?"

"We've been speaking, considering the possibility. She says she wants to take it very slowly."

"The only thing my wife takes very slowly is killing me," Reilly said.

"Look at that," Altman said. "Two teens looking guilty as hell just landed at a picnic table. They may be setting up shop."

"What ever happened to going to church with the family on Sunday mornings?"

Officers Landis and Mendez were on their second day of surveillance across from Il Colosseo on 18th Avenue.

They had been sitting in exactly the same spot for nearly twelve hours the day before.

"Talk about a waste of taxpayer's money," Mendez said. "A few more days of this and we'll have to start getting our mail delivered here."

"Is there somewhere you would rather be?"

"I could be at Sunday mass."

"You hate Sunday mass."

"Not as much as I hate this," Mendez said.

Landis' cell phone made the sound announcing a text message.

It came from Salina Mendez.

Call me when you get a chance. Please don't say anything to Rey.

"What the hell," Landis involuntarily said aloud.

"What?" Mendez asked.

"A *friendly* reminder that I'm late on my cellular phone bill. I know I paid it. Now I'll have to try getting in touch with a live representative."

"Good luck with that," Mendez said. "I would put in a prayer for you at church if I wasn't stuck here."

"Look at the bright side."

"What side is that?"

"Italian restaurants and barbers are usually closed on Mondays."

"Not this particular Italian restaurant, I checked," Mendez said, "and who the fuck would go to an Italian barber *any* day of the week?"

Senderowitz woke up hurting and disoriented.

For a moment he couldn't determine where he was. He finally realized he was lying on his bed, on top of the bed covers, fully dressed.

He had somehow managed to get out of his shoes.

A voice in his throbbing head asked, *When am I going to stop?*

Another voice answered, *Don't hold your breath.*

Bernie stumbled into the bathroom, threw cold water on his face, and opened the medicine cabinet looking for relief.

The cupboard was bare.

He moved to the kitchen and found the cure on the counter beside the sink.

He grabbed a glass a poured himself a scotch.

. . .

Marina Ivanov met Lorraine DiMarco for brunch at the Grand Canyon Restaurant on Montague Street in Brooklyn Heights.

Ivanov described the incident between her sister and Yuri Markov on Thursday night and Alex Holden's reaction.

Against all advice, Rachel's boyfriend had gone to the Lobnya Lounge on Friday night to give Markov what Alex called *a taste of his own medicine.*

"What did Alex say happened?"

"He said he confronted Markov in the parking area behind the club. Markov came at him with a knife, they wrestled for it, and Yuri lost the battle. Markov was dead when the police arrived."

"It sounds like self-defense, involuntary manslaughter maybe. Why the second-degree murder charge?" Lorraine asked.

"There were two witnesses, both employees of the club, who claimed Alex produced the knife and *he* assaulted Markov."

"How does Alex explain that?"

"He says they're lying."

"And why would they lie?"

"Fear of Yuri's father, the owner of the club, maybe a combination of fear and an early Christmas bonus."

"There were no other witnesses?"

"None we know about."

"Okay. I'll talk with Alex in the morning and decide if I can take on the case," Lorraine said. "In any event, I will at least advise a plea and represent him at the arraignment."

"Thank you."

"I'm not making any promises."

"I understand," Marina said.

"The waffles with fresh strawberries are very good here," Lorraine said when the waitress arrived at their table.

Ivanov took another quick look at the menu.

"I'm leaning toward the Sicilian omelet," she said.

. . .

Samson caught him just as he was about to rush out the front door.

"Jimmy, hold up."

"I'm sort of in a hurry."

"Come here and sit with me, I won't keep you long."

Samson and his son were alone in the house and Samson didn't want to blow the opportunity to get the talk over with, especially since Alicia had taken the girls out to Ally Pond Park for that very reason.

The boy reluctantly joined his father on the living room sofa.

"How are things with you?"

"Fine. Why?"

"You've seemed preoccupied lately," Samson said, "you are hardly ever home these days."

"School begins soon, we're all trying to cram in as much summer activity as possible while there's still time."

"Speaking of school, your mother is concerned about your grades."

"She worries too much," Jimmy suggested.

"*I* worry too much, your mother worries just enough."

"It was just a little slump. It happens to everyone from time to time. Have you checked Manning's passing percentage lately?"

"He makes millions of dollars whether he completes or not," Samson said, "and he's not hoping to get into a good college."

"I'll ace all my classes this year, guaranteed. Tell Mom not to worry. I really need to get going."

His father was about to ask *where to* as Jimmy headed for the door but he held his tongue.

Samson wondered instead how he was going to sell the football analogy to Alicia when he wasn't certain he bought it himself.

Jimmy rushed around the corner to the adjoining street and was relieved to see the car was still waiting. He jumped into the passenger seat.

"What took so long?"

"My father, he decided all of a sudden we needed to have a chat."

"About?"

"My grades last semester."

"Did you blame it on me?"

"Funny. Actually, I tried blaming it on Eli Manning."

"Is it alright? Do you want to skip this?"

"No, I don't want to skip it."

"Then we should go. Kenny will be home in a few hours."

A day after burying his only son, Detective John Cicero sat alone at the kitchen table. His wife and two daughters sat together in the living room.

Both girls would be leaving on Monday morning. Maryann to begin her first year at Rutgers University in New Brunswick, New Jersey. Lena returning to her home in Albany, New York, where she taught kindergarten.

Cicero knew Edward's death would hit Annie much harder once the girls had gone, if his wife could possibly become more distraught.

The *Sunday Daily News* sat on the table in an orange plastic bag. He removed the newspaper and looked at the front page.

KEVIN DONAHUE FOUND DEAD
IN BROOKLYN BASEMENT

The fact he had not received the news from Samson or Murphy only served to reinforce his belief that the 61st Precinct was not interested in having him meddle in *their* investigation.

Fuck the Six-one.

Nothing was going to stop him from finding his son's killer.

He owed it to Annie and the girls, he owed it to Eddie.

He owed it to himself.

. . .

Ripley had called his sister's house early Sunday morning to invite her husband to join him in Box Seats at Citi Field for the afternoon game.

He had received the choice tickets as a gift from Senderowitz who in turn had obtained them when visiting with a friend at what Bernie had described as an *Exclusive Sicilian-American Social Establishment.*

Ripley had gladly accepted the gift, no questions asked.

"Take Kyle with you, he'll love it and love the time with you," Connie had said. "Mickey can stay here with us and the girls. And anyway, Philip has had issues with the Mets since they traded Carlos Beltran."

"That's ancient history."

"Phil can hold a grudge."

"I hope he hasn't become a Yankee fan."

"Worse," Connie said. "He likes the Phillies."

Kyle was very excited. Mickey was not very disappointed.

They sat watching as the Mets' first baseman tossed ground balls to the other infielders and the Mets' starter threw warm-up pitches from the mound.

"Dad?"

"Yes, son."

"When you are a policeman do you fight the bad guys?"

"Something like that."

"Like the Cowboys and the Indians?"

"Well we don't call them Indians anymore, Kyle," Ripley said. "And with the cowboys and Native-Americans it was not always clear who the bad guys were."

"But you're the good guy, right?"

"If you put it that way, I guess so."

"Do you ever have to kill the bad guys?"

He had no idea how to answer the question from his eight-year-old. Kyle was becoming more perceptive every day, and the boy's inquiries were becoming more personal and much trickier to address.

Ripley was saved by the bell when the umpire yelled *Play Ball* and Kyle's attention was averted to the playing field.

Ripley knew the subject would come up again and decided he needed to be better prepared the next time it did.

"How about a hot dog, chief?" he asked after the first batter flied-out to short right field.

"Okay," Kyle said. "Thanks for bringing me, Dad."

Detective Jack Falcone phoned Marina Ivanov late Sunday afternoon.

"Just called to see how it's going with Alex Holden."

"We'll know more tomorrow," Ivanov said. "I talked to an attorney who has agreed to speak with Alex and said she could at the least be with him at the arraignment."

"I hope it goes well."

"Thank you, and thanks for your help."

"Listen," Falcone said. "Would you be interested in joining me for a cup of coffee sometime?"

"You never invited me for coffee when we worked together."

"I was off coffee for a while."

"Sure. Call me," Ivanov said.

The Lafayette High School varsity football team was practicing offensive plays late Sunday afternoon. The Patriots would be playing their first game of the season in less than two weeks.

Along the sideline, the cheerleading squad was rehearsing an elaborately choreographed halftime show.

As the sun began to set the two groups broke up.

Jenny Greco and Patty Bolin were about to get into Patty's Camry when Peter Donner rushed up to them.

Donner was the new wide receiver who was predicted to put the school in contention for the Borough Championship. His family had relocated from Utah where, in his junior year, Donner had led the state in receptions. His addition to the Patriot's roster was the talk of the school, and his good looks had all the girls talking.

"Jennifer, right?" Peter said.

"Jenny."

"Can I buy you a soda or something, Jenny? I can drive you home."

"I don't know. My parents will be expecting me."

"Go ahead," Patty said. "You can tell them we went over to my house, I'll cover for you."

"Can you give us a minute?" Jenny asked Peter.

"Sure."

Jenny dragged Patty away from the car.

"Are you sure?" she asked.

"Are you kidding? Look at him. My parents won't be home until eleven. If anyone asks, you were with me. Just be home before then."

"Thanks," Jenny said. "You're great."

"And you're lucky."

Stan Landis was very uneasy about keeping the secret from his partner.

When he called Salina Mendez after surveillance duty at the restaurant, Rey's wife was very upset.

She said she had to see him in person.

Landis agreed to meet Salina at her house at nine.

Rey would be out bowling with friends.

He hoped he wouldn't be hearing Rey's wild doubts about his wife's fidelity were correct.

The three small children were asleep when Landis arrived.

"What's wrong?" he asked as soon as he walked in. "On the phone you sounded like the sky was falling. Are you okay?"

"No, I'm not okay, Stan. Rey did it again."

"Did what again?"

"I'm pregnant."

"Congratulations?"

"No. We can't have another child. I have much too much on my hands as it is and we definitely can't afford it."

"And Rey doesn't know."

"Rey doesn't know, but he is going to be able to tell soon. I don't know what to do. Rey will never agree to an abortion and I'm terrified to go behind his back."

"Wow."

"I was hoping for a little more wisdom from you, Stan. What am I supposed to do?"

"How much time do you have?"

"Not much."

"I need to think about it."

"Please think fast."

"I'll call you," Landis said.

Josh Altman watched from his car as Sandra and Murphy walked into Rosen's house.

Rosen had told Josh, just before Christmas no less, she couldn't see him outside of work anymore.

Sandra claimed it was much too difficult having a romantic relationship with another detective in the same precinct.

He had tried for weeks to change her mind.

It only made their working together more uncomfortable as the time passed.

Altman suspected the situation was a big factor in Rosen's decision to transfer out of the Six-three.

Now here she was with a detective from the Six-one.

Altman had heard a little about Thomas Murphy. How Murphy couldn't even protect his own brother from being killed by a rookie cop.

What could Sandra possibly see in the clown?

Josh Altman allowed himself several minutes to calm down before speeding off.

Peter Donner had a cold six pack in his car.

He drove onto Shell Road.

The street was deserted at that time on Sunday night.

The businesses, predominantly auto salvage yards and tire dealerships, were all shut down.

The baseball field was dark and vacant.

Peter parked in the shadow of a large Norway maple away from any of the streetlamps and reached for a Budweiser.

He asked Jenny if she cared to join him and she accepted.

After a few beers Jenny let him kiss her. Before long Peter's hand moved between her legs.

"Don't," she said.

"Come on, I thought Brooklyn girls liked to have fun."

"I said stop."

When he didn't comply Jenny pulled herself away and jumped out of the car, seriously scraping her upper arm on the door frame as she did.

She moved away, hurrying down the desolate street.

"Jenny, I'll behave," Peter called from the car. "It's not safe out here. Let me give you a ride home."

When she didn't stop walking he punched the accelerator and raced off. Minutes later Jenny could hear a car approaching from behind.

She imagined Peter had changed his mind about leaving her out there alone.

Jenny put her head down and picked up her pace, unable to decide what to do.

The car came to a stop and she heard the car door opening, then quick footsteps following her.

The dimly lit street was menacing and her arm was bleeding.

"Swear you won't touch me again and take me straight home," Jenny said as she turned to face him.

TWELVE

Rose Greco had not notified the police yet, but she had made a number of anxious phone calls late Sunday and early Monday morning.

One of the girls who had been to cheerleader practice the previous day told Mrs. Greco that Jenny had left the field with Patty Bolin.

When Patty got the call from Jenny's mother she was about to lie, to tell Mrs. Greco Jenny had stayed with her for a while after rehearsal, but the serious concern in the woman's voice was unmistakable and alarming.

"Is Jenny alright?" Patty asked.

"She didn't come home last night. Carla Jackson said she was last seen with you."

"She took a ride with the new boy on the team. They were going to have a soda. He said he would take her home."

"How could you let her go off with a stranger, Patty?" Rose asked. "What is the boy's name?"

"Peter Donner. I think they live on West Second near Quentin Road."

Rose hung up on Patty and found a phone number for the Donners.

Jenny's father had stayed home from work, sick with worry. He told his wife *he* would talk to the boy.

"We picked up a few bottles of pop and I drove her home. It was around nine," Peter said.

"Where exactly did you leave her?" Andy Greco asked.

"West Thirteenth Street, across from the elementary school."

"That's not where we live."

"That's where she asked me to drop her, sir. Is she alright?"

Andy Greco hung up on Peter and called 9-1-1.

. . .

Landis and Mendez were back in their vehicle across from Il Colosseo at eight Monday morning.

It was unusually quiet in the car.

Landis was trying to come up with something to do or to say that might help Rey's wife with her dilemma.

It was Rey who broke the silence.

"Do you ever wish you weren't gay?" he asked.

"Do you ever wish you weren't Hispanic?"

"No sense wishing for what you can't change."

"There's your answer."

"Got it."

"Do you ever wish for another child?" Landis asked, biting his lip.

"I did before we had the boy. Now that I have satisfied *that* Latino requirement, I think we're good. Jesus, we can't even afford the three we already have."

"What if Salina got pregnant again?"

"She's not going to get pregnant again. Unless you know something I don't know."

"The only thing I know that you don't know is my birthday," Landis said, deciding he was not yet prepared to take it any further.

"June nineteenth," Mendez said.

"You're unbelievable."

"No, just attentive. It's this stake-out that is fucking unbelievable."

Lorraine DiMarco met with Alex Holden at eight-forty-five, just before the arraignment scheduled for nine.

Lorraine elected to believe Alex, and consequently concluded the two witnesses of record were not being truthful.

And giving false testimony that could ruin the life of an innocent young man, regardless of the reason, was something Lorraine found impossible to tolerate or ignore.

She told Holden she would argue his case.

At the arraignment he pleaded not guilty to second-degree murder.

The press conference was scheduled for ten. Stanley Trenton considered, if only for a moment, dropping the ball into Captain Samson's lap. But the Chief of Detectives understood the buck stopped with him.

Trenton did decide, however, to hold court at the 61st Precinct on Coney Island Avenue. He laid out the ground rules immediately.

The statement had been drafted by Jennings, Munro and Trenton less than an hour earlier.

"I will make a short statement. I will relate all we currently know about the death of Kevin Donahue and its probable connection to other events that have occurred over the past week. When I say *all we know* I mean everything, so I will not be wasting valuable time fielding questions I cannot answer.

"Kevin Donahue was last seen alive on Tuesday night. He was found dead late Saturday. The apparent cause of death was deprivation of fluids and air. Donahue had been gagged and tied into a chair and abandoned.

"We have determined DA Investigator Bill Heller, who was killed on Tuesday and discovered Wednesday, was held for a period of time in the same vacant apartment where Donahue was found.

"We also know Donahue and Investigator Heller had a meeting on Tuesday night to discuss an ongoing investigation by the DA's Office that we are not at liberty to speak about at this time," Trenton added, causing a good deal of commotion in the crowded room. He had to raise his voice to plead for silence before he could continue.

"Finally, we have found evidence suggesting Lee Wasko and Paul Gallo, named earlier as the perpetrators in the Lake Street double homicide, may have been involved in the death of Heller or Donahue or both.

"The NYPD is committed to addressing all unanswered questions related to these events and will be working around the clock to do so.

"The Public Information Branch of the Deputy Commissioner's Office will provide you with timely updates when information deemed reliable is available. Please, do not inundate the office or the New York Police Department with premature inquiries. It will only serve to encumber our efforts. Thank you for your time."

And that was that. There was no mention of a tape recording.

Trenton left the floor as questions were shouted from the audience.

He hurried up the stairs to the second floor and disappeared.

Trenton, Jennings and Munro had literally stonewalled the media and run for cover, leaving behind a roomful of bewildered and angry reporters.

But they were hoping to bait an unnamed man who was accountable for the deaths of Angela Salerno, Edward Cicero, Bill Heller, Kevin Donahue, Paul Gallo and Lee Wasko. They had concluded, at great risk to their careers, that in certain cases the argument *the public has a right to know* was not sacred.

They were banking on the belief that if a killer was ultimately discovered and brought to justice their deception would be vindicated.

Other than the brass, only Captain Samson and his team knew all that had been omitted in Trenton's report.

Samson, Senderowitz, Murphy, Rosen, Ripley, Ivanov and Richards held the power to redeem the Chief of Detectives, the District Attorney and the Deputy Commissioner, or bring them all down.

Trenton had great faith and trust in the abilities and integrity of Samson and the detectives of the Six-one.

What Trenton was forgetting about was Detective John Cicero of the Six-eight.

. . .

All morning he had been fighting the impulse to watch the live broadcast of the press conference, to find out if the other shoe was about to drop. He felt like a tightrope walker battling the urge to look down.

He lost the battle and tuned into the New York One airing at ten.

After hearing Trenton's statement, and watching Trenton rush off the stage, he felt as if a great weight had been lifted from his shoulders.

They still hoped to bring him out into the open with the tape recording and he would not be baited. He knew they had nothing.

He could now concentrate all of his time and energy into the important work ahead of him.

An emergency call from a panicked city trash collector was transferred over to Desk Sergeant Kelly at the Six-one. Kelly kicked it up to the Detectives' Squad and Murphy caught the call.

"Saddle up," he said to Rosen.

"What?"

"A dead girl in a dumpster at Gil Hodges Baseball Park on Shell Road."

"I hate Mondays," Rosen said, collecting her gear.

"Every fucking day is Monday around here," Murphy said.

PART TWO

THE HANGMAN

Every blade has two edges.
He who wounds with one,
wounds himself with the other.

—Victor Hugo

THIRTEEN

Rosen was holding the digital camera, scrolling through all the shots Investigator Joan Michaels had taken looking down into the dumpster at Gil Hodges Ballpark.

"Can you get these photographs to Detective Senderowitz at the Six-one?" Rosen asked.

"No problem."

Derek Fielder was inside the dumpster with a flashlight and evidence collection paraphernalia.

Two more CSU investigators were walking a grid inside the boundaries of a large area of the ball field cordoned off by police tape.

Uniformed officers were posted at all entrances, keeping civilians out of the park.

The girl had been carefully removed from the dumpster and laid out on a large sheet of black construction grade poly-ethylene.

Murphy stood at a safe distance watching Batman examine the body.

"Do we have an ID?" he asked the M.E.

"Not yet."

Murphy called the precinct.

"Kelly. I need a list of Caucasian females, approximately sixteen years old, reported missing in the past few days. If nothing turns up, get a photo from CSU Investigator Michaels and shoot it off to all the local high schools for identification. Lafayette, Lincoln, Dewey, New Utrecht, Coney Island Prep, Bishop Kearney, and so on," Murphy said. "We need to find out who the girl is, and soon."

"The schools are still out for another week or so."

"The administrative offices should be up and running by now."

"I'm on it," Kelly said.

Dr. Wayne stood up and walked over to Murphy. Rosen joined them.

"So," said Murphy, "what can you tell us about the red mark around her neck?"

Investigator Fielder had climbed out of the dumpster and was busy at the CSU evidence van.

"Fielder," Wayne called.

"Yes?"

"Please show Murphy and Rosen the rope."

Fielder pulled a large plastic bag from the back of the truck and carried it over to Wayne and the two detectives. The bag held a four-foot length of quarter inch white nylon rope. For all practical purposes, an everyday piece of clothesline. Except for the loop tied at one end.

"A noose?" Rosen asked.

"More precisely a Gallows Knot," Fielder said.

"The victim was strangled," Batman said. "There were bruises on her back in the areas of the left and right deltoid muscles. The girl would have been face down on the grass. Apparently the perpetrator was standing with a foot on each of her shoulders pinning her to the ground and pulled on the rope until she was dead."

"Why go through the trouble?" Murphy asked. "The killer had to be fairly strong to get her up into the dumpster. Assuming it was a man with two good hands, why not just choke the poor kid or snap her neck? Why bother with a noose?"

"To simulate a hanging?"

"I had the same thought, Detective Rosen," Wayne said.

"Why not just hang her?" Fielder asked.

"It might have kept him out in the open longer than he would have liked," Rosen suggested.

"Maybe the fuck wanted to save rope," Murphy said.

Rosen took a long look at the young girl on the ground.

"Let's hope he's not saving rope for another victim."

. . .

Detectives Murphy and Rosen stood in the ballpark not knowing exactly what to do.

The body was gone, Batman was gone, and all they could do for the CSU team was get in the way.

Murphy's cell phone rang.

The detectives might have been thankful Sergeant Kelly had found something for them to work on if it wasn't the name of a family who had reported a missing teenage daughter.

Jennifer Ann Greco, a sixteen-year-old Junior at Lafayette High, who never made it home from cheerleading practice the night before.

Kelly gave Murphy an address on West Street between Village Road North and Gravesend Neck Road.

"Isn't that near Our Lady of Grace Baseball Field?" Murphy asked.

"Just up the street."

"Time to roll," Murphy said after the call from Kelly.

"Where to?" Rosen asked.

"From one ballpark to another. And me without my mitt."

Samson called Ivanov into his office.

"I spoke with Lorraine. She told me she agreed to represent your friend."

"Yes. Thank you again for pointing me her way."

"Marina."

"Yes."

"I don't have to tell you to stay out of it. We can't appear to be in opposition to the prosecution."

"Alex Holden is like one of the family, Captain. My sister expects me to do something."

"Tell me about Pavel Vasin, Marina, you've mentioned his name more than once."

"He is my father's cousin, more like a brother. He came over from Russia when I was in my teens. Uncle Pavel was MUR,

Moscow Criminal Investigation. He would tell me about his cases and go on about how much he missed the work. Why do you ask?"

"You have told me it was Pavel Vasin who inspired you to go into law enforcement."

"And?"

"Lorraine said she may need a private investigator on the Holden case."

Murphy and Rosen elicited two names from Rose and Andrew Greco.

Patty Bolin and Peter Donner.

They asked the couple for a photograph of their daughter. Sadly, the detectives concluded the girl in the photo was the girl in the dumpster.

They had talked with Samson before going in to see the Grecos and agreed they would treat the visit as a follow-up on the missing person report, and not as a death notification, until they had an opportunity to speak with the last people to see Jenny Greco alive.

They chose to see Patty Bolin first.

After looking over photographs emailed from Michaels at CSU, Bernie phoned the medical examiner.

"Wayne."

"This is Senderowitz from the Six-one, do you have a minute?"

"Only a minute."

"The girl found in the ballpark."

"I'm with her now."

"Can you tell me anything about the gash on her upper left arm?"

"Not a knife, it wasn't that sharp. I would say metal of some kind. Something that came to a point."

"Could she have snagged her arm on the corner of an automobile door frame?" Senderowitz asked.

"Possibly," Batman said.

"Thanks, I'll let you go."

"Two more things while I have you on the phone, Detective."

"Yes?"

"The girl had been drinking alcohol shortly before her death."

"I'll let Rosen and Murphy know. And the second thing?"

"If it's any consolation, the girl was not violated sexually."

"As a matter of fact it is consoling," Senderowitz said.

Patty Bolin did not have much to add beyond what the detectives had learned from Rose Greco.

The last time Patty had seen Jenny Greco was when Jenny and Peter Donner drove away from the football field the previous evening.

"Donner's car? Make? Model? Color?" Murphy asked.

"Ford Explorer. Dark blue," Patty said.

Rosen received a call from Senderowitz as they were returning to their vehicle.

"The girl had a nasty gash on her upper left arm. She may have cut herself on a car door. She had been drinking alcohol and wasn't sexually molested," Bernie reported.

The detectives headed out to Peter Donner's address on West 2nd Street.

They saw the SUV in the driveway when they arrived at the house.

Murphy took a quick walk around the Explorer.

"Well?" asked Rosen.

"There appears to be blood on the front passenger door."

"Are you just seeing what you would like to see?" Rosen asked.

"What I would like to see is Dublin in August."

"Tommy."

"I said *appears* to be blood. It should be enough for a search. CSU can confirm before they go into the vehicle."

Rosen called Kelly at the precinct, read him the license plate number, and told the sergeant they needed a search warrant for the Ford.

"Probable cause, the appearance of blood on the exterior of the vehicle," Rosen said. "And we need it as soon as possible."

"I'll move it right to the top of my list, if I can get through all of this goddamn paper on my desk and find the place where the list begins."

"Well if it helps you with your work load, we identified the girl."

"It helps a little. Did you notify the parents?"

"We're putting it off until we talk to the boy she was last seen with, not that I'm in a big hurry to break the news."

"I'd rather be begging a judge for a vehicle search warrant than have to tell a mother her daughter is never coming home," Kelly said.

"How about having to tell two mothers in less than a week?"

"I'd rather have an impacted wisdom tooth."

"Can you transfer me up to Samson?"

"Sure. Hold on."

"Thanks Kelly."

"Don't mention it."

Samson stepped out of his office and called Ripley and Richards over.

"Rosen called, we have a possible suspect. I need you to locate the Lafayette High School football coach and get his impressions of Peter Donner. Also ask the coach for names and numbers of some of Donner's teammates and talk to whoever you can about Peter, particularly about how the boy described his luck with the girls."

"And if anyone wants to know what all the questions are about?" Richards asked.

"I'll tell them it's classified," Ripley said, "I'm very good at it."

"Call Rosen if anyone raises a red flag," Samson said.

. . .

Peter Donner answered the doorbell.

The detectives identified themselves and Murphy cut to the chase.

"When was the last time you saw Jenny Greco?"

"It was around nine last night," Donner said. "What's going on?"

"Let us ask the questions for a while. Where was that?"

"It was where I dropped her off," Donner said. "On West Thirteenth, across from the elementary school."

"Why there? Jenny doesn't live there."

"I didn't know that. That's where she asked me to take her."

"Had you and Jenny been drinking alcohol?"

"No."

"We know she drank alcohol last evening, Peter," Murphy said.

"Not with me. Maybe she met with some other friends afterwards. Are you going to tell me what this is about?"

"We will," Rosen said, "but we would like to continue this conversation down at the precinct."

"Am I under arrest?"

"Not really," Rosen answered, "but cooperating with us would be in your best interest."

"My parents aren't home, I need to call them."

"You can phone anyone you like when we reach the precinct," Murphy said. "So, how about it? Will you take a ride with us?"

"I have a car. I can meet you there."

"Your car is fine where it is, Peter, why waste the gas? Think of it as a courtesy shuttle, we'll have you back here in no time."

Twenty minutes after the detectives left for the precinct with Peter Donner, Fielder and Michaels arrived at the Donner residence.

Michaels watched as Fielder scraped a sample from the door

of the SUV onto a piece of filter paper with the small blade of a Swiss army knife.

"Nice evidence collection tool," Michaels said.

"Hard to beat."

"How are you testing? Luminol?"

"Kastle-Meyer."

Fielder added a drop of ethanol followed by phenolphthalein and finally hydrogen peroxide. The paper turned pink.

"Blood?"

"Most likely," Fielder said, "if it isn't horseradish."

"Do we enter the vehicle?" Michaels asked.

"Call for a tow truck. We'll go into the vehicle at the CSU garage, better to get the car off the street before we attract an audience."

Peter Donner sat in an interrogation room at the 61st Precinct. Samson, Senderowitz, Rosen and Murphy stood in a small adjoining room observing the suspect through a one-way mirror.

"He's asking for a phone call to his parents," Rosen said.

"Can we interrogate him before we give him a phone?" Murphy asked.

"We'll call it an interview," Bernie said, "but we don't have much time."

Murphy received word from Fielder at CSU.

"There was blood on the car door, empty beer cans on the floor in back. They ran an absorption-elution test on the blood sample, Batman confirmed it matched Jenny Greco's blood type," Murphy reported.

"It should be enough to arrest the boy if he won't cooperate otherwise," Samson said. "Let's try to get something out of him. If he refuses to talk, we will have to let him notify his family."

"He'll call his old man and they'll lawyer up," Murphy said.

Samson's cell rang. Ripley.

"I talked with a few of Donner's teammates. They said during practice Peter was going on about how hot Jenny was and betting he could score."

Samson related the news.

"Would you mind if I talk to the boy?" Senderowitz asked.

"Not at all," Rosen said.

"Try finding out if they discovered rope in the boy's car, and call Ripley back for the names of the teammates who said Peter was eyeing the girl. Let me know if you get anything I can use in there."

Senderowitz sat down at the table opposite Peter Donner.

Samson, Murphy and Rosen watched and listened.

"I'm Detective Senderowitz, Peter. Can I get you something to drink?"

"I want to call my father."

"And you will be able to call him very soon. I was hoping you could help me out first, just a few quick questions."

"Can I have a Coke?" Peter asked.

"Certainly."

"I've got it," Murphy said in the adjoining room.

"How well do you know Jenny Greco?" Senderowitz asked.

"I never met her before yesterday. I spotted her during practice and I asked who she was. A teammate gave me her name and told me not to waste my time. Jenny wouldn't give any of the boys on the team the time of day. I made a little bet that I could get her to take a ride with me."

"So you took her for a ride."

"I invited her out for a soda, said I would drive her home."

"Did you stop anywhere?"

"At a grocery store for a couple of soft drinks."

"What store?" Senderowitz asked.

"I don't know the name, on Eighty-sixth near the train station."

There was a light tapping on the glass.

"That must be your Coke. Give me a moment."

"I know someone is watching through that mirror," Peter said.

"They watch me constantly, waiting for me to screw up," Bernie said. "Give me a second."

Bernie stepped out of the room, Murphy handed him a can of soda.

"No rope in his car," Rosen said. "Adam Jackson and Carl Douglas."

"Get a phone up here for the kid," Senderowitz said before going back in.

Bernie placed the Coke on the table and sat again.

"We have a phone on the way."

"Thank you."

"Who gave you Jenny's name and told you she was not very friendly?"

"Adam. Carl agreed."

"We are very concerned about Jenny, Peter, and her parents are very worried. She never arrived home last night. As far as we know, you were the last person to see her. We only want a little help."

"I told you everything I know. I dropped Jenny exactly where she asked me to. I hope she's alright, but I can't help you."

"Do you have any idea why Jenny's blood was found on the door of your SUV?"

Donner looked the detective in the eyes and then looked down at the table.

"I want to call my father."

"Bring in the phone," Senderowitz said, rising from his seat.

Rosen entered and placed a phone in front of the suspect.

"When you speak to your dad, Peter," Senderowitz said as the detectives were leaving the room, "tell him you are under arrest."

"Nice try," Samson said. "Tommy, when he's done with his call, go in and read him his rights."

"I don't like him," Senderowitz said.

"I'm not too fond of him myself," Rosen said.

"I mean I don't like him as a murder suspect."

"He's been lying through his teeth all day," Murphy said.

"Blatantly," Senderowitz agreed. "Something obviously happened between Peter and Jenny last night, but I don't believe he strangled her with a piece of clothesline. I think he will be very surprised and shocked when he learns the girl is dead."

"What do you think, Sam?" Murphy asked.

"I think it's time to notify the girl's parents."

FOURTEEN

On Saturday the Labor Day weekend began, three days marking the official end of summer vacation.

New York City public school teachers and administrators would start work on Tuesday. Students would begin classes on Friday, following the observance of Rosh Hashanah.

Peter Donner was out on bail. The new hope of the Lafayette Patriots had been *temporarily* suspended from the varsity football team. His parents were looking into transferring Peter to a different high school to avoid certain recrimination.

Jenny Greco had been buried.

Rosen and Murphy went on an unhurried excursion up to Cooperstown for the weekend.

Murphy for the Baseball Hall of Fame, Rosen for the early fall foliage.

Marty Richards took his wife and daughter to Connecticut to visit his parents.

Ivanov had declined an invitation to join her parents, her sister, and Alex Holden for Sunday brunch. She knew the talk would be about Alex's case and she had been told to steer clear.

Marina accepted an invitation to have coffee with Detective Jack Falcone instead.

Ripley rented a bungalow in Ocean City on the Jersey Shore and enjoyed the weekend watching Kyle and Mickey climb aboard every single amusement park ride on the boardwalk and frolic on the beach.

Samson stayed close to home with his wife and two daughters, his son Jimmy was not around much.

Senderowitz spent most of the weekend with Johnnie Walker.

. . .

156

The stake-out at the Italian restaurant had been called off. Chief Trenton and District Attorney Jennings had unhappily agreed it was a dead end. Pressure from the media regarding the Donahue case had eased off considerably, their interest redirected first to an eighteen car pile-up on the Long Island Expressway and later to the high school girl in the dumpster.

Mendez would have enjoyed the weekend celebrating the decision to terminate the stake-out if he wasn't busy trying to figure out what was bugging his wife.

Landis knew what was plaguing Salina Mendez and had no idea how to help her.

Salina managed to sneak a phone call to Landis on Monday.

"Stan, I need your help."

"I've been wracking my brain, Salina. I don't know what to tell you."

"I understand you and Rey are on a later shift tomorrow, now that your surveillance duty is done."

"Yes, eleven to seven."

"I told Rey I needed to go shopping for food and household supplies tomorrow and I would take the children over to my mother in the morning."

"And?"

"I made an appointment at Planned Parenthood on Court Street for nine."

"Salina, think about this," Landis urged. "It's not a good idea going behind his back."

"I've thought enough about it and there are *no* good ideas. I'm damned if I do and damned if I don't. Rey will blame me either way, for terminating the pregnancy or for getting pregnant in the first place. And he can't know about this, Stan. You have to swear you will never tell him."

"So why tell me?"

"Because there is no one else I can ask to come with me to the clinic," Salina said. "Please, Stan, I can't do this alone. I can't."

. . .

Samson insisted Jimmy join them at the park on Monday afternoon, to spend time with the family.

Samson and his wife sat on a bench watching the boy push Kayla and Lucy on side-by-side swings.

"What's on your mind, Sam?"

"The girl found at the ball field. She was sixteen, not much younger than Jimmy. It's scary out there, Alicia. Do we need to lock our children up to keep them safe?"

"We do what we have always done. We implore them to be careful. We teach them to be alert. We ask them to beware, without frightening them. And then we say our prayers."

"It doesn't guarantee their safety."

"There are never guarantees, Sam."

At the swings, Jimmy's cell phone rang.

"Hey."

"Can you come over?"

"Push me, Jimmy," Lucy said.

"Hold on," he said to the caller. "Pump your legs, Lucy. I'll be back in a minute."

Jimmy walked away from the swing set.

"Sorry."

"Can you come over?"

"I don't think so. My father is planning his annual Labor Day barbeque and he wants me to be at home."

"Kenny called from somewhere in Ohio. He said he'll be back midday tomorrow. Then he's driving locally for a few weeks. This could be our last chance to be together for a while. Can you try to get away later, after the festivities?"

"I'll try. I'll call you."

"Try hard. Save me a hotdog."

"You are a great little traveler," Marty Richards said, taking his daughter from the car seat.

"She really loved seeing your parents," Linda said.

"It's no wonder. Every time we see them it's like Sophia hit the lottery. I could barely get all the gifts into the trunk. They're spoiling her."

"She's their only grandchild. And we could all use a little spoiling every once in a while."

"She's out like a light," Richards said. "How about we empty the trunk later, put Sophia in her crib, and try spoiling each other a little?"

"How about a lot," Linda said.

Ivanov and Falcone rose from their table at the New Times Restaurant on Coney Island Avenue.

"I need to walk over to the Six-one and check in. Everyone else is doing the holiday weekend thing."

"I'm glad we got together," Falcone said.

"It was nice. I'm glad you're back on coffee."

"If you're curious about why I gave it up for a while, I would rather wait to talk about it."

"Take your time. Do you do dinner?"

"Almost every day."

"Maybe I can whip us up a meal sometime."

"This is Lorraine DiMarco, Mr. Vasin. I'm representing Alex Holden."

"Yes, Ms. DiMarco. May I call you Lorraine?"

"Please do."

"Then I insist you call me Pavel. Marina informed me I might be getting a call from you, that you might need some assistance."

"I was hoping you could meet me tomorrow morning to talk about it, around ten, at my office in Brooklyn Heights."

"Please give me the address and I will gladly see you then."

They were driving north on the Garden State Parkway, headed back to Queens early Monday afternoon.

"Are we there yet?" Mickey said from the back seat.

"Soon, son," Ripley answered.

"He asks every two minutes," Kyle said, seated beside his father.

"So did you when you were his age, every time we took a trip."

"When Mom was with us?"

"Yes son, when Mom was with us. And she always told you the same thing. *We're not there yet but we're here together and I wouldn't want to be anywhere else.*"

"Do you wish Mom was here now?" Kyle asked.

"She is, Kyle. She always will be."

"Are we there yet?" Mickey asked.

Eileen Kaplan walked with her niece out of Mt. Hebron Cemetery in Flushing after the burial ceremony.

"Why wasn't your father here?" Eileen asked.

"I don't know."

"Sarah."

"I didn't tell him."

"How could you not tell the man his wife has died?"

"I don't know. She wasn't his wife anymore. Why should he care?"

"Your father always cared for her, and for you. He was a good husband and he always treated your mother with respect. When did you last speak with him?"

"It's been a long time."

"I thought so."

"What?"

"He didn't know she was dying."

"Mom didn't want him to know."

"Foolish pride. She didn't even want *you* to know, yet I told you. Do you regret you had the chance to spend time with her before it was too late?"

"Of course not."

"Your father would have wanted to be here. They loved each

other very much and were very happy until his work took its toll. Your mother couldn't handle it, and your father couldn't change who he was. There was no one to blame. Listen to me, Sarah, I knew my sister. I know she would want you to be a part of his life, more than ever now that she is gone. And I knew your father very well, ever since we were all younger than you are today. I am certain he wishes to be part of your life as well. Did you feel you needed to choose one above the other?"

"I don't know."

"He is your father and he loves you. Reach out to him before it is too late."

"I don't know," Sarah said as they arrived at the black limousine.

"You grill a mean burger, Mr. Samson," Alicia said as they finished washing and drying the dishes. "Although you may have gone a bit overboard with the jalapeños."

"I thought you liked it hot."

"I'm joking, Sam, everything was perfect."

"Thank you."

"And Kayla said it was the best hotdog she *ever ever* had."

"That's because we only allow them to have hotdogs twice a year. Where *are* the girls?"

"Upstairs, in their pajamas, teeth brushed, waiting for you to come up and read *The Little Prince*."

"When they're a little older and they start asking me about my work, I can read *The Little Finger Prince*. Why did Jimmy have to run off?"

"It's the last weekend before school begins."

"And?"

"And he wanted to see some friends," Alicia said. "He promised he would be home early."

"We're ready, Dad," Kayla called from the top of the stairs.

"Hurry, Daddy," Lucy chimed in.

"I'm coming, girls, get into your beds."

Samson's eyes locked on his wife's eyes for a moment before he started up to the girls.

"What?" she asked.

"It's a poor excuse for not staying home with his family for a change. It's the last weekend before school begins for all five of us."

Murphy pulled up in front of Rosen's place in Park Slope.

"I had a great time," she said.

"Being dragged through the Hall of Fame for three hours?"

"It was worth every moment," Rosen said. "Watching you stand in front of the plaque of Sandy Koufax, like a little boy."

"Koufax was a Brooklyn kid. When Sandy was at Lafayette High School he was better known for basketball. He started baseball as a catcher. My father always told us Koufax was the best left-handed pitcher to ever play in the big leagues. Dad hated Walter O'Malley with a passion for taking the Dodgers and Sandy away from Brooklyn. My father didn't see Koufax pitch until the Mets came along in sixty-two and the Los Angeles Dodgers were the visiting team. The way Dad talked about watching Sandy on the mound was intoxicating. Koufax became a legendary hero to me, even though he stopped playing years before I was born."

"I like that story, Tommy. You don't often talk about your father."

"He loved baseball," was all Murphy said.

"Would you like to come in?"

"I'm thinking about going over to Joe's Bar and Grill. I haven't seen Augie since his nephew's funeral and we didn't really have a chance to talk. And if it's not too late I need to pick up Ralph."

"I'm sure your mom won't mind having him for another night."

"I need to get him out of there before he decides he doesn't want to give up her cooking."

"I'll see you in the morning."

"You will."

"Don't drink too much," Rosen said as she left the car.

Murphy watched Sandra get into the house before he drove off.

On the opposite side of the street Josh Altman watched her also.

Maureen Rose watched her husband anxiously pacing back and forth across the living room floor.

"David, what's wrong?"

"Nothing is wrong."

"Are you nervous about tomorrow?"

"I suppose I am," he finally admitted, "Meeting new colleagues and students. Wondering how I will be received, wondering if leaving Newton was really a good idea."

"We agreed we had to leave, David. We decided it was too difficult to stay there, to be constantly reminded. And it was much too hard on Jason, with all of the questions at school. It's a new start for all of us."

"Are you sure?"

"David, you're a wonderful counselor. They will be lucky to have someone with your experience. Those kids will need your help."

"I sometimes wonder if I can help anyone anymore."

"You can, David, and you will. Jason is busy with a James Bond movie and it's a beautiful evening. Take me out for a walk."

"Sam. Wake up."

Samson opened his eyes and saw his wife Alicia standing in the bedroom doorway. He glanced at the bedside clock.

It was after one in the morning.

"What wrong?"

"Jimmy hasn't come home, Sam."

FIFTEEN

The boy had been shot twice. He was rushed to the Emergency Room at Long Island Jewish Medical Center in New Hyde Park Monday night and taken into the Operating Room immediately.

He was now in recovery, still unconscious.

His condition was listed as critical.

The victim was not identified until Detective Jesse Fulton of the Hundred and eleventh Precinct in Bayside, called to the hospital to investigate the shooting incident, was allowed entrance to the Intensive Care Unit following the surgery.

Fulton recognized the boy. He had worked on a number of community service projects in Northeastern Queens with the boy's father. The two men took part in a friendly poker game once a month.

Fulton phoned the boy's parents shortly before two in the morning.

Bernie Senderowitz and Silvio Batale left the Palermo Club just past two in the morning. After Batale locked the front door, the two men exchanged farewells and walked off in opposite directions.

Almost immediately, Silvio changed his course and he began following Bernie. He wanted to make sure Senderowitz arrived home safely, but did not want to insult his friend by suggesting the need for an escort.

Less than ten minutes later, Silvio watched Bernie slowly negotiate the front steps, using the handrail to steady himself. Bernie emptied the mailbox, fumbled with his keys and somehow managed to get through the door. When Senderowitz had entered the house, Batale continued on his way home.

Once inside, Bernie dumped the mail onto a table, adding it to a pile of papers and magazines already spilling over to the floor.

Senderowitz passed through the front room, walked back to the kitchen, drank a few tall glasses of water, stumbled down the hallway to his bedroom, kicked off his shoes and fell into his bed.

He was out cold in no time.

Samson arrived at the hospital at two-thirty.

Alicia had stayed at home, not wanting to wake the girls in the middle of the night. Not wanting to frighten them.

Samson was told Jimmy was listed as critical, but his vital signs were beginning to stabilize and he would survive the gunshot wounds.

The extent of permanent damage to Jimmy's right ankle and left shoulder would not be determined for weeks, if not months.

The boy remained unconscious in ICU.

After talking with the doctor and looking in on Jimmy for a moment, Samson hurried off to find Detective Fulton.

Ripley felt a tugging on his arm and opened his eyes.

It was near three in the morning.

"What is it, son?"

"I hear noises."

"In your room?"

"Yes."

Ripley sat up, turned on the table lamp and lifted the five-year-old up onto the bed.

"What kind of noises, Mickey?"

"Like scratchy noises."

"What do you think it is, son?"

"Like an animal or something. It's scary."

"Would you like me to come take a look?"

"Can I just stay here with you?"

"Who will look after Kyle?"

"What?"

"He's your brother. Even though he is bigger, you need to watch out for each other. Do you really want to leave Kyle there all alone?"

"I better not."

"I'll be right here if you need me, son. I'll never leave you."

"Can you walk me back to our room?"

"Of course I can."

Samson found Jesse Fulton sitting in the visitor's lounge.

Fulton rose to offer his friend a handshake and the two men took seats facing each other.

"How is Jimmy?"

"He'll live. They can't say anything yet about permanent disability," Samson said. "What happened, Jesse?"

"We received an emergency call just before ten last night. A man in the neighboring house heard gunshots. Uniformed officers responded and found a young woman, DOA. Jimmy was discovered beside her, bleeding badly. He was rushed to the ER before I got to the scene. They found no ID. No one knew who he was until I arrived here."

"Were they found inside the house?"

"They were found in bed together, Sam."

"Who was the woman?" Samson asked, once it sunk in.

"I'm sorry, Sam. I can't reveal her name before her family has been properly notified."

"I understand," Samson said. "Can you tell me anything *about* the woman?"

"I can tell you she was an English teacher at Bayside High School. Twenty-six years old, Caucasian, married, no children."

"Jimmy's school," Samson said.

"Yes."

"Do you have a suspect?"

"The neighbor saw the woman's husband run from the house

166

after the gunshots and drive off. We assume he surprised his wife in bed with your son and shot them both. We put out a statewide APB."

"I need to call my wife," Samson said.

"If there is anything I can do, Sam."

"Thank you, Jesse. I'll let you know."

Samson walked off and called Alicia. He told her all he knew. She said she would drop the girls off with her parents and be at the hospital by eight.

Samson walked back to ICU and stood silently at the bedside looking at his damaged son.

He recalled what his wife said the previous afternoon at the park, when they talked about the safety of the children.

There are never guarantees.

Samson turned when he heard someone approach and stop at his side.

"Alicia phoned me," Murphy said.

Sandra Rosen sat up in her bed, reacting to the noise.

Not fully awake, she glanced toward the sound and thought she saw a silhouette framed in her bedroom window.

A shadow that quickly disappeared.

Her bedside alarm clock told her it was past three in the morning.

Rosen left the bed, went to the window, parted the sheer curtains and looked out to the back yard.

Nothing. No one.

She wondered if the events of the past week or so were messing with her mind, stimulating her imagination in less than pleasant ways. She thought the dangers and deaths she confronted on the job were putting scary visions in her head, making her hear bumps in the night that weren't there.

Rosen returned to her bed and tried to shake off the uneasy feeling, but she couldn't.

Because she knew she *had* heard a sound and *had* seen something outside her window. And it *did* scare her.

. . .

Samson and Murphy sat in the visitor's lounge, drinking coffee in paper cups from a vending machine.

"I would have been here sooner, Sam, but when Alicia reached me I was helping Augie close his place. How are you holding up?"

"I'm managing," Samson said. "How is Augie?"

"It helps that he's back to work and keeping busy at the bar. His sister Rosie is having a rough time," Murphy said. "Her daughters had to leave after the funeral to return to work and school. And John Cicero is not being much help to his wife. Rosie told Augie her husband is always very angry. I can understand. Cicero is totally convinced there is someone behind his son's death who got away clean and he can't do a thing about it. He can't even talk about it."

"I'm sure it's very painful," Samson said. "Even with what happened to Jimmy, I can't imagine what Cicero is going through."

"What did happen to Jimmy?"

Shortly before four Tuesday morning a brick shattered the bay window at the Donner residence on West 2nd Street, landing in the living room.

The crash woke the entire family, Peter and his father jumped from their beds and ran out to the front room of the house. Peter's mother followed.

"Go back to bed, Sybil," Paul Donner said to his wife, "Peter and I will clean up the mess."

"I can clean up."

"Please, go back to bed," her husband insisted.

After his mother left the room, Peter's father asked the boy to sit.

"Tell me what happened that night, son."

"I never hurt the girl. I swear. After she got out of the car I drove away. Then I felt bad about leaving her all alone and I went back for her. She wasn't there, I couldn't find her."

"Why did you feel bad about leaving her where she asked you to, Peter? You said she asked you to take her to West Thirteenth Street. Didn't you take her there?"

"We had a disagreement. We were on Shell Road. She was upset and bolted out of the car."

"Shell Road, Peter, near the ballpark where she was found?"

"It's not the way it sounds," Peter said.

"Then tell me the way it *was*, and don't leave out a single detail."

Alicia found her husband and Murphy just after four in the morning.

"I couldn't wait. I woke up my mother. She drove over to the house to look after the girls, they're still asleep. I want to see Jimmy."

"I'll take you to him," Samson said as he turned to Murphy. "Thanks for coming down, Tommy. You should go and get some rest."

"Thank you, Tommy," Alicia said, giving Murphy a hug.

"Let me know if you need anything," Murphy said. "Anything."

When Murphy left, Samson took his wife's hand and led her to ICU.

"Will Jimmy be all right," Alicia asked as they walked the hall.

"Jimmy will be all right," Samson said, "but he may never be the same."

SIXTEEN

Landis and Mendez sat together in Rey's car parked opposite the Planned Parenthood Clinic on Court Street in downtown Brooklyn at nine.

Mendez looked as if he was about to crawl out of his skin.

Landis was reluctant to say a word.

"You promised me you would control your temper, Rey," Landis finally said.

"I'm not angry with Salina. I blame myself."

Landis looked toward the building.

"There she is, Rey."

Salina Mendez stood at the entrance, waiting for Landis to appear.

She saw her husband approach instead.

"Oh my God, Rey."

"Salina, we don't need to do this."

Mendez took his wife into his arms.

"I didn't know *what* to do. I'm so sorry, Rey," she said.

"No. I'm sorry. I'm sorry I made you feel you could not come to me with this. We will welcome this child, Salina. We will make it work. And I promise I'll be more help."

"You'll have to be, Rey."

"Count on it. Let's pick up the children and tell everyone the good news."

"Are you very sure, Rey?"

"Absolutely. I love you, Salina. This pregnancy is a blessing. Trust me," Mendez said. "I'll call the precinct and request the day off to celebrate."

"Did Stan come with you?"

"Yes. We can drop him off before we go for the kids," Rey

said. "Don't be mad at Landis, Salina, he did what he thought was right."

"I want to thank him," Salina said as they walked to the car.

Lorraine DiMarco and Pavel Vasin sat facing each other in the attorney's office on Tuesday morning.

Vicki Anderson brought coffee and quickly disappeared.

"As you know, Alex Holden was charged with second degree murder," Lorraine began, "we pleaded not guilty at the arraignment. Alex is presently out on bail. He put up his business, a bakery in Crown Heights, as collateral. A preliminary hearing has been scheduled, two weeks from tomorrow. This hearing will determine if we can avoid a trial, by having the charge dropped or by proposing a plea bargain."

"How may I help?"

"There are two witnesses who claim Holden produced the murder weapon and attacked the victim unprovoked. Alex told me they were lying and I believe him. The victim's father, Vladimir Markov, is a very powerful and intimidating man. His influence is far reaching. We suspect Markov coerced the witnesses into giving false testimony."

"Coerced?"

"Threats or hush money, or both," Lorraine said.

"And if the witnesses were somehow persuaded to reconsider their account of the incident?"

"I believe we would be looking at self-defense, involuntary manslaughter with a suspended sentence."

"I will see what I can do," Vasin said.

"Thank you."

"Lorraine."

"Yes?"

"Let me give you a warning, which I will share with my niece, Marina. Whether or not his son was the aggressor, Vladimir Markov will hold Alex responsible for his son's death. As well as anyone who tries to protect Alex. It is the Russian way, when a father loses a child, to settle the score."

"That particular sentiment is not exclusive to the Russians," Lorraine said.

Murphy and Rosen had arranged to meet for breakfast at the New Times before going in to the precinct.

They were both suffering from lack of sleep.

"Listen to this," Murphy said. "Jimmy Samson was found in bed with a twenty-six-year-old school teacher."

"Sam told me."

"When?"

"Early this morning. I went to the hospital to see how they were doing."

"Why did Samson ask me to keep it quiet and then turn around and tell you?"

"Maybe he was afraid you might accidently talk out of school."

"Are you saying I'm a blabbermouth? I wasn't planning to tell anyone else. And I wasn't trying to raise your eyebrows."

"Please don't be angry, Tommy, I'm not criticizing you. I'm flattered you chose me as a confidant. But it *is* a story that begs to be gossip. If it slips out before Samson and Alicia are prepared to address it, it could cause the family unnecessary grief. I know you will keep it under your hat, and so does Sam. And I'm really sorry if I was out of line."

"No, you're right," Murphy said. "I need to be more careful about talking before thinking."

"Sam was only asking you to keep your hat on for a while."

"I can do that. Did you hear Salina Mendez is pregnant again?"

"You're impossible."

"And you look tired."

"I had trouble sleeping last night."

"Do you want to tell me why? Or are you afraid it will wind up on the front page of the *Post*?" Murphy said, and then quickly added, "I'm kidding, Sandra, what kept you awake?"

"Lately I've had this unpleasant feeling someone is watching me."

Lafayette High School teachers, administrators, staff and volunteers reported for orientation late Tuesday morning.

A half-day designated for meeting new colleagues, visiting assigned class rooms and discussing curriculum for the new school year.

William Pabst had asked for a private meeting with David Rose at eleven in Pabst's office.

The principal wanted a few words with the new school psychologist.

"First, I wanted to personally welcome you to Lafayette High School and tell you how fortunate we feel having you aboard," Pabst began, "especially in light of the tragedy a week ago Sunday. There will be many questions. There will be anxiety and confusion. We are certain you will be of great help."

"Thank you for your show of confidence."

"Jenny Greco was a very popular student. She had many friends, she made friends easily. Until classes resume on Friday, we don't know how her death will affect friends and classmates or the student population in general. We will be monitoring the situation very closely. At the moment, we are most concerned about the young women who were with Jenny last. They all came very close to unsuspected danger."

"I understand your concern," Rose said.

"We have asked the other members of the cheerleading squad to come in for a special assembly at five. We would like you to meet them, talk with them and answer questions. Help them get through this shocking event in a positive and healthy manner. Can you do this for us, David?"

"I will do my best."

Paul Donner met with his son's lawyer early Tuesday afternoon.

"From what I have heard, the search for Jenny Greco's killer is ongoing," the attorney said. "This tells me the District Attorney doesn't truly believe Peter committed the crime or doesn't believe there is enough real evidence to make a case."

"Then why haven't they dropped the charge?" Donner asked.

"For the time being they need a suspect, to alleviate pressure from the media, the public and the Mayor. Peter fits the bill. He was the last known person to see the girl, he has no alibi for the time of her death, and there's a general feeling he lied to the police."

"Peter *did* lie to the police."

"Lied about what?"

"About what happened with the Greco girl that night."

"What did happen?"

"Peter is a teenager. Boys his age have trouble controlling their libidos. He and the girl parked and shared a few beers. Peter got a little fresh. The girl was not interested. She became upset and left his car. He drove off. He went back to apologize and to take her home, but she was gone."

"Where was this?"

"On Shell Road, close to where they found her."

"Why did he lie?"

"Peter was afraid his aggressive behavior would blemish his reputation at the new school, and jeopardize his high school football career."

"And now he is a murder suspect."

"But if he's cleared, if the killer is found, he may be able to regain his status. Could we wait awhile to see how the police investigation develops?"

"I wouldn't recommend it. Withholding the facts is an obstruction of justice. It could make a bad situation worse. Your son should talk with the police and tell the truth."

It was a perfect early September day in Brooklyn.
Temperature in the mid-seventies, sunny and dry.

Ivanov and Richards sat in a car up the street from the Donner home.

"Remind me why we are stuck here inside this vehicle on a remarkably beautiful afternoon," Richards said.

"I can sum it up in three words. It's our job. Some nut hurled a brick through their front window. Someone could have been badly injured."

"As I recall, it's Rosen and Murphy's case."

"And that is why Rosen and Murphy are out trying to find anyone who may have seen Jenny Greco, Peter Donner or both after they left the football field. And in the Six-one, every case is *everyone's* case." Marina stopped and took a deep breath before going on. "Look, Richards, I didn't mean to snap at you, but there are places I would rather be also. Complaining won't make it any easier to be here. If we are going to talk, let's talk about something else."

"Bad news about Samson's son," Richards said to change the subject.

"Yes, it is."

"Have you heard anything about the circumstances?"

"No, I haven't. It's personal. We'll know more if and when the captain wants us to know. Damn it. I'm barking at you again. I'm sorry."

"Are you having trouble working with me, Marina?"

"No, I'm not, Marty. I have a lot on my mind, I'm a little edgy. I do like working with you, in fact I was going to ask a favor."

"A favor?"

"When the relief team arrives at five to cut us loose," Ivanov said.

"Yes?"

"I was hoping you would take a ride with me over to Brighton Beach."

Murphy and Rosen had been at it since breakfast.

They went up and down West 13th Street for the third time in less than a week. They worked off a long list, visiting homes where no one had come to the door on their two previous attempts. Not one person had witnessed a young girl being dropped off the night Jenny Greco went missing.

"We're wasting our time. Donner never brought her here that night."

"You think he's lying?" Rosen said.

"I'm sure of it."

"Do you think he's guilty?"

"He's guilty of something."

They cruised Shell Road with lower expectations. Most of the businesses would have been closed that Sunday. Those that did open were shut down by mid-afternoon. If you were not searching for a used carburetor, or attending a Little League baseball game, you had no business on that stretch of Shell Road. Particularly after dark. There was no pedestrian traffic and there were no train stations between Avenues U and X.

No one ventured out to Shell Road without a car.

"As morbid as it sounds," Murphy said, "this is a perfect place to dump a body."

The detectives pushed on, interviewing the football coaches and players again, asking this time around if anyone had seen someone strange or out of place hanging around in or near the practice field.

Nothing.

They finally decided to revisit some of the girls who had been with Jenny before she left practice that night.

Rosen suggested they speak with Patty Bolin first. They caught her just as she was leaving home for a meeting at the high school.

Patty had nothing to add to what she told them in the earlier interview.

"So, you saw no one during rehearsal who looked suspicious?" Murphy asked, repeating himself.

"I already told you, no," Patty said, "and I have a few questions too."

Murphy turned to Rosen. Rosen nodded a go-ahead.

"What questions?" Murphy asked reluctantly.

"The first time we talked, why didn't you tell me Jenny had been killed?"

"We weren't sure it was Jenny at the time," Murphy lied. "We had to wait for her parents to identify her."

"And why are you asking about suspicious looking people now? Are you thinking Peter Donner didn't kill Jenny?"

"We are not at liberty to tell you what we think," Murphy said.

"What do *you* think, Patty?" Rosen asked.

"I was supposed to take her home that night," Patty Bolin said. "I can't stop thinking it was my fault she never got there."

"You shouldn't think that way," Murphy said.

"That's easy for you to say."

"Not that easy," Murphy said. "Thank you for your time. Take care of yourself."

The detectives turned to leave.

"Hey?"

"Yes?" Rosen asked.

"I'm running late, could you give me a lift to the school?"

"Sure," Rosen said.

Ripley drove over to his sister's house to fetch Kyle and Mickey after a relatively quiet day at the precinct.

"I'm still planning to ask Justine Turner over for dinner, and I would still like you to join us," Connie said.

"Are you going to torture me until I say yes?"

"Definitely."

"Okay. When?"

"Friday night?"

"Fine. I'll bring wine."

"Don't forget to bring the boys," Connie said.

"I'll try not to."

. . .

He was sitting in his car, watching the front entrance of the school.

When he saw Patty Bolin exit, he stepped out of the vehicle.

"Miss Bolin?" he said, when she reached the sidewalk.

"God. You scared me," she said.

"I'm sorry. I didn't mean to. Why are you still here?"

"I was feeling anxious after the group counseling session," Patty said. "I went to the gym to work out, work off the tension. Why are you still here?"

"I stayed to take care of paperwork. I was about to get into the car when I noticed you coming out."

"What time is it?" Patty asked.

"A little after eight."

"Shit. I totally lost track of time. And I forgot my cell phone. My mom will be really worried. Sorry about the language."

"I've heard it before. Would you like to use my phone? Let your folks know you are on the way?"

"At this point it would be better if I just showed up. After what happened last week, I think a call from an unknown number might scare my mom more."

"Well, in that case, I'm leaving now. Can I give you a ride home?"

"I don't want to take you of your way."

"It's really no problem."

Patty looked around. There was no one else on the street.

"Are you sure?" she asked.

"I'm sure. Let's get you home before your mother becomes too alarmed."

"Okay, thanks," Patty said.

SEVENTEEN

Murphy's cell phone jolted him awake. He quickly grabbed it off the side table and fumbled to kill the annoying sound.

"What time is it?"

"It's Landis."

"What time is it?"

"Almost four."

"Not good. What happened?"

"A dead girl. Kings Highway subway station at the Highlawn Avenue end of the platform, west side of the tracks. That's all I can say. I have to get off the phone."

"We're on our way," Murphy said.

"What time is it?" Rosen asked, sitting up in the bed.

"Time to suit up."

The MTA had stopped service on the N Line as soon as the call came in.

The body hung from the top of a retaining wall that separated the train station from the houses on West 8th Street.

Officers Landis and Mendez were above, in the back yard of a house near Highlawn Avenue. They held the rope at one end and slowly lowered the girl to the ground, trying their best to keep the body from banging against the concrete wall.

CSU had spread a large black tarp across the train tracks.

Before the girl's feet touched the ground, Michaels took her by the legs and Fielder held her under her arms. They gently placed her on her back, in the center of the tarp.

"Same knot," Fielder said, looking at the noose around the young girl's neck.

Rey Mendez met Murphy and Rosen when they arrived at the

179

Highlawn Avenue entrance to the subway station. The two detectives followed Mendez around to West 8th. He led them to the back yard where Landis stood at the wall looking down. Landis pointed out the six-inch piece of white clothesline tied to the metal rail running along the top of the wall.

"We were asked to leave this end tied on, we cut it here and had to add our own rope to get the body down to the tracks," Landis said.

Murphy moved to the back of the house, the officers followed.

"Have you spoken with the residents?" Murphy asked.

"There was no answer, we pounded on their door. I doubt they could have slept through the racket."

"Neighbors?"

"Four uniforms have been waking people up. Nothing yet."

"The girl is found hanging off the wall on the end of a rope and no one sees or hears a thing? Who called it in?"

"A transit worker, he was walking the tracks picking up debris," Landis said. "The victim wasn't visible from the platform or the street."

"Has CSU been up here?"

"They've been busy down there," Landis said.

"No one comes back here until they do."

Rosen had been quietly looking down at the activity below.

Murphy, Mendez and Landis joined her at the wall. They looked down to the tracks. Dr. Wayne was on the tarp, down on his knees working, blocking a clear view of the body.

"Do we have an ID?" Murphy asked the two uniformed officers.

"Tommy," Rosen said, as the medical examiner stood up and stepped away from the girl.

"What?"

"It's Patty Bolin."

When Murphy and Rosen got down to the tracks they saw Chief Trenton talking to the medical examiner. Two EMTs were moving the girl's body onto a stretcher.

Trenton motioned for the two detectives to follow him to the east side of the station platform.

"We believe the girl was murdered. She was hung with the same rope using the same noose as the girl found at the baseball field last Sunday. We never released the information about the rope to the press in the Greco case. If we do now it will cause the sort of media frenzy and public unrest that can seriously impede our investigation."

"What are you suggesting?" Rosen asked.

"For the time being, we report this incident as an apparent suicide."

"You're asking us to tell the girl's parents she killed herself when we are thinking otherwise?" Rosen said.

"Yes."

"Excuse me for saying it, sir, but this sucks."

"I agree, Detective Rosen. But I feel it needs to be done." Trenton said. "And I am afraid I have to insist."

They were heading to the Bolin residence to notify the girl's parents.

Rosen had not said a word since speaking with Trenton.

"What is it?" Murphy asked.

"What is it? Patty was alive twelve hours ago. She was sitting in the back seat of this car."

"Your point being?"

"I don't have a point," Rosen said. "There is no fucking point."

After breaking the news to Patty Bolin's parents, having to uncomfortably witness yet another inconsolable mother and stunned, helpless father, Murphy and Rosen elicited enough information to point them in the direction of William Pabst.

"Messengers of death."

"What?" Rosen asked.

"Nothing," Murphy said, as they pulled up to the home of the Lafayette High School principal.

William Pabst answered the doorbell in a bathrobe over a white T-shirt and cotton pajama bottoms. And a pair of moccasin styled house slippers.

Murphy and Rosen identified themselves.

"It's early," Pabst said. "Something has happened."

"May we come in?" Rosen asked.

"Of course."

"We need to ask some questions and would prefer you don't question *us* for the time being," Rosen said, once they had settled into chairs in the living room.

"Go ahead."

"There was a meeting at the high school last evening at five. Can you tell us who attended," Murphy said.

"There were the nine girls, all the members of the Patriots' cheerleading squad."

"We will need their names, their addresses and phone numbers," Rosen said.

"I can supply all of that information when I get to the school."

"Good," Murphy said. "When did the meeting end?"

"Shortly after six."

"Who else was there at the meeting?"

"Our Assistant Principal, Walter Kelty. The girl's gymnastics instructor, Marsha Calhoun. Our dance instructor, Emily Bledsoe, who choreographs the cheerleading routines. David Rose, the school psychologist. And myself."

"When did you leave the school?"

"Immediately after the meeting."

"And the other adults?"

"Calhoun and Rose walked out of the school with me. I watched David drive off in his car and I walked Marsha to her vehicle before I continued on to my own. Emily teaches an adult education dance class on Tuesday nights that starts at eight. She brought her dinner and planned to wait at the school until the class began. Walter said he had work to do in his office, he's been putting a memorial assembly together for Jenny Greco."

"And the girls?" Rosen asked.

"Emily asked the girls if they would remain for a while, to talk about how best to go forward with their work in the cheer-leading squad in light of Jennifer Greco's death. Emily asked for fifteen or twenty minutes of their time. I believe all of the girls agreed to stay."

"When will you be arriving at the school today?" Murphy asked.

"I plan to be there by nine."

"And the others?"

"They should all be in by ten. Except the students, who will not begin classes until Friday. However, as I said, I can give you all of the information you need to contact the girls."

"We would like to meet you at the high school, pick up that information and talk with Calhoun, Bledsoe, Rose and Kelty," Murphy said, looking at his notes. "Would nine-thirty be alright?"

"Nine-thirty would be fine. Can you tell me now what this is about?"

"Not quite yet," Murphy said.

"What do you think?" Rosen asked when they were back in the car.

"I think we need to talk to everyone who was at that little get-together last evening, starting with the staff at ten. We find out who saw the girl last and go from there."

"And meanwhile?

"What time is it?"

"Just past seven."

"I think it's time for coffee and something to eat."

"We need to find out where Peter Donner was last night."

"It shouldn't be difficult," Murphy said. "Donner's house has been under surveillance since the brick went through his window. We can call Kelly at the precinct. He should have an answer before our breakfast order is up."

"And after breakfast?"

"We get back to my place. Now that I'm finally awake I realize we ran out so fast Ralph never had his morning constitutional. And he is pissed off at me already for dragging him away from my mother's cuisine."

"Shouldn't we take care of Ralph before we eat?"

"He can hold out a little longer," Murphy said, "and I'll pick up a takeout order of bacon as a peace offering."

"And then?"

"And then it should be just about time for Sandy and Tommy to go back to high school."

Just before nine-thirty, Rosen and Murphy arrived at the school.

Murphy's phone rang as they passed through the front door.

"Gangster Squad, Murphy speaking."

"I thought you might be interested in knowing where Peter Donner was between six and seven last night," Ripley said.

"As a matter of fact we were about to call for that very information."

"He was here at the precinct. He walked in with his father and lawyer and he changed his statement about what happened with Jenny Greco that Sunday night."

"Oh?"

"They parked on Shell Road, he put the moves on, she dashed from the car and he never saw her again. He thinks she cut her arm on the way out."

"He feared he wouldn't be as popular if he was exposed as a creep, so he lied," Murphy said.

"That about sums it up. I spoke to the boy's father this morning. After arriving home from the precinct, Peter stayed in all night. The stake-out team confirmed it."

"It doesn't help us much. I never made the Donner kid for a killer, just a shitty liar."

"Looks like you'll need to find another suspect."

"We're working on it. Has Samson checked in?"

"He called Senderowitz, said he would be at the hospital if needed."

"Do me a favor."

"What do you need?"

"Find out if there's a record of anyone who died by hanging in the past year who wasn't a suicide. Check the tri-state area."

"Got it, I'll let you know."

"Thanks," Murphy said, ending the call.

"What was that?" Rosen asked.

"Peter Donner copped to not understanding that *no means no.*"

The principal handed a list to Rosen. The names, addresses and phone numbers of nine girls. Including Patty Bolin.

"Should I summon David, Walt, Marsha and Emily," Pabst asked.

"We would prefer speaking with them individually," Murphy said. "Could you direct us to where we might find each of them?"

Pabst jotted down names and room numbers. They thanked him and left the office.

"They'll want to know what it's about," Rosen said when they were out in the hall.

"Then we tell them what we told Pabst earlier."

"Something like, *We understand your curiosity, but we'll be asking the questions.*"

"Or, *it's none of your business but thanks for asking,*" Murphy said. "As long as they get the message."

"Where do we start?"

"Pabst said he left the building with Rose and Calhoun. Let's begin with them and see if their recollections jibe."

"Rose or Calhoun?" Rosen asked. "Eeny meeny miny mo?"

"Let's start with Calhoun," Murphy suggested. "Gym was always my best subject in school."

. . .

Marsha Calhoun's account matched Pabst's story like they were reading from the same page.

They had both watched David Rose drive away from the school before Pabst accompanied Calhoun to her car.

"And you left?" Murphy asked.

"Yes. I drove straight home, my husband and children were waiting on me to start dinner."

"Did you see Mr. Pabst enter his vehicle?"

"Yes, he was parked a few spaces in front of me. When I passed he was getting into his car. When I was waiting on the traffic light at Stillwell Avenue and Avenue V, he was stopped right behind me."

"And did you see anyone from that meeting, other than Mr. Pabst and Mr. Rose, after you left the school last night?" Rosen asked.

"No. Can you tell me what this is about?"

"Nothing to worry your head about," Murphy said. "Thank you for your time."

"*Nothing to worry your head about?*" Rosen said when they left the gym.

"Give me a break, it was the first thing that popped into my mind and I caught myself."

"Caught yourself?"

"I nearly said *pretty little head.*"

"Let me question Rose," Sandra said. "Psychology was always *my* best subject in school."

EIGHTEEN

They found David Rose in his office. He told the same tale. He walked out of the school with Pabst and Calhoun just after six and drove off before they did.

"Drove home?" Murphy asked.

"Yes."

"How are the girls responding to Jennifer Greco's death?" Rosen asked.

"Generally?"

"Okay."

"Generally speaking, in cases such as the unexpected death of a friend or fellow student, we often witness sorrow due to feelings of loss, sympathy for the family and thoughts about mortality."

"What about fear?" Rosen asked. "Fear of harm, fear of death?"

"Not really. These are young adults. Sadly, they have been exposed to violence. It is pervasive in our culture. Books. Movies," Rose said. "Some of the girls may have experienced violence personally. I'm reluctant to suggest they are jaded, but teens today are not easily shocked. They're not as afraid of death as they are fascinated by it. Events like Jenny Greco's death are far more frightening to the parents of these girls than they are to the girls themselves."

"Fascinated?" Murphy said.

"Death is a profound mystery to the living, Detective."

"I don't think about it much," Murphy said. "The mystery that intrigues me is who killed Jenny Greco and why."

"So," Rosen said, "you don't see Jenny Greco's death as potentially traumatic?"

"Again, certainly for Jennifer's parents and family," Rose

said, "but not necessarily for the girls. It is not as if they witnessed a gunman killing others in front of their eyes, survived the ordeal of meeting death face-to-face. It is disturbing, without doubt, but not as shocking. It may inspire them to be more careful, but it won't make them afraid to leave their homes."

"Even if they fear there is a killer of young girls out there?" Rosen asked.

"Is there reason to believe that's the case?"

"No. Not at all. It's a hypothetical question."

"If that *were* the case, it could be a different story."

"Did any of the girls you met with last night appear to be particularly affected by Jenny's death?" Rosen asked.

"Patricia Bolin, perhaps."

"How so?"

"Apparently, she was supposed to drive Jennifer home that night and failed to do so. I sensed remorse. She may be feeling somewhat responsible, feeling it was somehow her fault. I will plan to meet with her privately to help her put aside any misguided feelings of guilt."

"Thank you," Rosen said.

"Any time."

"Did that help us at all?" Murphy asked when the two detectives left the school psychologist's office.

"Not very much, but I found it provocative. And it stimulated unpleasant thoughts."

"I find the *Sports Illustrated* swimsuit issue provocative. I nearly dozed off in there. Let's find out what kept Walter Kelty after school last night."

"Detectives?"

Murphy and Rosen turned to find William Pabst standing beside them.

"Yes?" Rosen said.

"Can I have a word with you in my office?"

"Of course."

"A summons to the principal's office," Murphy whispered to Rosen as they followed Pabst. "Now that stimulates all sorts of unpleasant thoughts."

. . .

"I just received word that Patty Bolin committed suicide last night," Pabst said when they were behind closed doors.

"Terrific," Murphy said.

"Excuse me?"

"Can you tell us how you heard?" Rosen asked.

"Your Chief of Detectives called me, he asked me to please cooperate with you and keep the news quiet for a while."

"Then you understand why we couldn't say anything earlier."

"Why are you questioning my staff?"

"We are simply trying to establish when Patty was seen last and if she seemed alright. Clumsily avoiding the subject of her death," Rosen said.

"I wasn't told how she killed herself. When will it be made public?"

"That's entirely up to Chief Trenton," Murphy said, "unless it leaks to the press before he can make a statement. We are trying to wrap up our interviews as quickly as possible. We were about to visit Walter Kelty."

"Go ahead, I will keep this to myself," Pabst said. "I only ask you keep me informed. I am responsible for every student in this school."

"We understand," Rosen said.

The detectives headed out to talk with the Assistant Principal.

"Can you tell us when you left the school last night?" Murphy asked.

"Can I ask why you want to know?"

"We would prefer you didn't," Rosen said.

"The girls and I left shortly before eight."

"The girls?"

"Classes begin Friday. It will be the first time the entire student body will be present since the death of Jenny Greco. We are planning a memorial assembly at four Friday afternoon. Two of Jenny's friends have been helping me organize the program.

We met in my office last evening to work out details."

Murphy was about to ask if one of those girls was Patty Bolin when a look from Rosen stopped him cold.

"Who were the two girls?" Rosen asked.

"Susan Fleming and Andrea Fazio."

"They're not on the cheerleader squad," Rosen said, looking at her list.

"No. They are not."

"And when did you last see any of the girls from the squad?"

"There was a meeting, which I am sure you have heard about. I left the meeting just after six. The girls stayed behind with Emily Bledsoe. I did not see any of them afterwards. Has something happened to one of those girls?" Kelty asked. "Or is it none of my business?"

"Thank you for your time, sir," Murphy said, answering Kelty's question.

"He wasn't too happy with us," Rosen said, when they left the office.

"None of them were. We're treating them like children, keeping them in the dark. The way my mother did when I was a kid."

"Oh?"

"She would tell me we were going out for ice cream and the next thing I knew I was sitting in a dentist's chair."

"I bet you got the ice cream afterwards."

"In fact I did. So?"

"So, let's see the dance teacher and get it over with. Then I'll treat you to a double-scoop."

"The meeting was here in my home room last evening," Bledsoe told the detectives. "The girls remained with me. They all left shortly before six-thirty."

"And that was the last time you saw any of the girls?" Murphy asked.

"All except Patty Bolin."

"Tell us about seeing Patty Bolin," Rosen said.

"I had my dinner here in the room and caught up on some reading. At seven-forty-five, I walked to the gym to set-up for my dance class. Patty was there, working out. We talked for a while."

"About?"

"She said she was thinking about leaving the cheerleader squad. I asked her to give it more thought before making a decision. When my dance students had all arrived, I asked them to begin their warm-ups and escorted Patty to the front exit. I watched her leave the building a few minutes past eight."

"And after that?"

"I instructed the class in the gym. The session ended at ten and I went directly home," Bledsoe said. "Why are you asking about Patty and the other girls, and about who did what and when last night? I assume you're looking into Jenny Greco's death. What does last night have to do with Jenny? Has something happened to one of the other girls? Is it Patty?"

"Miss Bledsoe, you need to promise you will not repeat this to anyone for the time being," Murphy said. "Patty Bolin committed suicide last night."

Emily Bledsoe sat at her desk. She placed her hands over her face and she wept.

"We have to go," Rosen said. "Please, you must keep this quiet."

Bledsoe remained seated, perfectly silent.

"We couldn't lie to her," Murphy said when they left the room.

"We did lie to her, Tommy."

Murphy called Samson's cell.

"Where are you?"

"At the high school, but it's a dead end. Do you want to hear about it?"

"I'm back at the precinct," Samson said. "Come in and we'll talk."

"How is Jimmy?" Murphy asked.

"Come in and we'll talk."

"Do you mind driving?" Murphy asked. "I'll phone our guys at the scene."

"I'd love to drive," Rosen said. "Where am I driving to?"

Once in the car and rolling, Murphy called Landis.

"Get anything?" he asked.

"The residents of the house are out of town, they have been away since Friday. We got that from the neighbors to the south, who were out until after ten last night. The man in the house to the north is a widower. He's at least eighty years old and had trouble hearing me from a foot away. No witnesses, just a lot of people not very happy about a wake-up call at four in the morning."

"CSU?"

"Nothing. But I spoke to the M.E. a few minutes ago."

"And?"

"Wayne places the time of death between seven and midnight. The fall snapped the girl's neck, she would have died instantly. He discovered traces of chloral hydrate in her blood, probably administered by injection."

"So, she was unconscious when she was dropped and she didn't suffer dangling on the end of the rope."

"That's what Batman said. We're still going door-to-door and will stay at it until people start arriving home from work."

"Keep me posted," Murphy said, as they pulled up to the Six-one.

Rosen and Murphy found Samson, Ripley and Senderowitz gathered around Bernie's desk.

"Grab a chair," Samson said.

Murphy filled them in on the visit to the high school.

"So, the last person to see the girl has her leaving the building at eight," Ripley said, "and the neighbors on West Eighth Street arrived home soon after ten. That's only two hours."

"Only two hours?" Rosen said.

"Two hours to abduct the girl, knock her out, get her to the scene, carry her to the back of the house, tie her to the rope, drop her and get out."

"He must have chosen that train station beforehand," Senderowitz said.

"He may even have chosen the yard, known somehow the residents were away," Ripley suggested, "mail in the box, newspapers on the lawn."

"He did his homework," Murphy said.

"I believe so, which means someone may have seen him scouting around the street before last night," Ripley said.

"What is his motivation?" Rosen asked the former FBI agent.

"When we suspect one killer is responsible for two murders at different points in time, the first thing we look for is a connection between the victims. These victims had *too much* in common," Ripley said. "They were both female, both teenagers, and both from the same school."

"And both cheerleaders," Murphy added.

"Very specific. And there is the method, the hangman's noose," Ripley said. "I put out the query you requested, Murphy, incidents of hangings that were not considered suicides. Nothing yet, but it's a good call. And I agree we need to be looking at the cheerleader angle also."

"Okay," Samson said, finally jumping in. "We re-canvass the neighbors. Ask about anyone seen on the street in the past few days who didn't belong there."

"I'll get word to Landis and Mendez," Murphy said.

"Did the girl drive to the school?" the captain asked.

"No," Rosen said.

"Then she planned to walk or she got a ride. Speak to anyone who may have seen her outside the school after she left the building. Talk with all the other girls. Maybe she mentioned arranging a lift."

"We'll have to go to their homes, classes don't begin until Friday," Murphy said.

"Then we go to their homes. And we send uniforms along the route she would have walked."

"It's not fun questioning people who keep asking what it's about, and not being able to tell them," Murphy said.

"No one said it was going to be fun, and it is natural curiosity," Samson said. "It would be more surprising if they didn't ask. By five you won't have to play dumb."

"Meaning?" Rosen asked.

"Trenton will be reporting the girl's death before the news at five. He can't hold off any longer."

"Apparent suicide?" Murphy asked.

"Yes."

"So we have to play a *little* dumb," Rosen said.

"One of the things I'm best at," Murphy said.

"Tommy, can I see you in my office in five minutes?"

"Sure, Sam."

After Samson entered his office, Rosen asked about Richards and Ivanov.

"Out on a call," Senderowitz said, "trying to sort out a stabbing incident."

"Drugs?" Rosen asked.

"Pizza. There was a fight about who was first in line at L and B. The winner stabbed the loser four times, with a fork."

"Humans," Murphy said. "How many wars have been waged over religion, political ideology, territory and fast food?"

"Not to mention Helen of Troy," Ripley said.

"I might call Richards, ask him to bring me a sausage and peppers hero," Murphy said.

"Murphy," Rosen said.

"What? Am I being too cynical?"

"Not at all," Rosen said. "I'll take eggplant parmesan."

"Have a seat," Samson said when Murphy came into the office. "You asked about Jimmy."

"Yes."

"I'll make it short. Jimmy is awake and stable. That's the good news. But he's now aware of the extent of his injuries and knows Rebecca Ramirez was killed. It's a lot for a seventeen-year-old boy to deal with. Frankly, it is difficult for *us* to get a handle on. Thankfully we've managed to keep Jimmy's name out of the press for the time being. I've told only you and Sandra about Jimmy's involvement with the school teacher. Alicia and I need some time to figure things out."

"It won't go any further, Sam. How is Alicia doing?"

"She's coping. She's stuck answering questions from Kayla and Lucy about their brother."

"Any word on the teacher's husband?"

"Disappeared."

"If there's anything I can do."

"There's not much *I* can do," Samson said. "Let's change the subject."

"Sure."

"At the school today?"

"Yes?"

"Was anything said that hit a nerve? Was there anyone you talked with who struck you as wrong?"

"Whatever I have to offer would be subjective."

"Noted."

"Walter Kelty seemed very stiff, a stuffed shirt," Murphy said, "David Rose seemed, I don't know how to put it. Detached?"

"Administrators are formal, counselors are clinical. It's the nature of their jobs, and it's not how *you* operate. You tend to be more informal and personal. Maybe you simply didn't like them. Not your type. However, give it some more thought. There might have been something disquieting you just can't put your finger on."

"Talk to Rosen about it. She tends to be more psychological."

. . .

Murphy and Rosen spent the late morning and early afternoon on the telephones or in and out of their car until they eventually spoke to all of the girls who had been at the meeting the previous evening.

Asking who saw who last and when.

Carefully avoiding any mention of Patty Bolin specifically.

Skillfully deflecting questions thrown back at them.

Learning nothing new.

They drove to the scene.

The subway station had been reopened and the trains were running on schedule.

"Everything back to normal," Murphy said.

"Not for everyone," Rosen said.

Landis and Mendez brought them up to date.

No one had seen Patty Bolin outside the school, getting into a vehicle or otherwise. No one had seen a girl along the route she would have taken to her home, alone or otherwise.

"We did get something," Mendez said.

"What's that?"

"A neighbor saw a man walking up from the Kings Highway end of West Eighth very early Tuesday morning. He was placing flyers into the mailboxes, or stuffing them behind door handles. When he reached Highlawn Avenue, he turned the corner toward West Seventh and was gone."

"Description?" Murphy said.

"White male. Late-thirties, early-forties. It was all he could make out from across the street," Landis said.

"The witness said junk ads are dropped in the neighborhood all the time, but usually by young kids," Mendez added. "He said this particular type of flyer is usually found stuck under windshield wipers, and he thought it odd the man never hit his side of the street. Here's the flyer."

"EXPERT AUTO REPAIR IN YOUR OWN BACK YARD," Rosen read. "Did you call the phone number?"

"It's the number of a florist in Midwood," Mendez said. "And by the way, the house that backed up to the wall where we found the girl."

"Yes?"

"The mailbox was full, and there was a stack of newspapers at the front door."

"Reconnaissance," Murphy said. "Try getting a better description. This is our fucking guy."

When Murphy and Rosen reached the precinct, they caught Samson on his way out.

"Make it quick," Samson said.

Murphy ran through it.

"He planned it. He found the spot, and he gave himself a time limit. He took a chance not waiting until the middle of the night. Maybe he needed to be somewhere by ten or so. I'll be at the hospital," Samson said. "Would you give me a moment with Sandra, Tommy?"

"Sure," Murphy said, heading into the building.

"What?" Rosen asked.

"I dropped a copy of the Patty Bolin press release on your desk. Share it with Tommy. You probably won't like it, but it's your case. I thought you might want to see it before hearing it on TV, and we all need to be on the same page."

"Thanks for the warning," Rosen said. "Give Alicia my regards."

"Fuck this," Rosen said, after reading the press release.

"What?"

"Take a look," Rosen said, handing the one-page statement to Murphy. "You're a big fan of crime fiction."

"Neatly done," Murphy said, scanning the page.

"A flawless example of spin artistry. *Patricia Bolin, a sixteen-year-old Lafayette High School student, committed suicide last evening. Investigators speculate her action was motivated by the death of Jennifer Greco last week.* Speculate? Patty Bolin was hung by the neck off a wall and they're painting her as a mixed-up kid who couldn't live with the guilt she felt letting her best friend drive off with the high school heartthrob. One more of the thousands of teens who kill themselves each year. No mention of how she did it, and still no mention of the noose around Jenny Greco's throat. Jesus, Murphy, if I didn't know any better, this bullshit propaganda could have fooled me."

"Some facts need to be held back, you know that."

"I know it's what the brass thinks, but what about the families? What good did all of the secrecy do for the Lake Street investigation? There is still someone out there responsible for six deaths, and a pair of mothers who still don't understand why their children were murdered."

"Okay, calm down. They don't want anyone outside the investigation to know the deaths of Greco and Bolin are connected. It would cause a panic."

"There is someone outside the investigation who knows very well the two deaths are connected," Rosen said, "and I hope he's not out there thanking us for keeping his secret."

NINETEEN

"Happy New Year," Senderowitz said, when Murphy and Rosen walked into the squad room at nine on Thursday morning.

"Did I miss Christmas?" Murphy asked.

"It's Jewish New Year," Rosen said, "the first day of Tishrei."

"Well, that explains it," Murphy said.

"Today is Rosh Hashanah," Bernie said, "the first day of the new year. It corresponds to the sixth day of creation in Genesis, the first book of the Torah, in the Old Testament. It is supposedly the day God created Adam and Eve."

"And we all know how that turned out," Ripley said, coming into the room. "Isn't Rosh Hashanah the *Day of Judgment*?"

"On Rosh Hashanah, according to Jewish tradition, God inscribes each person's fate for the coming year into a divine book of judgment. The wicked, the righteous, and those in between. During the Days of Awe, a Jew attempts to amend his or her behavior and to seek forgiveness for wrongs done against God and other human beings. On the tenth day, all fates are sealed," Bernie said. "The evening and day of Yom Kippur are set aside for public and private petitions, confessions of guilt and repentance. At the end of Yom Kippur, one hopes they have been forgiven by God."

"Removed from the shit list," Murphy said.

"So to speak."

"Could God forgive whoever is killing these young girls?" Rosen asked.

"That could depend on whether or not he stops," Bernie said.

"I thought no work was allowed on Rosh Hashanah," Ripley said, "that observers spent the day at Synagogue instead."

"This precinct is my synagogue," Senderowitz said.

He sat alone on a bench in Manhattan Beach Park watching three men playing the card game Durak at a nearby picnic table.

The oldest of the three appeared to be in his late-fifties, close to his own age. The two younger players looked to be in their mid-twenties.

One of the younger men, the last player to have cards remaining in his hand and therefore the loser of the game, shuffled the deck. The *durak,* or *fool,* as the loser of the previous game was called, always dealt the following game.

He rose from the bench and approached the table.

"Izvinite," he said, "please forgive my intrusion."

"What can we do for you?" the oldest of the three players asked.

"I was hoping you would allow me to join the game. It has been quite some time since I have had the pleasure of a good contest."

"Do you still remember how to play, old timer?" one of the younger men asked.

"Please excuse my son, he means no disrespect," the older man said. "I am Mikhail Gagarin. Come, sit with us. You and I will play as partners and show these young *fools* a thing or two about old timers."

"Spasibo, I would enjoy it very much. I am Pavel Vasin."

The two men shook hands and Pavel sat opposite Mikhail at the table.

"Now, Lev."

"Yes, Father."

"I believe it is your turn to deal," Mikhail Gagarin said, giving his guest a sly wink.

After several games, which the older men won handily, Lev Gagarin and Roman Churkin excused themselves and left the park.

"Would you care to continue playing, two-handed?" Mikhail asked when the younger men were gone.

"I would like to offer you a cup of tea," Pavel said, "perhaps lunch. I wish to show my appreciation for your hospitality."

"I never say no to tea," Gagarin said, collecting the deck of cards.

Sarah Sanders and Eileen Kaplan left Temple Beth El of Bensonhurst, following a prayer service which had included a reading of Genesis XXI. The passage told of the birth of Isaac to Abraham and his young wife, believed to have occurred on Rosh Hashanah.

"Thank you for joining me, Sarah," her aunt said.

"I value every opportunity to spend time with you."

"Even in synagogue?"

"Why not in synagogue?"

"I sometimes worry you have lost interest in our history and traditions," Eileen said.

"Is it because I chose to call myself Sanders? I changed my last name, wisely or unwisely, for professional reasons," Sarah said. "It wasn't meant to imply a rejection of my Jewish heritage."

"What do you think about the story of Abraham and Isaac?"

"At the risk of sounding blasphemous, which is truly not my intention, Abraham was not exactly a candidate for father-of-the-year."

"His faith and acceptance of God's will ultimately spared the child."

"Granted. But I've always felt God cut it a little too close."

"Have you reached *your* father?"

"I've tried."

"You called him?"

"I dropped him a note, asking him to contact me."

"When?"

"Three days ago. No response."

"Are you certain he received the note?"

"It would have been hard to miss."

"Give him time, Sarah."

"And if I hear nothing?"

"Make another attempt, don't give up on him."

"I'll think about it, Aunt Eileen."

Ivanov and Richards were called to Coney Island Hospital early Thursday afternoon.

The detectives found Paul Donner in the Emergency Room waiting area.

"What happened?" Richards asked.

"My son was brutally beaten. He's in there with a broken nose, cuts above both eyes, and two fractured ribs."

"Who?"

"Peter was devastated by being banned from playing ball. He went to the school to watch practice and he was assaulted. He wouldn't say who."

"If he won't name names, there's not much we can do," Richards said.

"It's not a question of who, but why. He is being treated as a murderer. What you *can* do is clear his name."

"He tried to take physical advantage of a young female student," Ivanov said. "That alone would create animosity toward your son."

"Are you saying Peter deserved this severe punishment?"

"I am not saying that, and I don't condone it. And again, if he names his attackers we will deal with them firmly. But, let's not forget, he forced that girl from his car and he abandoned her in a dark, unsafe place," Ivanov said. "Your son could be feeling somewhat responsible. He may have turned up at practice today *looking* for punishment."

"How do we check alibis without suggesting Patty Bolin's death was more than a routine adolescent suicide?" Murphy asked.

"I never said teen suicides were routine, I said they were prevalent. What really upsets me is, in this particular case, it's a fabrication," Rosen said. "How can we expect to find the truth by telling lies? And what might we risk by not warning the public there is someone really scary and dangerous out there?"

"I'm sorry, Sandra, I used a poor choice of words. I do understand your argument. At the same time I can appreciate the company line. And at the end of the day the brass wins the debate. We may live in a democracy, but we don't work in one. And, you never answered my question."

"What was the question?"

"How do we confirm everyone went directly home when they claimed they did the night Patty Bolin was killed, without raising red flags?"

"I don't know," Rosen said.

"Thank you for the meal, and of course the tea," Mikhail Gagarin said.

"It was my pleasure," Pavel Vasin said. "It was wonderful talking with someone from my generation. And someone from the old country who is not a thug or a criminal."

"Surely you don't believe all the new Russian immigrants are gangsters."

"There are so many here in Brooklyn, it gives the rest of us a bad name. Forgive me. I will avoid the subject if we have the good fortune to meet again."

"Let us plan on it. Do you enjoy Prokofiev?"

"Very much."

"I have a pair of tickets to the Brooklyn Academy of Music this Saturday afternoon, a program of his work including the orchestral suites from *Romeo and Juliet*," Gagarin said, "if you would care to join me."

"I would be delighted. But surely you have family or a friend who would be as pleased."

"Since my dear wife passed away, I have been looking for someone with an appreciation for fine music and a good card game. My son does not fit the bill, and my daughter is away. And I believe I may have found a new friend."

"Very good," Pavel said, "But I insist on treating you to dinner after the concert. There is a restaurant I have wanted to try. The Volga. I have heard many good things about it."

"I know it, and I know the woman who operates the restaurant. She is the mother of my son's friend, Roman, who you met earlier."

"It's settled then. Let's speak Saturday morning to make arrangements."

The two men exchanged phone numbers and went their separate ways.

Mikhail Gagarin, home to his apartment on Ocean Avenue.

Pavel Vasin, off to discover what he could about Roman Churkin, the second of the two younger men playing cards in the park.

Samson and his wife left the hospital on Thursday afternoon to pick up Kayla and Lucy at Alicia's parents' house.

"What are you thinking?"

"It must have been going on for months," Alicia said, sitting beside her husband in the car, "since last spring, or winter."

"It would explain his falling grades, his distraction."

"How could we have been so unaware?"

"You knew *something* was going on. Don't blame yourself for not being able to guess what it was. He hid it well, which leads me to believe he knew what he was doing was not acceptable."

"I could never have guessed a relationship with an older woman, a school teacher. He's just a boy."

"He is a young adult. Mature enough to be tempted and excited by the prospect, but not experienced or wise enough to have anticipated the possible ramifications."

"Honestly, Sam. Do you feel Jimmy is responsible for the teacher's death?"

"Only as much as we are all responsible for our actions if they prove to be harmful, even if not intentional. And the effects of this disaster reach far beyond Jimmy, the woman, and her husband. The decision he and Rebecca Ramirez made changed everything, and everyone. It set all of our lives on an entirely different course. What they did was wrong in so many ways. It's fair to say she should have known better, as an adult who was employed to guide our children, but Jimmy had to realize it was wrong as well. The woman lost her life, her husband lost his freedom and Jimmy may have lost the ability to pursue his passion for athletics. So now, we need to work at adjusting to the new reality and put questions of responsibility aside."

"Jimmy has also lost his innocence," Alicia said.

"An inevitable human experience."

"Has he lost your confidence and respect?"

"Absolutely not, and he has not lost our love. If Jimmy trusts that fact, we will all work through this together. Which brings me to the subject of the girls. We can't be distracted from their needs. Tomorrow Kayla begins second grade, and Lucy begins kindergarten. They must both be feeling anxious, we need to assure them there's nothing to worry about. Assure them they will be fine, and Jimmy will be fine."

"Thank you, Sam."

"For?"

"For being a strong and compassionate parent to our children."

"I am learning day to day," Samson said, "and I am very fortunate to be learning from the best."

Vladimir Markov entered the kitchen of the Lobnya Lounge to speak with Lev Gagarin and Roman Churkin. The two chefs were busy preparing for what was expected to be a very hectic evening, a large number of dinner guests who would abstain from cooking at home on the holy day.

"I understand you are scheduled to make a sworn statement this coming Monday morning," Markov said.

"Yes, a deposition. At the defense lawyer's office," Roman said.

"Are you nervous?"

"It is not something to look forward to," Lev admitted.

"Do not be concerned. Simply repeat what you said to the police on the night my son was brutally attacked and killed. Can you do that?"

"Yes, sir," Lev said, without hesitation.

"Good. Then there is nothing to worry about."

The two young men remained silent until Markov left the kitchen.

"Did he ease your anxiety?" Roman asked Lev.

"Not much."

He followed the woman to the Shop Rite Supermarket on McDonald Avenue at Avenue I in Bensonhurst.

He waited for her to leave her car and start toward the store entrance before parking his car beside hers in the lot.

He walked the short distance to the Dunkin Donut shop, where he had a clear view of the supermarket exit. He purchased a coffee, watched and waited.

Thirty minutes later he saw her exit the market, pushing a shopping cart loaded with groceries.

He timed his approach, reaching his vehicle just as she arrived at hers.

"Good day," he said, as she opened the trunk of her car. "May I offer my assistance?"

"You are kind," she said, placing a bag into the trunk. "I welcome your help. Do I detect a Russian accent?"

"I am from Moscow," he said, helping to unload the shopping cart.

"Yes, the big city. I was a country girl, raised in Bykovo."

"I know it well, I worked at the airport there as a younger man. I am Pavel Vasin," he said. "Perhaps I knew some of your family back home."

"I am Irina Churkin, but my maiden name was Andropov."

"I knew a Sergei Andropov from Bykovo."

"And I knew two or three, none related."

"Of course, it is a common name. I sometimes forget it is not such a small world."

"It is and it is not," Irina said, as they loaded the last grocery bag.

"What does your husband do, if I might ask?"

"He is not with us any longer."

"I'm sorry."

"No need to be sorry, I'm not, he did not pass away he simply *went* away. I am fortunate to have a grown son, Roman, who still lives with me. Although I am sure it is an embarrassment to him at times. Now, I must be going. Thank you for your help, it was good meeting you. Next time you are in the mood for authentic Russian country cooking, please visit The Volga, my restaurant in Gravesend."

"It was good meeting you also," Pavel said, "perhaps we will meet again."

"Perhaps so, after all it is a small world."

Ripley and Senderowitz walked out of the precinct Thursday afternoon.

"Would you care to join me for a holiday drink?" Senderowitz asked.

"Sure. I'd love to check out the Sicilian-American social club."

"I'm afraid there would have to be a meeting of the tribunal before I could get you through the door, but I have a good bottle of scotch at home."

"I can't stay very long, the boys start school tomorrow and they'll need a pep talk."

"It's on your way home. You can be on the BQE in minutes from my door."

Ripley followed Senderowitz to his place in Carroll Gardens.

Bernie collected the mail and ushered his guest into the house.

Senderowitz threw the mail onto the table near the door, spilling most of it onto the floor.

"How do you find anything in that pile?" Ripley asked.

"There's not much worth finding. Bills and junk mail. Applications for credit cards, invitations to start magazine subscriptions, Chinese menus, the weekly AARP membership plea. I go through it at the end of every month, pay the bills, and recycle the rest. If I could afford the postage, I would send all the crap back to them. I'm tempted to get a bird, so I could line the cage with it. The scotch is in the kitchen."

"Lead the way."

"Tell me about your family," Senderowitz said, pouring drinks at the kitchen table.

"Kyle is eight, going on thirty. He is beginning to ask the questions a youngster would not have to ask if we didn't live in a very confusing world. Mickey is five. In fact, he turns six next week. Kyle calls his little brother a goofball. I think Mickey is hilarious. Kids his age are natural comedians."

"And their mother?"

"We lost her two years ago, automobile accident."

"I'm sorry," Bernie said.

"So are we."

"How are you finding the change of venue?"

"Judging by the first week or so, I am guessing it can get busy. I imagine I'll be spending less time behind a desk. And this case, a possible serial, is not unfamiliar territory. The only real difference is, if the FBI was already involved, the perpetrator would probably have a nickname by now."

"The Hangman?"

"Something like that."

"You said *if the FBI was already involved.* Will the Feds jump in?"

"If there is another killing linked to these two, and the Bureau gets wind of it, they definitely will."

"We men in blue don't do well with G-Men looking over our shoulders," Bernie said, pouring them both another scotch. "No offense."

"No offense taken, I'll probably feel the same in time. But..."

"But?" Bernie asked, draining his glass and filling it again.

"But sometimes it's not a bad idea to accept help, no matter who makes the offer."

Marina Ivanov sat in her car across from the Lobnya Lounge, pointing a Nikon SLR digital camera equipped with a 55-200mm f/4-5.6G telephoto zoom lens.

Detective Ivanov focused on the two men who were standing at the club entrance, engaged in an animated conversation. She rapidly snapped a dozen shots.

One of her subjects was the night club owner, Vladimir Markov.

The second subject, younger than Markov and very well-dressed in an expensive business suit, was unknown to her.

Through the viewfinder, Ivanov had clearly seen the younger man accept a thick envelope from Markov and slip it into his inside jacket pocket. The two men then moved into the club.

Ivanov placed the camera on the car seat and pulled out her cell phone. She called Jack Falcone to ask if he was free to meet her at the New Times.

Twenty minutes later, the two detectives sat at a table in the restaurant. Ivanov brought a picture up on the LED display and passed the digital camera across to Falcone.

"Do you know the man on the left?" she asked.

"No. But I recognize the man on the right, and I recognize the location. What is this, Marina? What are you doing?"

"My job."

"It's not your job to run an unauthorized surveillance on Vlad Markov, and I'm sure you've been advised to stay clear of this case. You're asking for trouble, Marina."

"I'm worried Markov will try to retaliate against Alex Holden, to avenge the death of his son."

"There are witnesses who will testify Alex was the aggressor, Markov can let the law deal with Holden."

"I think the witnesses were bought, or threatened. You know the kind of man Markov is. Do you truly believe he'll be satisfied with conventional justice? And I saw him pass an envelope to the other man. It could have been a payoff. What if Markov has hired an assassin?"

"The envelope could have been anything, or nothing. Even if it was full of cash, which you seem to be implying, there are countless possibilities that have nothing to do with a contract to kill Alex Holden."

"I need to find out who the other man is, Jack. I need to be sure I'm not just being overly imaginative, or paranoid. If I put in a request for an ID search myself, I will find the trouble you say I'm looking for. Will you help me?"

"You're asking a lot, Marina."

"I know. And I don't mean to put you on the spot."

"And if I can't help you, is the invitation for a home-cooked dinner off the table?"

"It's not like that, Jack. I honestly do want to spend time with you, apart from all of this drama. Whatever you decide, I will understand, and the dinner invitation still stands. I look forward to it."

"I need to think about it."

"Okay."

"I need to go," Falcone said, rising from his seat.

"Okay."

"Send me the photo when you get a chance," Falcone said, just before turning to leave.

Ivanov left the restaurant shortly after Falcone and drove directly back to the Lobnya Lounge. She pulled into the rear parking area and sat. Twenty minutes later the man who had accepted the envelope from Vlad Markov walked out of the back door. He climbed into a Cadillac and drove off. Marina followed. He parked in front of an apartment house on Avenue T in Gravesend, left his vehicle, and entered the building. Marina made note of the address and returned to the 61st Precinct. She uploaded the photo of the man to her computer and emailed a copy to Falcone at the Sixtieth.

. . .

Carla Jackson stood on West Sixth, near the corner of Avenue T, looking up the street toward Avenue U. She had just walked out of the Cusimano and Russo Funeral Home, having come for Patty Bolin's wake.

"Carla?"

She turned to the man's voice, surprised to find he had come up so close and so quietly behind her.

"You startled me."

"I'm sorry. I didn't mean to."

"I saw you arrive," Carla said. "You didn't stay very long."

"I was uncomfortable."

"I didn't see a person in that room who looked comfortable."

"Can I give you a ride somewhere?"

"No thanks. My father is on his way to pick me up. I normally walk, but my parents are freaked out by what happened to Jenny Greco. They won't let me go anywhere alone. I think they worry too much, and it's not convenient at times."

"They want to be vigilant. It's important for parents to feel as if they can protect their children."

"I guess so," Carla said, turning away to look up West Sixth Street. "Here's my father now."

As the car pulled up to the curb in front of Carla, she turned back to the man to thank him for offering her a ride.

He was gone.

TWENTY

Senderowitz walked into the detectives' squad room at the Six-one at nine on Friday morning. He was a bit hung-over from celebrating the Jewish holiday with a group of Sicilian-Americans who wouldn't know Rosh Hashanah from Luxembourg Independence Day. The room was deserted.

According to Desk Sergeant Kelly, Samson was at the hospital and could be reached if needed, Richards and his wife were taking their daughter to the pediatrician for the child's routine check-up, Ripley would be in after escorting his boys to their first day of school and a trip to the shooting range, Murphy and Rosen had already hit the streets getting nowhere on the Jenny Greco and Patty Bolin investigations, and Ivanov was due in any time.

Senderowitz looked around the empty office, wondering what the hell he would be doing if he wasn't there. The phone rang twice in ten minutes, both calls for Detective Ivanov. Jack Falcone and Lorraine DiMarco.

Bernie gave Ivanov the two messages as soon as she walked into the squad room a few minutes later.

Ivanov called Lorraine first.

They made arrangements to meet for lunch at the New Times Restaurant on Coney Island Avenue. It was close to the precinct but not *at* the precinct. Ivanov had been advised to stay away from the Alex Holden case, no sense making it obvious she was ignoring what was probably good advice. Marina and Lorraine decided to meet at eleven, to beat the noon crowd.

Ivanov then called her former partner at her former precinct.

Jack Falcone had identified the man in Ivanov's photo.

"Ivan Gogol. Gogol is paid muscle, which makes me as curious as you are about his business with Vladimir Markov.

And, on top of that, Gogol shouldn't be out on the street."

"What do you mean?"

"He's wanted for two felony assaults, suspected of murder, and no one has been able to track him down. We'll stake out the Lobnya Lounge, hope he shows his face there again, and pick him up. Let us handle it, Marina."

"Sure," she said. "Thanks. I'll give you a call when I'm ready to do some serious cooking."

"I'm looking forward to it," Falcone said before ending the call.

Ivanov thought about it for only a moment.

"Bernie?"

"Yes?"

"Are you busy?"

"Yes. I'm busy wondering what to do with myself."

"I just got a tip on the location of a wanted felon. He's holed up here in Gravesend. Would you ride with me?"

"Sure. Do we need to take back-up?"

"I don't think so. We can always call it in if we find out otherwise."

"Let's go," Bernie said.

Murphy and Rosen walked into Midwood Florists at Kings Highway and East 14th Street near the B Train Station.

The woman behind the counter was arranging red and white roses.

"Good morning, can I help you?"

"Good morning," Rosen said. "Are you the owner?"

"Yes. Can I help you?"

"Have you ever seen this before?" Rosen asked.

"I don't know if I've seen that particular flyer, but I've seen too many like it under my windshield wiper or slipped under the door."

"Do you know why *this* particular flyer has your phone number on it?" Murphy asked.

The woman took the flyer from Rosen.

"I have no idea, but it would explain why I've had a few calls about brake jobs and oil changes."

Murphy took a similar handbill from the counter. It included a coupon for a discount on gerbera daisies.

"I don't go around littering the streets with *my* leaflets," the woman said. "They are there for customers who come into the shop."

"Anyone seem unusually interested in this one lately?" Murphy asked.

"Funny you should ask."

I'm funny even when I'm not trying, Murphy thought.

"Someone asked where I had them printed."

"Someone you know?"

"No."

"Could you give us a description?"

"White male. Five-ten maybe. One-eighty. Nicely dressed, casual. Brown hair, brown eyes. Sorry, I'm sure that would describe a million people."

"I'm surprised you remember that much detail," Rosen said.

"I remember because he was in here with a teenager. I'm guessing his son. Very nondescript also, but the boy was wearing a spanking new Midwood High School jacket. I asked if the boy was new to Midwood and the father thanked me for my help, took the flyer, and ushered the boy out. Just like that. The boy never said a word. If his father came in to buy flowers, he changed his mind. And that's really all I can tell you."

"Did you tell him where you had these done?" Murphy asked.

"The Print Shop. It's just up Kings Highway at East Eighteenth."

"Do you think you would recognize the man if you saw him again?" Rosen asked.

"Maybe, certainly if the boy was with him."

"If you do, could you give us a call?" Rosen said, offering a business card.

"Sure. Did this man do something wrong?"

"If he had these car repair handbills printed," Murphy said, "he got the phone number *wrong*. Thanks for your help."

"Well?" Rosen said when they walked out onto Kings Highway.

"I don't know. Let's go talk to the printer."

Senderowitz and Ivanov turned onto Avenue T, heading for the apartment building Ivan Gogol had entered when Marina followed him from the Lobnya Lounge the night before.

"Bernie."

"Yes?"

"I need some counsel."

"You kid's make me feel ancient. What's up?"

"This guy Gogol, it has to do with the Holden case and the captain told me to stay out of it."

"Are there warrants out on Gogol?"

"Yes."

"Then if we find him it will be a good collar."

"Yes, but the captain might consider it too much a coincidence."

"We were going for a bite to eat. I spotted the guy going into the building. I thought I recognized him from a wanted bulletin, we were within our precinct borders, and I was pretty sure he was carrying. So we went in to check it out."

"That might wash with Samson, and I really appreciate you climbing out on the limb with me—but then there's Jack Falcone."

"Your old partner at the Sixtieth?"

"Yes."

"What about him?"

"He's not big on coincidences either. Jack identified Gogol from a photo I took last night, and I didn't tell him I knew where Gogol was stashed."

"I can handle Sam. You will need to handle Falcone. If you feel it's a problem, call Jack. Otherwise, here we are," Bernie said as they pulled up in front of the building. "Let's at least find out if the bird is in his nest."

. . .

The man behind the counter looked up at Murphy and Rosen when they walked into the Print Shop.

"You came at the perfect time," he said. "We're running an incredible special on wedding invitations."

Rosen and Murphy threw each other a quick glance.

Rosen tried to suppress a smile.

"Just kidding, Detectives. What can I do for you?"

"How did you make us?" Murphy asked.

"I spotted your gun. We don't get many armed robberies in this business. There's nothing to steal but paper. What can I do for you?"

"Do you know if you printed this flyer?"

He took a look.

"This wasn't printed. It's a photo copy."

"Was it done here?"

"I couldn't tell you. We don't do offset printing for anything less than one hundred copies. Someone comes in with something like this wanting fewer and I point them to the self-service copy machine. They make twenty copies, I make two bucks, done deal."

The superintendent jumped when he felt the tap on his shoulder. He turned to find a photograph held up to his face. He shut down the vacuum cleaner and pulled out his earplugs.

"Know this guy?" Senderowitz asked.

"You scared the hell out of me."

"I didn't mean to. I rang but there was no answer. Know this guy?"

"Not really. He comes in to visit his brother."

"Is he here now?"

"He left thirty minutes ago."

"And the brother?"

"Out of town. He lets your guy stay in his place while he's

gone. I don't like the idea, but these are characters you really don't want to say no to."

Ivanov stayed quiet, just watching the veteran detective work.

"What apartment?"

"Three B. Third floor. Far end of the hall."

Senderowitz pulled out a business card.

"You'll call me if my guy shows up?"

"Sure."

"And you never talked with us."

"Right."

"Thanks. The carpet looks good by the way."

"The carpet looks good?" Ivanov said when they were out on the street.

"We all want to feel pride in our work. What now?"

Before Ivanov could answer, Bernie's cell rang.

"Senderowitz."

"Where did you disappear to?" Sergeant Kelly asked.

"We grabbed a snack. What's up?"

"Richards and Ripley are not in yet. I need you to check out a lead."

"Did you call Rosen and Murphy?"

"I called you."

"That's right, you did. What's cooking?"

"Kenneth Ramirez."

"Who?"

"The guy who killed his wife and shot Jimmy Samson. We found out his mother lives in Brooklyn. He could be hiding out with Mom."

"Where?"

Kelly gave Bernie the address. Bay 38th Street and 23rd Avenue.

"And, Detective."

"Yes, Sergeant."

"This guy is armed."

"Noted."

"What?" Ivanov asked as they moved to their car.

"Off to see the mother of a wanted murderer. I'll let you do the talking this time. I'll drive. It's up the street from Angelo's Bakery. I'll treat you to a cannoli."

Ripley walked into the 61st Precinct at ten-thirty. As he passed through the lobby he nodded to Kelly, who appeared to be up to his ears in paperwork. He walked upstairs to the detectives' squad room and found no one there. He rang the desk sergeant.

"Where is everyone?"

"Out," Kelly said. "I could run down the list of exactly who is where, but I'm too busy sitting on my hands."

"Got it. Thanks."

Ripley cradled the handset just as his cell rang. His sister, Connie.

"Hey."

"I just got a call from Justine Turner. Something came up and she can't make it to dinner with us tonight."

"That's too bad. I was looking forward to it."

"I doubt that. Anyway, you and the boys are still on the guest list. We'll eat around six. I can pick the boys up from school."

"Sounds good," Ripley said. "I'll call when I'm on the way. I'll grab some wine."

"We're having enchiladas, better make it beer."

"Ten-four."

"Have a good day."

"You do the same," Ripley said, ending the call.

He still wondered what everybody else in the gang was up to.

Senderowitz parked across the street from the address. It was a small, neat looking house—with two floors above a garage.

"Do you know how to use that thing?" Bernie asked, indicating the technology built into the unmarked squad car. "It's like rocket surgery to me."

"What do you need?"

"See if you can pull up the APB on Ramirez. I'll be right back."

Senderowitz climbed out of the car and crossed Bay 38th while Ivanov played with the computer.

"What did you get?" he asked when he returned.

"Light skinned Hispanic. Five-nine, one-sixty, brown hair, brown eyes, twenty-eight years old, works for a long distance trucking company out of Long Island City."

"Drives a late model Toyota Corolla. License plate L647AN."

"The car is in the garage?"

"Should give us some leverage when mom insists she hasn't seen her little boy. Let's go ask. Stay alert."

Ivanov glanced at the clock in the dashboard.

"Shit."

"What?"

"I'm supposed to meet someone near the precinct in five minutes, and I don't have a cell number for her."

"Call Kelly," Bernie suggested. "If Richards or Ripley made it in, ask if one of them can get to her."

Kelly put Marina through to Ripley.

"Can you do me a favor?"

"Sure."

"Can you please run down to the New Times, find Lorraine DiMarco, and tell her I'm really sorry I couldn't make it. Please tell her I'll call later."

"Sure. How will I know her?"

"She's an extremely attractive attorney."

"That should narrow it down considerably. I've got you covered."

"Thanks."

"Well?" Senderowitz said.

"Let's do this."

"You're running out too?" Kelly said as Ripley was rushing past.

"I'll be right back."

"That's what they all say. And I'm certain Richards will show up any minute, go up to the squad room, and then call down with twenty questions about where everyone went and why."

"Tell him we all went to the bathroom. Let him guess why. " Ripley said, as he sped out the door.

He spotted her as she reached the restaurant entrance.

"Ms. DiMarco?"

"Yes?"

"Detective Ripley, from the Six-one."

"Did you catch me jaywalking?" she said, showing a big smile.

And big bright green eyes.

"Detective Ivanov got stuck out in the field. She wanted me to give you her apologies. She said she'll catch up with you later."

"Are you hungry?"

"Hungry?"

"Like, have you eaten?"

"No."

"Well, I still need lunch. Would you care to join me?"

Irene Ramirez insisted she hadn't seen her son. When confronted with the Toyota in the garage, she said he was there two days ago, left the vehicle, and she hadn't seen him since. The detectives could have written the script.

"There are a lot of people looking for him. He shot a police captain's son, made a lot of people angry. He would be a lot better off if he turned himself in before something really bad happens," Ivanov said.

"If he shows up, will you call us?" Senderowitz asked.

"I will," the woman said.

Sure she will, Bernie thought.

"Well?" Ivanov asked when they were back at the car.

"I think he's still here, in Brooklyn, staying with Mom or with someone else. It will be harder to spot him with the car in the garage. We'll request a stake-out here, update the all-points bulletin, and try to find out who else he knows in the neighborhood. I suppose we can get a search warrant for the house. We'll run it by Sam. I trust the super on Avenue T will call if Gogol shows his face. We may as well get back to the precinct before they think we drove to Philadelphia for a cheese steak sandwich."

"I wouldn't mind," Ivanov said.

Officers Landis and Mendez were sitting at a table outside a fast food restaurant drinking coffee.

"McCafé," Mendez said, "what a concept. What's next—McCabernet?"

"How are things at home?"

"Great. I'm pricing Tough Sheds for when the new kid arrives."

"Make sure it's big enough for your beer refrigerator and a big screen for your NFL Package."

Stan's cell rang. Rey could hear his partner's end of the exchange.

"Landis...shoot...hold on," he said, and then scribbled something on a paper napkin. "On it...will do."

"What?"

"That was Kelly. They need us to stake out a house on Bay Thirty-eighth. We're looking for the guy who shot Jimmy Samson."

"Do you sometimes feel as if all we ever do is wait for something that never happens?"

"That's not necessarily a bad thing," Landis said.

Rosen and Murphy walked to a pizzeria on Kings Highway, picked up a slice each, and ate off paper plates on the way back to the car parked in front of the Print Shop.

"This could be our guy," Murphy said. "And he might live around here."

"And if pigs could fly."

"Where the hell did that expression come from?"

"It's debatable—either from an ancient Scottish proverb,

from Puritan John Winthrop of Massachusetts, or from a Pink Floyd album."

"How do you know this stuff?"

"Do *you* know who played first base for the nineteen-eighty-three Mets?"

"Dave Kingman. Keith Hernandez took over at first base in eighty-four."

"There you go. And what that tells me is we could both use a recreation break."

"I would settle for a break in this fucking case."

PART THREE

SONS AND DAUGHTERS

*I prefer peace. But if trouble must
come, let it come in my time, so
that my children can live in peace.*

—Thomas Paine

TWENTY ONE

Kenny Ramirez had been hiding out at his mother's house since shooting his wife. He couldn't really remember how he had felt when he found them in the bedroom. He couldn't really remember pulling the .357 Magnum from the hall closet. All he could clearly remember was the terrible roar of the shots.

And as he raced to Brooklyn that night, Kenny could remember wishing he could turn back the clock.

Ramirez had been waiting since late Tuesday night for his mother to dig up the money.

On Friday morning, she had come back from the bank with ten thousand dollars in cash.

"What will you do?" his mother asked.

"I'll change the plates on the car, wait until dark, and run."

"Where?"

"I don't know. I'll give it some thought when and if I make it to Jersey."

And then Ramirez spotted the man snooping around his mother's garage.

He grabbed the cash, kissed his mother, and went out the back door.

He called her an hour later.

"They were detectives, Kenny. They saw the car. And they are watching the house," his mother said. "You can't come back here for the car, and I'm sure they will be watching the buses and trains."

"I'll figure something out."

"I love you, son."

"I love you, Mom. I'm really sorry."

. . .

On Friday afternoon they had all returned to the Six-one—with the exception of Captain Samson.

Ripley came in first, after his unplanned lunch with Lorraine DiMarco.

Richards arrived next. Sergeant Kelly was glad Ripley was already there to satisfy Marty's curiosity.

When Ivanov and Senderowitz walked in, Marina approached Ripley.

"Did you see Lorraine?"

"Yes. I told her you would call her."

"Thanks."

"No problem at all. In fact it was one of my most pleasant assignments," Ripley said, just as Rosen and Murphy came in.

"Hail, hail, the gang's all here," Murphy said.

"Learn anything?" Senderowitz asked.

"If you know anyone planning to get hitched, we can steer you to a great deal on wedding invites and probably get you a discount on flowers."

"That bad?" Ripley said.

"Worse. The pizza was cold."

"Do you have a minute, Murphy?" Ripley asked.

"Sure. Give me a minute to grab a cup of yesterday's coffee."

Ivanov didn't want to talk about what she and Bernie had been up to all morning, so she asked Richards about the visit to the pediatrician instead.

"It was okay," he said.

Marina sensed something was wrong.

"What's up?"

"The doctor heard something."

"Heard what?"

"An irregularity in Sophia's heartbeat."

"Jesus, Richards. What does that mean?"

"He's not sure. They'll need to run some tests."

Ivanov didn't know what to say so she said what she always said when she didn't know what to say.

"Try not to worry, Marty. I'm sure everything will be all right."

"I had lunch with Lorraine DiMarco."

"Oh?"

"It was circumstantial."

"Okay, whatever that means."

"I would like your opinion."

"About Lorraine?" Murphy said.

"Yes."

"She is one of the most remarkable women I have ever met."

"I would like to see her again."

"Did you tell *her* that?"

"No. I wanted to speak with you first."

"You don't need my permission."

"I was thinking about Lou Vota."

"Lou was like a brother to Sam and me. We think about him and talk about him often. But we've moved on—and I hope Lorraine has been able to do the same. That's all I have. You'll have to get the rest from her."

"Okay. Thanks."

"This coffee really sucks," Murphy said.

Kenny Ramirez had been sitting in the movie theater for hours, with ten thousand dollars in his pocket and no real plan. All he knew was he needed a vehicle—and stealing a car would be a lot trickier than pulling plates off one.

And he knew he would have to wait until dark.

Ramirez slid down in his seat as the film began for the third time.

Kelly transferred the call up to Senderowitz just after five.

"This is Harry," the caller said.

"Harry?"

"We met this morning when you interrupted my carpet cleaning."

"Did our guy show up?"

"A few minutes ago."

"I'll be right there."

"I think I'll stay in my apartment."

"Good idea."

"The lobby door will be unlocked. Three-B."

"End of the hall, got it. Is there another way out?"

"There's a fire escape off the kitchen window in the back of the building."

Of course there is, Bernie thought.

He caught Ripley heading out.

"I received a tip on the location of a fugitive. Can you ride with me?"

"Sure. It will make up for the time I missed this morning. Give me a minute to call my sister and tell her I may be late for dinner."

Sarah Sanders stood on the porch for nearly five minutes before finding the courage to ring the doorbell. No answer. She knocked on the door, waited a minute, rang the doorbell again and knocked again. No answer.

She had come this far, so back in her car she called Staten Island. She was told he wasn't there anymore, had transferred to a job in Brooklyn. She was given another phone number.

She was about to call but hesitated long enough to decide she would think about it over a cup of tea.

"What are you doing for dinner?" Murphy asked.

"Whatever you're doing," Rosen said. "We could pick up something to cook at my place, try to find a comedy on HBO, and go from there."

"I promised Augie Sena I would take him for a drink later tonight."

"So, let's eat at Joe's Bar and Grill. We can take both cars and I can go home from there."

"Sorry, it's been planned all week."

"No problem. I could use some down time, and I know you're not a big fan of comedies anyhow."

"Give me a minute," Murphy said. "I want to check in with Sam."

Samson and Alicia had run to the hospital after dropping the girls off at school and had sat at their son's bedside all morning. Jimmy had been in and out of sleep. When Jimmy was awake, they talked about anything except what happened at the Ramirez house a few nights before. Later, they went back to the school to pick up the girls. They talked with Kayla and Lucy about their school day, and told them Jimmy sent his love.

Alicia stayed at home to prepare dinner for the girls, and Samson returned to the hospital.

"How's it going?" Murphy asked when he reached the captain on his cell.

"He's been in and out of sleep. He's feeling stronger. The doctors think he might be ready for mild physical therapy in a few days. How about you?"

"Rosen and I ran down a few dead end streets."

"I heard we got a lead on Kenneth Ramirez."

"Bernie and Ivanov visited the mother. She stonewalled them. Landis and Mendez are sitting on the house."

"Are you done for the day?"

"Well done. Off to dinner with Rosen followed by drinks with Augie."

"What about the others?"

"Ivanov and Richards are out—robbery assault at an ATM on Avenue V. Senderowitz and Ripley took off, I don't know where to."

"I'll be in tomorrow," Samson said.

. . .

229

At six, a replacement team of two plain clothes officers arrived at the Ramirez house on Bay 38th Street to take over surveillance.

"I can't fucking wait to get home for some real food," Mendez said, just as Landis' cell rang.

"Don't hold your breath," Landis said, after the call from Kelly. "Ripley and Senderowitz need backup."

The memorial assembly for Jenny Greco, and now Patty Bolin, ran late.

It was just after six when the cheerleader squad met for a rehearsal in the gym with their dance instructor, Emily Bledsoe, following the assembly.

The cheerleader squad was two members short, and the football team was missing a star receiver, but the first home game for the Lafayette Patriots was still scheduled for the following Saturday.

Sergeant Kelly grabbed the phone before it could ring a second time.

"Sixty-first Precinct."

"I'd like to speak to Detective Senderowitz."

"Senderowitz is not in. Can I help you?"

"When do you expect him?"

"Can I ask who is calling?"

"His daughter."

"Detective Senderowitz was rushed to Coney Island Hospital," Kelly said. "I'm very sorry. I haven't heard anything more yet."

TWENTY TWO

Samson raced from one hospital to another. When he arrived at Coney Island Hospital he found Ripley waiting.

"How is he?"

"He's alive. The doctors and nurses aren't saying anything yet about his condition."

"What happened?"

When Ivanov and Richards arrived at the scene, the ATM bandit had already been collared. The victim had chased the perp down, tackled him, taken his gun, and held him until two uniforms took him into custody.

"Got to love civilians who do our job for us," Richards said.

"He could have got himself killed."

"Better one of us should get killed for someone else's sixty dollars?"

Before Ivanov could decide what to do with that one, her cell rang.

"What?" Richards asked.

"Senderowitz had a heart attack."

"Is he alive?"

"Yes, but it was a close call. He's at Coney Island," Ivanov said. "Jesus. This is my fault."

"I won't even ask what that means," Richards said.

"I was at the back of the building, Bernie was in front. I had called for backup and was waiting," Ripley began. "Then the guy climbs out onto the fire escape, spots me, takes a few shots, and I return fire. I hit him, he fell, and he was dead when he hit the ground. Mendez came running up to me. Rey said Landis was with Senderowitz, and they had called for an ambulance. Bernie must have been impatient and gone up alone. He'd been shot at through the apartment door. Luckily he wasn't hit but Landis and Mendez found him unconscious in the hall. The emergency medical technician said it was his heart."

"Who was this guy?" Samson asked.

"Ivan Gogol. There were a couple of warrants out on him, felony assault. Bernie said he was tipped-off to Gogol's location."

"By who?"

"The superintendent called to tell Senderowitz that Gogol had entered the building."

"How did the super know Bernie was looking for Gogol?"

"I don't know."

"Where are Landis and Mendez now?"

"They went to the morgue with the body to take care of paperwork."

"I want you to call them, send them back to the super, and find out how he came to call Senderowitz. And I want to know right away."

"There's something else."

"What?"

"There's a woman in the visitor's lounge who was asking for you."

"Who?"

"She gave me her business card," Ripley said, handing it to Samson. "She's a freelance journalist. Sarah Sanders."

"How did media get on to this already?"

"I don't know."

"Call Landis and Mendez." Samson made a quick call to Murphy and then headed for the lounge.

"Should we be at the hospital?" Rosen asked.

"Sam said there's nothing we could do there but get in the way. And I'm sure Bernie wouldn't want us to let the calamari get cold and soggy on his account," Murphy said, as Augie set the plate on their table.

"Ms. Sanders."

"Yes," she said, as she looked up from the book she was reading.

"I'm Captain Samson. I don't know why you are here—but the NYPD is not ready to make a statement."

"I'm here to see my father," she said.

"Sarah?" he said, once it sunk in. "My God. I'm sorry I didn't know you. The last time I saw you, you couldn't have been more than eight years old."

"I remember *you* very well. You were so gigantic to an eight-year-old—my mother had to constantly remind me you were a friendly giant."

"I think I scare my own girls at times. How *is* your mother?"

"Mom passed away Sunday."

"I'm very sorry to hear that. Bernie didn't say anything."

"He didn't know. I haven't seen my father in long time. My aunt finally talked me into trying to see him before it was too late. And it just might be."

"It would take a lot more than one heart attack to finish Bernie."

"How much scotch will it take?" she asked.

"I don't know, Sarah. But maybe you can help your father address that question. Let me buy you a cup of coffee and we can talk about it."

"Excuse me," Ripley said, coming into the lounge.

"Give me a minute, Sarah."

Samson followed Ripley into the corridor.

"The superintendent said Senderowitz and a woman detective had come looking for Gogol this morning. Gogol had just left. Bernie asked him to call if Gogol came back."

"Who was riding with Bernie this morning?"

"Ivanov."

"Where is she?"

"She and Richards just walked in. They're at the nurses' station."

"Tell her I need to talk to her. I'll be there in a minute."

"Sarah," Samson said, when he returned to the lounge.

"Do what you need to do, Captain Samson. Don't worry. I'm not going anywhere for a while."

All but one of the girls left after the rehearsal in the gymnasium.

Carla Sanchez stayed behind to talk with Emily Bledsoe.

"I've decided to leave the squad," Carla said.

"I understand what you're feeling. Everyone is confused, and probably a little frightened. But I truly believe it would be better for all of us, and the entire school body, if we work at moving forward as quickly as possible and not allow these tragic events to control our emotions and undermine our goals. I understand cheerleading for a school football team is not fighting for world peace or crusading against world hunger, but there is something to be said about tradition and school pride and keeping our morale up, particularly in times of turmoil. Will you think about it?"

"Okay."

"Are you in a hurry to leave?"

"Not really."

"Good. I *am* in a hurry. And if you will help me get all of this gear put away, we can both be out of here in twenty minutes."

Captain Samson led Detective Ivanov out of the hospital and to a bench across Ocean Parkway.

"Tell me about Ivan Gogol. And don't say anything that could make me angrier than I am already."

"What do you want to know?"

"Everything."

Ivanov ran it down.

"Why were you snooping around the Lobnya Lounge in the

first place and, if you knew where Gogol was, why didn't you tell Falcone when you spoke to him this morning?"

"Gogol was holed up in our backyard, Bernie was handy, and I thought it would be more expedient. The guy was a wanted felon."

"That's not the way we work, Detective. I asked you to stay away from the Holden case. It belongs to the Sixtieth precinct. You should have given it to Detective Falcone."

"It's about *my* family, Captain," Ivanov said. "If Detective Senderowitz had been shot at in the Sixtieth, and the shooter was still at large, would *you* stay away from that?"

"If you had followed protocol, or at least let me know what you thought was *expedient*, would Detective Senderowitz be up in that recovery room?"

"I've made you angrier. I'm sorry."

"I'll call the CO at the Sixtieth, tell him there is reason to believe Alex Holden may be in danger, and suggest they keep an eye on both Holden *and* Markov. And I'm not looking for apologies. I want to hear that you understand you acted wrongly, and I want to be assured it won't happen again."

"I know I screwed up and it won't happen again."

"I'll let it go with a warning this time, and a three-day sabbatical. But *that* won't happen again either."

"Great dinner, Augie," Rosen said.

"Augie?"

"Yes, Murphy?"

"Can we take a rain check on boy's night out? I'm feeling we should get to the hospital to check on Senderowitz. How about tomorrow night?"

"Sure, Tommy, whatever works for you. I hope he will pull through all right. Do you have time for dessert?"

"That works for me," Murphy said.

. . .

"Do you need a ride home?" Emily Bledsoe asked.

"I have my mom's car. They went to the city and they won't let me walk anywhere at night any more. I'm parked right out front on Bay Forty-third."

"I'm parked in back. I'll see you Monday. Give some thought to what we talked about."

"I will," Carla said.

Samson sent everyone home.

Senderowitz was moved to a private room. Samson called his wife to say he would be staying for a while, waiting for permission to see Bernie.

"They say he was very lucky," Sam told Alicia. "It was a serious cardiac arrest and he suffered a concussion when his head hit the floor. They're doing tests to determine if he'll need bypass surgery or a pacemaker. In any event, the doctors are recommending two to three weeks of home recuperation."

Samson joined Sarah Sanders in the lounge, and they talked over coffee in paper cups.

An hour later a nurse came in to let them know the patient was awake and they could go in for a *very brief* visit.

"Can you give me a few minutes with him alone?" Samson asked.

"Sure," Sarah said.

Senderowitz smiled weakly when Samson came into the room.

"Come to tell me what an idiot I am? I identified myself and when there was no answer I stepped in front of the door to listen for movement. He started shooting and then I felt my chest explode. I'm getting too old for this shit."

"You should have waited for backup."

"That too. Did they get Gogol?"

"Ripley shot him on the fire escape."

"Dead?"

"Yes."

"Ripley's two for two."

"I don't think he's looking to break records. Everyone was here, and I chased them away. The doctors want you to rest, but there's someone I think you should see before the lock down. I'll check in with you tomorrow."

Sarah was waiting outside the room when Samson walked out.

"Go ahead," Samson said.

Carla Sanchez swore out loud and turned the key again.

The same clicking sound and no go.

"Sounds like the starter."

She looked up to the car window.

"Jesus, you scared me."

"I'm sorry, I didn't mean to. It's dead, it would be best to deal with it tomorrow morning. I suggest you call your parents, I can wait with you until someone comes to pick you up."

"I can't call my parents."

"No phone? You can use mine."

"They went to a Broadway show. They won't have their phones on during the performance."

"I can give you a ride."

"Thanks. I'll call a cab."

"It's really no trouble."

She gave it a moment's thought.

"Can we stop at the deli on Stillwell Avenue? I told my mother I would pick up milk on the way home."

"Sure," he said. "My car is just across the street."

Kenny Ramirez had been walking 86th Street looking for a vehicle he could get into without alerting the entire neighborhood.

Where's an old beater with no alarms when you need one?

As Kenny approached Stillwell Avenue he spotted a car double-parking.

A young girl climbed out of the vehicle and ran into a deli.

Ramirez rushed up to the car, pulled out his .357, opened the door, and dropped into the passenger seat.

"Drive," Kenny said.

TWENTY THREE

Samson began the day on Saturday preparing breakfast for his wife and daughters. Lucy helped him mix the batter while Kayla helped Alicia cut fresh fruit and set the table.

"Can you make a horse, Daddy?" Lucy asked, standing beside him at the stove.

Using a teaspoon he dribbled batter into the center of the pan in a long oval, trying to approximate a body. He added two legs, a neck, and a head. It wasn't bad until the batter began to spread and transform into something very different.

"How about an elephant?" he asked his youngest.

"Okay."

Murphy was still in bed when Samson called. Rosen was in the kitchen preparing to cook omelets.

"I'm heading to the hospital to check in on Jimmy, then over to see Bernie. Can you keep things in order until I get in?"

"Sure."

"Ivanov is taking some personal time. We'll put Ripley and Richards together for a few days. Anything on Ramirez?"

"Not a thing. I'm sure his mother tipped him, and there's no reason for him to go back there if he can't get to his car."

"Let's keep the surveillance going until this afternoon. Then arrange to have the car impounded. Ramirez used it to flee the scene after the shooting so it's fair game. Anything on the Greco or Bolin cases?"

"We can't catch a break. And Sandra is losing patience."

"What do you mean?"

"Rosen doesn't agree with holding information from the

public that might help generate leads. And she's really having a hard time lying to the families."

"It's the company line. Whether I agree or not it isn't my call."

"She knows that. But it doesn't make her any cheerier."

"I'll talk to her."

"Maybe you can talk to Chief Trenton before you talk to Sandra. She's going to ask you if and when the company line might be redrawn."

"I hope to be in by noon," Samson said.

By the time Ripley was ready to leave the hospital the night before he had missed dinner at his sister's place by more than three hours.

He had called to apologize.

"Can the boys stay there tonight? I don't want to drag them home this late."

"Of course," Connie said. "Why don't you come here? I'll fix you some food and you can stay over also."

"I'm beat, and I've already had something to eat," he lied. "I'll come over in the morning and we can have breakfast—if that's all right."

What he didn't say was that he had killed another man and knew he wouldn't be sleeping like a baby.

When he reached home he fixed a sandwich and washed it down with a lot of Irish whiskey.

It knocked him out but it didn't chase away the bad dreams.

He woke up in the morning with a decent headache. He was scheduled for duty Saturday. He drank enough water and coffee to make it to breakfast with his boys before heading in to the Six-one.

"I heard you took care of the felon who shot at Senderowitz," Kelly said as Ripley passed the sergeant's desk.

"All in a day's work," Ripley said, and he went up to the squad room hoping for a better day.

. . .

Marina dropped in on her parents Saturday morning in time to join them for breakfast. As her mother prepared the food, her father asked for a talk.

"You don't work today?"

"I went off the reservation yesterday and the captain gave me three days off to think about it."

"I am as angry as you are about Rachel being assaulted and about what is happening to Alex."

"He's being framed, Dad. And he could be in danger."

"You can't help Alex by breaking the rules yourself. And if you keep stepping on toes, you will be shut out completely."

"You're probably right."

"I am right. Leave it to the proper channels and respectfully ask to be kept informed. Trust Captain Samson and Detective Falcone. They both care, and they are both good at what they do. It will work out, Marina."

"Are you just saying what you think I want to hear?"

"I'm saying what I believe."

"Thanks, Dad," Marina said.

"See if your mother needs help in the kitchen."

Her father *was* right about Sam, and about Jack. They did care. And she owed Falcone an apology. She thought about asking Jack to dinner.

"How do you feel?" Samson asked.

"I feel like a hospital patient," Senderowitz said. "How is Jimmy?"

"I'm sure he is feeling trapped also, but he seems to be doing much better. At least physically."

"The head stuff will take time. But he needs to get on his feet first so you two can stand eye to eye when you get down to it."

"How was seeing Sarah?"

"It was a shock. I almost had another heart attack. You should have warned me."

"I was afraid you might try crawling under the bed."

"Or going out the window? She has a lot of anger, Sam. I wasn't a good father or husband."

"I was very sorry to hear about Susan. They should have told you she was sick."

"Susan's sister might have advised it, but she wouldn't force it. It was Sarah's place to make the decision. And if I knew, I don't know that I would have had the courage to see Susan. And it could have got in the way of Sarah and her mother spending the time they needed to say goodbye."

"What now?"

"We wait and see. But I'm a little too old to change, Sam. So unless Sarah is willing to meet me halfway it won't work."

"Meeting halfway goes both ways," Samson said.

When Murphy and Rosen arrived at the precinct they found Ripley and Richards in the detectives' squad room.

Murphy called Richards over to Ripley's desk.

"Ivanov is out until Tuesday. While she's gone, you two can ride together. When Marina comes back, Samson will find a temporary partner for Ripley until Bernie returns from medical leave. For starters, we need the names of anyone who purchased a new Midwood High School jacket in the past month or two."

"It's Saturday, the school is closed," Marty Richards said. "How are we supposed to find that kind of information today?"

"Do some detecting."

"Do you have any idea how many names that could be?" Richards asked.

"No, I don't. But once you get them all we can count them together."

"We're on it," Ripley said, to end the exchange.

Murphy walked over to Rosen's station.

"Having fun?" she asked.

"Telling other detectives what to do is not one of my favorite things. I prefer bright copper kettles and whiskers on kittens."

"What are *we* going to do today?"

"I'll let you decide."

When Samson reached the precinct the first thing he did was call Rosen into his office.

"I know you are frustrated. I called Trenton to find out where the brass and the politicians stand at the moment. They are not ready to make public the suggestion that a government official was somehow responsible for the deaths of Angela Salerno and Edward Cicero."

"Because they don't want to admit there are no suspects."

"Exactly. And they are not ready to talk about the rope around Jenny Greco's neck. They're afraid of a panic."

"We could use some panic. Compel young women and their parents to be more vigilant in avoiding unsafe conditions and situations. Have more eyes on the street watching their neighbors' backs. We're getting nowhere."

"It is *our* job to find the guilty, Sandra, not the job of the bureaucrats. They can tie our hands, but we still have our heads and our legs. They can't stop us from scratching at the dirt. And we can't make excuses for failure. We need to work with what we have and keep digging. We can only do our best. So do that."

"You know I will," Rosen said.

After a very entertaining concert of Prokofiev works at the Brooklyn Academy of Music, Pavel Vasin and Mikhail Gagarin moved on to the Volga Restaurant.

When Irina Churkin spotted them walking in, she was very surprised to see the men together. She waited for them to be seated before greeting them at their table.

Not wishing to ruin what he expected would be a wonderful meal, Vasin decided to wait until after they had dined to confront Mikhail and Irina.

He handed the waitress cash to cover the bill plus a generous gratuity and asked the woman to please send Irina to the table.

"It is important that I speak with you both," Pavel said. "I will explain. Is there somewhere private we can talk?"

"We can talk in my office at the end of the back hall. I will be right there," Irina said.

The two men were silent while they waited.

Mikhail sat uncomfortably, not knowing how to ask or even what to ask.

Irina came into the room with coffee, cream, sugar, and homemade Russian tea cakes on a silver tray.

"First, I must sincerely apologize for deceiving you. I did not meet you by chance. I sought you both out, with the intention of bringing the three of us together. I would understand perfectly if you took offense to my dishonesty, I would feel betrayed also without an acceptable explanation. I can only assure you that my actions were inspired by very grave concerns, and I beg you to hear me out."

"If you are looking for some kind of trust from us, you chose a poor way to begin," Mikhail said. "I am willing to listen, but cannot guarantee indefinite attention."

"Please tell us what this is about," Irina said.

"Alex Holden is an honest and hardworking young man. Alex owns a bakery here in Brooklyn."

"I know Alex," Irina said. "He supplies desserts for the restaurant."

"What is your impression of him?"

"He has always been fair and courteous. I consider him a good man."

"Alex has been charged with second degree murder, for stabbing another man to death. Alex swears the other man came at him with a knife, they struggled, and it ended fatally. I believe him. But there are two witnesses who claimed Alex produced the knife and that *he* was the aggressor—and I do not trust their account."

"Why would two separate witnesses lie?" Mikhail asked.

"I believe they are afraid to tell the truth."

"Honesty is not a matter of convenience," Mikhail said.

"I agree."

"What does this have to do with you?" Irina asked.

"Alex is hoping to be my niece's husband and I consider him family. If Alex is convicted of this crime, it will ruin his entire life. The man Alex Holden killed in self-defense was Yuri Markov. You know who his father is. Vladimir Markov would want his son to be seen as the victim. And he would go to any lengths to see Alex punished. He wants, at the least, to see Alex convicted and imprisoned."

"At the least?" Irina said.

"Markov lost a son, and in his mind there are no special circumstances. And there is reason to believe he may be planning a more absolute retribution."

"I can understand your concern for your family," Mikhail said, "and I hope you find justice. But what does this have to do with us?"

"The two witnesses I spoke of are your sons, Lev and Roman."

There was a minute of dead silence until Mikhail finally spoke.

"Please give us a short time to talk alone," Gagarin said.

"Of course. While I am gone, please take a moment to consider what you know of Vladimir Markov and his reputation."

Jack Falcone arrived at Ivanov's apartment with a bottle of expensive imported Chianti.

"How did you know I was cooking Italian?" Marina asked.

"I didn't. But I know nothing about Russian wines."

"There's not much to know about Russian wines," Marina said. "Jack, I'm really sorry if I caused you any grief on account of my actions yesterday."

"Larimer chewed me out for running Gogol's photo without running it past him. I took it on the chin."

"How is Captain Larimer?"

"He still has sharp teeth, but I have tough skin. And we got Gogol, which helped curb the captain's appetite. Captain Samson called Larimer. We can't be certain Markov paid Gogol to harm Alex Holden but, if he did, with Gogol out of the picture Markov will need to find a replacement unless he takes it into his own hands. And that's not his style. In any event, Larimer has patrols watching both Markov and Holden, at least for a while."

"Samson read me the riot act and gave me a three-day vacation."

"Well then, we can eat slowly. It's pretty gutsy of you to cook Italian food for a police detective with an Italian mother."

"I'm sure I can't cook as well as your mom, Detective, but I bet I look as adorable in an apron. Are you going to open that wine?"

Pavel Vasin slipped out to the sidewalk in front of the Volga to have a cigarette and give Mikhail and Irina time to talk. When he returned he found that Mikhail had been chosen to be the spokesperson.

"You are suggesting our sons lied. That they were warned by Vladimir Markov against truthfully telling what they saw."

"Yes. I believe Markov threatened the young men."

"What could he intimidate them with that would compel them to lie, loss of their jobs? We know Lev and Roman. They are honorable men. Even if they were threatened with personal harm, they would not put their own safety above that of an innocent man. They were not raised to allow harm to come to others in order to protect themselves."

"But they may have been raised to protect their families, at all costs."

"Do you believe Markov threatened harm to us?" Irina asked.

"I believe that is the one warning even honorable men might find difficult to ignore."

"What are you asking us to do?" Mikhail Gagarin said.

"Lev and Roman are scheduled to sign statements Monday morning. If they put their signatures to false testimony they could be doing great harm to an innocent man and, if found out, could risk prosecution for perjury and obstruction of justice. If they did, in fact, witness Yuri Markov as the aggressor, I am asking you to encourage your sons to tell the truth before it is too late."

Murphy and Rosen walked out of the precinct at seven on Saturday evening.

"Try not to get too crazy with Augie Sena tonight," she said as they parted ways.

Rosen had her evening at home well planned out. A brisket sandwich and Cole slaw from Mendy's Deli, a Pilsner Urquell or two from her refrigerator, a hot shower followed by a single malt scotch and a book.

Sandra Rosen was partial to crime novels, and she was particularly fond of Elmore Leonard.

Rosen's apartment was a railroad flat on the first floor of a brownstone in Prospect Heights. When she arrived home she dropped the deli bag on the kitchen table, set her firearm and shield on the dresser in her bedroom, got out of her street clothes and into a plush terry cloth robe monogrammed with the words *Brooklyn's Finest*—a gift from Tommy Murphy.

Then she returned to the kitchen to give the sandwich the attention it deserved.

Murphy and Augie had a quick bite to eat at Joe's Bar and Grill to start the evening.

"We could stay here and drink," Murphy said. "It would be a lot more economical and I'll buy."

"My objective is to get out of this place for a change."

"I'm hip."

"That's funny, you don't look hip."

"How about My Father's Place on Cropsy?"

"Perfect."

. . .

Detective Josh Altman had been sitting in his car across from Rosen's building for nearly thirty minutes before she finally arrived home.

He sat for another hour before getting out of the vehicle.

Altman crossed St. Mark's Avenue and rang Sandra's doorbell.

Rosen put down her book, looked through the peephole, and opened the door.

"Josh. What are you doing here?"

"We need to talk."

"This isn't the time or the place. Call me Monday at the precinct."

"We need to talk *now*."

"Please, Josh. You have to leave."

Altman violently pushed her to the floor and stepped inside. He closed and locked the door behind him.

When Rosen looked up he was standing over her pointing a gun.

A pair of handcuffs dangled from Altman's other hand.

TWENTY FOUR

"How is your sister Rosie holding up?" Murphy asked.

"All right I guess, considering. She went to visit her daughter in Albany this weekend. Every time I see John he asks if there is anything new with the case. He must believe I have a phone tap at the Six-one. But I would be more worried about John's state of mind if he *wasn't* asking."

Augie Sena's observation reminded Murphy of something Samson had said with regard to all the questions thrown back at Murphy and Rosen when they were conducting interviews at the high school.

It would be more surprising if they didn't ask.

"You put a bug in my head," Murphy said. "Do you mind if I call Rosen to run it by her?"

"Go for it. I'll grab another round."

Augie returned to the booth with two whiskeys and a couple of bottles of Sam Adams.

"Did you reach Sandra?"

"No answer. She must be taking one of her legendary thirty minute showers. Remind me to try again later."

Kenny Ramirez was carefully staying within the speed limit on the Staten Island Expressway, heading to the Goethals Bridge and New Jersey. He had realized immediately after jacking the car that he needed to be in the driver's seat. Pointing a gun from the passenger seat at a driver doing sixty miles an hour would not give Kenny much leverage.

Kenny had told the driver to find an isolated spot where he could set the man free. They found a deserted side street off Stillwell Avenue at West 16th under the Belt Parkway. Of course,

Ramirez couldn't let the driver walk away if he hoped for a head start out of New York in a stolen vehicle. So, when they pulled over to the curb, Kenny hit the man square in the temple with the .357, knocking the man unconscious.

Ramirez put the man in the trunk of the vehicle, hands and feet bound with clothesline he had conveniently found in the back seat. He gagged the man with a handkerchief he pulled from the guy's jacket pocket.

He also found the man's wallet.

As he closed the trunk, Kenny Ramirez noticed the blood dripping from the man's ear.

By the time he came off the bridge into Jersey, Kenny had already stopped thinking about the man in the trunk.

Detective Rosen sat in a chair at her kitchen table. Hands cuffed behind her back, feet secured to the cross brace at the chair legs with a leather belt, a strip of duct tape across her mouth.

Detective Altman sat across the table, watching Rosen, looking for any sign of fear. He found none. His weapon sat on the table near his hand.

"We can't talk with you gagged like this," Altman said. "If I let you speak, will you promise not to make a racket?"

Rosen nodded her head. Yes.

Altman gently removed the tape from her mouth.

"Josh, you need to end this now, before it's too late."

"I still love you, Sandra."

"You have a funny way of showing it."

It was classic unrestrained Rosen, and she knew immediately it was the wrong thing to say.

"What am I going to do with you?" Altman said.

Rosen couldn't help wondering the same thing.

"I think it's time to cry uncle, Augie. I need to drive home without being pulled over by a police patrol car and having to convince a couple of uniforms that detectives are allowed to break the law."

"Are you sure you're not there already?"

"Not so I can't fake it. We need to do this more often."

"Next time I'll bring a bottle home to my place, I have a very comfortable couch. Be careful. And you asked me to remind you to give Rosen a call."

In his car, Murphy phoned Rosen. There was no answer.

Murphy fired up the engine, pulled out onto Cropsy Avenue, and soon found himself driving to Prospect Heights.

"What's your plan, Josh? Are you waiting for me to say I'm glad you dropped by? I'm glad you dropped by."

"This is not a joke."

"You're right, it's not. It's a disaster. If you cut me loose now, and can convince me you'll commit to getting help, I will let you walk out of here instead of taking you in."

"You're not saying what I want to hear, Sandra."

"I *can't* say what you want to hear, Josh."

"Okay, then," Altman said.

He put the tape back over her mouth and sat staring at her.

Murphy would be asked many times why he didn't simply ring the doorbell when he reached Rosen's house.

He could never come up with a reasonable answer.

In any case, Murphy chose to walk to the back of the building instead.

And he looked into the kitchen window.

Rosen was bound and gagged in a chair, Josh Altman was sitting with his palm resting on the butt of a nine millimeter handgun, and Rosen's cell phone sat in the center of the table between them.

No one ever questioned why Murphy decided to do what he did next.

. . .

Soon after crossing the Pennsylvania state line, Kenny Ramirez could see the lights of Philadelphia.

He wanted to put at least one more state between him and the police so he continued driving south.

The cell phone rang. Rosen and Altman watched it vibrate on the table. Altman reached for the phone and looked at the display.

"It's your boyfriend again. He must be worried about you. Maybe he'll decide to come by."

"I did. Put your hands in the air. Now."

Murphy was standing in the doorway that separated the kitchen from the mud room off the rear entrance. He held his weapon in both hands, trained on Altman's chest.

Altman hesitated for a moment and then went for his gun.

The shot knocked both Altman and the chair to the floor.

Murphy moved quickly to the table, grabbed Altman's weapon, and tossed it into the kitchen sink.

Murphy handcuffed Altman, arms behind the man's back, and secured Altman's legs with the hobble strap he had retrieved from his car.

He un-cuffed Rosen and phoned for backup and an ambulance while she removed the tape from her mouth and freed her legs.

When he finally turned his attention back to Rosen, Sandra was rubbing the bruises on her wrists.

"Miss me?" she asked.

Kenny Ramirez stopped at a department store off Interstate-95 north of Wilmington, Delaware. He purchased a large gym bag, a few pair of jeans, three long sleeved cotton shirts, T-shirts, socks and underwear.

He located the Wilmington Amtrak Station and left the car in the long term parking lot.

It was a short walk to the Doubletree Hotel on King Street. Ramirez paid for a room with a credit card from the vehicle owner's wallet.

He pulled up a number from his cell and called Raul Sandoval in Denver from a public pay phone outside of the hotel.

Kenny used a complimentary internet station in the hotel lobby to check train schedules.

He went up to his room, phoned the front desk to request a wakeup call at six in the morning, took a hot shower and fell into bed.

Ramirez was asleep in minutes.

The man in the trunk would not survive the night.

TWENTY FIVE

Sunday had been relatively quiet at the 61st Precinct. On Monday, the joint was jumping.

The Six-one was keeping the Internal Affairs Bureau very busy.

Monday morning, IAB detectives would be interviewing Senderowitz at the hospital and then talking to Ripley at their offices at 315 Hudson Street in Manhattan concerning the shooting death of Ivan Gogol.

Rosen and Murphy were summoned to visit IAB on Hudson Street later that morning to talk about Josh Altman.

"And that's why I don't like Mondays," Murphy said to Rosen after they received the call.

"Well then, next time you decide to shoot an NYPD detective, don't do it on a Saturday."

Monday morning, Lev Gagarin and Roman Churkin arrived at the Kings County District Attorney's Office on Jay Street accompanied by each of their parents. The two men were scheduled to give sworn testimony in the case of the State vs. Alexander Holden. A court officer outlined the procedure. They would be giving oral depositions, individually. The statements would then be transcribed and the written affidavits would be signed and notarized.

Lev was randomly chosen to be seen first, and he was taken into an interview room.

Also present in the room were Lorraine DiMarco, Attorney for Alexander Holden, Assistant District Attorney Mark Caldwell, and a court appointed legal secretary.

Lev Gagarin stated under oath that Yuri Markov had attacked Alexander Holden with a lethal weapon and Holden had acted in defense of his own life.

Soon after, Roman Churkin stated the same.

Both witnesses signed transcripts of their testimony.

Lorraine escorted the two men and their parents out of the building and thanked them on behalf of her client.

She then joined ADA Caldwell over a cup of coffee.

"Well?" Lorraine asked.

"The state will agree to reduce the charge to involuntary manslaughter by reason of self-defense. After that, under the Rules of Affirmative Defense, the charges will be dropped entirely."

"I'm not looking to throw a monkey wrench into the works, and I hope you will forget I ever brought it up, but I'm curious."

"What?"

"You never asked them why they failed to tell the truth to the responding officers at the scene."

"I could guess," Caldwell said. "Vladimir Markov won't be happy, but his happiness is not my concern. I need to get back to cases I can win, and you might want to give your client the good news. And recommend he stay alert."

Vladimir Markov sat at the kitchen table of his Sea Gate home over a cup of heavily sugared black coffee. His wife placed a plate of buttered black bread on the table. Markov was reading an article in the *New York Daily News* regarding the shooting death of Ivan Gogol in Gravesend. The newspaper story was short on details. The report named the two 61st Precinct detectives involved in the incident—but there was no mention of any connection between Gogol and Markov.

Markov's wife summoned him to the telephone. It was a courtesy call from the Kings County District Attorney's Office, informing him of the results of the morning's depositions by his employees, Lev Gagarin and Roman Churkin, and the reduced charges against Alexander Holden.

The legal system would not be punishing the killer of his son.

Markov returned to the kitchen table, sat, and hurled the plate of bread against the wall.

Kenny Ramirez had been up at six. He took another shower and dressed in fresh new clothes. He had shoved his old clothing under the bed, left the room key on the dresser, taken his bag and gone down to the hotel restaurant for breakfast.

Ramirez had walked back to the Amtrak Station and paid cash for a one-way ticket.

At eleven on Monday morning Kenny was sitting in his seat on the train, three hours out of Wilmington headed toward Chicago.

He would be arriving in Denver, Colorado at eight Tuesday evening.

Lorraine DiMarco's first call was to Pavel Vasin.

"The witnesses changed their testimony and I'm sure all charges will be dropped. I don't know how you did it, but thank you."

"I am glad it worked out. Lev and Roman are good men. All they needed was a reminder from *very* good parents. Some things are far more persuasive than threats from gangsters."

"I guess they'll be looking for new jobs."

"They'll have no trouble. They are both fine chefs."

"Let me know where I can send payment for your services."

"I did this for the family. However, if you have need of my assistance in the future, I would be glad to be of service. The work would be good for me."

"I'll keep it in mind," Lorraine said. "Thank you, again."

Lorraine called Alex Holden at his bakery.

"Thank you," he said when he heard the news.

"You can thank Rachel's uncle, Pavel."

"I will."

"Alex."

"Yes?"

"Watch your back."

"The NYPD has two officers following me everywhere I go. I don't know whether to feel privileged or stalked."

"Feel privileged."

Lorraine finally called the 61st Precinct to speak with Ivanov. She was connected to Ripley.

"Marina is out until tomorrow. You might try her at home."

"Thanks, I will."

"Lorraine."

"Yes?"

"Would you like to have dinner?"

"I have dinner almost every night."

"I meant would you like to have dinner with me."

"Sorry, I can't help trying to be clever sometimes—particularly when I'm feeling good. I know what you meant. Would Wednesday work for you?"

"It would work fine," Ripley said.

"Then it's a date. Give me a shout Wednesday afternoon."

Earlier that Monday morning, Maureen Rose had called the front office at Lafayette High School to report that her husband was ill and would not be coming in to work.

Just past noon, Principal William Pabst called the Rose home to check on his new school psychologist.

"How is David feeling, Mrs. Rose?"

"Not very well, thanks for asking. Hopefully it is only a late summer cold. If he is not feeling better in the morning, he plans to see a doctor."

"I am sorry to hear it. We will put him on day-to-day sick leave. Please keep us updated, and tell your husband we wish him a speedy recovery."

"I will, and thank you again for your concern."

Rosen and Murphy walked out of their meeting with two IAB detectives after clearing up the details regarding the altercation with Joshua Altman on Saturday, and after being given a clean bill of professional health.

"How about lunch?" Murphy asked.

"What a total waste of time that was," Rosen said. "Could they have come up with even one more stupid question?"

"They could have asked if you were in fear for your life."

"Are *you* asking?"

"I guess I am."

"Not for a moment. I have envisioned a number of ways I might meet my maker, Tommy—but that was not one of them. Lunch sounds great."

Samson and his wife, Alicia, sat in a small conference room at Long Island Jewish Medical Center with Dr. Alan Jackson. Jackson was the surgeon who had been in charge of tending to Jimmy Samson's gunshot injuries six days earlier.

"As you are aware, your son has been removed from the critical list and released from the Intensive Care Unit. His condition is stable. As I mentioned before, the extent of long term disabilities will take some time to determine—weeks if not months. It will be a gradual and strenuous process. Jimmy is a strong, athletic young man—but the damage was considerable. I suggest he be transferred to New York Hospital in Flushing as soon as it is safe to move him."

"Why is that?" Samson asked.

"Their resources for physical and psychological rehabilitation are at least as comprehensive as those at this hospital and, as an employee of the City of New York, you would be afforded better insurance compensation if he was treated in Queens as opposed to here in Long Island."

"Psychological rehabilitation?" Alicia asked.

"It is strongly recommended that Jimmy undergo both physical therapy *and* psychological counseling," the doctor said. "Your son experienced both types of trauma. Psychological effects are more difficult to evaluate and easier to conceal—and can be equally debilitating. Please trust me on this."

"Of course," Samson said, gently squeezing his wife's hand.

The Avenue Bakery had been serving residents of Crown Heights in Brooklyn for more than thirty years, and had gained a reputation which now brought customers in from all parts of the borough. The shop sat nestled among a variety of retail store-fronts on Nostrand Avenue, between President and Carroll Streets. The bakery had been established by Saul Holden, who apprenticed his only son in the business from the time the boy was in grade school. When illness left Saul too weak to manage the strenuous day-to-day duties of running the business, his son Alex took over the operation.

When his father passed-away two years earlier, Alex inherited the well-established enterprise—lock, stock and apron.

Alex and his two baker assistants arrived at four in the morning, seven mornings a week, to prepare the breads, rolls and pastries needed for opening inventory. His helpers remained until noon, continuing to prepare additional pastries, pies, cakes and special orders. Two more employees, Katherine and Susan, arrived at seven to open the bakery and manage the front of the shop. Both left at three. Alex remained to run the bakery, alone, until closing at six.

That Monday afternoon, Alex was whistling as he worked, feeling good. He had just learned he would not have to serve time in prison for defending his own life.

Just before one, a man walked into the shop and approached the retail counter. He greeted Katherine with a hearty "good day" and a broad smile.

"Good day to you, sir," Katherine said, returning the smile. "How can we help you?"

"I would like to order a birthday cake for my dear mother."

"We have a number of excellent choices in the display case at your right."

"I was hoping for something special, something custom made perhaps."

"Would you be needing that tomorrow?"

"I would need it today."

"I'm not sure we could have a special order ready for you today. I would need to check with Mr. Holden."

"Would you do that?"

"Certainly, sir, give me a minute," Katherine said, and she headed back to the kitchen.

Alex followed Katherine from the kitchen a minute later and walked around to the front of the counter to greet the customer.

"Alex Holden," he said, extending his hand.

"Pleased to meet you," the man said, accepting the hand shake. "You have a wonderful shop—highly recommended."

"Thank you. Please follow me," Alex said.

He led the man to a small table at the front window while Susan and Katherine attended to other customers.

"We usually require more time for special orders," Alex said.

"I was supposed to come in yesterday, but I was occupied with my two very demanding children. And I was tied up with business all morning. If I fail to provide one of *your* cakes for my mother's birthday this evening, my sisters will kill me. I would be more than happy to pay the full cost in advance."

"Would six this evening work for you?"

"I may be a few minutes late."

"I can wait a short while past six. Let me show you some photographs so we can get started."

Murphy and Rosen left Clemente's Maryland Crab House in Sheepshead Bay, crossed the parking lot, and climbed into the car.

"How can you eat that much and not need a nap?" Rosen asked.

"Who said I don't need a nap?"

Murphy put the key in the ignition and let it rest.

"What now?" Rosen asked.

"I don't know how many more times we can ask the same people the same questions without losing our audience appeal. I suppose we could go back to Avenue J and look for the one of hundreds of kids wearing Midwood High School jackets like the one in the flower shop."

"You never told me what was so important you had to run over to my place Saturday night after trying to out-drink Augie Sena. Not that I'm sorry you showed up."

Murphy told her what had been on his mind.

"Not very much, thinking back on it," he said.

"*Not very much* sounds promising right now. Let's go talk to him again."

"Can we take that nap first?"

Samson walked into a deserted squad room just past one.

Everyone is out making headway, he thought, optimistically.

He moved into his office and began attacking the pile of paperwork that had been accumulating as a result of his frequent visits to hospitals.

He was anxious to get home to his wife and his two young daughters, but needed to wait until the troops reported in.

Chief of Detectives Trenton phoned to speak with Captain Samson thirty minutes later.

"We will be releasing the details of Jennifer Greco's death tomorrow, and introducing the suspicion Patricia Bolin's death may not have been a suicide. We need to encourage parents and young women to be more vigilant, and the suggestion that the two deaths could be related may elicit useful testimony."

"I can think of at least one of my detectives who will be glad to hear that."

"Please tell *all* of your detectives their discretion thus far has been greatly appreciated. I am not so far removed to have forgotten how terrible it is to have to lie or withhold information from a victim's family."

"I will."

"The parents of the two girls will be informed before the announcement. I will take care of it, personally."

"Thank you."

"I have chosen a detective to temporarily replace Bernie Senderowitz."

"Who?"

"Danny Maggio. Maggio earned his shield a year ago, and has already been decorated. I spoke with his CO at the Fifth Precinct in Manhattan, *and* with Maggio. They are both agreeable to a temporary transfer. Danny grew up in Gravesend."

"I knew his father," Samson said.

"Maggio will report to you at the Six-one tomorrow morning at nine."

"Good."

"Now," Stan Trenton said, "tell me how your son is doing."

Her son arrived home from school and began asking questions she had no answers for.

Questions about why his father had been out the entire night before, and had not yet returned home.

"Your father had to leave town on business, he received a call late last night and left very early this morning."

"When will he be back?"

"He wasn't sure, he will let us know. Now, take care of your homework. If you get it done before dinner you can watch a movie later."

After the boy went to his room, she sat at the kitchen table staring at the wall telephone—not sure if she was waiting for it to ring, or waiting to find the courage to use it.

TWENTY SIX

Richards and Ripley had spent most of the morning and early afternoon scouting the neighborhood with the faint hope they would come across Kenny Ramirez strolling down the street enjoying the sunny September day. Every twenty minutes they circled back to Bay 38th Street on the chance Kenny had decided on one more of Mom's home cooked meals before skipping town.

A call from Officer Landis sent them to West 7th Street to investigate a shooting incident. Landis met them at their car as they pulled up.

"Twenty-nine-year-old male victim, seated at the kitchen table, two fatal gunshot wounds in the back. We found the suspect, his wife, sitting on the front porch with the weapon in her lap," Stan Landis said. "She is handcuffed in the back of the squad car. Mendez is inside waiting for you and the medical examiner and forensics."

"Did she say anything?" Ripley asked.

"She said he had called her a *fat pig* one too many times."

"Stay with the woman," Ripley said.

The two detectives entered the house.

Thirty minutes later they were heading back to the Six-one.

When Ripley and Richards popped into the squad room at three, Samson threw them an arm wave through his office window—but stayed put. He had decided he would wait until Rosen and Murphy came in, so he could avoid having to say everything twice. When Sandra and Tommy finally appeared, the captain called them all together for a pow-wow.

"I spoke with Chief Trenton," Samson began. "The true

nature of Jenny Greco's death will be officially revealed tomorrow."

"It's about time," Rosen said.

Samson let it pass, he understood Rosen's frustration.

"It will also be suggested that Patty Bolin's death was not a suicide as previously considered."

"I will not go back to those parents and tell them we lied."

"Detective Rosen, don't say you will not do something before you are asked to do it. It could easily be perceived as premature insubordination. Chief Trenton will be handling the notifications. He asked me to thank you all for sitting on this for so long. Ivanov will be rejoining us tomorrow," Samson continued, promptly changing the subject. "We will also be joined by Daniel Maggio of the Fifth Precinct. Danny will partner with Ripley until Senderowitz, hopefully, gets back on his feet. He is a well-respected young detective, and he knows Gravesend. I worked with his old man before most of you kids climbed into your first uniform. I'll leave it at that for now—you will learn more when you meet him in the morning. Any luck today, Murphy?"

"I guess we were lucky at Internal Affairs, but after that luck slipped out the back door. We did try to do a follow-up interview at the high school, but the subject was out for the day."

"What was that about?"

"It was about something *you* said," Murphy answered. "One of the staff was much less inquisitive than the others when we spoke with them earlier. It got me wondering why."

"I remember what I said, but it is often just a matter of personality. It may be nothing."

"When you ain't got nothing, you got nothing to lose. We can go back to see him in the morning."

"Let me think about it. Is there anything new on Kenny Ramirez?"

"Nothing," Ripley said. "I think he flew the coop and could be halfway to anywhere by now."

"Let's reach out to neighboring states with an APB and a warrant," Samson said. "New Jersey, Connecticut, Pennsylvania,

Delaware, for starters. I suggest we all go home and get some rest, tomorrow will be another busy day—beginning at nine sharp."

"Captain," Rosen said.

"Forget it Sandra. Just do your job and don't try to do Chief Trenton's. Believe me, you wouldn't want Trenton's job."

Kenny Ramirez sat alone in the crowded dining car of the Amtrak Capitol Limited, working on a cheeseburger with the works and a Coors Light.

Ramirez occasionally gazed through the window, out over the countryside surrounding Alliance, Ohio. An older man approached and politely asked if he could share the small table.

Wise enough to know that rudeness was often recalled more clearly than courtesy—Kenny invited the man to join him. Ramirez was in no mood for chit-chat, but his table companion was a talker. He started running his mouth the moment he was seated opposite Kenny.

"Jim Spencer," he said, extending his hand in greeting.

"Dave," Kenny said, accepting the handshake.

"Where are you headed, Dave?"

"Chicago."

"Business?"

"Home. Returning from a conference in D.C."

"What do you do?"

Ramirez reached into his pocket, pulled out a wallet, and produced a business card. He passed it across the table. Spencer gave it a quick look.

"It must be interesting and rewarding work."

"It has its moments," Kenny said. He finished what was left of his beer and rose to leave the table. "Enjoy your meal and the rest of your trip."

"Thank you. Good meeting you, Dave."

"Likewise," Kenny said, and he exited the dining car.

On his way back to his seat, Ramirez tossed the wallet out through an open window.

. . .

By five-thirty, Samson was sitting at the dinner table with his wife and their two daughters.

The girls had not seen their big brother Jimmy in nearly a week.

"When is Jimmy coming home?" Kayla asked.

"It may be awhile, sweetheart," Samson told his eight-year-old.

"Can I have his room? Lucy snores."

"Do not," her five-year-old sister said.

Kayla began giggling and soon Alicia and Samson joined in laughing.

"Do not," Lucy said.

Richards kissed Linda as soon as he came through the door, then he immediately went to Sophia's crib. Richards gently lifted his eight-month-old daughter up into his arms as his wife came up behind him.

"I'm worried, Martin," Linda said.

"No sense worrying too much before the follow-up tests on Wednesday."

"Will she be alright?"

"If she has a heart as strong and true as her mother's, she will be just fine," Richards said.

Murphy and Rosen took Ralph down to Shore Road Park.

They strolled beneath the Verrazano Bridge near Fort Hamilton while the dog chased squirrels.

"Does he ever grab one?" Rosen asked.

"Never. He just likes to show them he could if he wanted to."

"I think I pissed the captain off this afternoon."

"Not even close," Murphy said. "Sam knows you, trusts you, and he gets it. And he has developed a high threshold of tolerance working with me for so long. It would take a whole lot more than *premature* insubordination to make Samson blink. Speaking of which."

"What?"

"Are you ready for that nap now?"

Ripley picked his boys up from his sister Connie and took them to a kid-friendly pizza restaurant on Queens Boulevard.

He was a little preoccupied looking forward to meeting a new partner in the morning and dinner with Lorraine DiMarco on Wednesday.

"Dad?"

"Yes, Kyle."

"Can I borrow forty-two thousand dollars?"

"What for, son?"

"I want to buy Mickey a BMW for his birthday so when he is old enough to drive he'll have a sweet ride, and a classic," Kyle said, grinning.

"Good thinking. Let me check what I have in my piggy bank," Ripley said.

"Don't talk," Mickey said. "It's *my* birthday."

"Yes, it is, son. In four days."

"I'll be six."

"Yes, you will, son," Ripley said, finding it hard to believe how time flew.

Marina Ivanov was anxious to get back to the job after her involuntary three-day sabbatical. Aside from a very pleasant evening with Jack Falcone on Saturday, she had been going stir crazy waiting for Tuesday morning.

Monday evening she was sitting beside her sister on the living room sofa at her parent's home as their father entertained his two girls with tales of *his* father's adventures as a circus performer in pre-World War II Russia.

Their mother was busy in the kitchen, preparing a special

dinner to celebrate the good news about Alex Holden's exoneration.

Marina's sister Rachel glanced at the grandfather clock in the corner of the room, brought over by her grandparents from Leningrad. It was forty minutes past five. Alex usually stayed at the bakery for at least an hour after closing shop to take care of miscellaneous business but this evening, for the occasion, he would be on his way as soon as he locked up at six. He would be joining them very soon.

"Did grandfather really put his head into a lion's mouth?" Marina asked her father.

"He had to."

"Why?" Rachel asked.

"Because the lion's head could not fit into *his* mouth," their father answered, and had his daughters laughing hysterically.

Two police officers sat in their vehicle across Nostrand Avenue opposite the Avenue Bakery. They had been sitting there all afternoon.

Farley sat in the driver's seat watching the front door of the shop, while Kenton was buried in the sports section of *The New York Post.*

Kenton looked up from the newspaper.

"I don't know about you, but I could eat a horse," he said.

"Pinto or Appaloosa?"

"I say we run down to the delicatessen at the corner and grab dinner. Sit down and eat like human beings."

"We can't both leave. Bring a brisket sandwich back for me."

"You're no fun," Kenton said, leaving the vehicle.

At six, a man entered the bakery shop.

Kenton returned later with a sack full of food.

"A customer walked into the shop about twenty minutes ago and hasn't come out," Farley said.

"Let's eat while this food is still warm and before the bread turns into bread pudding," his partner said. "Then we can check it out."

. . .

At six, as Alex headed to the front to lock up, the customer who had special ordered the birthday cake earlier that afternoon walked in.

"Sorry if I kept you waiting."

"Actually you are just in time. The cake turned out very well. I thought you might like to see it before it was boxed. It's in back, give me a moment."

Holden returned, and carefully placed the cake on the counter between them.

When Alex looked up, there was a gun pointed at him.

"Open the cash register," the man said.

Alex complied without hesitation.

"Empty the contents into a bag, and don't do anything stupid."

Alex did as he was told, trying to avoid looking at the man's face.

"That's all of it," Alex said. "I have nothing else to offer you, unless you would like the cake."

"Is there a back door?"

"Yes. Locked from inside, a simple twist of the dead bolt and you're out to the alley."

"Good. I guess I'll be on my way."

With that, he shot Alex Holden three times in the chest.

TWENTY SEVEN

Samson called Chief Trenton from his office very early Tuesday morning.

"What made you think I wasn't asleep?"

"I wasn't thinking about it. Good morning."

"We'll see. What is it?"

"Alexander Holden was shot to death in his bakery shop last evening."

"I heard the news last night. And you want the Six-one to handle the investigation."

"What are you, a mind reader?"

"Am I wrong?"

"No."

"The crime was perpetrated in Crown Heights, Sam."

"I'm aware of that. I'm asking a favor. You owe me at least one. And, at the end of the day, you have the power to assign any case to any precinct in the borough at your pleasure."

"And if I agree, I will be in debt to Captain Anderson at the Seven-seven. And frankly, Sam, I'd rather owe you. I'm damned if I do, and damned if I don't. And *pleasure* is not exactly how I would describe the power."

"It's what you signed on for, Chief."

"Do you find this funny?" Trenton asked.

"No. I don't find anything very funny lately."

"I'll call Anderson and make a humble request."

"Thank you, Stan."

"I'll ask when two of your detectives can meet with the primaries at the Seventy-seventh who caught the case, and I will let you know."

"Good."

"Sam," Trenton said.

270

"Yes?"

"Make sure one of them is not Detective Ivanov."

"I wouldn't think of it. Sorry if I woke you."

Principal William Pabst was gazing out of his office window when the phone rang.

"Mrs. Rose is on the line for you, sir."

"Thank you, Millie, please put her through."

Pabst settled into the chair behind his desk.

"Mrs. Rose, good morning. How are you?"

"Fine, thank you. I am afraid my husband is not doing so well, he was diagnosed with strep throat. David suffered head-aches, high fever and throat pain all day yesterday and was given a rapid antigen test. He is now taking antibiotics. He may be out for a few more days."

"Tell David to take all of the time he needs. There is no reason to risk impeding a full recovery, or risk exposing others to possible contagion. Please give him our best wishes."

"Thank you, I will."

Pabst replaced the phone in its cradle.

There is absolutely no reason to think the woman was not being entirely truthful, he thought. *So what is troubling me?*

All hands were on deck when Samson called the troops together at nine on Tuesday morning.

He began by welcoming Ivanov back, and introducing Danny Maggio to the squad and to his new partner.

"As some of you have heard, Alexander Holden was shot to death in Crown Heights last evening. Chief Trenton has granted my request to run the investigation out of the Six-one. Ripley and Maggio will visit Detectives Maddox and Lombard at the Seven-seven later this morning, get everything they have collected thus far, and hopefully take over the case. It is presently being considered a robbery/homicide, and until we know more it will be treated as such. If there are any questions or problems concerning this arrangement," Samson said, looking at Marina Ivanov, "speak now."

No one did.

"Ivanov and Richards are on Kenny Ramirez," Samson continued. "I agree he has probably fled New York, so we will need to get word out to the surrounding states I listed last evening. Get photos out to the state and county officials, and politely ask that they filter the information to the locals. Let's get photos out to news services in all of those states, and ask them to run a photograph of the subject in the major dailies. Ramirez knows we are looking for him, so we may as well let everyone else know. Ramirez is wanted for murder, so we should get cooperation. It is trying to find a needle in a larger haystack, but it is all we have unless Ramirez turns himself in. I have put in a request for real time reports on all phone calls in and out of his mother's home, and I expect it to be granted. You should also speak to his co-workers at the trucking company on the chance he has made contact, and try to find out if there is anyone outside of New York he may reach out to for help.

"Rosen and Murphy, you will continue on the Greco/Bolin cases. With any luck, the announcement from the department later today will shake a tree or two. I would like to talk with you about the uneasy feeling you expressed last evening before you do any follow-up interviews at the high school.

"We have a lot on our plates. We are a team, but will we make more progress if you all remain focused on your particular investigations—please do so, unless an emergency necessitates otherwise. We will meet every evening at five to make sure everyone is updated on all of the ongoing cases. If there are no questions, go to work. Sandra and Tommy, let's have a quick word in my office."

With that, Murphy and Rosen followed Samson, and the others got down to business.

Kenny Ramirez sat looking out of the window as western Iowa raced by beneath him. Nebraska and Colorado lay ahead,

Illinois safely behind. Moving into and out of places where he had never been.

Passing through.

He played with the burner cell phone he had picked up at an all-night kiosk at Chicago Union Station. He wanted very much to call his mother, but he knew better. He wished he would have thought to get her a phone like it before he left New York.

Kenny tried remembering the night a week earlier that had changed his life forever, but the visions were hallucinatory and surreal—it was like trying to recall a terrible dream, like trying to make sense of something senseless. When he saw the two of them through the open bedroom door in *his* bed in *his* home, he lost himself. He went to find his gun without thinking, and shot them both without hesitation.

Kenny tried to understand why he had acted so quickly, so instinctually. It was *their* fault, *they* asked for it, *they* had it coming, *they* made him do it. It was rage, shock, disappointment, retribution, any of an endless list of emotions that may have pushed him to act so rashly, so fatally.

And then, for a moment, Kenny Ramirez toyed with the idea it was love. He acted as he had because he truly loved his wife. But he quickly chased the thought away, terrified by its implications and its irrationality.

As the Omaha skyline came into view, all Kenny was left wondering was how long he could survive.

"I would like you to postpone visiting the high school for the time being," Samson said.

"What do you suggest we do *during* the time being," Murphy asked.

"I suggest you write up individual statements concerning the events of Saturday night. You have a meeting with ADA Randall Washington at his office at eleven-thirty. Washington will being handling the prosecution's case against Josh Altman."

"What will the charges be?" Rosen asked.

"Something like abduction and forced imprisonment with the

threat of serious physical harm, and armed assault against an NYPD detective. It will not go well for Altman. I realize it is difficult to testify against one of our own, but Altman crossed the line, and he is clearly dangerous. Do not be tempted to sugar-coat your statements."

"Understood," Rosen said.

"If, afterwards, you still feel compelled to follow up on your concerns about an employee at the high school regarding his failure to bombard you with foolish questions—wait until the school day is over. Perhaps you can visit the subject's home."

"Are you trivializing my instincts, Captain?" Murphy said.

"I would never, Detective."

Sarah Sanders walked up the stairs leading to Bernie Senderowitz's door.

She emptied the mailbox, pulled the key from her pocket, and walked into her father's apartment.

What greeted Sarah was disheartening.

Her plan was to quickly clean the apartment, to have it look and feel like home when her father was eventually released from the hospital—but as she looked around she realized there would be nothing quick about it. The place appeared as what it was—somewhere to sleep and drink and not much more.

The refrigerator held various fast food leftovers, the kitchen sink held empty glasses sticky with alcohol, the bed was unmade, and articles of clothing were dropped haphazardly on the bed-room floor. The bathroom was relatively clean, but the hamper overflowed with laundry.

A small table at the front entrance was piled high with mail, with more mail spilled onto the floor at its feet.

Sarah realized she would need some time and supplies to do the clean-up job, and decided to tackle the task later in the day. Instead, she gathered all of the mail, moved it to the kitchen table and began going through it. Discarding junk mail, and sep-arating those correspondences she would bring to Senderowitz when she visited the hospital.

She found the note she had left in her father's mailbox nearly two weeks earlier.

"Oh, Bernie," she said aloud. "What do I do about you?"

Ripley and Maggio sat in an interview room with Detectives Lombard and Maddox at the 77th Precinct in Crown Heights.

"Alexander Holden was fatally shot, three times in the chest, at close range—almost certainly across the display counter in the bakery shop. The cash registered had been emptied. Holden and the shooter were alone in the shop, all other employees having left by three. He was killed between six and six-thirty. The shooter exited the rear door to the alley. There were no known witnesses and no reports of gunshots," Lombard began.

"How did you establish the time?" Ripley asked.

"As you are aware, there were two officers stationed outside the shop to guard Holden from possible threats. Holden traditionally closed the shop at six, and then remained to do whatever it was he did until leaving an hour or so later. Officer Farley saw a customer arrive just as Holden was about to lock up at six. Holden welcomed the man into the shop, Farley had the impression Holden knew the man. At around six-forty, when no one had exited the shop, Farley and Officer Kenton left their vehicle to investigate. They found the front door unlocked, and Holden behind the counter," Maddox said. "If it is determined the officers were in any way derelict in their duty, it will be dealt with accordingly—however that will be the one aspect of the investigation which will remain with the Seventy-seventh. We take care of our own house cleaning here, as we are sure you do in the Six-one."

"Understood," Maggio said.

"Anything to add?" Ripley asked.

"We have been canvassing the area since last evening and into this morning with no results. I think we pretty much exhausted the field. We can give you a list of all of the people we spoke with—so you do not have to duplicate our efforts if you decide to continue interviewing," Lombard said.

"We trust you covered the bases," Maggio said, "but we *will* take the list, and all of the evidence collected thus far, to insure the case file is complete going forward. It wasn't our idea to take the case away from you—we do what we're told."

"No sweat," Maddox said, "we have our hands full as it is."

"Do you think it was a robbery?" Ripley asked.

Before either could answer, the Desk Sergeant was at the door.

"Detectives, there is a man here who says he knows something about the shooting last evening."

"Bring him down here, Coleman," Maddox said.

Maddox looked over to Lombard, both rose from their seats, and started out of the interview room.

"It's all yours," Maddox said, and they were gone.

The squad room of the Six-one was a hive of busy bees.

Captain Samson was sequestered in his office, painfully putting together a budget for the precinct, knowing his final proposals would be cut to pieces.

Rosen and Murphy sat at their respective computer terminals, hunting and pecking at their keyboards, writing statements regarding the shooting and arrest of Detective Josh Altman.

Ivanov and Richards were running between phones and the fax machine, alerting four neighboring states about a wanted fugitive named Kenny Ramirez.

Samson called down to Sergeant Kelly at the front desk.

"Is Officer Mendez in the house?"

"He and Landis just rolled out in their cruiser."

"Get word to Mendez when you have the chance, I'd like to see him in my office at four this afternoon."

Coleman escorted a man of about sixty years old into the interview room.

He was unshaven, poorly dressed, but clean.

He clutched a leather bound bible in his two hands.

"This is Noah Booker, no address," Coleman said. "These are Detectives Maggio and Ripley, Mr. Booker—they will be taking your statement."

Coleman quickly exited.

"Take a seat, Mr. Booker," Maggio said. "Please tell us what you can about what happened last evening on Nostrand Avenue."

"Will it matter what I say?"

"What do you mean?" Ripley asked.

"I live on the street. I've had a little trouble with the police, once or twice. So, will it matter what I tell you?"

"Are you wanted for anything right now?" Maggio asked.

"No."

"Any felony convictions?"

"Never."

"Anything wrong with your eyes or your ears?"

"No."

"And you didn't come all the way down here to waste our time with a load of bullshit."

"I did not."

"Then, it *could* matter what you tell us."

Booker settled into a chair opposite the detectives.

"The boy, Alex, he was good to me. Every evening I knocked at the back door of the bakery, between six-thirty and seven, after he locked up the front. He always gave me something to eat from the shop, bread, cookies, whatever, sometimes he had other food for me, sometimes he threw me a few dollars. I don't drink or do drugs."

"And last evening?" Ripley asked.

"As I was coming up the alley toward the back of the shop, a man came out the rear door. He held his hand down to his side—he may have held a gun."

"Did you get a look at his face?"

"No. He was walking away from me. It was dark in the alley."

"Can you describe him at all?"

"White, six feet, well dressed."

"What then?" Maggio asked.

"I followed the man up the alley. He turned right onto President Street. I turned after him and saw him climb into a car and drive off."

"Can you describe the vehicle?"

"Mid-size. Black."

"That's it?" Ripley asked.

"I got the license plate number."

Booker pulled a small piece of paper from his jacket pocket, torn from a Chinese take-out menu he had picked up off the street. He passed it across the table.

"Son-of-a-bitch," Maggio said.

"I always carry a pencil," Booker said.

"Why didn't you call the police?" Ripley asked.

"First thing I did was go back to the bakery and rap on the back door. No one answered, and it was locked. Then I went around to the front, and the police were already there. And I wasn't sure I wanted to get in the middle of any kind of bad business. But when I heard Alex was killed, I decided it *was* my business."

"Thank you for stepping up, Noah," Ripley said, pulling a business card from his wallet. "What you had to say matters a great deal. If you ever need a hand with anything, give us a call and we will do what we can."

"We would like you to come with us to the Sixty-first Precinct to write up a statement?" Maggio said. "Then lunch is on us."

"Can you give me a ride home after?" Booker said, without irony.

"Anywhere you like," Ripley said.

Ivanov and Richards sat in Al Gerard's office at Eastern States Moving and Hauling in Farmingdale, Long Island—asking the Chief Dispatcher what he knew about Kenny Ramirez.

"I have no idea whether Ramirez has talked to anyone. I haven't heard from him since it happened. And you're not going to find anyone here in the terminal, they are all out driving. We go as far south as Florida, as far west as Illinois and Missouri, and often pick up more cargo on the other end. Drivers are sometimes out for days. The best place to catch a trucker is at home, and they're never at home."

"Is there anyone who Ramirez was particularly friendly with?"

"Ramirez was not the friendly type, and the drivers rarely see each other or buddy up. But, come to think of it, there was one guy who Ramirez seemed pretty tight with."

"Name?"

"Raul Sandoval."

"Can we get an address?"

"I don't have one. Sandoval was from Colorado. His mother had some serious medical problems and he moved back to Denver about six months ago. I can give you his SSN and a photocopy of his CDL license if it would help."

"It could," Richards said.

The meeting with the Assistant District Attorney went quickly, and the two detectives were back in their car just after noon.

"He is going to lose his job, probably serve time."

"He had you in handcuffs, took a shot at me."

"Josh has serious psychological problems."

"He does, but I don't think that will help him much."

"Am I that irresistible?"

"Except first thing in the morning before coffee," Murphy said.

"It's not funny."

"I know, Sandra, it is sad—but we didn't write the script, and we're lucky it played out the way it did."

"What now?"

"I guess we go back to the high school, but I agree with Sam about waiting until school is out. If we can't catch him there, we can try getting a home address from Pabst."

"And now?"

"Now we take Ralph for a quick run, and then do what we usually do at this time of day."

"Lunch?"

"Lunch," Murphy said.

"Thank God for tradition."

Ripley and Maggio escorted Noah Booker into the Six-one as Samson was headed out. Maggio took Booker up, Ripley stopped to talk to the captain.

"What do you have?"

"He got a license number on a suspect in the Holden shooting. He's here to write up a statement."

"Hold weight?"

"I think it is good."

"Run the plates, but don't move until you talk to me. I need to run out to Long Island Jewish, Jimmy is being moved to New York Hospital in Queens tomorrow and I need to sign some papers. I should be back by three, no later than four. Call me if you think we need to move sooner."

"I don't believe this was a robbery, Captain."

"Nor do I. It was a hit. And if it leads back to Vladimir Markov, we need to do this right."

Ivanov and Richards were heading back to Brooklyn on the Southern State Parkway. Richards drove. Ivanov was quiet.

"Can you keep your nose out of the Holden case?" Richards asked.

"Can you keep your nose out of my business?"

"Sorry."

Ivanov took a deep breath before speaking.

"No, I'm sorry. I was out of line. I know what you were asking. I fucked up once already, you're trying to offer sound advice and I hear you. I'm glad the case came over to the Six-one. I have total confidence in Ripley, and Maggio has a good rep. I'll trust them to do their job, and we'll do ours. So let's reach out to the Denver PD and see if we can catch a break. How is your daughter?"

"We'll know more after tomorrow," Richards said.

"Good luck."

"Thanks, but I don't know if luck has much to do with it."

"Luck has something to do with everything," Ivanov said, "and sometimes it's actually *good* luck."

Chief of Detectives Stanley Trenton called a press conference at one on Tuesday afternoon. It was televised live on New York One.

Trenton never actually stated the deaths of Jenny Greco and Patty Bolin may have been related, but the insinuation was impossible for the news hungry reporters and a public hungry for answers to ignore. Trenton had been ordered to refuse questions.

The families of the two girls were somewhat prepared. They had been forewarned and asked, emphatically, to avoid or deflect any questions from the media—for the sake of the investigations.

In an apartment in Midwood, a woman who was *unprepared* stood in front of the television as Trenton made the announcement. Her legs went out from under her, and she grabbed onto the couch to keep from crashing into a coffee table.

She pulled herself up onto the sofa and wept.

TWENTY EIGHT

After Maggio helped their witness write up a statement, and Ripley put in a request to run the license plate, the two detectives took Booker to the Del Rio Diner on Kings Highway.

"Why are you living on the street?" Ripley asked.

"I can handle the rent. I was working in the meat department at the Shop Rite on Bay Parkway. They laid quite a few people off. I was expendable. I've been looking for work, but it's difficult to land a job when you have no address, a phone booth for a contact number, and you're closing in on sixty."

"Were you any good?" Maggio asked.

"Modestly speaking, and I have nothing if not humility, I could have run that department a lot more efficiently and successfully—but I didn't have the job seniority and the manager was someone's son-in-law."

"I can't promise anything, but my Uncle Vito owns a butcher shop on Eight-sixth Street. I'll give him a call, see if he is looking for help and willing to give you a shot," Maggio said, pulling a business card from his wallet. "Keep this with Detective Ripley's card. Give me a call in a few days—I'll let you know if Vito is game. And call either of us if you run into any unforeseen dilemma."

"Thank you," Booker said, before going back to the hefty menu.

"What would you like to eat?" Ripley asked.

"Everything," Booker said.

Officers Landis and Mendez were patrolling the neighborhood in their cruiser.

Mendez was driving.

Landis was humming.

"What's with you?" Mendez asked.

"I have a date tonight."

"Someone new?"

"Met him in a bar a few nights ago."

"In a bar?"

"It's either a bar or the supermarket, Rey."

"Do you know much about him?"

"School teacher, lives in Park Slope, great sense of humor."

"He know you're a cop?"

"Yes."

"What's on the agenda?"

"Dinner and a movie."

"Nice. I hope all goes well. Tell the guy if he ever does you wrong, I'll rip his lungs out."

"Thanks, Dad. I'll be sure to mention it."

Mendez answered a call on his cell. He listened, said okay, and put the phone away.

"Salina?" Landis asked.

"Kelly. Samson wants me in his office at four."

"Did you fuck up?"

"It would be pretty hard for me to fuck up without you knowing about it before the captain."

When Ripley and Maggio returned to the Six-one from dropping Noah Booker at a run-down housing project on New York Avenue, Ripley found a fax on his desk.

"Katrina Popovich. Doesn't sound much like a man's name."

"No, it doesn't. What do you have?" Maggio asked.

"The word on the license plate number Booker gave us. Katrina Popovich, twenty-eight years old, Brighton Beach address, black BMW."

"Do you think Booker got it wrong?"

"I really don't."

"Then this guy borrowed a car to go rob a bakery?"

"Stranger things have happened," Ripley said.

"Do we really need the captain's permission before we make any move?"

"I think we can safely get away with having the woman and the vehicle watched, very discreetly, strongly prohibiting any contact."

"You know the captain better than I do."

"Not much better, I've been here less than three weeks, but I think he'll be fine with it as long as no one knows they are being watched. I'll call Jack Falcone over at the Sixtieth—ask him what they can do."

Samson had some time before his scheduled meeting with Rey Mendez.

After taking care of arrangements for the transfer of his son to New York Hospital in Queens the next day, he ran over to Coney Island Hospital for a quick visit with Senderowitz. When he reached the hospital room, he bumped into Sarah Sanders coming out.

"He's doing a lot better. I brought some mail from his place. I'm on my way back there to try making the place look like something other than a war zone."

"Do you need anything?"

"I picked up everything I should need. The back seat of my car looks like a janitor's closet."

"I'm really glad you're with him now."

"I'm willing to give him a chance," Sarah said, "but it's the only chance I have left to give."

Murphy and Rosen met with Principal Pabst in his office.

"We had a few more questions for David Rose," Murphy said, "and we didn't want to barge in on him before seeing you first."

"Mr. Rose has been out the past two days."

"Oh?"

"His wife says he has strep throat."

"What do you think?" Rosen asked.

"Excuse me?"

"You didn't say *he has strep throat,* you said *his wife says* he has strep throat. Any reason to believe it is not the case?"

"Not really."

"Not really? Well that settles it," Murphy said. "Is he sick often?"

"I couldn't really say. Mr. Rose just started here last week. He transferred from a high school in Boston."

"Could you give us a home address?"

When Samson arrived at the Six-one just before four, they were all in the squad room. He stopped at Murphy's desk.

"I'm expecting Mendez any minute. Shouldn't be more than a ten minute meeting. Afterwards, I want everyone together to recap the day. If we get an early start, maybe we can get out of here at a decent hour. Spread the word."

Ten minutes later, Officer Mendez was sitting in Samson's office.

"I hear you and your wife are expecting another child. Congratulations."

"Thank you."

"I'll get right to the point. I put your name in for Detective Third Grade. You've put in the time, and if my request is approved I think you have the talent and determination to keep moving up very quickly. I'll know something by next week."

"If it goes through, will I stay here at the Six-one?"

"It's not up to me, but I'll do what I can."

"I'm going to miss riding with Stan Landis."

"Believe it or not, before I was bumped up I rode with Murphy—and I felt the same way. You get over it."

Four hours out of Denver, Kenny Ramirez phoned Raul Sandoval.

"Where are you?"

"On the Amtrak. Should be there by six-thirty, seven latest."

"Listen, bro. I wanted to be there for you but I caught a haul. I'm on my way to Oakland, and then I have a pick-up in Portland returning to Denver. I won't be back until Thursday morning. You have a phone?"

"A burner."

"Give me the number. Grab a hotel for a few nights. I'll call you when I get back and come pick you up."

Ramirez gave him the cell number.

"I'm really sorry, bro. That's why they call it fucking work."

"It's okay."

"We'll have a serious party when I land."

"Sounds good, Raul," Kenny said.

And then said *fuck,* when Sandoval was off the line.

"All right," Samson said when they were all gathered. "Let's try to make this thorough *and* quick. Ripley, Maggio, you're up."

"We have a witness who saw a suspect exit the rear door of the bakery at the approximate time of the shooting," Maggio said.

"Okay."

"He didn't see the man's face, but made the plate number of the car the man drove off in. We had the plate run. It came back registered to a woman named Katrina Popovich, residing in Brighton Beach."

"Who is she?"

"Don't know yet."

"Well, we need to find out, and find out who might be using her vehicle. She needs to be watched, to see where she goes, and who might be with her or show up."

"I reached out to Falcone. He said he could have the woman, her place and the car watched starting now for at least a day or two," Ripley said.

"Good call. But it's just a car, and who else drives it isn't going to help us if there is no one to positively identify the guy who left the scene."

"There's the cake," Maggio said.

"The cake?"

"All of Holden's employees were interviewed when they arrived to work today, two baker assistants arrived at four in the morning, and the two women who run the front of the shop were in at seven. They showed up for work like any other day, none of them knew about the shooting. But the two women said a man had come into the shop, early yesterday afternoon, ordered a birthday cake, and was supposed to pick it up before closing. There was a birthday cake sitting out on the counter when Holden was found."

"And you think it might be our guy?"

"It's possible," Ripley said. "And both women said they would know him if they saw him again. I asked Falcone to have their watchers try to get photos of any men who show up at Katrina Popovich's place, so we can run them by the women from the bakery for an ID."

"That's a little better. We still need to know who Popovich is, get on that first thing. And ask Falcone to let us know if and when they need to pull their men away, so we can send our own team down to take over. Anything else?"

"No."

"Richards, Ivanov, what have you got?"

"We went out to the trucking company where Ramirez worked before he jumped. There was only one guy he was tight with, Raul Sandoval," Richards said. "Sandoval moved back home to Denver. The Denver PD will keep an eye on Sandoval, and be on the lookout for Ramirez, but for only so long. The detective we spoke with said they were pretty thin on manpower."

"And you got all of the other notices and photographs out?"

"Yes," Ivanov said.

"Murphy, Rosen?"

"We went over to the high school to talk with David Rose again," Murphy said. "We waited until half past two, thought we could catch him at the end of his day."

"Teacher?"

"School Psychologist," Rosen said. "The principal told us Rose had been out sick two days, so we went to the house."

"And?"

"Spoke to the wife. She said he was asleep, had taken sleeping pills. We never got past the door. We gave her a card, asked that he call."

"Okay."

"We get to our car and see a kid in a Midwood High School jacket go in. The guy who was asking about printing services at the flower shop, where the phone number of the auto repair flyers we found around the Bolin crime scene led us, was with a kid in a Midwood jacket."

"Those jackets are not unusual in Midwood."

"In the car we ran Rose's name, and his wife's, through DMV for registered vehicles. They show one car, a late model silver Camry. It's not in the driveway, and it's not on the street. If the guy is knocked out in bed and his wife is at home, where's the car?" Murphy said.

"In the repair shop or parked around the corner? If you are thinking this guy Rose is involved in the Greco and Bolin killings you're reaching."

"What we're doing is working the case, we're trying."

"How long has Rose been at the school?"

"He just started—moved over from a school in Boston."

"Find out where and why before you go back to the house."

"Got it."

"If there's nothing else," Samson said, "I'd like to blow this pop stand."

There was nothing else. Gradually, they all left the precinct.

Kenny Ramirez walked out of Union Station in Denver with no idea about where he was or where to go. Kenny did what you do when you blow into a strange city with no clues, he approached a taxi driver.

"Where can I find a hotel around here?"

"A hotel down here is going to set you back two-fifty, minimum."

"Two hundred and fifty dollars?"

"Minimum."

"You've got to be fucking kidding me."

"Down on East Colfax you can get a room for around eighty-five. It's not far, two miles or so."

"Take me," Kenny said.

When Ramirez left the cab, in front of the hotel, he looked around. A 7-Eleven store just to the east. A bar on the west side which, by the looks of the congregation at the entrance, was a gay club. A row of shops across the avenue including a Middle Eastern restaurant, a smoke shop, and a Wendy's.

At the check-in desk he asked for a room for two nights.

"Eighty-four-ninety-nine a night," the girl said.

The cab driver knew his stuff.

Kenny put two one-hundred-dollar bills on the counter.

"Do you have a credit card, sir?"

"No."

"Then you will have to put down a refundable two-hundred-dollar room deposit to cover any additional charges. Damage, mini-bar, phone calls."

In no mood to argue, Ramirez dropped two more C-notes on top of the first two.

"Keep the change," he said.

He filled out a form, using the name James Spencer. Where it asked for an address, he simply wrote Chicago. The desk clerk didn't ask for ID. He took his key and went up to his room on the second floor.

He took a shower, changed clothes, and went out to stretch his legs after the thirty-six-hour train ride.

Four blocks west of the hotel, Kenny spotted a restaurant and bar called The Irish Snug.

He went in.

. . .

After putting the girls to bed, Samson and Alicia sat together on the living room sofa. Samson had said hardly a word since arriving home.

"What is it?" his wife asked.

"We have at least four open homicide cases, and Kenny Ramirez is in the wind—God knows where," Samson said. "Sometimes I wish I was buried in a basement somewhere, clerking an evidence room."

"No you don't."

"It's all the violence, Alicia, all the death."

"James?"

"Yes?"

"What would you have done if you were Ramirez?"

"What do you mean?"

"If you came home one day and you found your wife in bed with another man, what would you do?"

"That's a foolish question—like asking what I would do if the sun rose in the west. It could never happen."

"Try to forget me in particular for a moment, my unquestionable fidelity. Try to put yourself in his shoes for a moment."

"I try putting myself into the shoes of every felon who comes into my world. That is what makes the job so terrible, and so intoxicating. It is how I form speculation about motive, how I develop assumptions about what the criminal was thinking before the crime and *is* thinking after, come up with ideas on how to outsmart him and bring him in. But if I were really in his shoes, found myself in a situation where reason doesn't necessarily prevail, I don't know what I would do. And I doubt Kenny Ramirez knew what he would do until it actually happened."

"Do you feel sorry for him?"

"I feel sorry for all of them."

After a very enjoyable evening, which included a fine Italian dinner in mid-Manhattan and a laugh-out-loud French comedy at the Angelica Cinema in Greenwich Village, Stan Landis and Steven Wallace sat in Stan's parked car in front of Wallace's residence, which sat above a beauty salon on Fifth Avenue in Bay Ridge.

"Your partner sounds like quite a character."

"Rey Mendez is one in a million. He is impossible, totally loveable, and a great cop. I trust him with my life. I'm going to miss riding with him."

"Did something happen?"

"A promotion is about to happen. Rey is up for a detective's shield. When it comes through, as I am certain it will, we'll be riding in different types of vehicles."

"What about you?"

"Me?"

"Detective Landis has a nice ring to it."

"It does, but I'll need to put some more time in first. I'll get my turn, as long as sexual preference has nothing to say about it."

"Could it?"

"It's a lot better in the department than it was, but we're not quite there yet. Bottom line is, one never knows but can always hope."

"That's pretty much the bottom line for everything," Steve said. "Would you like to come up for a drink?"

"What do you have to drink?"

"Almost everything, and there is a liquor store just across the street if I don't have what you like."

Landis looked across the avenue and then turned to Wallace.

"Call nine-one-one, Steve, now. Report a ten-twenty, a robbery in progress, and give the location of the liquor store. Tell the operator it's a ten-thirteen, an officer needs immediate assistance, and give my name. And, Steve, please do not leave this vehicle. "

"What are you going to do?"

"Whatever I have to do," Landis said, and he climbed out of the car.

TWENTY NINE

Murphy was staring at the screen of his desktop computer Wednesday morning when his cell phone rang.

"Miss me, Rosen?"

"I guess I did, wait a minute while I reload."

"Nice."

"I thought I would swing by your place and pick you up, we can grab breakfast before we go in."

"I'm already in, been here since six."

"What got into you?"

"It was the meeting yesterday afternoon. Every time I opened my mouth, Samson seemed to shoot me down."

"That's Samson," Rosen said. "He's famous for playing devil's advocate."

"I think it was his way of telling me to do the work."

"Find anything?"

"Maybe. But there is still something missing. I'll show you what I found when you get in."

"I'm on my way. I'll bring coffee and bagels."

"See if you can find me a scrambled egg, bacon and cheese on hard roll."

Samson walked in ten minutes later.

"You're in bright and early," Murphy said. "Can I show you something?"

"Not this minute."

"What's wrong?"

"Stan Landis was shot and killed last night."

"Jesus Christ, what the fuck happened?"

"I'll tell you what I know when everyone else gets in. Right now, I have to call Rey Mendez and ruin his fucking day too."

. . .

"I said stay home for a couple of days, Rey. Don't make me have to say it a third time."

"Yes, sir."

"I'll see you this evening at the wake."

"Yes, sir."

Mendez had already been in uniform when Samson called. He changed into a pair of cargo shorts, Nike running shoes, and a Brooklyn Nets T-shirt. He walked into the kitchen. Salina was trying to feed the three kids.

"What's with the homeboy outfit?"

"Stan Landis was killed last night."

"Oh my God, Rey, I am so sorry."

"The captain asked me to take a few days off. I need to get out for a while and clear my head. Run. I shouldn't be more than a couple of hours."

"I'll have breakfast for you when you get back."

Mendez took the elevator down to the ground floor, walked out of the building, got into his car, and went looking for Stump.

Rosen walked into the squad room holding two white paper bags. She spotted Samson in his office and came to Murphy's desk. "Kelly just told me about Landis. Fuck. How is Sam taking it?"

"He's angry."

"What do we know?"

"The captain said he'll fill us all in when the others get here."

"Fuck."

"Let's try to get our minds off it until he talks to us. This might help a little. Take a look," Murphy said, tapping his computer monitor.

"What am I looking at? I forgot my binoculars at home."

"It's a death notice from a rag called the *Newton Tab*, this past April."

"Newton?"

"Massachusetts. Mary Ellen Rose, seventeen, died in the home of her parents. She was survived by her father, David Rose, a school psychologist at Fenway High School, mother, Maureen Rose, and brother, Jason, fifteen."

"Cause of death?"

"Not mentioned, but I called the Newton PD and they sent this," Murphy said, handing Rosen a fax.

"Suicide by hanging, holy fuck."

"Nice colloquialism."

"Did you show this to Samson?"

"He wasn't ready for new business. But I would like to know why this girl decided seventeen years was long enough."

"It says here she was a student at Newton South High School," Rosen said, "give the school a call."

"I was waiting for you. To make the call, and for my egg sandwich."

Mendez found Stump on a bench at Seth Low Park in Bensonhurst watching a basketball game. The bench was the man's office. The man's street name was a consequence of a run-in with a pit bull belonging to a Brooklyn drug dealer, resulting in the loss of a right hand. Stump was Rey's confidential informant. Rey's CI was an encyclopedia of Brooklyn criminal activity. From behind the bench, Mendez placed a hand on Stump's shoulder.

"Jesus, Rey, you trying to give me a heart attack?"

"You need to *have* a heart for one of those," Mendez said, sitting on the bench.

"Is that a nice way to talk to a man when you about to ask a favor."

"Stan Landis was killed."

"Shit, Rey, I'm sorry to hear that. I liked Stan. I know you was tight."

"You know a guy named Jerry Paxton?"

"I heard the name. Bay Ridge I think. You need to talk to him?"

"I wish I could, but Jerry's dead. I'd like to know who he might have partnered with on a liquor store stick-up."

"I could ask around."

"Do it quietly, I don't want to spook anyone into going underground."

"I'll be extra careful who I ask and how I ask it."

"Thanks. You still have my cell number?"

"Right here," Stump said, tapping a finger to his forehead. "Listen, Rey?"

"Yes?"

"I hate to ask at a time like this."

Mendez pulled out his wallet and he placed two twenty-dollar bills into Stump's left hand.

"I'm in a hurry for this."

"Express delivery," Stump said. "I hear you."

"Why not just say I'm a police detective?" Rosen asked.

They had carried a desk phone into an empty interview room.

"Citizens who work in schools have mixed feelings about the cops. They hate admitting they can't handle all contingencies without outside help. Put it on speaker."

"Okay," Rosen said, punching in the number.

The call was answered after four rings.

"Newton South High School, this is Mrs. Mumford."

"Mrs. Mumford, this is Doctor Rosen calling from New York."

"How can we help you, Doctor?"

"I'm working with a young man named Jason Rose here in Brooklyn, psychological counseling. Jason was a former student at your school. He is having issues related to the death of his sister, Mary Ellen, and I am having trouble getting him to talk about the particulars."

"You'll want to talk to Sheila Kennedy. Sheila is the counselor here, and she worked with both of the Rose children."

"Can you connect me to Ms. Kennedy?"

"If she is in, please hold a minute."

"Thank you."

"Nice work, Doctor," Murphy said.

"Quiet."

"Doctor Rosen, this is Sheila Kennedy."

"Ms. Kennedy, Jason Rose is having trouble dealing with the suicide of his sister. If I knew more about why Mary Ellen may have taken her own life, I would be better equipped to help the boy."

"I thought I could help Jason, but I wasn't given enough time. I tried helping Mary Ellen, but I was in over my head. I'm glad to hear Jason is seeing a more experienced professional. Have his parents been much help?"

"They are a bit shy on the subject of their daughter."

"I had the same problem. It is so tragic, David Rose is a psychologist himself—and he couldn't help his own children."

Murphy was giving his partner a thumb up, she waved it off.

"Tell me about Mary Ellen, what was going on with her that would push her to such an extreme?"

"A very embarrassing photograph of Mary Ellen in the shower of the girl's locker room at the school turned up on the internet."

"How terrible—was it determined who was behind it?"

"She was sure it was a few of the other girls in the group who were jealous and often bullied her. Mary Ellen was group leader. She was a very smart young woman and extremely popular. After the photograph surfaced it was hell for her. I tried hard to help her through it, and thought I might be making progress, but then she just stopped coming to see me. A week later I heard the news. I hope you can do better helping Jason."

"I'm sure you did all you could," Rosen said.

"Thank you for saying so."

"Were the other girls ever held accountable?"

"There was never solid evidence of who was responsible."

"What kind of group was it?"

"I thought you knew," Sheila Kennedy said. "Mary Ellen was the leader of the school cheerleader squad."

. . .

Richards received a call from Detective Bob Espinoza of the Denver Police Department.

"Raul Sandoval is out of town until tomorrow morning. Driving a rig cross country."

"How do you know?"

"I called for him at work, didn't ID myself as police. I told them it was about a late credit card bill."

"How did you know he had a late credit card bill?"

"Who doesn't have one? Anyway, I was told not to call him at work."

"Okay."

"I don't believe your man will show up while Sandoval is away, and we can't afford having our guys in a car twiddling their thumbs all day, so we pulled them away. We'll send them back first thing in the morning, but as I told you before, there's a limit to how long we can sit on the place."

"I understand," Richards said. "Thanks for the help."

Kenny Ramirez woke up in the hotel with a killer hangover. He managed to raise his head from the pillow long enough to see where he was and notice there was a woman in the bed beside him.

"Fuck me," he said.

Then he dropped his head and slept more.

"Officer Stan Landis was shot and killed last night," Samson said, when he had them all together. "I am going to tell you *everything* I know. Landis was off-duty. He spotted a ten-twenty at a liquor store in Bay Ridge and went in. He and a suspect were both killed. The store clerk was discovered unconscious behind the counter. One suspect was also found behind the counter, two fatal shots to the chest. Officer Landis was discovered on the customer side.

"The clerk told investigators that two men came into the store, both in ski masks. One pointed a gun at the clerk, while the second came around to his side of the counter, had him open the cash register, and then knocked him out cold with a the grip of his weapon.

"The detectives who arrived at the scene following the first responders have made preliminary suppositions. Ballistic and forensic reports are pending and may confirm their theories—but right now it is all speculation. It appears Landis interrupted the robbery and he killed one of the perpetrators in self-defense. The second man came at him quickly from his right, one shot to the right temple at close range. Officer Landis obviously never saw it coming and, according to the medical examiner, he died instantly.

"Only one witness saw anything, and what he saw was a man fleeing the scene after the shooting stopped. He could not see the suspect's face.

"Now, please listen carefully, I am not going to say this twice. This case is in the hands of the Six-eight and will *remain* there."

"Who caught it?" Murphy asked.

"Detectives Roosevelt and Cicero. Now, you had something to show me, Murphy?"

"Yes."

"Bring it to my office," Samson said. "And if anyone else has anything to share with me afterwards, take a number. Otherwise, I'm sure you all have work to do."

Stump slipped onto a seat at the counter of the Bridgeview Diner at 3rd Avenue and 90th Street in Bay Ridge. One of the diner's veteran employees walked up with a guest check book.

"Still in time for the breakfast special," the waiter said.

"Seen Jerry Paxton lately?"

"Why do you ask?"

"I owe him money."

"You're a day late. Paxton was killed trying to take down the liquor store on Fifth last night. Guess you're off the hook."

"Was there anyone with him?"

"Two eggs, hash browns, bacon and toast. Four-ninety-five."

"Scrambled, well done," Stump said, "rye bread."

Ripley received a call from Jack Falcone.

"A man and woman showed up at the Popovich place in a black BMW and went inside. He walked out twenty minutes later in a different outfit."

"Get his picture?"

"Coming out, suitable for framing," Falcone said. "He went off on foot, one of our guys followed."

"And?"

"He went straight to the Lobnya Lounge. I'll send the photo over."

"Can you stay on him, and the house?"

"We're good for now. I'll let you know if and when we can't."

"Thanks, Jack."

Murphy and Rosen ran it all down for Samson.

"What a fucking thing," Samson said.

"It's fucking Shakespearian," Murphy said.

"I want David Rose in here for questioning—today. First, go down to see Kelly. Tell him we need the Rose house covered, front and rear. That's *two* units, in uniform, in marked patrol cars. We want them parked as close to the residence as possible, preferably where they can be clearly seen by anyone looking out of the house. If they see Rose leave the house, they are to pick him up. Also, tell Kelly to put out an all points on the Rose vehicle. Then go down to the Criminal Courthouse on Schermerhorn. I will call Trenton, he will call whichever judge is down there who owes him one, and you will pick up a search warrant for the Rose residence. It will get you into the house whether or not the wife says he's there. If he *is* there, bring him in. If he is not there, we'll question the wife. I don't want her near a phone, so bring her here. Have the two units stay with the house until a forensics team arrives, and then the rear unit can be cut loose. Do you have any questions?"

"Will we be good on PC for the search warrant?" Rosen asked.

"We'll let Trenton worry about probable cause, it's his forte. Get to work, Ripley and Maggio look like they're in a yank to get in here."

Richards and Ivanov watched Murphy and Rosen blast out of Samson's office and Ripley and Maggio rush in.

"Some folks have all the fun," Ivanov said.

"Are you good without me for a few hours, I need to take my wife and daughter over to the hospital for those tests."

"No problem, Marty. Nothing we can do on the APBs except wait, unless we send it out to the other forty-four states and Puerto Rico. And we won't be hearing from Denver until tomorrow, earliest. Do what you have to do, no need to rush. And I hope everything goes all right."

"What am I looking at?" Samson asked, looking at a photograph fresh off the printer, sent in an email attachment from Jack Falcone.

"A possible suspect in the Holden shooting," Ripley said. "Seen here leaving Katrina Popovich's place."

"Suspect is a strong word for a man walking out of a house."

"We want to take it to the two women who worked at the bakery," Maggio said, "see if they can place him at the shop that afternoon."

"Do you need my permission to show a picture to a witness?" Samson asked. "Or is there something else that has both of you looking like you found Jimmy Hoffa's body?"

"He was followed to the Lobnya Lounge."

"Okay, put the picture with four or five others from our files. If both women pick this guy out, it's a good start. But, we need to be very cautious. Getting the shooter would be commendable, but if Vladimir Markov is behind this we want to get him too, on conspiracy, and we need to cover all the bases. If this is our guy," Samson said, handing the photograph back to Ripley, "let's put our heads together before moving further."

When Kenny Ramirez woke again he found himself alone in the hotel bed. He breathed a momentary sigh of relief, and then the woman walked out of the bathroom straight from a shower.

"Breakfast, Romeo?" she said, wearing a towel wrapped around the top of her head and nothing else.

Jesus, Ramirez thought, *how much did I fucking drink last night?*

Murphy and Rosen rang the doorbell. A few minutes later the woman opened the front door.

"Mrs. Rose," Murphy said, "we need to see your husband."

"David isn't here."

"We'll need to come in and take a look," Rosen said.

"You can't do that."

"This warrant says we can," Rosen said, holding up the paperwork.

Maureen Rose looked at the warrant for a moment, and then looked at the patrol car parked across the street.

"Come in," she said. "I didn't know what to do. I don't know what to do."

Stump had been walking Bay Ridge for hours. Up and down, from Shore Parkway to 86th Street, along 3rd, 4th and 5th Avenues. He spotted Spike Cassidy going into Pete's Pizza on 4th and 97th. Spike knew the hood. Stump crossed the avenue and waited outside the pizzeria.

Cassidy came out with a slice a few minutes later.

"Spike, what do you know?"

"Stump. Long time."

"Hear about Jerry Paxton?"

"Everyone heard about the fool. The heat from the Six-eight been up and down here all day. They been grilling anyone who ever knew the man."

"They get anywhere?"

"Nobody knows nothing, or isn't yapping."

"You know anything?"

"Like what?"

"Like if anyone else went in the liquor store with Paxton."

"I might have a hunch."

"Mind sharing?"

"Can you spare twenty?"

Stump pulled a twenty from his pocket and handed it over.

"Nicky DeSantis," Spike said.

"Why you thinking DeSantis?"

"I happened to see Jerry and Nicky together last night, not long before the store was hit. But remember, it's just a guess. It's what it is."

"A hunch, right, I heard you twice the first time. Any police hit *you* up for an opinion?"

"Two detectives came in the Bridgeview. This cat Roosevelt stands up on a table like he's Popeye fucking Doyle, raises his voice so the entire place can hear, and asks if anyone can *help them out.*"

"And?"

"You could hear a pin drop. Like I said, nobody knows nothing. And me, I keep my opinions to myself when it comes to the police. I doubt anyone is going to know for sure if DeSantis was in that liquor store unless Nicky say so himself."

"You know where Nicky hangs?"

"What's that worth?"

Stump pulled another twenty from his pocket and passed it over.

Easy come, easy go, he thought.

"Nicky washes dishes tonight at the Bay Ridge Diner. He's

usually there until eleven. He has a crib on Eighth and Seventy-third, above the Purple Rose Bar."

"Don't tell anyone we talked," Stump said.

"Do you think I'm fucking crazy?" Spike said. "*You* don't tell anyone we talked."

THIRTY

Murphy and Rosen came into Interview Room One and sat at the table opposite Maureen Rose.

Captain Samson followed them in and took a seat in a chair against the wall near the door.

Detective Rosen led the questioning.

"I am informing you this interview is being recorded."

"Okay."

"And you have been told, you are entitled to have a lawyer present."

"That won't be necessary."

"Please state your full name."

"Maureen Helen Rose."

"Also present are Detectives Sandra Rosen and Thomas Murphy, and Captain Samson, of the Sixty-first Precinct, New York Police Department. Can we get you anything before we begin, Mrs. Rose?"

"No, thank you."

"When was the last time you saw your husband, David Rose?"

"This past Friday morning. David failed to return home that evening."

"To your knowledge, where was your husband prior to the time he was scheduled to return home."

"To my knowledge, he was at the high school."

"Lafayette High School."

"Yes."

"Were you concerned about his failure to return home?"

"The later it got, the more I was concerned. When he was out all night, I didn't know what to think."

"Had he ever spent the entire night away before?"

"David has had a very difficult time since our daughter died. There were a few times when he said he needed to get away, needed to be alone for a day or two. But he always told me his plans beforehand."

"On Monday morning, you called the school to report that your husband would be out sick. He had been gone for more than two days. Why didn't you report him missing?"

"He had just begun a new job. I didn't want the administration thinking David was irresponsible or had serious personal problems. I still had hope he would come home, or at least call. So I didn't report his disappearance to the school, or to the police. And then, when I saw the press conference on TV, I was so confused and frightened, I didn't know what to do."

At this point, the woman broke down, sobbing violently. Samson stepped out of the room.

"Take as much time as you need," Rosen said, "before we continue."

The two detectives waited, uncomfortably, while the woman worked at regaining her composure. Samson returned, placed a bottle of water and a box of tissues on the table, and returned to his chair.

Maureen Rose took a drink, and a deep breath.

"I am all right to go on," she said after a few minutes.

"Do you know where your husband is now?"

"No."

"Has he contacted you at all since Friday?"

"No."

"Do you have an idea about why we are interested in your husband?"

"I believe I do. God save him. God save us all," she said. "Can I go back home before my son returns from school?"

Rosen looked behind her to Samson, he gave Rosen a nod.

"We have a team searching the house. They should be done before Jason returns. We can let you go home if you allow an officer to remain with you, inside the house. We cannot allow you to try contacting your husband, and we need to know if he tries to contact you. It would be best for everyone, David included, if he came in."

"Please don't hurt him," Maureen Rose said.

Ripley called Katherine Grant and Susan Beck, the two women who worked at the Avenue Bakery, and asked them to come down to the Six-one.

Katherine arrived first, and the two detectives took her into Interview Room Two. Maggio placed six black and white photographs of the same size on the table in front of the witness.

"Can you identify the man you saw in the bakery Monday afternoon?"

She immediately pointed to the photo they had received from Falcone.

"Thank you," Maggio said.

"That's it?"

"That's it. Forgive us for any inconvenience."

"Is that the man who killed Alex?"

"We don't know," Ripley said. "We are investigating possibilities."

"He was very friendly, good looking, well dressed."

"We don't know," Ripley said.

A few minutes later, Susan Beck chose the same photograph.

"What will happen with the bakery?" Maggio asked.

"We don't know. Alex has a sister with business experience. We hope it will stay with the family and the staff will be asked to stay on. We won't know anything until after the funeral. But, the more I think about what happened, I'm not sure if I would be alright working there again."

Stump called Mendez. They met at the Del Rio.

Stump gave him Nicky DeSantis as a "possible," Nicky's work schedule that evening, and the apartment above the Purple Rose.

"How will I recognize him?"

"Nicky is hard to miss. He was a less than successful heavyweight. Has a face that looks like it was put into a blender. Cauliflower ear, a nose broken two or three times, and a Frankenstein scar above his left eye. He should be wearing a ski mask *all* the time."

"Will he be hearing that someone was asking about him?"

"Nope."

"Thanks, Stump."

"From what I know, there were no witnesses," Stump said.

"I'll get him to confess."

"Mendez?"

"Yes?"

"It cost me the forty you gave me for the dope on DeSantis."

Mendez handed Stump another sixty.

"Don't do anything I wouldn't do," Stump said.

"I'll do what I believe my partner would do."

"They both identified him?" Samson asked.

"Without hesitation," Maggio said.

"Was he followed when he left the Lobnya Lounge?"

"I just spoke to Jack Falcone. The suspect hasn't left the place. Falcone believes he might work there," Ripley said. "And we did a background check on Katrina Popovich. No criminal record, but Vladimir Markov is her uncle."

"Go to the Lobnya, bring two uniforms in a patrol car along, find him and bring him in for questioning. Tell him it is routine, but make sure everyone in the place knows he is being taken away, especially Markov. If he refuses to come, wait there for an arrest warrant. I'm going to send Ivanov to see Katrina Popovich, and question her about where she was at the time of the murder and why her vehicle was spotted on President Street off Nostrand at the time of the murder. I'll put in a request for a warrant to search the house and car so, if Popovich has no good answers for Marina, we will be prepared for a search of both. I'm sure Chief Trenton will be impressed with how busy we are doing our jobs on hump day."

"Got it," Maggio said.

"Thank Jack Falcone for the leg up. And do whatever you need to do, within reason, to scare this guy into fucking himself, and Markov, before he decides to lawyer-up."

Murphy was at Samson's door as soon as Maggio and Ripley left.

"What?"

"We just got a call from Central. They received a report of a vehicle with New York plates left abandoned in a parking lot at the Wilmington, Delaware Amtrak station. Twenty-ten silver Camry. The plates match Rose's car."

"Did the report come from the terminal or the Wilmington PD?"

"It came from Amtrak. Claim they've been waiting since Monday for the police there to respond and they're ready to have the car impounded."

"Call them. Tell them not to touch the vehicle, tell them we will get it out of there. Then find a towing company down there who will haul the car up to the Navy Yard for a forensics search," Samson said, "and, Tommy..."

"Yes."

"Good work, both of you."

Ripley and Maggio were on their way to Brighton Beach. Maggio drove, Ripley's cell rang.

It was Kelly calling from the precinct.

"I thought you might like to know that Lorraine DiMarco phoned looking for you. She said she's at her office," Kelly said, and he was gone.

Ripley pulled Lorraine's business card from his wallet and entered the office number. A receptionist put him through.

"Did you forget about me, or lose my card."

"I haven't had a moment, and I'm not sure about tonight."

"I understand. I heard the terrible news about Stan Landis.

Stan was a friend. Will you be at the wake this evening?"

"I'm planning to be."

"Then I'll see you there, and we can decide if we're still in the mood for dinner afterwards."

"We are convinced that we are dealing with mucocutaneous lymph node syndrome, or Kawasaki disease, so named for the Japanese pediatrician who first described it. It is most common in children under the age of five. There is no standard tool for diagnosing the condition. The diagnosis is clinical, that is diagnosis based solely on medical signs and symptoms. Sophia's symptoms, prolonged fever, swollen tongue and swollen lymph nodes, are indicative of Kawasaki disease, but are also symptoms of other conditions, including scarlet fever, juvenile rheumatoid arthritis and measles. The tests we did last week have ruled out those conditions. The chest x-ray we did today showed a slight inflammation of the arteries, and the fact that the fever has prevailed for five days, have given us confidence in our clinical assessment. The treatment is non-invasive, and presents no danger at all to your daughter. The prognosis is extremely positive. Total recovery is nearly always realized after several days in hospital with a regimen of aspirin and intravenous immune globulin, unless there has already been damage to the heart due to poor blood flow, which we will not be able to determine until the treatment runs its course and Sophia's symptoms subside. I understand this is a lot to digest, and I thank you for not interrupting, but now is the time for questions."

"I have one question, doctor," Marty Richards said. "Will our daughter be all right?"

"I truly believe Sophia will be fine, but I recommend we begin treatment immediately."

Richards turned to face his wife. Linda's cheeks were tracked with tears. She nodded her head.

"Do it," Richards said. "Where do we sign?"

. . .

309

When Katrina Popovich answered the door, Ivanov identified herself as a police detective, throwing in a few Russian words for good measure. She told Popovich she had a few questions and said if Katrina could help her out it could save the woman a great deal of serious trouble.

Popovich invited Marina in for tea.

"What is this about?"

"It would work a lot better if you let me ask the questions. Can you tell me where you were around six Monday evening?"

"Atlanta. I left early Monday and got back this morning."

"What's in Atlanta?"

"I'm a sales representative for a line of women's sporting and leisure clothing. I visited a number of retail stores."

"I imagine you flew."

"Yes. My boyfriend drove me out to LaGuardia in my car, around ten that morning."

"And he had the vehicle the entire time you were gone."

"I suppose so. I had no need of it, and he was going to be picking me up at the airport today anyway."

"What is your boyfriend's name?"

"Victor."

"And after Victor dropped you here this morning?"

"He changed clothes and walked to work."

"Does he live here?"

"He stays a lot, but he has his own apartment."

"You said he changed clothing."

"He keeps some things here, I gave him a drawer in the bedroom dresser and he keeps some clothing hung in the hall closet."

"Would you mind if I looked around?" Ivanov asked.

"Is Victor in some kind of trouble?"

"We're investigating a shooting incident that occurred Monday evening. We need to know Victor's whereabouts at the time."

"You think Victor shot someone?"

"We would like to be able to rule him out."

"Why don't you talk with him? Victor works at the Lobnya Lounge, he should be there."

"There are detectives on their way to see him, now," Ivanov said. "Listen carefully, Katrina. If we find out Victor was involved in a felony, and that you know anything about what happened Monday and are hiding something, you could be seen as an accessory and face arrest and prosecution."

"I don't know anything."

"Then you *won't* mind if I take a look around."

"Go ahead."

"There are two police officers sitting in a car outside, would you mind if I brought them in to witness your permission for a search?"

"Do what you need to do."

They found him behind the bar at the Lobnya Lounge serving drinks.

Ripley and Maggio made him from across the room as the man in the evidentiary photograph.

"What is your name, sir?"

"Who wants to know?"

Both detectives showed their shields.

"I'm Detective Ripley, and this is Detective Maggio, your turn."

"Victor Conrad."

"Can we see some ID?" Ripley asked.

He opened the cash register behind him, took out a passport and a work visa, and handed them to Ripley.

"Mr. Conrad," Ripley said, taking a quick look at the documents. "We would like you to come with us to the Sixty-first Precinct."

"What for?"

"For questions, part of an investigation you may be able to help us with."

"What investigation?"

"We'll tell you all about it at the station."

"Am I under arrest?"

"No."

"Then why should I come with you."

"Because we asked you nicely," Maggio said, as two uniformed officers made a perfectly timed entrance into the club and walked up to the bar.

"Why can't you ask your questions here?"

"That's not the way *coming in for questioning* works. Besides, you'll like our place. There's coffee, Diet Coke, and a terrific view of Coney Island Avenue."

Suddenly, an older man appeared at the bar.

"What is this all about?"

"And you are?" Maggio asked.

"Vladimir Markov. This is my place you have barged into, and this is my employee you are harassing."

"Will you come with us voluntarily, Victor," Ripley said, ignoring Markov.

"You have the right to remain silent, Victor," Markov said.

Victor slowly came around the bar, glaring at the two detectives.

"Take him in," Ripley said to the uniforms, "we'll be right behind you."

"It was good of Vladimir to read him his rights, don't you think?" Maggio said to his partner, loud enough for Markov to hear. "Nice place he has here, if you're looking for a perfect venue for the Bee Gees."

When they were in the car, Ripley sat in the passenger seat tapping the passport and work visa on his knee, a big smile on his face.

"What?" Maggio asked.

"In my years with the FBI, I saw hundreds of phony documents," Ripley said, "but these would make a three-dollar-bill look authentic."

Murphy tapped on Samson's door.

"The Rose car is on its way. It should be at the Navy Yard in two hours."

"Call forensics and ask them to be ready to move. Call the pound and ask them to let you and forensics know the moment the vehicle arrives. When you get the call, go down there with Rosen as quickly as you can."

Ivanov called Samson.

"Her boyfriend had the BMW Monday night."

"Does she know anything?"

"I don't think so, but I put a scare into her, the tried and true *accessory after the fact* routine, and she gave the okay to search the place."

"Find a weapon?"

"No, but we found a Russian passport. Victor Bronski."

"Bring it in, leave someone to watch the woman," Samson said. "Run the name through VICAP, Interpol and Homeland Security as soon as you get back. Maggio and Ripley picked him up at the Lobnya Lounge, and they should be in an interview room with him shortly. He gave them counterfeit ID, and I think there is a good chance he is wanted somewhere."

"On my way," Marina said.

"Ironic," Murphy said.

They were impatiently waiting to hear about David Rose's car, still on its way from Delaware.

"Are you referring to anything in particular or the state of the world in general?"

"John Cicero. We pulled the Lake Street murder case, and he caught the Landis investigation."

"I hope he does a better job than we did on Angela Salerno and Cicero's son."

"We got the doers."

"They were puppets," Rosen said. "The puppeteer is still out there."

PART FOUR

THE AVENUE

*...there are degrees of guilt, shades of innocence,
and they all congregate on the same avenue.*

—Thomas Murphy

THIRTY ONE

The indigenous Native American inhabitants of the region, the Lenape, called it Narrioch, the land without shadows, because of the geographical orientation which kept the shoreline in sunlight all day.

The Dutch called it Conyne Eylandt, and the English later called it Coney Island, both names derived from the corresponding words for rabbit. The land was a haven for rabbits and then a bountiful hunting ground, until the resorts chased the critters away.

Rabbit Island—not a very glamorous epithet and not really an island at all—its miles of beaches and its phenomenal theme parks made Coney Island a thrilling destination attracting millions of visitors from every part of the world from the late eighteen hundreds through the first half of the twentieth century.

Coney Island Avenue stretches for five miles, north and south, from Brightwater Court to Grand Army Plaza at the southwest corner of Prospect Park, passing through the neighborhoods of Brighton Beach, Sheepshead Bay, Gravesend, Midwood and Kensington along the way.

Heading from Prospect Park toward the Atlantic Ocean the cross streets are named alphabetically—Albemarle, Beverly, Cortelyou, Ditmas, Foster—until at Avenue H they take on the names of letters themselves, through Z. Just past Avenue Z, Coney Island Avenue crosses the Belt Parkway, and less than two miles further south it ends at the Boardwalk and the shadowless beach.

The 61st Precinct sits on Coney Island Avenue between Avenue W and Gravesend Neck Road.

. . .

When Ripley and Maggio came into the Six-one, Sergeant Kelly stopped them at the front desk.

"Your guy is sitting in Interview Room One, mumbling in some foreign language. Samson needs to see you before you get started."

When they reached the squad room, Captain Samson came over to meet them.

"Call Ivanov on her cell, she interviewed Katrina Popovich. Marina is on her way back, but you should know what she learned before you begin the questioning. What did this guy give you for ID?"

"A bullshit passport," Maggio said. "Victor Conrad."

"Ivanov found a passport at the Popovich place. Victor Bronski. She's bringing it in. We're trying to find out who the fuck he is."

The detectives sat down at the interview room table opposite the suspect.

"Can I have a lawyer?"

"If you feel you *need* a lawyer. As we told you before Victor, you are not under arrest. You are simply here to answer a few routine questions," Ripley said, "to help us eliminate you as a subject in an ongoing investigation so we can move on to other avenues of inquiry."

"What investigation?"

"Why don't we just get started? You will be hearing all you need to know in the course of the interview."

"I have nothing to hide, and I need to get back to work. So, let's get this over with."

Maggio led the questioning.

"Please state your name, for the record."

"Victor Conrad."

"Victor, hope you don't mind if we call you Victor," Maggio said. "Victor, where were you at six this past Monday evening?"

"I was having dinner with my employer, Vladimir Markov."

"Where was that?"

"At Mr. Markov's home, he is an excellent cook."

"I'm sure he is. I would ask what he prepared, but I missed lunch today," Maggio said. "Was there anyone else present?"

"No."

There was a light rapping on the door. Ripley stepped out, came back in almost immediately, returned to his seat, and whispered into his partner's ear.

Maggio let Ripley continue the questioning.

"What time did you arrive at Markov's home, and when did you leave?"

"I arrived no later than five, and left shortly before ten, does that answer all of your questions?"

"We have a few more, please bear with us. Where is Markov's home?"

"At Rockaway Beach, do you need the address?"

"No, the address is not important. Did you drive the BMW out there?"

"Excuse me?"

"According to Katrina Popovich," Ripley said, "you had her BMW from the time you dropped her at LaGuardia Monday morning until you picked her up and drove her back home *this* morning so, what I am asking is, did you drive her car out to Rockaway Beach Monday evening?"

"Yes, I did."

"We have a witness who spotted a man matching your height and build getting into a black car on President Street near Nostrand Avenue around six Monday evening. That witness noted the license plate number of the vehicle. We ran the plate number and it matched Katrina Popovich's registration. Is it possible you are mistaken about the time you arrived in Rockaway?"

"It is your witness who is mistaken. The car was with me all evening and, as I already told you, I was in Rockaway by five. I cannot remember *ever* being anywhere near Nostrand Avenue and, what was it?"

"President Street."

"I doubt I could find it."

"Well, if that's the case, you weren't anywhere near the Avenue Bakery that afternoon," Ripley said.

Victor was silent for a few moments before he spoke again.

"Was that a question?" he finally said.

"Sorry. I phrased it awkwardly. Were you in the Avenue Bakery on Nostrand Avenue between President and Carroll Streets on Monday afternoon?"

"No."

"The thing is, Victor, and I have to admit it puzzles us," Maggio said, "the thing is we showed six photos, including one of you, to each of the two women who worked the front of the bakery shop. They both quickly picked you out as the man who had been in around one on Monday afternoon to order a birthday cake for his mother."

"My mother is long dead, and the two women are mistaken. Either we are done with this nonsense, or bring me a telephone to call a lawyer," he said, rising from his chair.

"Sit down, Victor," Maggio said. "We're not quite finished here yet."

"We need to return your passport," Ripley said.

He took the passport from his pocket and placed it on the table.

"You may want to take a look at it before you leave, Victor" Ripley said. "Make sure everything is in order."

Victor opened the passport.

The color went out of his face.

"Victor Bronski," Maggio said, as he locked Bronski to the table restraint, "you are under arrest for the suspected murder of Alexander Holden."

"I don't know what you're talking about. I want to call a lawyer."

"Sit tight," Maggio said, "we'll send in a telephone."

The two detectives left the room, Samson met them outside the door.

"We arrested him," Ripley said, "I hope we didn't jump the gun, he wants a telephone."

"Fuck jumping the gun, everything he gave us was bullshit,"

Maggio said. "And the look on his face when I cuffed him to the table was priceless."

"Let him stew for a while, and then go back in and show him this."

Samson handed Ripley a fax.

Ripley held it up, so Maggio could read along.

"This guy is fucked either way," Maggio said.

"He is," Samson said, "but I have good idea which way he'll go."

After getting the call, it took them nearly an hour to reach the Brooklyn Navy Yard police impound—crawling at five miles an hour on the Gowanus.

"Expressway my ass," Murphy said, when they pulled into the yard.

When they finally located David Rose's car, the Crime Scene Unit was already there. Derek Fielder was watching as Joan Michaels was opening the driver side door.

"The door was unlocked," Fielder said when Murphy and Rosen joined them. "The keys are in the ignition."

Murphy spotted something in the back seat and went for the back door.

"Hands off, Detective," Michaels warned, as she passed the car keys to Fielder. "I hope you didn't come down here to get in our way."

"It's all yours. But could you please reach back there and hand me one of those flyers?"

Murphy quickly looked at the flyer and handed it to Rosen.

"Jesus, this is our guy," Rosen said. "We need to find him."

"I think we just did," Fielder said, looking into the opened trunk.

"Victor," Ripley said, when he and Maggio returned to the interview room, "this document states you are wanted in Moscow for the murder of two MUR inspectors."

"Where is a telephone?"

"It's coming. Meanwhile, Victor, let us tell you *now* what your choices are," Maggio said, "since they will not change when a lawyer gets here. Either you confess to the fatal shooting of Alexander Holden, help yourself by naming anyone else involved, and face prosecution here in the great state of New York or, if you prefer, we send your ass back to Moscow and you can pray they blindfold the firing squad."

Murphy and Rosen climbed into their car after notifying Maureen Rose that her husband had been found.

"That sucked," Murphy said.

"How do you think she took it?"

"I don't know, shock, relief?"

"What a fucking thing," Rosen said.

"That's one way of putting it. I feel sorry for the boy when all of the news hits the street."

"Let's get back and write it up. Maybe there's still a chance we can have a fairly pleasant evening."

"I'm sure the visit to Torregrossa will be enjoyable as hell."

The viewing room at Torregrossa and Sons Funeral Home was filled to capacity.

Mendez sat in the front row with his partner's immediate family—father, mother, two sisters and brothers-in-law. Chief Trenton and Captain Samson sat together a few rows back on the aisle, both in uniform. Detectives Murphy and Rosen sat together behind their captain. Additional members of the Landis family—uncles, aunts, cousins, were scattered throughout the room. Richards sat with Maggio, while Marty's wife was camping out at the hospital with their infant daughter. Bernie Senderowitz had sent his regrets from a different hospital, and Marina Ivanov was at a different funeral parlor. Detective Ripley and Lorraine DiMarco stood together against the rear wall.

The casket was closed.

"Is it too late for dinner?" Lorraine asked.

"I haven't had time to eat a thing all day."

"What about your boys?"

"Kyle and Mickey are staying over at my sister's for the night."

"Let's go," Lorraine said.

As they left the building, they nearly collided with a man rushing in. He nodded an apology, found the viewing room, walked briskly down the aisle, and said a few words to Mr. and Mrs. Landis. On his way back up the aisle, he stopped to greet Chief Trenton.

"My condolences, Chief," he said, offering a hand.

Trenton accepted the handshake, and the man was quickly gone.

"Who's the suit?" Samson asked.

"City Comptroller, Theodore Wilson."

"What is he doing here?"

"Campaigning," Trenton said. "Looks like a shoe-in to win the Democratic Mayoral Primary next week, and he's already started kissing babies. I heard you cleared two major cases today."

"It was my detective's squad," Samson said. "Rosen and Murphy found David Rose dead in the trunk of his car, with enough physical and forensic evidence to prove he killed those two high school girls. Ripley and your boy Maggio got a confession in the murder of Alexander Holden, and convinced the shooter to roll over on Vladimir Markov as a conspirator. We picked Markov up. They will both be arraigned in the morning."

"What about the fugitive who shot your son?"

"He may show up in Denver, we have eyes out there."

"Tell all your people I said they have been doing a great job, and I appreciate their diligence."

"I think you should drop by the Six-one and tell them personally."

"You're right, I'll do that."

When Samson and Trenton headed out, Murphy and Rosen followed.

Once out on the street, Chief Trenton walked off and the two detectives joined the captain.

"We're going to Joe's Bar and Grill up the street," Murphy said. "Drink to Stan Landis. Augie is setting them up as we speak."

"Did you invite Richards and Maggio?"

"Maggio is in. Richards said he needed to get to the hospital."

"Lead the way," Samson said.

"Who was the cat in the Armani suit that offered his hand to the Chief?" Rosen asked as they walked.

"Wilson, City Comptroller," Samson said.

"What does a comptroller do?" Murphy asked.

"Makes enough friends to run for mayor," Samson said.

Rey Mendez was last to leave the funeral home, other than the family. He said goodbye to Landis' parent's, made a quick stop at the casket, and walked out onto Avenue U.

It was just before ten.

Mendez climbed into his car, took U to Stillwell Avenue, and crossed Bay Parkway where Stillwell became 75th Street.

He turned right on 7th Avenue and parked on 8th at 73rd Street, against the fence that ran along the Staten Island Expressway.

He walked across the avenue and into the Purple Rose.

Mendez ordered a Corona at the bar, took it over to a table by the front window, and sat looking out for Nicky DeSantis.

Ripley and Lorraine sat at a booth in the Del Rio Diner.

Dessert and coffee had just arrived.

"I would have liked to take you to a fancier place," Ripley said.

"First of all, we are splitting the bill. I'm big into sharing. Secondly, this is my favorite place. There is nothing you could possibly want to eat that is not on the menu."

"I'm a fan of sharing also," Ripley said.

Ripley was feeling a bit self-conscious.

Lorraine found it charming.

"How are you adjusting to the new job?"

"Good. They do things differently than we did in the Bureau. Not better or worse, just different. I'm learning fast."

"I heard you broke the Holden murder case."

"We were very lucky. The suspect copped to the shooting because he was terrified of the alternative."

"I'm glad you got Markov," Lorraine said, "and I'll stop talking shop."

"Listen," Ripley said.

"I'm listening."

"My youngest, Mickey, has a birthday coming up. Six years old. It's hard to believe. Anyway, we're throwing a little party on Friday at my sister's house around six. Connie, her husband, their two girls—and Samson and his wife are coming with their two girls."

"And you were wondering if I would care to join you."

"Yes."

"I would love to. This chocolate cream pie is amazing."

Mendez had no trouble recognizing DeSantis. Nicky's damaged face was everything Stump had described, and worse.

A single entrance to the building served both the bar and the upstairs rooms. A door to the stairs leading up to the apartment stood at the end of the short entrance hall, the door to the bar was on the right.

Mendez quickly slipped on a pair of latex gloves as DeSantis entered the building.

When Rey stepped out of the bar he was close enough to touch DeSantis as Nicky unlocked and opened his door.

Mendez pressed his gun roughly into Nicky's back.

"I'm walking up behind you," he said. "If you try anything funny I will kill you right here on the stairs."

They reached the top and entered the apartment. The music

from the bar below made the floor vibrate.

"Are you carrying?" Mendez asked.

"No."

"Is there a weapon in this place?"

"Listen," DeSantis said.

"No, you fucking listen. I am an impatient man, and a have a very short temper."

"On top of the dresser. In the bedroom."

"Show me."

He followed DeSantis to the back of the apartment.

"Get on the bed," Mendez said. "Sit on your hands, and keep your mouth shut unless I ask you a question. Am I clear?"

"Yes," Nicky said.

Mendez moved his gun to his left hand, and picked up the .38 caliber handgun from the dresser with his right.

"Is this the weapon you brought into the liquor store last night?"

"I don't know what you mean."

"I warned you, Nicky, do not fuck with me. I am here to ask questions, and your job is to answer honestly. I am not leaving until you tell me what I need to know, or you are dead. Now, is this the weapon you brought into the liquor store last night?"

"Yes."

"Then this would be the weapon you used to kill Officer Landis. I am guessing you are aware of the penalty for killing a New York City police officer during the commission of a felony robbery."

"I didn't know he was a cop."

"He was my partner. I knew him as well as I know myself, so I know he identified himself and when *your* partner drew down on him he had to shoot the scumbag in self-defense. And then you, you miserable fucking coward, blindsided Officer Landis and put him down like a dog."

"If you are a cop," DeSantis said. "I want to turn myself in."

"Is this the weapon that killed my partner?"

"Yes."

"Show me how you did it."

"What?"

Mendez came up beside DeSantis, on Nicky's right.

"Show me your right hand."

DeSantis complied.

"Take the gun."

DeSantis didn't know what to do.

"Let me help you," Mendez said.

He placed the weapon in DeSantis' right hand, covered Nicky's hand with his own left hand, and raised the gun to Nicky's right temple.

"Careful," DeSantis said, "this thing is loaded."

"Put your finger on the trigger," Mendez said.

"You're fucking crazy."

"Do it," Mendez said, pointing his own gun at Nicky's forehead.

DeSantis put a finger on the trigger, and Mendez covered it with his own.

"Was it something like this?"

"The gun wasn't against his head," DeSantis said, he was as white as a ghost. "I was a few feet away."

"I prefer this," Mendez said. "No chance of missing the shot."

Then Rey Mendez pressed down on Nicky's finger and the gun fired.

THIRTY TWO

Samson had called a mandatory meeting of all Six-one detectives for ten Thursday morning. Chief of Detectives Trenton would be joining them.

After dropping the girls at school, Samson drove out to Queens to learn how his son was doing at the new hospital.

"It's okay. I begin physical therapy tomorrow. I can carry weight on my right ankle, but the cast is doing all the work. We won't know until it comes off if I'll be able to run again. They'll also be slowly working my shoulder. And I'm supposed to see a psychologist later this morning. Is that necessary?"

"It can't hurt," was all Samson would say.

"Have they found Kenny Ramirez?" Jimmy asked.

"There are some promising leads."

"I can't help thinking we pushed him. I don't see him as a murderer. I mean, I wonder about what I might have done in his shoes."

"Share those thoughts with the psychologist."

Richards stood at the bedside looking down at his daughter.

"It breaks my heart, tubes and monitors, she's so small."

Linda had been at Sophia's side all night, camped out in an extra bed courtesy of the hospital.

"She is doing very well. Her fever has been steadily coming down. They will do an X-ray later this morning to check the arterial swelling. The doctors are very optimistic about full recovery," Linda said. "She may be small, but she's a tough cookie. Like her father."

"And so beautiful," Marty said. "Like her mother."

· · ·

Senderowitz was sitting up in bed trying to read a crime novel—a police procedural written by a retired NYPD detective. At every turn, Bernie thought about how he would have handled the evidence. He finally gave it up, because all he could *really* think about was getting out of the fucking hospital.

The door of the room opened as Senderowitz put the book down.

"Well," he said, "look what the cat dragged in."

"I just heard what happened or I would have come down sooner," Vincent Salerno said.

"Good of you to come. I live for visitors, this place is hell. Thank God I get sprung tomorrow."

"Do you need a ride?"

"Thanks," Senderowitz said, unable to suppress a smile, "my daughter is taking me home."

"I didn't know you had a daughter."

"I had nearly forgotten myself. But enough about me—how are you?"

"I'm good. I'm still at the restaurant, but there's a new manager. Bobby Hoyle. Bobby is training me to wait tables. And I'm taking classes, studying for the electrician's apprentice exam."

"That's terrific, Vinnie. Are you still seeing Alison?"

"Every morning," Salerno said. "We got a place together. It's good."

"You're making my day, young man."

"Did they ever find the man on the tape with Kevin Donahue?"

"No. After the showdown in Chicago, the investigation hit a dead end."

"I can't stop thinking I brought it on Angie, and Eddie Cicero."

"You went to Angela for help *because* she was your sister. If *she* needed help, she would have come to you."

"Angie thought I was a fuckup, and I couldn't blame her."

"Try thinking of how proud and pleased she would be about how you have turned things around. What happened to Angie and Eddie was tragic, but it was out of our hands. How are your folks doing?"

"They're still hurting a lot. Angie was the light of their lives. But they've both told me it wasn't my fault. Sometimes I wonder if they say it because I'm all they have left."

"Trust them."

"I wish Eddie's father didn't blame me."

"John Cicero lost a son and he needs to blame someone."

"I still listen to that recorded conversation. Often."

"Why?"

"I don't know," Vinnie said, "looking for an answer there—somewhere. Jesus, I can recite the entire conversation by heart. I can even impersonate the voices, at least as well as I can do Christopher Walken."

Bernie reached over to a nearby table and grabbed a pen and paper.

"If you ever need to talk, Vinnie," Senderowitz said as he wrote, "here's my address and phone number. You are welcome anytime, I'm sure I will be craving company."

Ripley sat with Lorraine DiMarco at her kitchen table over coffee.

"You're looking a bit wrinkled, Detective."

"I have a change of clothes at the precinct."

"Pretty sure of yourself, were you?"

"It's an old habit from my bureau days," Ripley said, "as far as being sure of myself—when you asked me in last night."

"Yes?"

"I can't remember when I was so nervous. Probably sometime back in high school."

"I'm looking forward to meeting your boys tomorrow," Lorraine said.

. . .

Murphy and Rosen walked along the waterfront in Shore Road Park while Ralph was off chasing squirrels.

"So this guy loses a daughter and decides to take out a vendetta against innocent girls simply because they're cheerleaders," Rosen said. "It boggles the mind."

"Sadly, it is not an unusual story," Murphy said. "What boggles *my* mind is how he winds up in his car trunk in fucking Delaware."

An anonymous caller informed the desk sergeant at the 68th Precinct that the shooter in the attempted liquor store robbery Tuesday evening was Nicky DeSantis.

The caller gave an address on 8th Avenue and hung up.

The sergeant passed the word on to the primary investigator, Detective John Cicero.

"Look like a suicide to you?" Cicero asked, looking down at the body on the bed.

"Maybe," Detective Washington said. "Did he leave a note?"

"I doubt this fucking mope could write his own name."

At ten, all except Detective Ivanov were gathered in the squad room with Samson and Chief Trenton. Ivanov was attending Alex Holden's funeral.

"I am aware of the accomplishments of this entire squad. Yesterday was a remarkable day for the Six-one," Trenton said. "I am here today to learn more about those efforts. I have a meeting at eleven, so I may need to quietly slip away. But the main purpose for the visit is to express my appreciation and respect for your outstanding work. Thank you."

When no one had anything to say, Samson got things rolling.

"Rosen, Murphy, you're up."

"We can now say, with great confidence," Rosen began, "that David Rose was the man responsible for the deaths of Jenny Greco and Patty Bolin. The fliers in Rose's car matched those found on the street adjoining the subway station where

Patty Bolin was discovered. Clothesline in the vehicle matched the rope found at both murder scenes. Rose had motive, if you could call it that, a disturbed reaction to the suicide of his daughter. And Rose had opportunity—he worked at the school the girls attended and, since his wife has changed earlier testimony, there is no one to account for his whereabouts at the time of either murder. Forensics is still working the vehicle for prints, on the interior and on the doors and trunk, and looking for hairs or fiber which might put either or both of the girls in the car. How Rose landed in the trunk of the car, in Delaware, is still a mystery."

"Any theories?" Samson asked.

"Rose was found gagged, bound and DOA," Murphy said. "Preliminary findings by the medical examiner suggest he died of massive blood loss and hemorrhaging resulting from a severe blow to the head. Batman estimated the time of death at three to four days ago. We were glad to hear he didn't die while the vehicle was being towed back here. As to how he wound up where and how he was found—we played around with a few ideas. We considered an accomplice in the murders, who turned on him, killed him and dumped the car and the body—but we ruled it out as highly improbable. We considered the possibility that someone discovered he was guilty of the killings and took the law into their own hands—we both decided the thought was just too karmic. Bottom line is, we just don't know."

"I'm sorry, but I really need to run," Chief Trenton interrupted. "Can you get all of that on paper for me by early this afternoon?"

"Probably," Murphy said.

"We'll need it to prepare for a press conference," Trenton added. "We need to make an official statement as soon as possible."

"No problem," Rosen said.

"Thank you all again," Trenton said, and rushed out.

"Gee," Murphy said. "No one said *you're welcome.*"

"He came down here to sincerely express his appreciation, not to fish for a *you're welcome.* And no one should need to thank you for doing your job," Samson said. "Ripley, Maggio, your turn."

"Victor Bronski and Vladimir Markov," Maggio began, "are in custody—awaiting arraignments this afternoon. Bronski was arrested and charged with first degree murder, and he subsequently signed a full confession. Markov was later arrested and charged with solicitation of first degree murder after Bronski named Markov as the man who employed him to do the job. If indicted, neither will be granted bail. If convicted, both face the possibility of life imprisonment. Unless the D.A. seriously screws the pooch, neither will be seeing the outside of a prison for a very, very long time—if ever."

"Marty?"

"Raul Sandoval is scheduled to return to Denver from a two-day trucking assignment sometime this morning," Richards said. "We've been working with Detective Sonny Wasinger of the Denver PD. They'll be watching Sandoval on the chance Kenny Ramirez pops up in Denver. We're waiting for word. It's all we really have going right now."

"All right," Samson said. "We need written reports on the Rose case and the Holden case by this afternoon, but there is no need for two detectives to write each statement. Choose which of you will sit and write, and which will take off and be back at four to cover the evening watch."

"Isn't it your job to delegate?" Detective Murphy asked, before he could stop himself.

"No problem. Heads or tails," Samson said, fishing a quarter from his pocket.

"Heads."

Samson flipped the coin.

"Heads it is. Detective Rosen writes the report. Ripley, heads or tails," Samson said, retrieving the coin.

"Tails."

"Heads again, Ripley you're writing. Murphy, Maggio, beat it and be back here at four. Rosen, let me know if you hear anything more from forensics on Rose's vehicle. Richards, let me know if you hear from Denver. And thank you all again for the great work."

With that, the captain retreated to his office.

Rosen stopped Maggio and Murphy on their way out.

"Tommy, have a minute?"

"Sure."

"I'll see you at four," Maggio said, and headed out of the squad room.

"What's up? If you want to switch it makes no difference to me. A coin toss is not the law."

"I'm good," Rosen said. "It seems like Sam has been hard on you lately."

"Maybe a little."

"Have any idea why?"

"I'm afraid I know exactly why," Murphy said.

THIRTY THREE

Back in his office, Samson called down to Desk Sergeant Kelly.

"Thanks for holding our calls."

"Why does everyone wait until you begin your meetings before lighting up my telephone?"

"Why is the sky blue? Anything important?"

"Those determinations are above my pay grade. Detective Cicero phoned, he would like you to call him at the Six-eight. Michaels called from forensics for Detectives Rosen and Murphy, she is at the lab. There was a call from Denver PD for Richards or Ivanov."

Samson stepped out of the office.

"Sandra, give Michaels a shout at the forensics lab. Marty, Denver wants to talk with you," he called across the room.

Then he returned to his desk and phoned John Cicero.

"We found the scumbag who killed Officer Landis. Nicky DeSantis," Cicero reported.

"Are you sure?"

"We found the gun with DeSantis, according to ballistics it was a positive match. He matched the physical description from the liquor store clerk, and he was a known associate of Jerry Paxton."

"Did you get a confession?"

"We were too late. DeSantis was found in his place. Single shot to the temple. No sign of forced entry, nothing disturbed, the weapon was in his mitt, and he definitely pulled the trigger. I'm sure it will go down as a suicide. He was a cop killer and now he's fucking dead, it's good enough for us."

"Thanks for letting us know."

"It was the least I could do," Cicero said.

He's still angry at the world, Samson thought, *and who could blame him?*

Samson called Officer Mendez.

"Rey, I know I told you to stay away but I need to see you. Can you get down here to the precinct?"

"Sure. Give me an hour."

A minute later, Richards was at the captain's door.

"Sonny Wasinger is on the line from the Denver PD. They spotted Kenny Ramirez and he wants to know what we would like them to do. Since the decision is ultimately yours, I thought you should talk to him yourself."

"Sit down, Richards. I'll put us on speaker," Samson said, taking the call, "Detective Wasinger, this is Captain Samson."

"We followed Raul Sandoval to a hotel near downtown. He picked up your suspect and took him back to the house. They are both in the place now. Would you like us to take Ramirez in?"

"Ramirez is probably armed."

"This is Denver, not West Bumfuck. We even have a SWAT team."

"We would like him alive."

"I think we can take him alive. But if you're worried you could always come out here and take over. It's not like we don't have other business."

"I didn't mean to question your abilities, Detective."

"Forget it, I'm not easily offended."

"Please pick him up. Thanks for all your help."

"I'll let you know when we have him in custody. And, Captain."

"Yes?"

"You'll have to make your own arrangements for getting Ramirez back to New York. We don't have the budget or the manpower to spare."

"I understand. I'll make the arrangements."

After the call, Samson turned his attention to Richards.

"How is your daughter doing?" he asked.

"The doctors believe she will be all right. They want to keep an eye on her in the hospital for a few more days."

"When do we expect Ivanov?"

"The funeral was at ten, she should be in any time."

"Let's get a head start on this. Find out what you can about the earliest flights to Denver tomorrow morning while I work at getting authorization."

Danny Maggio walked into the campaign headquarters of Marco Acevedo on Kings Highway. He found his wife coaching a group of college kids on the art of cold calling. Annie spotted him as the group took to the telephones and she met him at the door.

"Half day?" she asked.

"Day and a half, I'm on the four to midnight. How's it going here?"

"We're not ready to throw in the towel. We'll hang on until the primary. But to call it an even contest would be like calling the Alamo a fair fight. The Wilson campaign is outspending us at least five to one. Money talks. And the City Comptroller, with his big office in Manhattan, is a lot higher profile than a state representative in a Brooklyn storefront."

"How about lunch?"

"What's the occasion?"

"Thursday?" Maggio said.

"Give me five minutes."

Samson had just received word that Kenny Ramirez was in custody when Ivanov arrived at the squad room. He waved her over.

"You're going to Denver in the morning," he said.

"Colorado?"

"That's the one. Richards will fill you in."

Samson spotted Mendez coming in as Ivanov walked off. He waved Rey over and brought him into the office.

Samson brought Mendez up to date on Nicky DeSantis.

"Suicide?" Mendez said. "Open and shut?"

"No one cares to even consider an alternative scenario. The prevailing attitude seems to be that the shooter did everyone a favor and we move past it as quickly as we can. I'm inclined to agree."

"Stan would probably agree as well."

"Trenton would like you to say a few words at Stan's funeral tomorrow morning."

"Of course," Rey said.

"And he said you should expect a call to go in to see him early next week. I'm guessing there is a detective's shield waiting there for you."

Rosen had waited until Samson was done with Mendez before going to his office.

"I spoke with Michaels. They found Patty Bolin's prints in Rose's car, and blood evidence matching Patty's blood type. They pulled prints from the doors, steering wheel and trunk that don't match David Rose. They are working as quickly as they can, going through all available databases for a hit."

"Good news. Add that to the report. Chief Trenton needs it as soon as possible. He wants to hold a press conference in time for news at five. He is visiting the parents of both girls this afternoon."

"I'll deliver the report to Trenton personally by two at the latest," Rosen promised.

"Thank you. Please get a copy to me also. You can call it a day as soon as Detectives Murphy and Maggio get back in. We have a funeral first thing in the morning. Everyone in blues."

"Sometimes I wonder," Rosen said, "about how fucked up things have become when finding out *who* killed someone is considered *good news*."

Rosen swung by the high school after dropping her report off at Chief Trenton's office. She felt Principal William Pabst should hear the news about David Rose before Trenton made it public.

"How terrible, so many lives affected," Pabst said.

Rosen had nothing to add.

"I bumped into one of our students in the hall today. Carla Sanchez. She asked about Mr. Rose, she seemed concerned about his absence from school considering last Friday night."

"What about last Friday night?"

"Carla left school late after a meeting of the cheerleader squad. She couldn't get her car started. Rose came along and offered her a ride home. She asked if they could make a quick stop at a convenience store on the way. She ran in to pick up a carton of milk and when she came back out Rose was gone. I didn't know what to make of it."

"According to his wife, Rose failed to return home Friday night and, as far as we know, it was the last anyone heard of him until his car was found."

"That would make Carla Sanchez one of the last to see David Rose alive," Pabst said.

"That makes Carla a very lucky young woman."

When Detective Murphy arrived at the Six-one, Rosen was waiting at his desk anxious to tell him about her talk with Pabst.

"What do you make of it? Did he decide to let her live?"

"Or something distracted him," Murphy said. "And whatever happened in the few minutes she was in the store, it got him killed. Fuck, Samson said he wanted to see me as soon as I got in."

"Will you call me tonight?"

"I'm stuck here until midnight, you'll probably be asleep."

"You'll never know unless you call," Rosen said.

"Have a seat," Samson said when Murphy entered the captain's office.

"If this is about why you have been on my case lately," Murphy said, slipping into a chair. "I think I have a pretty good idea."

"You do?"

"Either you have lost some of your great confidence in my abilities, or you have been prepping me. It's like knowing an ax is going to fall, but not knowing which one."

"I had a long talk with Trenton. We came to the agreement that it was time I didn't have to run the precinct *and* supervise the squad. We also agreed that if changes were to be made, they should happen before we have a new mayor, and possibly a new commissioner."

"How soon?"

"Two weeks from this Monday you will be Lieutenant Murphy and the detectives unit will be yours. I'll move to the Precinct Commander's office down the hall, and you will move your wall of fame in here."

"So," Murphy said. "What's the good news?"

Tillie Germano looked out of her window above the Empire Beauty Salon on Avenue U and West 9th Street and noticed a man come out of the pizzeria across the avenue and walk briskly away from her up 9th toward Avenue T.

Tillie glanced at the wall clock in her kitchen. It was twenty minutes past eleven. Mrs. Germano knew that Johnny Fazio locked the door at eleven every night. Religiously. Fazio was always in a hurry to get back to his wife and children after thirteen hours at a hot oven. She also knew Johnny was alone in the pizzeria from ten until closing, when they stopped deliveries and he sent everyone else home.

Something wasn't right, and there had been trouble in the neighborhood not long before. Tillie called 9-1-1.

Murphy picked up the call from the night desk sergeant.

"Avenue U and West Ninth Street, look for the patrol car."

Murphy looked at his watch.

"Jesus, Flynn. The night guys should be here any minute."

"Look for the patrol car," Flynn repeated, and rang off.

"What?" Maggio asked. "Don't tell me we caught one at ten fucking minutes before midnight."

"I won't tell you on our way to Avenue U," Murphy said.

"This is Johnny Fazio's place, I went to school with him," Murphy said, when they pulled up in front of the pizzeria.

Officers Janda and Mackay had been first on the scene.

"Looks like a robbery," Mackay said. "The register was emptied. I spoke with the woman who called it in. She saw someone leave, but couldn't see his face."

"What about John Fazio?" Murphy asked.

"In the men's room," Janda said. "He's gone, Murphy."

"Goddamnit. He had three young kids. God-fucking-damnit."

"It might be too late to start canvassing without disturbing everyone else in the neighborhood," Janda said.

"I want four uniforms here first thing in the morning going door-to-door."

"The funeral for Stan Landis is tomorrow morning," Mackay said.

"Right after the service, then, and I'm afraid you'll have to stay here until a forensics team and the medical examiner arrives," Murphy said.

He headed to the restrooms in back. Maggio followed.

Murphy looked down at the body. Speechless.

"Jesus Christ," Maggio said, coming up beside him, "how many times did the maniac need to kill him?"

"Motherfucker," Murphy finally said. "This was no robbery. I know who did this to him."

"Well, let's go get the fuck."

"The fuck is locked up at Riker's," Murphy said, "and I need a fucking drink."

THIRTY FOUR

Augie Sena was alone cashing out the register in Joe's Bar on Avenue U just past one Friday morning when Murphy tapped on the window.

Sena let Murphy and Maggio in and relocked the front door.

Twenty minutes later, Augie brought a second round of beers and joined them at the table. Murphy poured the scotch and held court.

"So here's to Johnny Fazio. We played ball together at Fort Hamilton. He was one of the best fielding third basemen I ever saw, high school or otherwise. His batting average senior year was third highest in the borough.

"Fazio goes straight from school into the Marines, and at eighteen he's with the Second Battalion Fourth in Kuwait waiting to see how Saddam would respond to the Desert Fox air attacks in Iraq.

"He comes home, opens a small auto repair shop, and marries his high school sweetheart. His older brother is a fire-fighter who dies at ground zero. His father runs the pizzeria. Johnny can't keep up with the new automotive technology, can't afford to buy the diagnostic equipment needed to service the late model vehicles, so he joins his old man at the restaurant.

"Two years ago his father has a massive stroke and Johnny has to take over the shop. He has two kids, seven and five, and a two-year-old. He works twelve, thirteen hours a day, only sees the kids in the morning because they are already asleep when he gets home at night."

Murphy took a breather and knocked down another shot.

"Then there is Joe Bando. Bando has been terrorizing the neighborhood since he was in grade school. He worked his way up to a mid-level position in the Colletti Family and when

Colletti and his sons were killed, Bando moved up. The only obstacle keeping Bando from being crowned the fucking *Prince of Gravesend* was Mario Crimi, a Brooklyn prosecutor whose major mission in life was to put Bando away, or at least make Bando's life miserable.

"Mario Crimi lives on West Ninth Street between U and T. Johnny Fazio leaves the pizzeria one night, walks to his car parked on Ninth, climbs in, and before he can turn the key he sees Crimi walk up to his house on the opposite side of the street and start up the stairs. A man with a handgun steps out of a car parked under a streetlight in front of the house and puts three in Crimi's back. When the shooter turns to get back into the car, Fazio can see his face clearly. And Johnny scribbles down the plate number as the car speeds away. Johnny calls it in and, when the uniforms arrive, he names Joe Bando as the gunman.

"Joe Bando is at Rikers awaiting trial, and Johnny was the prosecution's star witness. I have no doubt Bando reached out and had Johnny killed. He needed Fazio silenced and, judging from the brutal beating, he wanted to send a message to anyone who might ever think of crossing him. I need to find the motherfucker who beat Johnny to death and get him to finger Bando." Murphy said. "I need another fucking beer."

"What if we find no witness and the forensics team comes up empty?" Maggio asked, as Augie moved to the bar to grab another round.

"I'm going out to Rikers tomorrow after the funeral."

"You can't think Bando is going to give you anything."

"There's someone else out there who may be persuaded to lend a hand," Murphy said.

Just as Sena dropped three more bottles of Sam Adams onto the table, there was a tapping on the window. He walked over to the door and let Sandra Rosen in. The dog ran in after her and went straight for Murphy, tail waving like a flag in a hurricane.

"Augie woke me up—he thought you might need a ride. I stopped on the way to liberate Ralph, and he wanted to tag along."

. . .

Eight hours later, after the funeral service for Stan Landis at Holy Cross Cemetery, Murphy changed from his dress blue uniform into a suit, white shirt and tie, and drove out to Rikers Island.

Tony Territo was already waiting in an interview room at the prison when Murphy arrived just before noon.

"Well, what a surprise," Territo said. "Did you bring lunch?"

"I need your help."

"Give me a hint. Why would I help one of Brooklyn's fucking finest who put me in here?"

"I didn't put you here. A jury of your peers put you here after you gunned down Dominic Colletti, his two demented sons, and Sammy Leone."

"Didn't exactly break *your* heart, did it?"

"You help me and maybe I can help you."

"How can you help me? I'm up on four counts of voluntary manslaughter," Territo said. "If I ever get out of here, my son will have grandchildren, if the idiot can manage to find someone to marry him. Short of getting me a conjugal visit with Angelina Jolie, you can't do shit for me."

"Why weren't you convicted on first-degree murder?"

"Because the geniuses in the prosecutor's office couldn't put the murder weapon in my hand and offered me what some might call a bargain, unless they had to eat the fucking crap they call food here."

"And because you thought Leone and Colletti killed your daughter and everyone believed you believed it. You're eligible for a parole hearing in four years. You need to think more positively, Tony. With a little help maybe you can see daylight in time to broker a wife for Anthony Junior."

"You're so full of shit your eyes are brown, Murphy. But I have to admit I like your style. What is it you think I can do for you?"

"Johnny Fazio was murdered last night."

"I'm sorry to hear it, he was a good guy. Wasn't he set to

testify against Joe Bando—witnessed Bando gun down an assistant D.A.?"

"Johnny had a wife and three kids. He was viciously beaten to death, Tony."

"And you think Bando got to him?"

"I'm sure of it. Johnny was silenced and left in the toilet as an example. I need to find the mad dog Bando set loose on him."

"I don't have anything to do with Bando, he was a Colletti lieutenant and I'd just as soon piss on him as talk with him. But I'll snoop around—see if I can catch a whiff of anything here inside. Do you remember my cousin Stevie? I was holed up at his place when you picked me up."

"Sure."

"I'll ask him to put an ear to the ground also. He'll give you a shout if he hears anything and, if I do, I'll send word through Stevie."

"Thanks."

"If you want to thank me, next time you grace me with a visit bring a sausage and pepper hero from John's on Stillwell Avenue."

Murphy parked behind the precinct and phoned Detective Maggio before going in.

"Where are you?" Murphy asked.

"I'm down at the scene. Four uniforms have been bothering everyone out on the avenue, in storefronts, or at home in their apartments. No one heard or saw a thing other than the woman who called it in last night. And the crime scene unit found absolutely nothing in the pizzeria."

"Do you need me down there?"

"I'm about to head back to the Six-one. I decided to call a recess until people start getting home from work this evening. Although I would think if there were any witnesses we would have received a call from a conscientious citizen by now."

"I don't expect many citizens will be talking once they learn how Johnny Fazio was rewarded for *his* conscientiousness."

"How did it go at Rikers?"

"I'll fill you in when you get back. The short answer is *we wait and see.*"

When Murphy entered the squad room, Rosen was on him immediately.

"I just received a call from Derek Fielder at the forensics lab. If I have to say this twice it will be twice as unbelievable," Rosen said, and she led Murphy over to Samson's office.

"The fingerprints lifted from the steering wheel, trunk, and both front doors of David Rose's car match those of a bonded interstate CDL driver. The prints were on file with the Department of Transportation."

"Nice build up," Samson said. "Did you get a name?"

"Kenneth Michael Ramirez."

"Incredible. No question?"

"None."

"Unfuckingbelievable," Murphy added.

"Ivanov was on a plane to Denver at seven this morning. She was met at the airport by two detectives from Denver PD, Ramirez was placed into her custody, and they boarded a quick turnaround flight due to arrive at Kennedy around three. Kelly has the complete itinerary. Have him assign two uniforms to follow you out to pick them up at JFK, I want Ramirez to ride in the radio car, Ivanov can ride with you. I'll probably be gone when you get back, but I'll be waiting for my cell to ring," Samson said. "I would like you and Ivanov to lock Ramirez in an interview room and stay there for as long as it takes to find out what the fuck is going on."

"On it," Rosen said, heading out of the office.

Murphy made a move to follow.

"Tommy?"

"Yes?"

"Where have you been while Maggio has been running the show out on Avenue U?"

"I went out to Rikers to have a heart-to-heart with Tony Territo."

"Sit," Samson said. "I can't wait to hear about it."

. . .

Annie Maggio called her husband at the Six-one.

"What's up, Detective?"

"I'm getting ready to leave. How late will you be tonight?"

"I'm already home. We quit early because we have a big day tomorrow. The final debate before the primary is Sunday evening, and there's a world of preparation to deal with."

"Well, then, what do you want to do?"

"I'm doing it. I'm cooking dinner and uncorking a bottle of wine. Later I want to watch one of those South Korean crime movies you love so much so you can put your arm around me and tell me when I can open my eyes again. After that, it's all up to you."

Rosen called Samson's cell.

"Ramirez signed a statement. He jacked the car with Rose in it in front of the convenience store on Stillwell, while Rose was waiting for Carla Sanchez to pick up milk. Later, Ramirez decided he needed to be behind the wheel so he knocked Rose out, tied him up and put him in the trunk. He left the car at the train station in Wilmington, walked to a hotel, and forgot about Rose. We sent him over to central booking and lock up. Ramirez will be arraigned Monday on charges relating to the carjacking and abduction. A.D.A. Caldwell will be talking to the Queens County D.A. with regard to what they want to do about the homicide and attempted murder charges out there."

"Good work, tell Ivanov I said so. And do me a favor. I'm at a birthday party trying to keep six kids all under eight years old from assaulting the cake before dinner."

"Lucky you," Rosen said. "What do you need?"

"Try to get hold of Jesse Fulton at the One-eleven in Bayside and fill him in on Kenny Ramirez. Tell Fulton I'm sorry I couldn't phone myself, but will give him a call tomorrow."

. . .

"Do you need me to stay?" Sarah asked.

"No. I'll be okay," Senderowitz said. "Thanks for getting me home today, and for cleaning up. I hardly recognize the place."

"Don't kill yourself looking for a bottle, you won't find one."

"Thanks for the warning."

"I'll be back after work tomorrow, we'll cook dinner. If you need anything call me."

Sarah stopped at the door, came back to Senderowitz, and kissed him on the forehead.

"Goodnight, Dad," she said.

"Kayla, Lucy, get your things it's time to go."

"I don't want to go home," Lucy said. "I want more cake."

"It's very late and we have a big day tomorrow," Samson said. "Connie is giving us cake to take home."

"What big day?"

"Silly," Kayla chimed in. "We're going to see Jimmy tomorrow."

"Can we bring Jimmy some cake?"

Marina Ivanov and Jack Falcone sat drinking espresso at La Sorrentina Restaurant in Dyker Heights.

"That was a terrific meal," Marina said.

"Are you sure you don't want to try the gelato?" Falcone asked. "It's truly amazing."

"I'm stuffed, maybe next time. How did you find this place?"

"It opened the year I was born. I waited tables here part time when I was in college. Listen, Marina, I didn't want to bring it up over dinner, but how is your sister doing?"

"She's taking it hard. She had already been planning the wedding. And I think she is feeling some guilt, for getting Alex involved in the business at the Lobnya Lounge and with Markov."

"Yuri Markov assaulted your sister, and the man who loved her needed to do something about it. It was his decision, Rachel didn't encourage it, you and Rachel pleaded with him to stay out of it. You're her big sister. You should be able to help her understand she's not to blame."

"It might be easier to convince her if I didn't feel guilty myself."

"About what?"

"Not being able to protect Alex, when we knew Markov wanted revenge."

"We did all we could. If we have learned anything from history it's that when someone is determined to hurt or kill another person, they will find a way in spite of our best efforts to prevent it."

"You may need to keep reminding me."

"I'll be happy to. What would you like to do now?"

"Maimonides is not far from here. Marty Richard's daughter has been there for several days. Marty and his wife have been practically living in the hospital. It looks like the girl will be okay, but I've been meaning to stop in."

"Let's do it," Falcone said. "We can bring gelato."

"It was great meeting you," Connie said.

"It was great meeting you guys also," Lorraine said, "Thanks for having me. Your girls are precious."

Ripley thanked his sister and brother-in-law, scooped up the boys, and walked Lorraine out to her car.

"It was a terrific time," Lorraine said. "Call me."

"Dad," Mickey said, tugging at Ripley's leg.

"What is it, son?"

"Can Lorraine come to our house and read us a bedtime story?"

"I don't know," Ripley said, turning to Kyle for the older boy's reaction.

"It's okay with me," Kyle said, looking from his father to Lorraine.

"Well, in that case," Lorraine said. "I'd love to."

. . .

Murphy was in John Paul Jones park watching Ralph run. He was thinking about the meeting at Rikers, the absurdity of asking Tony Territo for help.

As much as absurdity seemed to be in fashion.

Murphy spotted three teenage boys standing near one of the cannon, talking in hushed voices like they were planning to rob Fort Knox. He could easily pick out the leader—animated, pleading, persuading, and finally earning agreement.

"Hey," he called, "whatever it is you are thinking of doing, don't do it."

Murphy whistled, Ralph ran to his side, and they walked home.

THIRTY FIVE

The telephone woke Murphy very early Sunday morning.

"What the fuck?"

"It's Stevie Territo. Meet me at the Del Rio at eight."

"Can I bring my partner?"

"Sure," Territo said, and hung up.

"What the fuck?" Rosen asked.

"Stevie Territo wants a meet at eight."

"Tony didn't waste any time."

"Tony is jonesing for a sausage and pepper hero. I need to call Maggio."

"I need to get some sleep."

Kayla and Lucy stood at their father's side as he worked on his famous elephant pancakes. His wife Alicia sat at the kitchen table with a cup of coffee and the *Sunday Times*.

"Is there anything worth hearing about?" Samson asked, turning from the stove.

"I'm reading about the Democratic mayoral candidates, the final debate is tonight."

"Don't talk, Dad," Kayla said, "you'll burn them."

"Daddy?"

"Yes, Lucy."

"When is Jimmy coming home?"

"It may be awhile, sweetheart, but we will visit him again soon."

"It was fun writing my name on his cast," Kayla said.

"Me too."

"You wrote Kayla's name on Jimmy's cast too?"

"No, Daddy, I wrote *my* name. L-U-C-Y."

"Well I'm glad you both did, it will help Jimmy remember you."

"Will Jimmy forget us?" Kayla asked.

"Never."

"You're burning the pancakes," Alicia said.

Stevie Territo slipped into the booth and poured a cup of coffee from the carafe on the table.

"We found your guy."

"Positive?" Murphy asked.

"Tony got it from the prison grapevine, and what I learned confirmed it. Al Bianca. He was muscle for the Colletti Family under Sammy Leone's wing, now he works freelance. The man is a beast, used to fight pro, nearly killed a guy in the ring once."

"Where?"

"Here's the address where he's been hanging lately," Stevie said, passing Murphy a slip of paper. "But I'd hurry, he moves around a lot."

Murphy called Samson at home.

"What?"

"How quick can we get a search warrant?"

"What for?"

"For the motherfucker who killed Johnny Fazio," Murphy said. "Maggio and I would like to pay him a visit, but we would also like to get inside his place and look around. We would hate to blow a prosecution on some fucking technicality."

"It's Sunday morning, can it wait until tomorrow?"

"If Bianca hears he's been asked about, he'll disappear."

"I'll have to wake Trenton, and owe him one, and he'll have to wake a judge, and we'll both owe the judge one."

"This animal beat a good man to death. I would ask you to wake up the fucking Pope if it would help collar the fuck—and then *I* could owe you all one."

"Give me an address," Samson said. "I'll call you back."

"So?" Maggio asked when Murphy put the phone down on the table.

"He'll call back."

"Well," Stevie said. "We may as well have breakfast."

Alison Davis was up early Sunday morning trying to make sense of the latest reading assignment in her statistics textbook. Alison was still working at a bridal shop on 18th Avenue while taking evening classes at Brooklyn College. She hoped eventually to give up fitting wedding dresses and take up teaching grade school.

Vinnie Salerno found her beating a pencil on the kitchen table when he finally made it out of bed himself.

"You don't look happy," he said.

"This book might as well be written in Chinese."

"What's the subject?"

"Probability, and if it doesn't begin to sink in soon, the probability of me making it through this class will be zero percent."

"I'm going out to throw a football with some friends. Why don't you take a break and come along, get some fresh air?"

"I would love to, but I really need to get somewhere with this before class tomorrow. Have fun."

"Can I bring you back anything?"

"Bring me a turkey, swiss and avocado club sandwich on sourdough toast and a Chinese interpreter."

Murphy grabbed the cell phone from the restaurant table and answered it after one ring.

"Mendez will be at the place at eleven with search warrant in hand," Samson said.

"Thanks."

"Don't do anything I wouldn't do."

"Thanks for the latitude."

Murphy checked the time before putting the phone away.

"The captain hooked us up. We need to be at Bianca's place in an hour."

"I'd love to be in on that party, but I'm late for Mass at Saint Mary's," Stevie said.

"Thanks for your help," Murphy said.

"Thank my cousin, it was all Tony."

"I'll do that."

"Do it in person, Tony likes visitors bearing food."

Mendez was waiting in plain clothes when they arrived.

"I'm off-duty," he explained.

"Are you going to stick around?" Murphy asked.

"I wouldn't miss it."

The place was a converted storefront, the entrance at street level.

"Should we knock?" Maggio asked.

"We did knock, and we identified ourselves," Murphy said. "I guess he didn't hear us. Can we get through this door?"

"I played soccer in school. If you both give me a shoulder, I can knock the door into next week."

Maggio stood between Murphy and Mendez, threw his arms around their shoulders, lifted his legs off the ground, swung a few times, and then hit the door with both legs fully extended. The door came off the hinges and traveled at least five feet into the front room. When they went in, Al Bianca was on the floor trying to crawl out from under it.

"What the fuck?"

"Get up," Murphy said, as Mendez and Maggio moved the door aside.

"Who the fuck are you?"

"Give him a hand," Murphy said.

Maggio and Mendez stood Bianca up in front of Murphy.

"Let me see your hands."

Bianca lifted his hands and Murphy hit him full force in the mouth.

Bianca went down again.

"Cuff this motherfucker to the radiator and find something to shut him the fuck up."

Mendez slapped on the handcuffs, Maggio grabbed a dish rag from the kitchen sink.

"That looks really nasty," Murphy said, as Maggio stuffed it into Bianca's mouth. "Mendez, show him the warrant. Al, nod if you need it read to you. Let's get this door up in the doorway before we attract an audience, and then we tear this fucking place apart."

They replaced the door, all pulled on latex gloves and they went to work.

Ten minutes later, Mendez called Murphy into the kitchen.

"Found these under the sink."

Murphy pulled a zip-lock from his jacket pocket and passed it to Mendez.

"Gallon size," Mendez said. "Nice."

"I'd like to put his fucking head in it. Please bag those and wait until I call you in."

Murphy went back to the front room and went down on one knee in front of Bianca. Maggio came in from a back room.

"You are under arrest for the premeditated murder of John Fazio. If you say you don't know what I'm talking about, we will hit you with the door again. In fact, don't say a thing until you answer one simple question," Murphy said, and he called Mendez.

He took the bag from Mendez and dropped in onto Bianca's lap.

"My question is, Al, did Joe Bando not pay you enough for new leather gloves to replace this pair soaked with John Fazio's blood or did you save them for sentimental reasons? Let's get this animal into a cage where he belongs."

"Should I pull the rag out of his mouth?" Maggio asked.

"No, I hope the motherfucker chokes on it."

A touch football game naturally led to several rounds of cold bottled beer and it was nearly three when Vinnie Salerno finally made it home on Sunday afternoon.

Alison was still at it, nose in the textbook, scribbling in a notebook.

"Sorry I'm so late. I brought your sandwich."

"I made an omelet."

"You can take the sandwich for lunch tomorrow."

"By then it will be so soggy I'd need to use a straw. We can share it for dinner, I'll make a salad."

"I was planning to order a pizza for dinner, for the game."

"The game?"

"The Giants are on NBC tonight. Cris Collinsworth, Al Michaels, and Big Blue. *The* game."

"I need to watch the debate tonight."

"What debate?"

"The Democratic Party candidates," Alison said.

"Who cares?"

"I have to write a report on the debate for my Political Science class so I'm guessing my professor cares."

"When is it due?"

"Thursday."

"I can record it, and you can watch it anytime you like before then."

"How do you do that?"

"The DVD machine Carmine sent from Chicago for a house warming gift records onto blank discs."

"And you know how to do that?"

"I program the time and the channel and the machine does the rest. And you can pause it, go back, go forward, whatever you want."

"I hope its *fool* proof."

"Cute. I'll make you a deal, you watch the Giants with me and I'll watch the debate with you."

"That sounds very romantic, how about I choose the pizza toppings?"

Thomas Murphy and Lorraine DiMarco sat at a table in Joe's Bar over drinks late Sunday afternoon.

Murphy had intended to schedule a get together for a long time—and had been putting it off for just as long for no good reason. After taking care of the business with Al Bianca, he impulsively called Lorraine on the chance she had a few hours to spare for an old friend. Lorraine hurried down to the bar.

The meeting was casual, comfortable. They shared a mutual respect, and more than that they truly liked each other. They had both faced life changing challenges over the past year or so— individually and mutually.

Lorraine asked about his mother, asked about Ralph, and asked about Sandra Rosen—allowing him to decide whether to talk about Sandra or about him *and* Sandra.

Murphy asked about her law practice, her parents, and asked about her health—allowing her to decide whether or not to talk about the brain tumor treated less than a year ago and if she still had a clean bill.

And they talked about Lou Vota who they had both loved. With the help of the time that had passed, it was easier to talk about Lou, they found they could talk more about his life than his death, and their reminiscences most often brought smiles and sometimes laughter.

"Rumor has it you're moving up," Lorraine said.

"Bad news travels fast."

"You're not pleased?"

Murphy poured another scotch before considering the question.

"First of all, its time, in the eyes of the department it's like growing up. And if I run the detectives squad it will lighten Samson's work load, so he can concentrate on all of the bullshit necessary to operate the precinct—budgets, personnel, vehicles, and the dreaded public relations."

"Are you worried it will change your relationship with the others?"

"It didn't for Sam when he moved up and I'm hoping it won't for me. I have great respect for the detectives at the Six-one. Not to sound too much like Popeye, I am who I am, I'm good with who I am, and for some reason I am well liked. I believe they will

357

all want me to succeed and will help me succeed. And I won't be locked in an office. I'll go out on calls with them whenever I can."

"It will still become you and *them*, Tommy, that's the nature of rank and authority. But I'm sure it will work out, if you don't let power go to your head."

"No worries. Power won't go to my head, I leave that to scotch and beer chasers. Speaking of rank, rumor has it you have been seeing one of my soon to be underlings."

Lorraine had to laugh.

"It's too soon to comment. So, for the time being, I'll plead the fifth."

"Would you like another beer?"

"Sure, why not?"

Murphy went to the bar and came back with two cold bottles.

"Lorraine, I hate to talk business when we're having so much fun being silly—but I could use some advice."

"Shoot."

"Do you remember Tony Territo?"

"Tony Territo is quite unforgettable," Lorraine said. "What about him?"

"He helped us out. I said I would try to help him."

"How do you expect to help him? He killed four men. He was convicted and they relocated him from a mansion in Bay Ridge to a cell at Rikers."

"But they didn't throw away the key. Look, I don't condone his actions, but he killed four men who nobody in their right mind would miss. And he had the mistaken idea they had killed his teenage daughter. He is not what I would call a role model, but he had no previous record of violent crime and I don't believe he is a menace to society. I believe there are degrees of guilt, shades of innocence, and they all congregate on the same avenue. And as far as blame goes, there is nothing to gain by assigning it. Bad things happen to good people as well as to bad ones. When you blame yourself you are being self-indulgent and when you blame others you are ducking responsibility. Territo will be eligible for a parole hearing eventually, maybe there is some way to get it moved up, but I don't know how to present the suggestion to the D.A."

"I won't be his attorney, but I'll look at his case and the trial record and share my thoughts on how you might approach the prosecutor."

"That would be great, Lorraine. Thanks."

"Is this so you can tell Territo you tried?"

"It's so I can tell myself I tried."

"Shades of innocence," Lorraine said. "I like that."

THIRTY SIX

Monday morning, detectives from the Six-one were scattered throughout the Kings County Criminal Courts Building.

The wheels of justice were spinning wildly.

Murphy and Maggio sat in on the arraignment of Al Bianca.

After considering a number of options presented by the District Attorney, Bianca had elected to name Joe Bando as his solicitor and swear to it at trial.

"So, Bando has a key witness killed and in the process creates another key witness," Maggio said. "Do you think Bando will try finding a hit man to silence the hit man?"

"I'm not that imaginative," Murphy said.

Across the hall, Detectives Ivanov and Rosen witnessed the arraignment of Kenny Ramirez, who was charged with the abduction and subsequent assault resulting in the death of David Rose.

Ramirez would be facing arraignment in Queens County later that day, charged with the murder of Rebecca Ramirez and the attempted murder of Jimmy Samson.

In a third courtroom, Detective Ripley attended a bail hearing for Victor Bronski and Vladimir Markov.

Bail was denied in both cases, and trial dates were set for both defendants who would be prosecuted separately.

Later that Monday morning, Annie Maggio and other members of the senior campaign staff were with candidate Marco Acevado preparing for the primary election scheduled for the following day.

Sarah Sanders was behind a desk at New York One, preparing questions for an interview with the winner of Tuesday's election.

Marty and Linda Richards brought their daughter Sophia home from the hospital.

And in a private service, attended by his wife and son, David Rose was unceremoniously put to rest.

On Tuesday morning, Officer Rey Mendez met with Chief of Detectives Stanley Trenton in Trenton's office.

"I am pleased to inform you that you will be among six members of the New York Police Department, including Thomas Murphy, who will be promoted to or within the Detectives' Division in a ceremony this coming Monday. You will be awarded your detective's shield at that time. You will be assigned to the Sixty-first Precinct under the command of Captain Samson, and your specific duties will be determined at Lieutenant Murphy's discretion. Congratulations and good fortune, Detective Mendez."

"Thank you, sir."

"You can, of course, invite anyone you wish to be at the ceremony."

The one person Rey Mendez *wished* could be at the ceremony was Stan Landis.

Senderowitz phoned Samson at the Six-one just before noon.

"I thought it would be good to catch up."

"I'm sorry I've been out of touch, Bernie, I've been buried in work here."

"Have you had anything to eat lately?"

"I can't remember."

"If you can sneak away for an hour or two, the Smith Street Canteen between President and Carroll is fairly quiet after the lunch rush, and the food is very good. I need to talk with you. I know it's out of your way, but I'm not up to driving yet and I can walk there."

"How about meeting there at two?" Samson asked.

"Perfect. I'll see you then."

. . .

Early Tuesday afternoon, Maureen Rose hand delivered a letter to the Administrative Office at Midwood High School.

Her son Jason would not be returning to classes.

They would be moving back to the Boston area, where her parents still lived, and Jason would be transferred to a third high school in less than four months.

Samson and Senderowitz sat at a window booth looking out onto Smith Street.

"How are things going with Sarah?"

"Sarah has been a great help, Sam, and she has been keeping a close eye on me."

"As in looking out for you?"

"As in looking in all the usual hiding places. Don't get me wrong, it's good having her back in my life," Bernie said, "but there is also the fear I'll disappoint her again. I haven't had a drink in more than a week, but it's not because I couldn't use one. What else am I missing?"

Samson brought Bernie up to date.

"The killer of Jenny Greco and Patty Bolin was identified and found dead, closing the 'Hangman' case. Peter Donner has been cleared of any suspicion in the first murder, but his inappropriate actions put Jenny Greco in danger and I doubt he will be very well-accepted at school, have much luck with the girls, or be allowed to remain on the football squad for that matter. Vladimir Markov employed someone to replace the man who shot at you, and Alex Holden was killed. Both Markov and the shooter are being held without bail awaiting trial for murder and conspiracy. Nicky DeSantis, who shot and killed Stan Landis, was himself found dead, an apparent suicide."

"I heard Kenny Ramirez was apprehended."

"Ramirez turned up in Denver and Ivanov had to fly out to fetch him."

"How is Jimmy doing?"

"We moved him to New York Hospital in Queens. He is doing physical therapy and getting psychological counseling. We're very optimistic. It was a traumatic experience, no question, but compared to the burdens Peter Donner and Jason Rose will have to bear, Jimmy could be considered relatively lucky."

"It sounds like it was an eventful week at the Six-one."

"Only because it is so insane out there. Ours is not a business where it is necessarily good to be busy," Samson said. "But enough of that, what did you *need* to talk with me about?"

"I heard Murphy and Mendez are being bumped up."

"Its official on Monday, Murphy will take over the detectives' squad and Mendez will join them."

"And how is Maggio working out?"

"Good, I like him."

"You might consider stealing him from the Fifth Precinct permanently."

"I've thought about it."

"It sounds like you're in good shape on Coney Island Avenue."

"What's on your mind, Bernie?"

"I'm planning to put in my retirement papers."

"I'm sorry to hear it."

"I no longer have the energy to be chasing criminals all over creation, Sam. The heart attack was a wakeup call."

"I would hate losing one of the best noses in the department."

"One of the biggest at least."

"Can I propose something?"

"Okay."

"Hold on to those papers for a while. Let me speak with Trenton while I'm in such good graces with him. See if we can work out limited duty, keep you in the department as a part-time consultant—bring you in when we are in need of your invaluable instinct and intuition."

"That sounds like a sure way to earn resentment for stepping on toes."

"Your input has always been welcomed, often solicited. I don't see why that would change."

"Let me think about it before you approach Trenton and then, if I decide to go for it, I can always hope he says no."

Shortly after the polls closed Tuesday evening the local television and radio stations projected a winner in the primary election.

At eight, from his campaign office on Kings Highway in Gravesend, Marco Acevedo conceded. Acevedo congratulated his opponent, thanked those who voted for him for their support, and thanked his staff of consultants and volunteers for their valiant efforts.

His concession speech was not televised live.

Although Marco Acevedo, a favorite son of Brooklyn, had received nearly sixty-five percent of the Kings County vote, his supporters in the remaining four boroughs were greatly outnumbered and, at the end of the day, he was defeated citywide by twelve points, fifty-six to forty-four percent.

Theodore Wilson celebrated his victory at a mid-town Manhattan hotel, in a ballroom packed with enthusiastic backers and with cameras from all of the networks rolling.

The City Comptroller thanked Acevedo for a well fought, dignified battle, adding he had learned much from the campaign about the issues which most concerned the citizens of *this great city.*

Wilson reminded the cameras that the general election was only six weeks away. He expressed his sincere hope that the esteemed Congressman from the Tenth District, along with those voters who so vigorously endorsed Acevedo, would all stand behind him in the tough fight ahead to keep a Democratic mayor in City Hall—more than once in his victory speech invoking the term *common cause.*

A regular visitor to Seth Low Park took a seat beside an old acquaintance later Tuesday night.

"What do you think of Wilson?" he asked.

"Wilson?"

"The Democratic candidate for Mayor—will you vote for him?"

"I'll vote for anyone who has any idea about how to help me get off this fucking bench," Stump said.

THIRTY SEVEN

The job of Police Commissioner in the city of New York is an appointed position. The Commissioner is chosen by the sitting mayor, can be replaced at any time, and so serves at the pleasure of the city's Chief Executive.

Wednesday morning, Mayor Fredericks phoned Commissioner Daniels on behalf of Theodore Wilson and explained to Daniels what Wilson had in mind. The commissioner didn't care for the idea, but was reminded by his honor that maintaining a Democratic Party hold on City Hall could have a profound effect on Daniels' position going forward. The Commissioner called Chief Trenton who in turn called Captain Samson at the Six-one. Samson in turn called down to Sergeant Kelly and then he scheduled a meeting of all detectives at ten.

Rey and Salina Mendez dropped their two daughters at school. Now that the younger girl had started kindergarten, Salina had it a little easier getting through her day. Still, their two-year-old boy was a handful.

Afterwards, they visited Salina's pediatrician for a routine check on her pregnancy. Rey kept the toddler at bay in the waiting room. Thirty minutes later his wife rejoined them.

"Well?"

"Everything is perfect, but she did do an ultrasound."

"And?"

"Would you like to know if it's a daughter or a son?"

"Do I?"

"Do you?"

"Sure. It's good either way."

"A boy."

"Another holy terror."

"Rey."

"Yes?"

"I would like us to name him for Landis."

"*Stanley* Mendez, that would be a family first."

"You don't like it?"

"I love it," Rey said, "and I love that you suggested it."

Mendez dropped his wife and his son at home and rushed down to the Six-one, arriving just as Samson began his presentation to the squad.

"Beginning Monday, following a ritualistic promotion ceremony to which you are all cordially invited, I will be moving down the hall to the *Captain's* office so I may attend to administrative duties without being distracted by all of your pretty faces. *Lieutenant* Murphy will be sitting in the office I have been trying to hide in lately, or standing on his head out here if he prefers, either way he will be responsible for the smooth and successful operation of the detective's squad at the Six-one. Try not to make his job as difficult as he made mine. Rey Mendez will be joining us as detective third grade and I will let Murphy flip a coin to determine who gets stuck having to wipe behind Rey's ears. I spoke with Detective Maggio earlier, inquiring as to his possible interest in joining us permanently. He indicated he would very much like to do so, God knows why. I will be cashing in a marker with Chief Trenton to try to make it happen. Bernie Senderowitz sends his Jewish motherly love. I am hoping he will eventually come back to work with us, at least in a limited capacity. If there are no questions, I will move on to the *really* bad news."

"Have you ever considered hosting the Oscars?" Murphy asked.

When the laughter died down, Samson continued.

"Everyone in the precinct works Saturday—as in *no exceptions*. Theodore Wilson, the Democratic candidate for mayor, will be staging a campaign rally in front of the Six-one at ten that morning."

"You have to be kidding," Rosen said. "Why here?"

"Because he needs Brooklyn if he hopes to win the general election in November, for that he needs Acevedo's endorsement and he wants to get it right here in the Congressman's district. Wilson also wants to make a big show of praising the Police Department. Finally, if a Republican candidate is elected, Commissioner Daniels will be out looking for another job. That is why. Coney Island Avenue will be closed to all traffic between Avenues X and V, as will Crawford and Lancaster Avenues between Seventh and Twelfth Streets and Gravesend Neck Road between Eighth and Twelfth. It is what it is, several hours of logistical hell. Then those who had a scheduled day off will go home, and the rest of us will take a deep breath and do police work."

Murphy and Rosen picked up sandwiches and soft drinks from a deli on Avenue V, walked over to Mellett Playground, found a park bench, and called it a late lunch.

"Samson was hilarious this morning, until he got to the part about the fucking rally on our doorstep," Murphy said.

"I was just thinking."

"What?"

"Today is four weeks since Angela Salerno and Eddie Cicero were killed."

"It seems like yesterday."

"It seems like a year ago," Rosen said.

"I've been meaning to reach out to John Cicero, and I keep putting it off. There's a problem between us, I could feel it when Maggio and I went out to the Six-eight and Cicero had to hand over the Holden investigation, and it needs to be dealt with. And I feel I brought it on."

"Cicero can be a hard case."

"And I can be a hard case myself. When my brother Michael was killed, I was prepared to crucify a frightened rookie cop who made an honest mistake, and when Lou Vota was killed I was ready to destroy the world. I was hard on John. His son was executed, and he was treated as if he was just someone who was in our way."

"I can't say what you should do, Tommy."

"I know you can't," Murphy said, "but what if you could?"

When Maggio arrived home Wednesday evening, his wife Annie was preparing dinner.

"How was your day?"

"Captain Samson asked if I'd like to remain at the Sixty-first Precinct permanently."

"And you said?"

"I said I would, and I would. It still has to go up the ladder for approval, but he seems certain Chief Trenton will sign on."

"You'll be missed at the Fifth."

"I'd like to think so, but I will be glad to be working the neighborhood. How was *your* day?"

"I received a flattering telephone call from Theodore Wilson's campaign manager asking if I would like to join their camp—on salary."

"And you said?"

"I politely declined."

"Why?"

"There's something about Wilson that bothers me, I can't put my finger on it but it's there and I can't shrug it off."

"What will you do?"

"I'll do what I have been doing, teach my Political Science classes at Brooklyn College and pick up high school history classes as a substitute," Annie said. "It's funny."

"What?"

"The assignment for my class tomorrow was a report on Sunday's debate, the result of yesterday's primary sort of diminishes the debate's importance."

"If you are examining the debate process itself, the outcome shouldn't really matter."

"You are perfectly correct, Detective."

"So do a get an A, Professor?"

Sarah was clearing the dinner dishes. She had been unusually quiet during their meal, and intuition told Bernie Senderowitz there was something plaguing his daughter.

Sarah brought coffee over to the table, then moved to the sink and began rinsing plates.

"Leave those," Senderowitz said. "Pour yourself a cup and come sit with me."

"I brought the sesame Regina cookies you like so much."

"Sit. Tell me what's on your mind."

Sarah sat, took a deep breath, and began.

"A good friend from journalism school was asked by CNN to cover the presidential debate in Chicago. She and her husband are expecting a child in a few weeks, so she decided to decline the offer and she recommended me. I guess CNN admired what I did for New York One on the last gubernatorial campaign and I received a telephone call today asking if I would be interested in the assignment."

"It sounds like a simple decision. I'm very proud of you."

"It would mean being away for nearly a week."

"And you're worried about leaving me to fend for myself. Sarah," Bernie said, before she could respond, "I'm doing fine, getting around well, and in any case I was going to suggest I was taking up too much of your time. Don't let me stop you—it would hurt me more than help me. And don't worry about the drinking. I haven't thought about a drink in some time, and if I thought for a moment it had anything to do with your hesitation in accepting a career changing opportunity it would make me very sad—and a bit angry."

"Are you certain?"

"Absolutely. On top of that, I will probably be back to work myself before long."

"I thought you had decided to get out."

"I had lunch with the captain yesterday. Samson is lobbying

to have me return, limited duty, as a consultant. Finish out my time so I can earn full retirement benefits."

"So you think it's a good idea?"

"I do. If I don't do something to keep busy, I would go stir crazy. And it will keep me out of mischief."

"If I sign on, they want me in Chicago on Friday."

"Well, then, you have a lot of preparing to do. But first, where are those sesame Regina cookies I like so much?"

Alison and Vinnie finally got around to watching the DVD recording of the Sunday debate on Wednesday night. Vinnie didn't really see the point of watching the thing after a candidate had already been chosen, but he didn't argue. Alison had sat with him to the bitter end of a heartbreaking loss by the Giants and he would hold up his end of the *deal*.

The final few minutes of the debate were devoted to closing statements. Theodore Wilson spoke last. He succinctly reviewed his visions for the future of the city, and he restated some of his ideas about how these goals could be realized. He ended with a call for a united effort. *"Working together to keep New York City great,"* Wilson said, *"should be our most pressing concern."*

Vinnie Salerno nearly jumped out of his skin.

"Are you alright," Alison said, "you just turned as white as a ghost."

"I just heard a fucking ghost. It's him."

"What's him?"

Vinnie crossed the room and took a CD from a bookcase shelf. The copy Carmine Brigati had made of the tape Bill Heller has passed to him at the restaurant a month earlier, the tape which held the conversation between Kevin Donahue and the unidentified second man. The conversation that had gotten Heller killed, and then Donahue. The tape recording that had led to the violent deaths of Eddie Cicero and Vinnie's sister Angie.

Vinnie inserted the disc into the CD player. His hand shook as he pressed the play button. "Listen carefully," he said.

Donahue: *Kevin Donahue.*

Unknown: *Good afternoon, Mr. Donahue.*

Donahue: *Are you crazy? I told you never to call me here. And why are you calling at all, our business is done.*

Unknown: *I need two hundred thousand dollars.*

Donahue: *You already got two hundred grand.*

Unknown: *My needs have changed. I saved you at least twenty times that amount and a good deal of bad publicity. I don't feel as if a ten percent commission is asking too much.*

Donahue: *We had a deal. I don't know what world you bureaucrats live in, but where I come from a deal is a deal.*

Unknown: *Spare me the lecture on business ethics, Mr. Donahue.*

Donahue: *Why should I give you another dime?*

Unknown: *Because just as easily as I made incriminating evidence disappear, I can make it miraculously appear again. We are talking about a scandal that could severely damage reputations and hurt the city. Working together to keep New York City great should be our most pressing concern.*

Vinnie stopped the CD there.

Then, using the DVD remote, Vinnie replayed the last several moments of Theodore Wilson's closing statement.

"My God, it *can't* be," Alison said. "Are you sure?"

"I've listened to this conversation so many times I hear it in my sleep. And there it is, word for word, without question. Alison, I have to tell someone about this."

"You can call Detective Senderowitz first thing in the morning."

"Senderowitz is out of commission, recovering from a heart attack, but there's someone else who needs to hear this and I feel I owe it to him."

Vinnie told Alison who he had to see. He took the DVD from the player, went to the kitchen, and put both the CD and the DVD into a plastic bag. Then he grabbed a jacket.

"You're going now?" Alison asked. "It is nearly eleven."

"This won't keep. Can I use your car?"

"The keys are in the candy bowl near the door."

"Don't wait up for me," Vinnie said, as snatched up the car keys and rushed out the door.

THIRTY EIGHT

Alison opened her eyes and glanced at the clock on the bedside table. It was half past three Thursday morning.

She couldn't say what woke her.

She climbed out of bed, walked out to the living room, and found Vinnie sitting silently on the sofa. "What happened?" she asked, "you look like someone hid the ice cream."

"He dismissed it."

"What exactly does that mean?"

"He said it was compelling, but not conclusive. He said Wilson has such strong support from the current mayor and the Police Commissioner that no one would touch it without an incontestable voice comparison, which no one was going to authorize."

"And?"

"He asked me to leave the CD and DVD, said he would try to go through the back door to get an analysis done."

"Was he convinced himself?"

"He said no, but not convincingly."

"And what does that mean?"

"Something in his eyes, Alison, it was a little frightening. He told me to keep it to myself. Tell no one."

"So?"

"I don't know."

"You did what you needed to do, you're not police."

"I don't know."

"Aren't you working a double at the restaurant today?"

"Ten in the morning until closing."

"It's almost four, Vinnie. You need to get some sleep. We can talk about it tonight. Come," Alison said.

She took Vinnie's hand and led him back to the bedroom.

. . .

Early Thursday morning Rachel Ivanov called her sister to ask if Marina had time for breakfast.

They sat at a window booth in the Del Rio Diner at seven.

"Alex's sister asked me to meet her yesterday afternoon," Rachel began. "Sonia has been here since the funeral, to be with her mother. She returns home to California later today. She asked to meet at the bakery. When I arrived, Katherine, Susan and Alex's two assistant bakers were there also."

The younger sister took a moment before continuing.

"Sonia would like the Avenue Bakery to survive. She sees it as a legacy to both her father and her brother. She has a family and a business in San Francisco, so she is out of the equation. She asked if I would be interested in taking over operation of the bakery. She expressed confidence in my ability to handle the business end, and said her mother could make a baker of me. The four employees wish to stay on."

"And?"

"We reopen Monday morning at seven."

"I'll be there," Marina said.

Lorraine DiMarco called her assistant Victoria Anderson into her office Thursday morning.

"We need some information on a Riker's Island inmate, Anthony Territo," Lorraine said.

"Go," Victoria said, legal pad and pencil in hand.

"The date set for his first parole hearing, whether or not he has been a good boy inside, and if there are any *respectable* citizens out there who can speak well of Territo's character. And reach out to his wife—find out where she stands."

"Got it."

"Thank you," Lorraine said

Victoria left the office to get to work.

Twenty minutes later, Victoria came back in and placed a dozen long stemmed roses in a cut glass vase on top of the barrister bookcase at the door opposite Lorraine's desk.

"These just arrived. I'm guessing they didn't come from the flower shop at Riker's."

"What does the card say?"

Victoria removed the card from the small envelope.

"Have a nice day—Kyle and Mickey Ripley."

"I believe I will," Lorraine said.

Detectives Rosen and Murphy were doing lunch at Nikki's Café on Kings Highway.

"Josh Altman called me," Sandra said.

"I understood the stipulations of his bail release were that he stay far away from you and *not* call you."

"He said he wouldn't bother me again. He said he needed me to know he was getting psychological counseling and that he was sorry."

"And you said?"

"I said I was sorry as well. And that was that. How are you feeling about Monday?"

"What's Monday?"

"The day after Sunday. The day *Lieutenant* Thomas Murphy takes over the detectives' squad."

"It is what it is," Murphy said, "an occupational hazard of a chain-of-command bureaucracy. I just hope they will all still like me."

"Who likes you?"

"Good point."

"Your father would be very proud, Tommy, and so would your brother Michael."

"Pride is earned, I'll do my best."

"Any thoughts about who will be teamed?"

"I thought about keeping Richards and Ivanov together, putting Mendez with Danny Maggio, and having you and Ripley partner—but I'm open to other suggestions."

"Actually, that sounds good. I was wondering."

"Yes?"

"What do you think about Ripley and Lorraine DiMarco?" Rosen asked, with a mischievous smile.

"I like them both," Murphy said, not biting.

Captain Samson watched from the sidelines while his son went through his physical therapy session.

Although the jury was still out on long-term prognoses, by all accounts the boy was making terrific progress.

When they returned to the hospital room, Jimmy handed his father an envelope.

"What's this?"

"I told my psychologist I was having trouble expressing my regrets about what happened. She suggested I try it in writing, so I wrote down my feelings in the form of a letter to Kenny Ramirez. I thought maybe he should see it."

"Did it help you to write it?"

"Yes."

"Then I am glad you did. Do you trust me, son?"

"Yes."

"Allow me to read it and if I believe it will help *him* in any way, I will make sure he receives it."

"Okay."

Later, in his car, Samson read the letter.

It was well-articulated and heartfelt, but he didn't see how it could be of any benefit or consolation to Kenny Ramirez.

He filed it in the glove box and headed for the Six-one.

Vinnie Salerno arrived home after fourteen hours at the restaurant, exhausted but determined.

"This thing has been eating at me all day," he said to Alison as soon as he walked in the door. "I need to talk to Detective Senderowitz. I need him to listen to the original Kevin Donahue tape again, and Theodore Wilson's closing remarks from the debate, and hear what *he* thinks."

"It's midnight, Vinnie, it can wait until tomorrow. What time are you done at work?"

"I should be able to get out by four."

"My class is out at five-thirty. I'll come pick you up here and we can drive over to see him together."

Bernie Senderowitz spent a few hours with his daughter on Friday afternoon before she had to head to the airport for her flight to Chicago.

"All set?" Senderowitz asked.

"I think so."

"Do you need anything done at your apartment? Mail? Plants?"

"Aunt Eileen's daughter just started graduate school at NYU. Deborah commutes from New Jersey. I told her she was welcome to use my place while I'm away. It will save her a little time and money."

"That is very generous."

"She's family. Speaking of which, you should visit with Aunt Eileen sometime soon, she would like that."

"Eileen reminds me so much of your mother."

"That doesn't need to be a bad thing."

"Will you let me know when your reports are scheduled to be aired?"

"I will."

"It will really be something to see the name Sarah Sanders beside the scrolling headlines at the bottom of the television screen."

"I hope you won't be too disappointed if it says Sarah Senderowitz."

When Alison pulled up in front of the apartment house, Vinnie was anxiously waiting at the curb. He quickly jumped into the passenger seat, a laptop computer tucked under his arm.

"I called Carmine in Chicago. He was able to email me a

digital copy of the telephone conversation. And I found the debate online. I'll be able to play both for Detective Senderowitz as soon as we get there."

"Are you sure we'll find him at home?"

"He's still recovering."

"Maybe you should call."

Vinnie dug into his pocket for his cell phone.

The unopened bottle of Glenfiddich single-malt scotch whiskey had been well-hidden far in the depths of his clothes closet. He had been thinking about it for days. Now it sat on the kitchen table, holding his full attention.

The telephone rang.

It was Ripley.

"I'm taking my boys to Coney Island to see a Cyclones baseball game. I have an extra ticket. We can swing by and pick you up."

"I can take the subway. I should be at the ballpark in an hour."

"Perfect," Ripley said. "We'll buy you a hot dog and a beer."

"We'll see about the beer."

Senderowitz threw on a windbreaker and a cap.

On his way out he took one more look at the bottle of scotch.

"I'll deal with you later," he said.

"The line is busy," Vinnie said.

"What's the quickest route?"

"Take the Belt Parkway to the Gowanus and get off at Hamilton Avenue. We should be there in twenty-five minutes."

Thirty minutes later, after getting no answer at Senderowitz's door, they returned to the car.

"Fuck."

"Relax, Vinnie. I'm hungry, let's find a restaurant. We can try calling again after dinner."

. . .

At the ballpark Bernie Senderowitz resisted beer—but then he was not very fond of beer.

During the game, he paid more attention to the interaction between Ripley and the boys than to the play on the field.

It reminded him of all of the time he had missed in his daughter's life.

Ripley insisted Bernie join them for a nightcap after the game.

"Root beer floats—and we'll give you a ride home."

"I'm in," Bernie said.

Vinnie tried reaching Senderowitz a few more times later Friday night with no luck.

"One more day isn't going to hurt," Alison said. "Let's get some sleep."

And they called it a day.

THIRTY NINE

At two on Saturday morning open trucks stacked with temporary police barricades began rolling out of garages and storage warehouses in Brooklyn and Queens.

NYDOT and NYPD personnel worked through the night to block off Coney Island Avenue, and the side streets feeding into the avenue near the 61st Precinct, from all vehicular traffic.

Eight twelve-inch high four-foot by eight-foot risers were arranged in front of the entrance to the precinct and covered with carpet—creating a thirty-two-foot wide, sixteen-foot deep stage. A podium was set at center stage front, and eight chairs were set at the back of the stage—four to the left and four to the right of the podium.

Candidate Wilson and his wife, along with Congressman Acevedo and *his* wife, would be seated stage left. The First Deputy Mayor candidate, his wife, Chief Stanley Trenton and Captain Samson would be seated stage right.

Detectives and police officers from both the 61st and 60th Precincts would be stationed at points throughout the cordoned area, handling traffic, pedestrian and crowd control.

Richards and Maggio, each with two uniformed officers, would be at the back of the stage to the left and right, behind the seated guests. Murphy and Rosen would be posted at the front of the stage—left and right of the podium.

Bernie Senderowitz woke up feeling the need to walk-off the Root Beer float from the night before.

He thought about Ripley's boys. Kyle and Mickey had called him Uncle Bernie when they dropped him off at home.

He thought about how proud he was of his daughter.

As he was passing through the kitchen, he spotted the bottle of scotch on the table.

Senderowitz picked it up and emptied it into the kitchen sink.

A few minutes after Bernie left for his walk, Vincent Salerno phoned Detective Senderowitz and got no answer.

By nine on Saturday morning everyone had found their stations.

Marina Ivanov and Jack Falcone, her former partner from the Sixtieth, stood drinking coffee at the corner of Coney Island Avenue and Avenue W. It was noticed by some that the two detectives had arrived together.

Rey Mendez and two other uniformed officers stood at the corner of Coney Island Avenue and Gravesend Neck Road. Rey's colleagues were joking, amiably, about his imminent ascendancy to detective—asking if Mendez had completed his thrift store shopping for a plainclothes wardrobe.

By nine-forty-five, hundreds of people had arrived—crowding the avenue from Avenue W to Gravesend Neck Road.

Detective Ripley and six uniforms stood behind the congergation at the opposite side of the avenue.

Shortly before ten, the guests-of-honor stepped up onto the stage—Theodore Wilson smiling and waving at the crowd as he found his seat.

Captain Samson looked as if he would rather be anywhere else.

At ten, Marco Acevedo came to the podium to introduce the newly chosen Democratic Party candidate for mayor.

Murphy spotted someone he knew, standing at the front of the crowd at center stage.

Murphy worked his way over.

"I didn't expect to find you here," he said, coming alongside.

"There was a call for volunteers, so I signed on."

"I'm glad I ran into you. I was hoping we could get together for a drink sometime."

"Sure, whenever you like."

"I'll give you a yell," Murphy said, as Wilson came to the podium.

Acevedo and Wilson shook hands, Acevedo returned to his seat, and Wilson greeted the crowd and began speaking.

"Tommy?"

"Yes?"

"Do you know a good criminal defense attorney?"

"Lorraine DiMarco. I know her well, there are none better."

"Do me a favor."

"Sure," Murphy said.

"Put in a good word for me."

With that, he stepped up to the podium, pulled out his service revolver, and fatally shot Theodore Wilson three times in the chest.

Then Detective John Cicero quickly dropped the weapon, threw his arms above his head, and went down to his knees.

ACKNOWLEDGMENTS

There are too many to thank here for encouraging and inspiring me to write and strive to become better at it—and as many to thank for supporting my humble efforts by spreading the word.

However, I will name those who have been particularly influential.

Linda Abramo—the best publicist a brother could wish for.

Sonny Wasinger and Daniella BaRashees—always first in line for each new book.

Andrea Cataneo—who has been on my side since day one.

Tom Arlow—for walking the walk.

Eric Campbell and Down & Out Books for unparalleled faith and loyalty and for working so diligently and professionally to make the writing as good as it can be.

J.L. Abramo
Denver, Colorado

ABOUT THE AUTHOR

J.L. Abramo was born in the seaside paradise of Brooklyn, New York on Raymond Chandler's fifty-ninth birthday. Abramo is the author of *Catching Water in a Net*, winner of the St. Martin's Press/Private Eye Writers of America prize for Best First Private Eye Novel; the subsequent Jake Diamond novels *Clutching at Straws, Counting to Infinity* and *Circling the Runway; Chasing Charlie Chan*, a prequel to the Jake Diamond series; the stand-alone thriller, *Gravesend*; and *Brooklyn Justice*.

Abramo's short fiction has appeared in the anthologies *Unloaded: Crime Writers Writing Without Guns; Mama Tried: Crime Fiction Inspired by Outlaw Country Music; Murder Under the Oaks*, winner of the Anthony Award for Best Anthology of 2015; and *Coast to Coast: Private Eyes From Sea to Shining Sea*.

Circling the Runway won the Shamus Award for Best Original Paperback Novel of 2015 presented by the Private Eye Writers of America.

For more information please visit:

www.jlabramo.com

www.facebook.com/jlabramo

OTHER TITLES FROM DOWN AND OUT BOOKS

See www.DownAndOutBooks.com for complete list

By J.L. Abramo
Catching Water in a Net
Clutching at Straws
Counting to Infinity
Gravesend
Chasing Charlie Chan
Circling the Runway
Brooklyn Justice
Coney Island Avenue

By Trey R. Barker
2,000 Miles to Open Road
Road Gig: A Novella
Exit Blood
Death is Not Forever
No Harder Prison

By Richard Barre
The Innocents
Bearing Secrets
Christmas Stories
The Ghosts of Morning
Blackheart Highway
Burning Moon
Echo Bay
Lost

By Eric Beetner (editor)
Unloaded

By Eric Beetner and
JB Kohl
Over Their Heads

By Eric Beetner and
Frank Zafiro
The Backlist
The Shortlist

By G.J. Brown
Falling

By Rob Brunet
Stinking Rich

By Angel Luis Colón
No Happy Endings

By Tom Crowley
Vipers Tail
Murder in the Slaughterhouse

By Frank De Blase
Pine Box for a Pin-Up
Busted Valentines
and Other Dark Delights
A Cougar's Kiss

By Les Edgerton
The Genuine, Imitation,
Plastic Kidnapping

By Jack Getze
Big Numbers
Big Money
Big Mojo
Big Shoes

By Richard Godwin
Wrong Crowd
Buffalo and Sour Mash
Crystal on Electric Acetate (*)

By Jeffery Hess
Beachhead

(*)—Coming Soon